Light Weaver

by

Lusine Torossian

Cover Art by *Teddi Black*

The Wild Rose Press, Inc.
PO Box 708
Adams Basin, NY 14410-0708
Visit us at www.thewildrosepress.com

Publishing History
First Edition, 2025
Trade Paperback ISBN 978-1-5092-6140-6
Digital ISBN 978-1-5092-6141-3

Published in the United States of America

This book is dedicated to...

My mother, Takui, a true queen among queens,
My first teacher about light and love.
My forever guiding star.

and to...

Vasken, Christina, and Stefanie
You're my compass, my sunshine, my shooting stars.

~*~

Author's Note

Dear Reader,

I hope this book finds a special place in your heart. As an author of Armenian descent, I've been inspired by the ancient myths of Armenia and the Caucasus, weaving these beloved threads into a tapestry of my own design.

This novel isn't meant to be an accurate reflection of history or mythology. It is an homage to my heritage. The world you're about to enter combines my favorite elements from childhood stories with invented history and magic that sprang from my imagination.

I welcome you to lose yourself in this blend of traditional and reimagined mythology. I truly hope it captures your heart as much as my childhood stories have captured mine.

With warm wishes,
Lusine Torossian

Acknowledgements

This story found its way to these pages through the unwavering support of countless hearts and minds.

A heartfelt thank you to The Wild Rose Press and to my brilliant editor, Nan Swanson, who believed in this story and helped refine every shadow and gleam. To Teddi Black for creating the beautiful cover art that captures the essence of this tale. To my wonderful critique partners—J.C. Cervantes, Jan Nerenberg, K. Robert Donovan, Mona Storm, Estey Nesmith, Pat Hauldren, and Tys Grenz, who helped polish both prose and plot with their insightful feedback. Special thanks to TF (Tammy) Burke and Day Leitao for our invaluable brainstorming and writing sessions, and to Gloria Ferguson for our inspiring café sprint sessions. To Shakira Gafar-Kirshnitz, for being both beta reader and dear friend. To my late mentor David Farland, whose wisdom still illuminates these pages.

To my husband, Vasken, for holding space for my dreams. To my beautiful and supportive daughters: Christina, whose insights threaded through this novel like golden light, and Stefanie, whose creative vision helped me shine in the digital realm.

To my ancestors—your strength flows through my veins like ancient starlight, carrying forward our Armenian heritage. And finally, to you, dear reader, for stepping into this world of light and shadow. My gratitude, like light itself, knows no bounds.

Chapter 1

When a thief has stolen from a thief, the gods laugh.
~ Ar-Haya Highlands Proverb

Death was the ultimate thief.

And if my father and I accomplished our task tonight, we'd be reclaiming what was once stolen from us.

We'd been crawling for hours through the narrow passageways of the Golden King's palace with its walls made of *tuffa* bricks and volcanic rocks the color of sunset. Even through the thick fabric of my tights, my knees were scraped raw. Dressed as a boy, I couldn't imagine how much more difficult this would have been in my long travel skirts.

We still hadn't found the entrance into the royal gallery of treasures—the room that, my father claimed, hid the resurrection stone. The hypnotic swishing of our cloaks scraping against stone lulled me into a dangerous trance.

My glowrock illuminated my father's figure crawling ahead. His muttered curses and groans echoed through the tunnel as we moved. At his age and girth, his ability to fit himself through such a tight space was remarkable.

Soft light slipped from hairline gaps in the walls, beyond which were dozens upon dozens of palace chambers. In this gray space between the jutted rocks of the old building and the newer structure built less than a century ago, the world outside felt as if it existed leagues away. Then muffled voices would echo into the tunnels—the palace guards, or any of the royals, or the royal priests, and we'd be reminded that we were far from alone.

The royal priests with their gleaming heads and long white gowns—they scared me the most.

Mingling with the scent of dank earth, the spicy aroma of roast kebab filled the air. We were passing the imperial kitchens. Stray curls had escaped my braid. I took a deep breath to blow them out of my eyes and dust clogged my nose and throat, caking in my mouth. The sneeze came unbidden, jerking my head into the low ceiling. I hissed at the shooting pain.

"Can you not control that?" my father snapped, glaring at me over his shoulder.

"No," I said, rubbing my head. "Are you sure we're going the right way?"

He huffed. "Satya, for the hundredth time, I know where I'm going. If I can do this, you certainly can manage." He turned and continued to drag himself through a narrow gap between the old and new structure.

And vanished.

A crash. A grunt. Then deafening silence.

Heart hammering, I slithered toward the ledge my father had fallen over. "Baba?"

The length of half a dozen steps beneath me my father stood and dusted himself off. He held up his glowrock toward the ancient, darker wall, then glanced up at me with a grin. "It's here."

In the ruddy light of the glowrock the *tuffa* bricks

were speckled with ancient lava rocks used centuries ago to build these walls. Beyond this barrier lay our greatest salvation or our doom, depending on whether we got caught. My chest tightened in the familiar way it did every time I accompanied my father on these missions—a concoction of dread and nerves, plus a glimmer of thrill that always shocked me.

I slid over the ledge and dropped. The fall jarred me straight through my soles. My father whipped out a hand to steady me, then pressed a finger to his lips. The cool damp air raised goose bumps to my sweaty skin in the tiny alcove no larger than our churning room back home. Here in the alcove the music we'd been hearing in the distance echoed into sudden clarity: the davul's soft melodic beat, accompanied by the zurna with its melancholy whine making one's heart tremble.

The walls surrounding me faded as an old memory surfaced. My brother, Caral's small hand wrapped around the mallet as he pounded the davul, a large drum nearly half his size. My father accompanying Caral's beat with a soulful melody, his cheeks swelling into balloons as he blew into the zurna's thin tube. My mother's eyes closed, her soft round features relaxed as she listened. The scent of patchouli that always clung to her…

I shook off the memory and the walls surrounding me came back into focus. Eyes stinging, I pressed my hand against the grainy bricks to steady myself. The Golden King had brought in musicians from the Ar-Haya Highlands of Sophene for the royal festivities. Sophene, *our* kingdom. Why would they play for that scum?

"Focus," my father hissed.

His slow hearing loss could be a curse, but now it

proved a blessing as he remained oblivious to the distant musicians. Tonight marked the beginning of Nurazard, an ancient spring celebration for Goddess Anahit. Legends said that during a particularly arid season, Anahit sent her firebird to paint the Ar-Haya Highlands with a vibrant array of colors, ensuring fertility for the soil and bountiful crops.

Tonight was a tribute to *our* history, *our* legends. Our stories meant nothing to the King, whose only revelry came from sacrificing other kingdoms like a lion devouring its prey. And he'd chosen this day to invite our musicians to his palace? I could only guess at his reasons, but I couldn't imagine it was to help our people celebrate.

Muffled voices drifted through the tuffa walls surrounding us. I joined my father by the wall and pressed an eye to a hairline crevice between the thick stones, and sucked in a breath. Beyond these gray tunnels lay a golden atrium filled to the high ceiling with treasures.

Past a column obscuring part of my view, three guards flanked a man with a shaved head and wearing a pallid, floor-length robe. A royal priest. The priest matched the pallor of his garments, and towered above the tallest guard. My nails dug into my palms.

"Eshi," Baba cursed under his breath, pushing off the dusty wall.

A glowrock pulsed with an ethereal light in his calloused hand, casting long shadows over the walls and his dirt-encrusted nails. From his pocket he produced a threadbare silk patch and a hollow, goblet-shaped crystal no larger than my palm. Draping the cloth over a gap in the wall, he slid the crystal over it and motioned me closer. As I pressed my ear to the crystal's smooth surface, the distant voices crystallized with clarity.

"...and all is accounted for," the priest's voice echoed through the crystal, his unusually high pitch ringing with authority. He spoke the language of the royals, each word enunciated with precision, and accented by a hint of northern heritage. "Be vigilant. There are many visitors at the palace today. Do not leave your posts, and report back to me if there are any urgent concerns."

I'd taught myself the language of the conquering Aurean royals using Baba's texts, behind his back. Despite my hatred of them. Despite their offensive control over our culture, our rituals, our ways of life. Despite their oppression.

He never said it, but I knew Baba now appreciated my defiance. It came in handy for a thief in the enemy's territory.

The priest walked out then, followed by the guards. The thick doors banged shut, a bolt slid into place.

"They're gone," I whispered, handing the silk and crystal back to my father.

Experience taught us never to enter an empty room right away. To wait, ensuring no one returned, before slipping in silent as phantoms to take what didn't belong to us.

Well, what didn't belong to us according to *them*.

Backs pressed to the grimy wall, we waited in agonizing silence. I'd counted to three hundred when my father finally unpacked his satchel. Releasing a sigh, I ignored the sharp jab in my chest. It was time.

My father unwrapped a silk cloth and produced a sharp silver tool as long as a dagger and as slim as a weaver's needle. He inserted it into the widest gap between the stones. Baba had acquired the Wall Splitter by methods he wouldn't tell me, from a place that wasn't even on a map. That had been before I began to assist him in his secret missions, and when he finally told me what he really did for a living. Or started doing after my mother's and brother's deaths.

I would have never considered a life of thievery, especially pilfering tools of forbidden magic, when my mother lived. Yet here I was on a mission that could change my life forever, or end it.

"Be equipped. Be observant. Be quick," Baba said, the motto he'd repeated to me countless times these past few years. His practiced sharp tone told me he may have heard the music of our homeland, but chose not to discuss it. He took much longer than me to process such emotions.

"Always," I whispered.

I willed my heart to stop racing. If my father and I were discovered here, we'd be dead by sunrise. Sophenians were not given the courtesy of a trial. Here in Vosk, the Aurean Kingdom's Golden City, with all its mines filled with riches, we were considered scum.

With a grunt, my father pushed the wall splitter into the wall. It entered as smoothly as a dagger slicing through feta. Soft light filled the tunnel, illuminating every stone, every grain of dirt. For a heartbeat the speckle of volcanic rocks that surrounded us transformed into the brilliant night sky.

The light intensified. A hiss filled the space as pebbles and sand showered us in a grimy downpour. Warm air touched my skin and the heavy scent of myrrh and frankincense filled the tunnels. The dust cleared, revealing a rugged gap in the wall large enough to crawl through. Before us stood a golden atrium of treasures beyond imagining. For a heartbeat we both stood there, gaping.

My father snapped himself out of his shock first. "We're here for only one item, understood?"

My mouth watered at the riches hidden here. Riches stolen from our people, our mines, our artisans and weavers. I sucked in a frustrated breath. "I know."

"Wait here," he whispered. Then he slid through the gap and into the royal gallery of treasures.

Baba's big form disappeared behind stone columns, the davul's muffled beat punctuating his fading steps. I hunched on the ledge between the tunnels and the treasure chamber, breathing deeply to calm my quivering nerves. The thick, stagnant air made my tunic cling uncomfortably to my back. And the zurna's distant whine tore at my already frayed nerves, sending shivers of foreboding down my spine.

Be equipped. Be observant. Be quick.

I extended my neck for a better view. Hundreds of glowrocks illuminated a chamber with archways and inner cavities at least five times the size of our bookshop in Mosatti. Tapestries in various sizes hung around the room displaying intricate designs from the regions where they'd been made, trophies left behind by the skilled weavers of Sophene who had given their sweat, blood and voices to weave them. Sophene weavers were now outlawed in the kingdom, falsely accused of using forbidden magic. The room around me wavered as my inner vision brought forth a memory.

My mother had been among the last of the Sacreds, ancient warrior healers and magic weavers. She perished in the massacre five years ago, the day our lives catapulted into what my father and I had now become. First my mother, then my little brother. The echoes of their cries reverberated through my skull. I could still feel Caral's lifeless hand in mine. It should have been me in the path of the dagger. He'd been too young to die. Then another dagger had found me.

I had fought so hard to protect them both. *You could have tried harder*, my inner voice, as always, hissed.

I dropped my gaze from the hanging tapestries, shaking off the dark memories and their disorienting way of tilting my world. They served no purpose now. I repeated my father's mantra until his shuffling steps grew louder and he slid silently back into the shadowy alcove.

In the room's soft glow, the lines on his face deepened, his black-silver beard grew more disheveled. I wondered for the thousandth time at his determination. What my father must be feeling now, after so many years of searching and planning, I could only imagine. But I also recognized that look. Eyes wide with excitement, shoulders stiff with worry, hands trembling with the need to move and to do. All with the hope that all this moving and doing would one day reunite our family.

This was the fifth of our missions in search of the resurrection relic. But each quest before, through the deserts of Amaranth, along the coast of Memmorah, or through the valleys of Santoria and Luth, felt as if it could be the last. *This* time, Baba insisted, was different. *This* time, he knew without doubt we'd find it. These missions bonded us, but they also trapped us in a vicious cycle of hope and disappointment.

And this time, as each time before, I held in the

anticipation, dread, and hope that twisted within my chest until I could barely breathe. I took his offered hand and slipped out of the rugged opening, landing with a soft thud. I'd been bent and cramped for hours, and pain spiked through my feet all the way to my thighs. My dirt-encrusted boots scuffed the polished stone floor. I stretched to unknot my back until my spine cracked with a pop.

My father held up an hourglass, an ancient time relic he'd acquired from only-the-goddesses-knew-where, and whispered, "When the top bulb empties, we're out of time. Make it count."

"Lovely," I grumbled. "So, where do you propose we start digging? Maybe under the throne? Or even better, under the King's own pillow."

Baba narrowed his eyes but didn't respond. As soon as he turned away, I frowned at the hourglass in his palm. I had never asked him where it came from or how it predicted our timing. But we'd embarked on enough of these missions together that I relied on his timing, at least.

We stepped into the main atrium, and the staggering display of treasures nearly brought me to my knees. Weapons lined the walls: jeweled swords and daggers fashioned from rare elephant tusks, crossbows with strings woven from gossamer-thin threads of gold, yet as tough as steel. Many of these items had been sourced and crafted by the most skilled metallurgists of Sophene.

The tools and weapons on one shelf alone could settle us comfortably for life. Why didn't the King secure such valuables in a tomb? Maybe he was confident that this atrium, the most heavily guarded room in the palace, maybe the entire kingdom, remained impenetrable. Any attempt would be pure suicide.

They clearly didn't know my father.

A sudden, high-pitched squeal jolted me. There, in the corner, a small gray creature writhed, its tail trapped under a tumbled basket of scrolls.

I slapped my palm over my racing heart. *It's just a mouse.*

The poor thing tugged and slid on the tiles, struggling to free its tail pinned beneath the basket's edge.

Bending down, I whispered, "How did you end up in this predicament?"

The creature's squeaks grew louder.

"Shh." I shot a furtive glance over my shoulder. Baba rummaged through an open basket with focused precision. Turning back, I whispered to the frantic creature, "I'm going to help you, but you need to leave. Finish your thieving elsewhere."

As soon as I righted the basket, the mouse freed its tail and twisted to face me.

I hopped back. "You're not a mouse."

I'd never seen anything like it. Its large milky-yellow eyes and sharp incisors were disproportionate to its tiny body. It bared its fangs, dropping its jaw nearly to the floor, and displayed rows of sharp, black teeth.

I grabbed a scroll and aimed it at the creature. "Shoo, go bite something else, demon-mouse."

With a mewling growl, it turned and skittered into a hole in the wall, its squeals fading.

"You're welcome," I whispered, fighting a shiver. Uneasiness crept over me. Even the mouse-creatures here were vicious.

"Stop dawdling," Baba hissed from up ahead. He'd

abandoned the basket to rummage through a table overflowing with trinkets. "Are you searching for it?"

"Yes," I said, with a last glance at the hole the little demon-mouse had disappeared through. "But it would be helpful to know its general location."

"Satya *jan*, it's a spool-shaped stone," he said. "There can't be many such objects here."

Jan. The term of endearment was lost in his curt delivery. I was nearly eighteen, and he still treated me like a child. Our previous searches had uncovered similar-looking spools, but those were used for collecting nothing more than plain old threads. Without a grain of magic.

The sand at the bottom of the hourglass had reached a fingertip thick. I pressed my nails into my palm, feeling the weight of our limited time.

As I sorted through a cabinet filled with gleaming trinkets, I muttered a popular Mosatti rhyme like a mocking prayer, "Basilisk King, cold and cruel, heart of stone, a gilded fool." If any of the guards heard me sing that out loud, I'd be dead. But it helped ease my nerves.

Where could the Spool be hidden? A secret nook? Behind a loose brick or beneath a floorboard?

This could be another dead end. I swallowed, refusing to entertain that thought.

The resurrection stone had been a myth until after the massacre when my father obsessively searched ancient records and found evidence of its existence.

"It's called the Weaver's Spool," Baba had explained. "Said to bring back the dead."

"Bring back the dead?" I'd asked. "Isn't that...*wrong*?"

He thought my questions rude. *I* thought he'd lost

his mind. But then, he'd shown me proof in the ancient texts he'd pilfered on one of his secret missions. Maybe it was my own burning desperation, or maybe I'd lost my mind too, but I believed him. Though even if we were fortunate enough to find this magical spool, where and how we'd find a Sacred to wield it remained a mystery. I wasn't sure he'd even thought that far.

"I still don't understand," I whispered, opening yet another cabinet drawer filled with...a giant palm-sized spider. Stifling a yelp, I quickly closed it. "If only a Sacred can wield the Spool, how do you plan to use it?"

The last of the Sacreds, revered warrior-healers who channeled magic through god-relics such as the Weaver's Spool, had been my mother. Even if she knew how, Mama would have *never* agreed to such sacrilege as raising the dead.

Baba's hands shook as he examined a stack of texts on a shelf. "How many times must I repeat this?" he snapped. "There's an old map of hidden temples in the Ar-Haya Highlands where Sacreds may have escaped the massacre. I have a friend who can acquire it."

I bit my lip. He still didn't answer the question. A friend. Who'd be so brave, or *foolish*, as to harbor such a map? Even if we found a hidden Sacred, how did he plan on convincing them to raise the *dead*? As if his answer wasn't vague enough, seeking a Sacreds' tool amidst these treasures...I scoffed. We may as well hunt for a single pebble in a hill of rocks.

Deep in thought, I brushed past a statue of a sword-wielding knight, its hilt snagging my tunic. As I stepped forward, the sword ripped through the fabric and swung back with a loud clang.

I froze. "Eshi."

My father whirled around, glaring. I bit my lip and tried to look apologetic.

Then both our gazes slid to the closed doors.

Chapter 2

Death is the ultimate thief.
~ Ar-Haya Highlands Proverb

I held my breath, trying to hear past the sound of my drumming heart.

I strained to listen for yelling guards, clanging weapons, or the sliding bolt. But the only sound was the distant music. After a few heart-pounding moments, Baba and I released simultaneous sighs and continued our search.

The sense of being watched crept over me, prickling my scalp. A barely-there tune, closer than the faint festive music, resonated across the chamber. My anxious gaze darted around, searching for its source.

To my right, against a tapestry depicting the epic clash between the god Vahagn and a serpent-dragon, stood a wooden glass-topped cabinet. The tapestry was an auspicious sign, maybe symbolically guarding something important.

As I approached the cabinet, the glass top shimmered with an ethereal melody, tugging at the fringes of a memory. My ears strained to capture it fully, but it remained just out of reach.

Beneath the glass lay a dazzling display of jewels, rings, and small trinkets upon a veil of burgundy silk. A delicate silver ring caught my eye, intricate swirls dancing around a sparkling blue gemstone at its center. My mouth watered at the price it could fetch. Enough to feed our entire town for a month. I tore my gaze away from the ring and scanned the assortment of objects.

And there it was. A frog among swans.

Nestled in the far corner of the casing lay a stone tube with disks at each end. A spool.

"Baba, here by the gemstones…"

He turned and strode toward me, his dark eyes flashing. "We aren't here for gemstones," he hissed. But when his gaze landed on the object I pointed at, his eyes widened. "Well done, my canary."

I clenched my jaw, the weight of the bittersweet nickname pressing against my chest. A reminder of what we had both lost. Baba hadn't called me that in a long time, not since before the massacre.

Your canary doesn't sing anymore.

But it was good to see him determined, rather than the lost look he'd carried since the last futile quest for the elusive Spool.

"Help me," my father whispered.

Placing the hourglass on a basket, he unsheathed his dagger and wedged it between the glass cover and wooden frame. I crouched down, swiftly retrieving the small knife from my boot.

With a determined grip, I inserted its sharp point into the lock. The familiar sequence played out in my mind. *Twist up, turn right, then left, and repeat.* The lock yielded with a satisfying click.

My triumphant grin mirrored my father's as we wedged our fingers under the glass cover. Just as we lifted it, the hourglass on the basket shattered with a thunderous crash. The cabinet cover imploded, unleashing the piercing screech of a hunting hawk. Glass shards flew in all directions.

I dropped my knife, shielding my face.

"Demon souls," Baba cursed. "They've spell-woven it."

"You said magic is forbidden in the castle," I cried.

"I was wrong." Baba's desperate gaze flicked to the doors, then back to me.

Our eyes met as the same realization hit us. We would not be getting out of here alive.

"Take it," he rasped, voice hoarse, eyes bright. "And go. *Go*, Satya, *jan*."

I snatched the Spool and stuffed it into my pack. Before I could change my mind, I grabbed the ring and shoved it onto my left pinky. The instant the delicate metal met my skin, a shudder spiraled through me, a soft tune echoing then fading in my head.

The strange sensation made me stagger, thoughts scattering like windblown leaves as my eardrums pulsed. Above the shrieking alarm, shouts echoed beyond the chamber. Dropping his knife into his satchel, Baba snatched up a bejeweled sword from a nearby table and rushed to the doors, wedging the blade across the locks.

The alarm screeched and screeched.

Other sounds joined the cacophony. Guards shouted. The doors shuddered.

The sword across the locks bent.

My blood turned to ice. "Baba!"

My father held the doors closed with the strength of his weak back. I gaped in a silent cry as my gaze slid to the sword. In his haste he'd grown careless. He'd grabbed a ceremonial blade too soft for combat.

"Save yourself." Baba nodded toward the alcove

where the wall splitter kept the passage open.

Grabbing his satchel, I sprinted to the alcove and scrambled back into the tunnel. From my concealed spot, I stole a lingering glimpse at Baba, etching his features into my memory. His face blurred. How could I do this without him? How could I do this *to* him?

"Baba, you can make it. Run." My voice cracked.

The doors trembled, hinges loosened.

I choked out a sob.

The doors splintered. A jagged crack tore through one side.

The sword warped, emitting a drawn-out, catlike yowl.

"Satya, you can bring us all back." Baba's face flushed crimson. "Find the map. Talk to Ra...."

A resounding crash cut him off. A cry of pain escaped my father's throat. His feet slipped.

"Baba," I whimpered.

The sword contorted, broke free, hitting the tiled floor with a resonating zing.

I jerked the wand from the wall. A gossamer-thin membrane quickly sealed the opening, gradually thickening but clear enough for me to see the nightmare play out.

The doors ripped from their hinges and slammed open.

Guards burst in.

My father snatched the bent sword and turned to face them. "I'm sorry," he roared, raising the tip to the nearest guard.

My fingers went numb against the satchel. *What is he doing? They'll kill him.*

The horror of what he'd done coiled around my

chest, squeezing, squeezing until I couldn't breathe. *That's what he wants.*

A Sophenian captured by the King's guards would have a far worse fate than death.

His apology was meant for me. I clapped my palm over my mouth.

Metal clanged as swords met in a burst of sparks. My father couldn't best a foe even in his youth. He wouldn't last a breath with a bent sword against three trained swordsmen.

One guard grabbed Baba by his collar. Another plunged a blade into his heart.

Chapter 3

Beware of an Enemy with Allies.
~ Ar-Haya Highlands Proverb

I bit my tongue, stifling a scream, the taste of blood and terror filling my mouth.

Chest heaving, I collapsed against the tunnel's wall. Through the thickening barrier my gaze locked with my father's, his eyes eternally fixed in shocked resignation.

Any moment, they'd spot the dirt by the wall that hid me. Every instinct urged me to flee, but I sat paralyzed, an observer watching some fantastically real production.

"How did he get in?" a guard yelled over the shrieking alarm.

"If anything's missing, the Enlightener will serve our heads to the King," another shouted.

The tunnel's thick wall now shrouded the room beyond in a haze, like looking through grainy glass. They couldn't see me in the tunnel's darkness. That's how the wall splitter worked. Insert the wrong side into the wall and the effect would reverse. I'd be left exposed and blinded to whatever lay on the other side.

I forced myself to watch as they dragged my father's body out the door, his blood staining the pale tiles. More guards entered, scouring every corner, case, and tabletop. They stepped over the dust and gravel by my wall, not even sparing the ground a glance.

The alarm continued to screech. I clapped my palms over my ears, trying to freeze my mind and heart from hearing and feeling too much. But it was no use. The sight of the blade protruding from my father's chest merged with the haunting images of my mother's and brother's lifeless bodies.

A man in pale robes entered, the same royal priest from earlier. The Enlightener. Clad in an elaborate white robe lined with gold thread for the Golden King's revels, he'd clearly been pulled away from the festivities. He barked insults at the guards, a relentless string of curses flowing when he noticed the open glass casing and the missing objects.

"The King will call for blood," he said, his voice rising over the alarm. "The healing spool and the ring are both gone. The thieving Sophenian knew something."

My hand instinctively sought the Spool inside my pack. *Healing* spool? Had my father been mistaken? A healing tool couldn't resurrect the dead. Goddess, had Baba died for nothing? I swallowed fresh tears in silence.

The Enlightener raised his palms, eyes fixed on the ceiling, and murmured inaudible words. *It's a spell.*

The alarm abruptly stopped. Then deafening silence.

I sat still, fearing the slightest movement would betray my location.

"Did you check his pockets?" the Enlightener asked.

"Empty," one guard said.

"Empty?" the Enlightener snapped. "He had an accomplice." He crouched by the glass case and scooped something off the floor. When he rose, I glimpsed the object in his hand. A knife.

My knife.

I'd dropped it in panic when the alarm had started to shriek. Baba often warned me against leaving personal objects behind during our thieving missions. Certain magic could identify someone through a regularly carried item. For the past five years, that knife had never left my side.

"Eshi," I whimpered, then clamped my hand to my mouth.

The Enlightener slipped my knife into his pocket and scanned the room with deliberate slowness. His narrowed gaze traveled over every object until settling on my wall. He stilled, eyes slitting. With determined steps, he strode toward my alcove.

Though I knew he couldn't see me, I sat unmoving as he neared. For a heartbeat those eerie eyes stared straight at me. Almost *through* me. I couldn't help but stare back through the thickening glass-like barrier, unblinking.

Those eyes. They weren't normal. A golden sheen gilded his pupils. I'd heard rumors about the royal priests and their use of dark magic. Could he somehow *see* beyond the wall?

He glanced down, and from the hiss that escaped him, I knew he'd noticed the dirt on the tiles. Then his unsettling eyes snapped back up, as if he sensed me there.

I stopped breathing.

A low snarl escaped his throat as he whirled around to face the guards. "Search every room, every corner, including the grounds. Now!" He stormed out, his thick robes billowing behind him.

The guards shuffled out, leaving only two posted by the doors. Their gazes scanned the room, repeatedly sliding over my wall. My limbs quivered with the urge to move, but I was trembling too much to attempt it.

I waited a few hundred frantic heartbeats until the wall solidified, sealing off any sight or sound. The thought of being trapped within these suffocating tunnels sent a wave of panic through me. The guards would soon discover our entry point and secure every possible entrance and exit to the tunnels. I pushed my brain into focus, willing my limbs into action.

Hauling myself and the two packs onto the high ledge, I slid through the winding tunnels, guided by the faint glow of a single glowrock.

****

For hours, I lost my way in the tunnel maze. Memories, fear, and exhaustion blurred into a suffocating fog. Each turn offered a glimmer of hope, but instead led deeper into the cold, cavernous labyrinth.

Chambers flew past, some bustling with music and dance, others echoing with emptiness. But none offered escape. Even if I used the wall splitter to break free from the tunnels, I'd still need to navigate the well-guarded palace. In my current state, I had 'thief' hennaed on my forehead. I'd have to chance the tunnels and hope to find an exit.

I struggled to recall our earlier route, but each turn led me into unknown channels behind the walls of unfamiliar rooms. Reaching the end of yet another passage, I dropped my bags and shook with indecision. A horrible realization hit me with the force of an anvil. The channel had narrowed, sloping upward. The path should not be rising.

My father had painstakingly outlined the tunnels on his map, but the folded parchment now lay in his tunic's hidden pocket. The tunic that I'd cleaned, folded, and packed for this journey now lay in tatters and covered in blood. *Baba.*

Swallowing a lump, I tried to center myself the way he'd taught me. *Be equipped. Be observant. Be quick.*

A shadow stirred to my left. I raised my glowrock and a small gray creature froze in the pale light. I scrambled back. Was this the same demon-mouse from the gallery?

The tiny beast drew nearer, its yellow eyes widening hungrily, fangs elongating toward the ground. I fumbled for my knife, only to recall that I'd lost it. Retrieving the Wall Splitter from my pack, I leveled it at the creature. It hissed.

"This thing is sharp," I warned, voice wavering.

Glancing between the creature and the identical branching tunnel paths on either side of me, I hesitated. Which would Baba take?

The demon-mouse growled, talons scraping as it drew closer.

"Get out of my way," I warned.

Its guttural snarls bounced off the walls. After a pause, other growls joined in.

Goddess, there are more?

One by one, they emerged from crevices, their numbers multiplying with every thunderous thud of my heart. An entire swarm converged, blocking the left passage. Over two dozen pairs of predatory yellow eyes locked unblinkingly on me.

Cursing, I shoved the Wall Splitter back into my pack. Baba's voice echoed in my head. *Run.*

Hoisting both bags, I veered right, scrambling on all fours with desperate speed.

The horde hissed in unnerving unison and charged after me. High-pitched snarls echoed through the labyrinthine tunnels. Each dead end revealed more of the creatures blocking one side or the other. After three right turns and a left, it dawned on me. I was being herded like a flock of sheep. *Eshi, they're leading me somewhere.*

My back ached, muscles quivering with fatigue, clothes plastered with sweat and caked mud. I grew disoriented, lost in the twisting, turning maze until a cool breeze brushed my overheated cheeks. Ahead, a rough-hewn ledge opened onto the dark night.

I stumble-crawled toward it in relief, packs swinging awkwardly. The demon-mice paused behind, blocking every path but forward.

I extended my hand as a feeble barrier. "Stay back!" I cried, voice quivering with exhaustion.

The creatures recoiled and hissed in unison.

I blinked. The stolen ring blazed brighter than my glowrock. Was it why they hadn't attacked me? Testing my theory, I thrust my hand forward. The little monsters growled, but did not advance. Exhaling a shaky breath, I peered out. Castle turrets pointed to the sliver moon, as if the gods spied upon me with a squinted eye. Below, clay slates of a rooftop slanted down, stopping many floors above the gardens. Baba and I had entered the tunnels through the city's sewer system. I'd obviously taken a wrong turn. Many wrong turns, thanks to the demon-mice.

From the distance, the palace music crescendoed, matching the rhythm of my racing heart. Soft growls emanated from behind me. The horde advanced, fangs elongating, blocking every path except the one that would plummet me to my death.

Calculating the distance between the roof and the castle gardens below, my mind raced with possible escape options. Maybe I could use the roof and potential balconies as steppingstones into the gardens. I glanced back at the multiplying crowd of demon-creatures.

"Not much of a choice, is it?" I muttered. "I'll take my chances with a fall."

Hefting both packs higher, I shuffled to the open ledge. And leaped onto the roof.

Chapter 4

Basilisk King, cold and cruel, heart of stone, a gilded fool.

~ *Sophenian Children's Rhyme*

The roof sloped down, steeper than I expected.

I struggled for traction, the weight of the two packs dragging me toward the edge, faster and faster. The clamor of my boots ricocheted into the empty gardens below.

My glowrock tumbled across the rooftop and vanished over the edge. I dug my heels into the tiles, attempting to decelerate, but the edge rushed closer… closer…closer.

Goddess, help me slow down!

As soon as the plea crossed my mind, a needle-thin vibration surged from my left hand, up my arm and down my spine. The edges of my vision grew hazy. Time slowed.

The air around me thickened. And suddenly I was gliding. My heels found brief purchase as I teetered at the roof's edge. *How is this possible?*

Don't look down. Don't look down.

Of course, I looked down. Vertigo blurred the dark gardens five floors below. A deserted balcony jutted out one flight beneath, bathed in faint light. Pressure pressed against my back. An invisible force shoved, propelling me into the air.

Wind snatched at my clothes as I glided down like a clumsy crow with wings made of weighty packs.

The fall stretched…endless. The burning sensation in my pinky intensified until, finally, I landed with a muffled thud on the terrace's terracotta tiles. I stared at my hand in disbelief. A soft glow emanated from the stolen ring. The same ethereal energy I'd felt in magical relics before. Silky power resonated through my skin and bones, almost soothing.

The haunting lullaby from the King's treasure gallery echoed softly around me, raising the hairs on the back of my neck, then fading into silence. Abruptly, the ring's light winked out.

Reality crashed over me like an icy plunge, and the night's fears came flooding back. I stumbled to the balcony's edge and retched over the side.

Several ragged breaths later, I wiped my mouth and gazed down at the dark gardens far below. How long before they swarmed with guards? If I attempted the jump, I'd break bones, or worse. I didn't trust the ring to save me twice. I wasn't even sure how to activate its power. But staying up here exposed by the towering turrets, or returning to the creature-filled tunnels? Not an option.

A resounding cry echoed from the chamber beyond the balcony. My heart thundered like a stampeding mountain ram as I flattened myself against the shadowy wall and slid toward the slightly ajar window. The rough stone scraped my cheek, but I barely noticed.

Through the narrow gap, I caught glimpses of the room's interior. Ornate furnishings…plush rugs… towering bookshelves. Glowrocks illuminated walls and rugs that glimmered as if woven with threads of stardust.

Across the window, an angry tapestry hung from the wall. Fashioned entirely from delicate silk, it stretched taller than two men and spanned the width of a ten-woman line dance. Intricately woven gladiolus flowers in various shades of blood-red and orange surrounded its borders, in stark contrast to the incredibly lifelike violent scene they framed. The centuries-old surrender of the Ar-Haya Highlands.

This rug could not have originated in the Aurean Kingdom, but had most likely been fashioned by a Sophenian weaver. It was in the carefully woven terror on the faces of mothers as their young daughters were brutally enslaved. In the horrified expressions of fathers witnessing sons impaled by enemy daggers. In the golden threads of silk woven through the captives, as if their souls were imprinted into the fabric.

Another cry shattered the night, jolting me. The chamber door swung open with a resounding crash. I crouched lower, peering through the partially open window, just as two men flew in, dragging a woman by her neck.

The victim, a heavy-set noblewoman dressed in finery, struggled, but she was no match for her two attackers' obvious strengths. They dropped her onto the thick carpet in the middle of the room with the carelessness of handling a tattered puppet.

The man who had his back to me wore the long festive robe of a noble, a silver hood covering his head. The other, taller man stood to the side, his face in clear view. The Enlightener.

I sucked in a sharp breath.

"I saw nothing, I swear!" the woman cried, but both

men ignored her.

"You allowed her to see?" the Enlightener asked the other man.

The hooded figure grunted, his head bobbing at an odd angle, as if his neck could barely support his skull.

"The girl was already dead," the woman yelled. "I saw nothing else. Please, please…"

"Then you know what must be done," the Enlightener told the other man, his voice rising over the woman's high-pitched cries. He drew a dagger from the folds of his robe, and with a swift hand, sliced the woman's throat.

I clamped my palm over my mouth, closing my eyes to the sight of blood spurting from her neck.

"The gods grow hungry," the Enlightener said.

My eyes snapped open at his strange words. The royal priest wiped his dagger on the dead woman's cloak. He sheathed it within his robe and retrieved an object from his pocket hidden from my view. Holding it over the lifeless body, he chanted in the dead language of the Ar-Haya Highlands, spoken only by devout worshippers of the old gods. He sang the spell with a discordant resonance that clung to the air, its sluggish weight crawling over my skin.

I clenched my fist until my nails dug painfully into my palm. This man was no priest. He was a master of forbidden magic.

His voice pierced the air as he repeated the spell with growing insistence. Most of the words eluded me, but two stood out. "Hoki…Ahriman…hoki… Ahriman…"

Hoki, the Sophenian term for one's light or essence. But it was the name, Ahriman, that sent an icy chill down my spine. The Archdemon of Despair and Chaos, the most feared god of the old pantheon. Transfixed, I teetered between the instinct to flee and the horrifying spectacle unfolding before me.

The Enlightener's pitch rose. Whispers ricocheted around the room, zinging through the glass. Shadows slithered from his body, coiling around him in a sinuous dance. A noxious energy pulsed through the air. I wasn't unfamiliar with such power, having witnessed my mother's spells for years before the massacre as a warrior-healer, a Sacred.

But where Mama's tune had been harmonious, the Enlightener's grated with discordance. Where her magic blossomed in hues of vibrant color, the Enlightener's spell merged into murky shadows that mimicked a storm. Unlike my mother's use of the ethereal force, this sorcerer's powers clearly came from a darkness beyond this world.

Baba's forbidden texts spoke of individuals chosen as vessels by benevolent deities such as Vahagn, Anahit, Astlik—the gods who aided and protected us. Mama had drawn a sliver of godforce through Sacred tools to heal others. How could the Enlightener channel so much dark power?

The dead woman's body shuddered and gyrated. Then grew still. A shimmery haze rose from her chest resembling pale smoke infused with specks of garnet embers. Her *hoki*.

I'd seen it before. The people of Mosatti had often called my mother when someone was about to pass. Mama had helped their essence transcend into the ether, where the departed continued their journey through the veil.

The Enlightener's voice dropped as ashen smoke

wafted from the tapestry's sides, the smoky tendrils sharpening into points that pierced the woman's body. Her shimmery essence intertwined with the smoky threads and wound through the relic in the Enlightener's grasp.

Searing heat gripped my finger. I fought back a cry of pain. Was the ring responding to the Enlightener's spell? I tried to pry it off, but it wouldn't budge.

With the Enlightener's final cry of "Hoki...Ahriman!" the woman's essence threaded into the tapestry's fibers. The screech of a thousand raised voices tore from the cloth and echoed into the courtyard below. I covered my ears but couldn't take my eyes off the hanging rug. What this spell evoked was worse than death. It tore the woman's spirit from its path and forced it into the violent world of the tapestry.

This was cruel. Evil.

I'd seen my mother trap the soul of a criminal once inside an embroidered tablecloth depicting a peaceful scene of the Highlands. She'd explained that the darkness in the soul would travel the peaceful landscape until only light remained. Then she'd gently lead the *hoki* out of the tapestry and through the veil.

The Enlightener had just doomed this noblewoman's soul to live and relive one of the most brutal battles in the history of the Highlands.

Ripples of power undulated over the cloth, ebbing and flowing like sea waves. As the swells subsided, a new figure sprawled on the cloth's battlefield, her eyes wide with terror, mouth frozen in an eternal scream.

The screeching abruptly stopped, leaving behind a haunting silence. My gaze darted over the other tapestries hung around the room of scenes portraying various battles. How many souls had the Enlightener imprisoned here? Or was the battle tapestry the only soul-trapping rug?

"Ah, the cry of spirits in fear," the Enlightener said with reverence. "Is there any better sound?"

A guttural noise echoed through the chamber. It came from the silver-hooded man. His body was contorted at a strange angle, one shoulder hanging lower than the other, head inclined to the left.

The Enlightener brushed his thin, long fingers over the tapestry as if patting a favorite steed. "Ahriman will be pleased with these countless Sophenian souls, along with a meddling noblewoman's."

I squeezed my palm against my mouth. *Sophenian souls.*

I swallowed the bile that rose up my throat. The spirits of my parents and brother weren't free in death. They were trapped!

The Enlightener pocketed the small relic he'd used for the ritual before I could see it. From his other pocket he retrieved a knife. *My* knife. My breath hitched. He'd use it to track me.

"Come, Malchus," he said. "I have a thief to track."

At first, I thought he was addressing the hooded man. But then a tiny creature scampered up the Enlightener's robes and settled on his shoulder. A demon-mouse.

I gaped at the creature. Had the Enlightener controlled the horde that had driven me here? But if he knew where I hid, he would have surely confronted me.

Turning to his hooded companion, the Enlightener added, "Enjoy the feast."

With those horrifying words, he walked out, softly

closing the door behind him.

As soon as he left, the other man lunged for the lifeless woman's exposed neck and sank his teeth into her flesh. Blood dripped onto the pale tiles, his entire body trembling as he feasted.

My scream resounded over the balcony.

The creature's head snapped up, his wild eyes narrowed on the window. Never in my worst nightmares had I seen such a monster.

He stood, his hood slipping off. Blood dripped from his chin. This wasn't just any noble. It was the Golden King himself.

His crown lay askew over matted yellow hair, his gilded festival robes stained with blood. He prowled toward me, a predator scenting new prey. Those eyes. Pupils covered in a thick golden sheen. I'd seen them before. On the Enlightener.

I scrambled back, not bothering to hide the sound of my scraping boots. He obviously knew I was here. For the first time I wished for the guards. At least their deadly blows would be swift and my soul would be free.

The balcony door flew open and the Monster-King paused in the doorway, framed by a halo of light from the room behind him. His terrifying eyes narrowed on me.

I swallowed another scream.

His head dipped lower and his crown slipped off, clattering onto the terrace tiles. His lips stretched in an ugly grin. "Come to save me, my sweet?"

He spoke in Sophenian, in an accent that sounded odd in his grating voice. Then he said in a sing-song way as if rehearsing a song, "Weaver of light. Weaver of souls. Come to tame the monster, have you?"

Unclenching my frozen limbs, I stumbled back until my bulky packs crushed against the balcony railing. "I…ah…" What did one say to a monster who could snap your neck in two?

"He's within us all, you know," he said, stalking closer. "Waiting. Just…waiting."

"Who?" I whispered.

His smile fell away.

The golden sheen of his pupils spread into the whites of his eyes.

His head twitched. Once. Twice.

Then his jaw dropped unnaturally low, revealing razor sharp teeth painted red with the noblewoman's blood.

The ring warmed my finger. Its enchanting melody resonated in my head. A milky calm settled over me. Time slowed. The Monster-King lunged.

Chapter 5

Beggar and king, beneath the same sky,
When tragedy strikes, both weep and both cry.
~ Sophenian Folksong

I vaulted over the balcony rails and dove into the gardens below.

The ring vibrated, and the air thickened, slowing my descent. I glided down, my braids floating upward as if submerged in water. A deafening roar pierced the night, overpowering the tune in my ears, the distant sounds of music, the entire kingdom.

My feet had barely grazed the ground before propelling me through the gardens. I maneuvered past crowded cobblestone streets, navigated corners, turns, around buildings, and through narrow alleys. Sprinting toward the looming city gates, I darted past armed guards. Shouts and screams echoed in my wake as I ascended the ramparts encircling the city. The Golden King's famous swinging bridge came into view. I did not stop until I'd crossed it and disappeared into the pitch-dark woods.

I ran until the Monster-King's roars faded, until the castle turrets vanished behind the hills. The ring remained warm. My vision blurred, making it impossible to discern day from night. The sky transformed into a kaleidoscope of lights and darks. I ran until wind roared through my ears, until the two packs became heavy stones rhythmically thumping against my back, until the distance stretched for leagues between me and that *creature* we called the Golden King.

It took hours of running for the realization to dawn on me that the demon mice had been sent by the Enlightener when he'd sensed me in the wall. They'd led me straight to where the Enlightener intended for me to go.

Except, by some miracle, or the influence of this magical ring, I'd managed to escape the clutches of the crowned monster.

****

I ran for what felt like hours, days, months, as the sky lightened, darkened, then lightened again. First, across the woods and over the barren hills surrounding Vosk. Then through Amaya Forest separating Vosk from the kingdom of Sophene. The towns of Edeys, Handeia and Tahish sped by in a blur.

Every crackle of wood, every whistling breeze and rustling leaf made my heart jump, propelling my fatigued body into fresh motion. My legs begged for rest and my lungs struggled for breath, but goddess help me, I couldn't stop. I couldn't stop. I couldn't stop.

At last, the sun broke over the distant hills and through the gnarled maples and soaring cypress trees that marked the southern edge of Amaya Forest. The glimmering necklace of Eugetz River wound around the hills, and the high walls of Mosatti came into view. I collapsed to my knees, whispering my gratitude to the gods for bringing me home safely.

Here, in the comfort of my beloved town, the creature king with his gold-sheened eyes felt like a distant nightmare. The empty feeling within me spread, and I had a sudden dark premonition. This could be the last time I gazed upon these hills, the veiled streams and rivers flowing from the mountains, the glinting metal rooftops of the only home I'd ever known. Now that I'd stopped running, my body trembled with exhaustion, and my shoulders ached under the weight of the packs. I pulled myself up within the copse, my hand on the rough bark of an oak, quivering with indecision.

Laughter and music rang from behind the town wall. The roads leading to Mosatti were filled with people dressed in their finery. Girls and women, garbed in gowns of burgundy, rich green, and gold, with white and gold headdresses fashioned in silk and finely embroidered. Men and boys in their best tunics and vests, carrying leather sheaths encasing iron swords and daggers to show off their metallurgy skills.

I surveyed my own travel-worn boy's garb. Sweat clung to my skin despite the chill, my braids hung in a mess of tangles down my back, and dirt coated my clothes and face. In this crowd, I'd stand out like a frayed rug among silk arras.

Frayed rug or not, I needed to get home.

Pulling my grimy cloak from my pack, I wrapped it around myself and raised the hood to conceal the grime coating my hair and face. Descending the incline toward the bustling path, I slipped into the festive crowd and headed down the narrow path toward home.

No one spared me a glance. People strolled by, their smiles, laughter and songs echoing over the lively crowd, oblivious to the horrors lurking just beyond Sophene. For them, this was another celebration, an occasion to share joy with family and friends, forge new acquaintances, trade goods.

I wished, wished, *wished*, I were in their shoes.

All around, squeaky carts groaned under the weight of their bounty. Baskets overflowing with pastries and fruits, jostled precariously against crates with bleating goats and honking geese. These strangers from all corners of the Ar-Haya Highlands continued with their lives.

While my own had come to an abrupt halt.

Numb to any feeling but the burning in my thighs and the stitch at my side, I fixed my gaze on the dirt path leading to the town gates from the valley, as if I'd just arrived from Lumya, a town leagues away from Vosk. Best no one saw me approaching from the direction of the Golden King's city.

I rounded the north wall to a commotion near the gates. A wagon, adorned with a vibrant array of silks, blocked the entrance. Roamers.

"You can't come in this way," Hrant, the main guard, yelled at the coachman. "Go around to the side gates."

I stopped with the line of people waiting to enter Mosatti, positioning myself next to a large family who spoke Sophenian in the accent of Zepure, a coastal town bordering the Sable Sea.

An elderly woman pulled aside a flap at the back of the colorful wagon and stuck her head out, fluttering her hand in the air. "But *why*, my good man? We've come for the market and celebrations, same as everyone here."

Hrant removed the sword from his scabbard and held the point toward the cart, his voice rising. "You know the rules, *digin*. Go to the side gate or leave."

The woman, likely a fortune teller, rolled her eyes

and addressed her driver, grumbling in frustration. "You heard him," she said before disappearing inside and closing the flap.

Our guards often directed those deemed suspicious through the side gates for searching. I bit my lip. Baba often purchased unusual relics from roamers throughout the Highlands, the only people unafraid to defy the laws of the Golden King, and many paid with their lives.

Could they have the forbidden map I needed? If the guards allowed them entry, these roamers might set up shop somewhere on the market road in town. I'd search for them later if the "Ra-" my father mentioned did not materialize, or worse, refused to help.

Wheels squeaking, the colorful cart made its slow turn through the crowded street. While the irritated guards eyed the roamers, I slipped through the gates behind the family from Zepure.

"Better to enter unseen than to be questioned," Baba's rumble echoed into my head.

No one in Mosatti knew of my father's and my secret life. They simply thought we sold rare books and valuable artifacts in our shop. Zakaya, the Regent's son and my betrothed, trusted me. It burned that I lied to him by omission. I never told him the truth about where we went and what we sought when we left for weeks at a time and returned exhausted. I couldn't bear the thought of him seeing me as a thief with blood on my hands. My father's blood. But I couldn't bear the thought of him seeing me as a liar either.

My heart lurched. I'd taken two valuables from the Golden King's palace, and they'd seen Baba, knew he came from Sophene. Knew Baba hadn't been alone. Fear sliced through me as I followed that train of thought. The

Enlightener had my knife. He could use magic to track me, identify me.

The Monster-King had pursued me through the night, but after a few hours he'd stopped, as if he'd miraculously lost my scent. And what about those demon-mice that led me to the crowned-monster? What in the name of the goddesses was happening in Vosk?

On instinct I glanced over my shoulder, beyond the crowds filling the road, beyond the town walls. Mount Massisa's peaks glistened white in the far distance, hovering over the wooded hills. A soft breeze fluttered my hood. It all appeared so peaceful, so ordinary. Would the Monster-King even show himself in such a crowd? Did he look that way all the time or only at night, like the myth of the *soulless*? Would his bite transform his victims into creatures like himself? Where had I read that?

Baba's texts.

Baba.

Panic seized me. I should have forced Baba into the tunnel with me, forced him to go without the Spool. Baba would have known what to do when faced with the blood-sucking creature.

I quickened my steps. The market road was carpeted in the flowering willow's tiny violet petals. Shops and dwellings lined the cobbled streets, their open doorways welcoming. I half-walked, half-ran, hefting the two packs on my back, keeping my head low to avoid meeting anyone's gaze.

Slipping past the cluster of shops at the town center, I veered onto the uphill path. Laughter and chatter filled the air as people swarmed shop doorways. The familiar sweetness of rose-kissed sugar cookies wafted from the corner bakery. Countless mornings had begun with me rushing there for Baba's and my favorite treats. My steps began to drag.

Outside the baker's shop, overflowing baskets displayed the season's first fruits. My gaze lingered on the hard green apricots. Baba's favorite snack, dipped in salt. My eyes stung.

Sweet and pungent aromas assaulted my senses. My mouth watered. I'd eaten nothing since yesterday morning. Had it been yesterday morning? I rubbed my temples. How long had I been on the road? But my stomach churned with nausea at the thought of food. How could I eat Baba's favorite treats when he lay dead at the King's palace? Yanking my hood lower, I hurried past before the baker could notice me, call me inside. Ask about Baba.

Our shop, wedged between the butcher and seamstress, stood in stark contrast to its neighbors. Their freshly painted entrances bloomed with potted flowers, doors open and welcoming. While our once-red doorway stood locked, and flaked like peeling sunburn. My matted braids and clothes clung to me as I stood frozen before our entrance.

Just two stairs…and I couldn't do it.

I stared at the lower step, the one with the crooked stone as far back as I could remember. The one Baba tripped over every time he climbed it, his mind often leagues away. My vision blurred. A couple passed by, hand in hand, their laughter pulling me from my haze. Too late, I realized someone had paused behind me.

"Satya?"

My stomach lurched as I turned. "Lana." My voice rasped like grated stone, rusty from disuse. But I couldn't ignore Zakaya's sister, my closest friend.

"May the gods and goddesses bless you," she said in acknowledgment of the holiday.

"May you always be in the light," I replied automatically.

"Are you just now returning from your trip?" Her eyes raked over my dishevelment. "Are you…all right?"

Her deep frown proved just how unkempt I looked. As the Regent's daughter, she wore silk dresses and self-crocheted lace. Her current gown was a deep burgundy rimmed in gold, reaching her leather sandals.

As twins, she and Zakaya shared the same high forehead, same curly, jet-black locks. But where his chin was square and prominent, hers was pointy and delicate. Where his dark eyes held specks of gold, hers were wide and tinged in green. Where his gaze softened at the sight of me, hers often crinkled in mirth. I loved her like a sister. My heart dipped at the way she studied me now. Had she heard about the thievery?

"I…fell asleep in the wagon," I said.

She glanced up at the shop door. "And your father…?"

"Stayed behind," I said quickly. "I returned with one of Baba's merchant friends."

Her eyes softened. "I'm glad you're home. Hurry and get ready. Zakaya will be horrified to see you in this state." She smiled to soften her words. "You should see how handsome he looks."

I forced myself to smile back.

"I cannot wait for the dance tonight," she said, pressing her hands together and bouncing on her toes.

My mouth slackened. Her solo performance was tonight? But the dancers were to perform on the last day of Nurazard. My insides went cold. Was *today* the last day of Nurazard?

Impossible. How could I have taken a three-day journey in one night?

That would mean I hadn't slept or eaten or done anything but run for days!

I rubbed my temples. What type of magic caused one to lose so much time?

Lana stared at me strangely. "Are you sure you're all right, Satya?"

My cheeks flushed. I should have asked her about the dance, and it was obvious from the way she studied me that she'd expected me to.

"Your performance is going to be amazing," I said, sidestepping her question.

Her smile widened. "Go rest. I need to get ready. The gown they have me wearing is absolutely stunning, and a bit indecent." She giggled.

"I'll see you tonight." The lie slipped off my tongue.

"Hurry, then." She flung her arms around me, ignoring my sweat-soaked, grimy clothes, then jogged off to prepare.

My throat tightened. I almost called her back. Almost confessed everything. Almost.

Instead, I dragged my feet up the crooked steps and grabbed the rusty key from my pocket. Hands shaking, I struggled with the lock until it finally yielded. The door groaned open.

Through the shadows, echoes of my father's voice reached me. *Satya jan, are you home?*

I forced myself to step into the empty shop, to close and lock the door behind me. I stared around blindly, half-expecting him to emerge from a crouch by a bookcase or his workshop in back. I wove through cluttered shelves, past tables laden with books and artifacts, toward our family quarters at the rear. Pausing, I leaned my forehead against the worn wooden door leading to our empty dwelling. With a loud sigh, I pried it open, hinges creaking.

My footsteps echoed into the empty rooms. "Baba?" My whisper cracked.

For a silent moment I stood waiting. Waiting.

Only the dust particles suspended in sunbeams peeking through shuttered windows stirred the silence.

****

Once, patrons crowded our shop, drawn to the texts, rare relics, and Mama's intricate tapestries. Most of my mother's handiwork was gone now, seized by the Golden King's soldiers five years ago.

I stepped through the archway of the room I once shared with Caral. We'd kept his small bed in the corner, covered in his favorite blanket. His clothes lay neatly folded in the open wardrobe, frozen in time for five years. A reminder that our thievery had a purpose.

Baba had been that sure of the Weaver's Spool.

Above Caral's bed hung a tapestry barely an arm's length, the sole survivor of the Golden King's raid five years ago. Woven by Mama to soothe Caral's nightmares, it depicted legendary gods. In the center stood Anahit, goddess of healing, a lotus blossoming from her outstretched palms. Vahagn, the Dragon Reaper, sat astride a serpent-dragon, sword raised high. To their left, the Sable Sea stretched into the horizon, watched over by the sea gods, Nar and Tsovian. The scene was so lifelike, one could reach out and expect to slip into the woven world. A testament to Mama's extraordinary gift.

Slipping it from the wall, I stumbled down the corridor and paused on the threshold to my parents' bedchamber. Darkness crept at the edges of my vision. Whispers, ghosts of their laughter. Years hadn't erased Mama's scent—a mix of rose-lavender soap and the familiar tang of leather, parchment, and Baba. It smelled like home.

With a sob, I crumpled the silken tapestry against my chest and sank to my knees. "Mama, Baba, tell me what to do."

Silence.

A primal screech ripped from my throat.

I screamed and screamed my rage and grief into my brother's tapestry.

Chapter 6

Any fool can tell the truth, but it requires some sense to lie well.

~ Ar-Haya Highlands Proverb

"You can bring us all back. Find the map. Talk to Ra-" Baba's resigned eyes wavered before me.

I wove wraith-like through the throng, Mama's silver cape hood pulled low over my face. After a panicked cold bath, I'd dressed in my most comfortable travel garb. A burgundy tunic covered my ankle-length woolen skirt. My belt-pouch held the essentials: Baba's pocket knife, picks, a coin case, and Caral's dream tapestry, rolled neatly into a thin tube. Blocking all thought, I'd packed methodically, leaving the large satchel, with the Weaver's Spool hidden inside, beneath a stack of rugs at our shop to retrieve once I had the map.

Then I'd be on my way.

The town's main cobbled path swarmed with crowds and the clamor of horse carriages. The scent of *bonchik* wafted from a nearby tent. The mere thought of the syrupy dough curdled my stomach. *Focus. I'm not here for food.*

Baba knew two people whose names began with "Ra-." Master Raman, my former schoolmaster, frequented our shop. Advisor to the Regent, he and my father had often argued lately. Baba could not have meant him. That left Ralondu, the carpet merchant Baba traded with. Ralondu's shop, two roads down from the corner of our block, stood closed. He'd likely set up a tent tonight at the market.

I strode past tents brimming with wares, strangers' faces blurring as I sought Ralondu's tent. Above, on a hill overlooking the joyous chaos, the Regent's dwelling gleamed in the twilight, a gilded symbol of the present tyranny. It hadn't always been this way. Decades ago, Sacreds had tended tranquil gardens and temples dedicated to the gods. The Regent's manor had claimed the location where a temple once stood. A Sacreds' garden remained at the hill's base, transformed into a memorial for those lost in the massacre. Within it, a stone wall bore the names of the fallen. My mother's and brother's names were etched on that wall.

"Goddess, watch over them," I whispered as I dragged my feet past the sacred space. If my plan worked, my family would no longer be empty names on a stone wall.

At the center of town, carriages had been transformed into colorful shops that snaked around the central fountain, their canvas awnings weaving a rainbow tapestry around the bustling square. Flowers of every color carpeted the cobblestones, a battlefield lost by laughing children armed with blossoms.

A group of men near me burst into a celebratory song of the Highlands. "Copper, bronze, and iron, smelt 'em and then mold 'em. Shape 'em into smolderin' knives to bring with us for huntin'."

A few people behind me joined in. Their laughter scraped at my raw nerves, harsh as fingernails against stone. Baba had often sung that tune under his breath, except he'd changed the last stanza to, *to bring with us for plunderin'*. Saliva slid down my throat like sand.

Merchant tables overflowed with pastries, drinks, and a variety of fruits and sweets. The scents of grilled lamb on iron skewers mingled with dripping syrupy sweet breads. My stomach continued to growl with a mix of hunger and queasiness as I rounded a corner and the scent of burnt wood grew pungent in the air.

A round firepit had been set up at the center of one of the wide avenues, long flames bursting from the blackened wood. A small crowd surrounded the fire and a line dance had formed to the music played by three musicians nearby.

A few young men had already started attempting their "fire jump" to impress the town girls or gain a promise of a bonding from the one they loved. A boy sat on the ground, holding his bare foot in his hands, wincing. He'd obviously tried and failed to jump over the fire. The sharp tang of smoke stung my nose and throat. I coughed and quickly walked by, holding my palm over my mouth and nose.

"Satya?" a deep voice said from behind me.

Fear froze me as I turned. The veil of smoke thinned to reveal my old schoolmaster, Raman, dressed in his burgundy festival robe. His silvery hair reached past his shoulders and his full beard covered his mouth and chin. When he spoke, the mound of hair moved up and down resembling a bird's nest caught in the wind.

Prior to our journey to Vosk, I'd entered our shop to find my father and Master Raman in a heated argument. Though they both quieted as soon as I entered, I'd wondered ever since what had caused the two friends to disagree. Could he be the "Ra-" my father had named?

But why would Baba confess to Raman, not only my former schoolmaster, but also among the Regent's closest advisors? When our eyes met, his own shuttered.

"May the gods and goddesses bless you, Master Raman," I mumbled the formal greeting for the holiday.

"May you always be in the light," he said, bowing his head. Then he stilled, his eyes cast down at my hand.

The ring! Goddess, I'd forgotten I still wore it. Cursing my carelessness, I jerked my hand into the folds of my skirt.

Raman straightened, his eyes crinkling in a forced smile. "The gods and goddesses have plans for us all on this beautiful evening. Enjoy the festivities."

"You as well," I said.

Leaning on his walking stick, he hobbled away.

I stared at his retreating back with a prickling feeling that he'd recognized the ring. I'd often wondered if he knew more about forbidden relics than he let on. But if he did know or guess, he'd kept his silence. My heart lurched in panic as he disappeared into the crowd. Would he go straight to the Regent?

I froze with indecision as the smoke from the fires surrounded me, stinging my lungs. Had my father meant Master Raman, or his merchant friend, Ralondu?

A vision of the hourglass sitting on Baba's palm flickered in my mind's eye, the sand at the bottom thickening at an impossible pace. If Raman recognized the ring, he'd tell the Regent. Heart racing, I pushed through the swarming crowd.

Every whisper, every glance felt like scrutiny. This had been a foolish idea. I shouldn't have come. No map was worth the price of a hanging.

But without the map I'd wander lost in the Ar-Haya

Highlands' forests and caves, blindly hunting hidden temples that might house a Sacred, someone capable of wielding the Spool.

Trembling with indecision, I surveyed the town center. Bodies jostled from every side until I felt trapped. Air rushed in and out of my lungs in panicked bursts. The cacophony of chatter, laughter and song merged into a deafening roar.

I couldn't breathe. I needed air. I needed space.

A gap in the crowd revealed a canopy of shimmering silks before a vendor wagon. Rugs?

The air filled with patchouli and bergamot as I moved closer, and the full wagon came into view. My heart sank. Not Ralondu, but the roamers. They must have bribed their way in from the town's side entrance. A breeze parted the wagon's curtains, revealing stacked tapestries and scrolls. Baba's words echoed in my head, *"Roamers know everything...for a price."*

Before I realized it, I found myself sheltered beneath a vivid tapestry, shielded from prying eyes. Two women in kaleidoscopic silks dealt divination cards at the wagon's entrance. The older woman, the one who'd argued with the gate guards earlier, sashayed over.

"See something you fancy, dear?" She waved at the wagon's flapping curtain.

I moistened my lips, casting a quick glance around me, then whispered, "I need...a map."

Her sculpted brows arched. Leaning forward, she matched my hushed tone. "What type of map?"

I swallowed tightly. These roamers smuggled forbidden items. Only the Regent's ignorance spared them during festivals. If the King's guards were here, they'd seize them, *and* me. "A map of...ancient temples."

Her eyes narrowed. "A banned map, then."

"I didn't say that…" This was a mistake. I should leave.

But before I could decide what to do, she flashed me a one-toothed grin, grabbed my right hand in both of hers, and shut her eyes. I tried to tug my hand free, but her grip tightened.

Her eyes flew open, and she blinked at me. "Dear, dear," she said, clucking her tongue. Her gaze grew hazy as if she could see through me. "There are many paths that entice, yet only one will lead you to what you seek. Beware the false path, for a fierce evil dwells within…a sacrifice you must make." Her tight grip sent a wave of pain through my hand as she whispered, "Harness the woven light and the sacrifice will be undone."

I gaped at her. *Harness the woven light? Sacrifice?*

She leaned forward. "What you seek is seeking you. But what you seek now is not true."

I tugged my hand free and rubbed my burning fingers. A riddle?

Her grin widened as she extended her open palm. She wanted payment.

"That isn't the information I asked for," I said, my chest tightening with frustration.

"And yet I gave you the information you need." She pushed her palm closer.

Sighing, I dug into my pouch and dropped a few coins into her hand, more to keep her from making a fuss than for the nonsense she'd spewed.

"The truth is hidden in plain sight, my dear," she said, as she pocketed the coins. "You don't need a map for that."

Her cryptic message grated on my nerves. Plain sight? Here in Mosatti or here at the celebration? Or in plain sight at our shop? *Why am I even considering her words?*

I walked away, my mind reeling with the roamer's strange words. *What you seek is seeking you. But what you seek now is not true.*

Utter nonsense, as Baba would say.

"I'd stay away from those people, Satya," a voice said from behind.

My stomach caved as I slowly turned to face my betrothed. "Zakaya."

"You came," he said, grinning. He took in my clothes, but didn't comment on the fact that my mother's silver cape clearly hid my travel outfit. "I'd hoped you would."

I cleared my throat. "You look amazing."

He did. Even through my haze, I couldn't miss his regal garb. Black hair slicked back, tied in a bun at the nape of his neck. His suit, a mixture of emerald-green and black, brought out the dark olive of his skin and the brown of his eyes. A ceremonial sword in a scabbard hung from his belt. He was tall enough that the emerald gems around his collar made him look kingly. Tonight, he truly looked like the Regent's son, more so than ever.

My heart lurched. How could I tell him what I'd done? What I'd seen? Would he believe me? Would anyone? How could I say goodbye?

With a laugh, he pulled me into his arms. "I missed you."

"I've missed you too," I said, swallowing.

We'd known each other for years, but this, *this* was new. During the past few months our feelings had grown into something more. Right before Baba and I had left, Zakaya'd secretly asked me to marry him and had given me a ring. I'd gifted him a silver-encased amulet of Vahagn, the Dragon Reaper. It had cost a small fortune, but I was so high on love I hadn't cared. It hung from his neck now, proudly displayed on a leather cord. He followed my gaze as he pulled back.

"You always reminded me of the god of courage," I said.

Zakaya smiled. "My parents almost named me Vahagn for just that reason."

Inside, *inside* I pleaded for him to find that courage when he learned the truth. The courage to trust me. The courage to wait for me.

Zakaya took my right hand and lifted my fingers to his lips, then stared down at our betrothal ring with a smile.

I still couldn't believe we were to be married. We'd planned on telling our families when Baba and I returned. We'd told Lana, though. We couldn't hide news like that from her.

But now, everything had changed. I slipped my other hand, the one with the magic ring, within the folds of my skirt.

Just then, two men walked slowly past us, their voices carrying.

"…thievery at the king's palace…" one said.

"I heard a few valuables were stolen."

"They'll blame it on Sophenians. They always do."

"They killed one thief. The king's guards searched our village this morning for the other, who escaped."

I stood rooted as the men passed us, fearful of meeting Zakaya's probing gaze. My empty stomach lurched and I had to swallow a few times to avoid vomiting.

Goddess, news spreads so fast.

A group of children ran by us, tossing flower petals into the air, their laughter fading as they ran down the avenue.

Zakaya leaned forward as the petals rained down on our heads, and whispered, "If it's a Sophenian from this town, I'd hang him myself."

Chapter 7

A betrayer betrayed is like a thief who's been robbed.

~ Ar-Haya Highlands Proverb

Zakaya's fierce words pierced me, sharp as daggers.

What would he do when he found out *I* was the thief? For the first time in our relationship, I feared him. Not Zakaya. But the Regent's son.

Pretending to be studying a frayed thread on my cape, I asked, "Do you think the royal guards would have already come if they suspected Mosatti?"

"They may still come," Zakaya muttered, his eyes scanning the crowd. "But this is a celebration. Let's not dwell on that." When I didn't respond, he gently squeezed my hand. "I can hear the musicians starting up again. Lana is about to dance."

Lana's dance! She'd never forgive me if I missed it. But how could I stand there watching a dance when my world crumbled and crumbled and crumbled?

Violet twilight crept across buildings and tents as a troupe of musicians in shimmering red-orange attire parted the crowd.

Just as I thought of an excuse to slip away, a flapping rug down the road snagged my gaze. Ralondu's tent. My heartbeat quickened.

Maybe the dance offered the perfect distraction.

A lone duduk player stepped forward. Lifting the thin woodwind to his lips, he unleashed a melancholy lament. The duduk's mournful cry bled through the air, each note a sob.

Three children in stark white robes emerged, glowrocks casting ethereal light on their bowed heads. A weighty hush settled over the crowd, pressing my chest. Heads dipped in mute tribute for those silenced during the massacre.

Tears glistened like scattered stars among the gathered faces. My own eyes stung with bitter fire and shared sorrow. Beside me, Zakaya's hand found mine, gripping tight as he bowed his head in silent salute for my loss.

As the duduk's final note faded into a whisper, the music shifted. The other musicians joined, and the davul's drumbeat accelerated defiantly, met by the double-reeded zurna and stringed kanon's cheerful tune.

Dancers in crimson and gold glided hand in hand into the clearing, rhythmic feet scattering flower petals. Silken skirts swirled like flames, matching the men's sharp, precise booted steps. The crowd, caught between mourning and celebration, slowly responded, clapping to the davul's pulsing beat. My chest constricted. *This*. The Sophenian union of grief and joy braided into the same tapestry.

I slipped my hand from Zakaya's, ready with an excuse, when a ripple of unease spread through the crowd. The Regent and his wife emerged, escorted by four guards. The Regent's silk robes, vibrant against the darkening sky, whispered against his legs as he strode toward us. His searching gaze lingered on me, but I avoided eye contact, focusing instead on the dancers.

The white-robed children had melted into the crowd. How would the Regent have reacted to the commemoration of our loved ones, had he arrived moments before? Carving names on a wall in a secluded memorial garden completely differed from openly acknowledging those the King marked as rebels. A defiance the Regent couldn't ignore.

Despite his Sophenian heritage, the Regent acted as the King's puppet. His own son Zakaya had just participated in the memorial moments ago, a stark contrast to his father, who would have ordered arrests instead. One day, Zakaya would prove a far fairer ruler for his people than his father.

The Regent angled his head to the performers, then his gaze met mine. "Is your father well?" Even above the music and dancing, I heard a tremor of suspicion in his tone.

I opened my mouth to answer, but my throat squeezed shut.

Zakaya answered for me, "Her father hasn't returned yet."

"Zakaya," the Regent said, his voice dropping to a hushed tone. "We need to speak."

My gaze snapped back to the Regent, but his eyes were scanning the outskirts of the crowd.

Zakaya tensed. "About the thievery?"

The Regent nodded, lowering his voice. "Be alert, my son. If they suspect a Sophenian…" He glanced at me again.

A shiver of ants crawled over my scalp. He *did* suspect me, or at least he suspected my father.

Zakaya's mother patted her husband's hand. "Your daughter is about to dance. Enough talk about guards and danger. Please, let us try to enjoy this." She turned and offered me a smile.

I forced myself to smile back, my heart growing heavy with all the secrets I kept from Zakaya. He pulled me close, one hand gripped tight on his amulet, betraying his own anxiety.

I swallowed my guilt and glanced back at Ralondu's tent, trying to think of a reason to slip away. The crowd had thickened around us. The performers raised their arms, hands linked as they swayed. I spotted Lana toward the back. Our gazes met and her face lit up with a happy smile.

The main davul player banged a fist to his small drum and the dancers yelled, "Haya!"

The davulist's fists blurred, flaying the drum into a frenzy. The ground throbbed with the dancers' stomping, the crowd's clapping. The rising rhythm hammered against the walls of my chest, my mind. My breath hitched, each gasp a scream I choked back. The world narrowed.

I couldn't do this. I couldn't just stand here watching a performance. I needed to talk to Ralondu. Now.

"I'll be right back…" I whispered to Zakaya and stepped out of his embrace.

Zakaya frowned, his arm slipping off my shoulders. "Now?"

I cleared my throat. "I'll only be a moment."

He pressed his lips together. "Lana will be so upset…"

"I'll return before her solo performance," I said quickly.

I bit my lip. If Ralondu helped me, I doubted I'd return at all.

"Hurry back," Zakaya said, his frown deepening.

I nodded, blinking back the sudden burn in my eyes. Before I could change my mind, I slipped through the crowd. I could feel Zakaya's worried gaze following me.

The fortune teller's words echoed through my mind. *A sacrifice you must make.* Her eerie words followed me as I quickened my steps.

The farther I walked away from my betrothed, the thinner the cord between us stretched. How long before it snapped?

****

Ralondu's small tent teemed with carpets piled to my mid-waist. A man and a woman stood inside, loudly bargaining over a small woolen rug. His belly protruded, straining the buttons on his tunic, as Ralondu argued with the couple over the price. I stood to the side, jittery with nerves, and waited impatiently for them to finish.

The customers finally left, the man carrying the rolled rug under his arm and a smug smile on his face.

Ralondu's face lit up when he saw me. "Satya!" he called, waving me to the back. "Is your father here?"

I shook my head as I approached. "No, he wanted me to speak with you."

He frowned. "Do you need more rugs for the shop?"

More rugs for the shop?

I bit my lip and my words flew out before I thought too deeply about his reaction. "Baba said I can come to you if we're in trouble."

His frown deepened. "What kind of trouble are you in, Satya?"

I hesitated. Had I made a mistake? "I-I need help."

Ralondu's forehead wrinkled in confusion, but I pressed on. "Baba said you have a map of hidden temples…"

My voice tapered off at the horror slowly dawning in Ralondu's gaze.

"The thievery," he hissed. "Your father?"

I shook my head, stumbling back until I bumped against a pile of rugs.

A voice called out from outside the tent. "Satya?"

Zakaya. He'd followed me? I turned to see my betrothed standing at the tent's opening, his worried gaze on me.

Ralondu's eyes flitted between Zakaya and me, his face turning red.

I retreated away from the rugs, putting distance between me and the man who I'd thought was my father's friend. Just as I reached Zakaya, a shout rang over the thick crowd outside.

"King's guards," Zakaya hissed, taking my hand. "My father thinks…" He cleared his throat. "Satya, we need to talk."

"Get her out of my tent," Ralondu yelled at him. "I had no part in it."

"Zakaya, I need to explain…" I sputtered.

But Zakaya wasn't listening as he pulled me from the tent. A disturbance scattered the crowd down the road. Zakaya pushed me behind him, hand gripping his sword hilt.

My heart stabbed at my chest. A woman screamed, a child began to cry. Clanging sounds neared as dozens of Aurean guards tore through the throng, dispersing people in all directions. The line dancers down the road broke formation and the musicians stopped abruptly. A hush fell.

Fear choked me. These guards were not here to

make a request. They were prepared to kill.

A loud, booming voice rose over the crowd. "Where is Satya Lumian?"

The sides of my vision blurred. How? How did they know my name? Had their magic stolen it from my blade?

Gasps resonated from the crowd.

"The Sacred's daughter," someone yelled. "Haven't they done enough?"

"Never trusted that family," another said.

Zakaya turned around, his horrified gaze meeting mine.

Before I could react, a silent figure emerged between the Aurean guards. His bald head glistened in the ruddy blaze of the glowrocks. His pale robes swished as he stalked forward, scattering flower petals.

The Enlightener.

His metallic-yellow gaze levelled over the crowd.

I bolted in the opposite direction.

Footsteps pounded behind. Zakaya grabbed my arm, pulling me behind a wagon to face him.

"Satya?" His eyes lowered to my hand where the stolen item glistened accusingly on my pinky.

I wanted to deny it. Oh, how I wanted to lie. "It's…Baba and I…we…"

His fingers dug into my arm, his eyes tearing. "You told me your father was away…"

"Please, Zakaya. Please don't…"

A distant voice echoed over the crowd. The Regent. "Zakaya!"

"How can you do this to me, to *us*?" Zakaya hissed.

"Please, please trust me," I pleaded, tugging at his vise-grip. "Let me explain…"

"Zakaya," the Regent called again, fear marking his voice. "Where is she?"

Zakaya towered over me. For a moment, uncertainty wavered in his eyes. Then a cold glint hardened his gaze. Gone was the boy who'd given me a betrothal ring, the boy who wanted to spend the rest of his life with me. In his place stood a stranger with betrayed eyes.

This, this angry man, was the Regent's son.

"I won't let you bring another raid upon our town," Zakaya said, his voice cracking. "You've betrayed your own people." *Betrayed me.* His unsaid words hung between us. His eyes filled.

I had never seen him cry. *I* caused those tears. My heart broke again and again.

"Please, Zakaya, please listen…" With my other hand I reached out toward him, trying to make him understand, but he snatched his hand away.

"Zakaya," the Regent screamed.

"I'm sorry," Zakaya whispered, eyes overflowing. "I just…I'm sorry."

His red-rimmed gaze still pinned to me, Zakaya did the last thing I expected him to.

"She's here, Father," he yelled over the crowd. "Satya Lumian is here."

Chapter 8

A secret is a key that unlocks a door,
not to new treasures, but to what hid there before.
~ Ar-Haya Highlands Proverb

The air left my lungs.

For one frozen heartbeat, I stared at Zakaya. Waiting…for what, I didn't know.

I should have been prepared for this, should have anticipated Zakaya's reaction. But some deep, selfish part had hoped his love would protect me. I should have known. Should have expected that he was the Regent's son first and foremost.

Zakaya, who loved his father, but feared the Regent; who respected the law and took the responsibility of caring for his people above all else. Above *me*.

A surge of heat flooded my face. I tugged hard. "Release me."

Zakaya's grip tightened. He pulled me into the crowd, avoiding my eyes as I struggled.

"You're hurting me," I cried, wedging my feet against the ground.

Sniffling, Zakaya swiped at a tear with the back of his hand and continued to haul me like a wheelless wagon. The crowd thickened around us. Some pointed to me in recognition. My gaze remained fixed on Zakaya's back. Until I spotted Lana.

Still in her stunning dance gown, she stood on the outskirts of the crowd beside her shocked mother, palms covering her mouth. Shame warmed my cheeks.

When my father first proposed this insane quest to return our family from the dead, it wasn't the fear of getting caught that had made me pause. It was *this*. Being ostracized by my own people, my closest friends.

I yanked with all my strength and finally jerked free of Zakaya's grip. The ring he'd given me suddenly felt too heavy on my finger. Hands shaking, I pulled it off and flung it at his chest.

"Keep the amulet," I cried, my vision so blurry I could barely see him. "To remind you of your faith in me."

The delicate ring bounced off his chest and clinked to the ground. Zakaya blinked at it, eyes brimming as he met my gaze. His hands clenched into fists, anguish and guilt mingling with the fear in his eyes. For a moment he almost looked as if he'd changed his mind. "Satya..."

But too late. The crowd parted as the Regent stalked toward us, face marked with rage and terror. A dozen King's guards in Aurean maroon followed, weapons drawn, boots pounding the ground as if prepared for battle.

Numb, I stared at their metallic chainmail armor, golden helmets, swords and daggers. At the symbol etched into their shields—the sun encased within a diamond-shaped eye.

Baba's voice speared into my thoughts, *"Be equipped. Be observant..."*

I can't! Those words won't help me now.

The townspeople and some of our own guards surrounded me, blocking my escape. Among them were familiar faces. The baker, who often gave me an extra *bonchik* on Sunday mornings. The seamstress who had mended my mother's and my gowns for years. Bennik, one of our loyal patrons who visited our shop at least once a week.

My eyes overflowed until I could no longer recognize faces and turned away from their accusing glares.

One of the king's guards shoved aside the Regent and stalked toward me, his eyes a steely gray beneath his helm. The tall form of the Enlightener followed.

"Satya Lumian?" the guard growled.

I stepped back, wanting to deny it, but a woman behind me yelled in a trembling voice, "That's her!"

I glanced wildly around and at first couldn't see Zakaya. Then I spotted him behind the crowd. The people had pushed him out of the way of the guards. Of course they would. The Regent's son needed protection. The royal guards had no respect for the people of Sophene, no matter their rank. I, on the other hand, would be handed over to them as a peace offering. A sacrifice.

The fortune teller's words pierced through my terror. *For the right path, a sacrifice you must make.*

Would the sacrifice be my own life?

"Now," the Enlightener said, twisting and twirling a knife in his hands. *My* knife. "Let us begin with you returning the objects you stole."

I stared at my knife in his hands. The weapon that had never left my side for the past five years. The weapon that had betrayed me as surely as Zakaya had.

When I didn't answer, the Enlightener tipped a long finger to someone behind him. A guard stepped up, a thick chain dangling from his grip.

I stumbled back, but multiple hands pushed me forward.

I'd be subjected to a public beating. Then death. I knew their methods, had seen it countless times during the massacre. How many innocents had died at the hands of these chain-bearing barbarians? But in their eyes, and in the eyes of everyone here, I was no innocent. I'd stolen from the wretched King.

What would the people of Sophene do if they knew the truth about *him*?

The truth. I had nothing left to lose.

"Your king is a monster," I cried, my voice thick with hate. "He devours people, steals their souls. The Enlightener *helps* him." I pointed an accusing finger at the tall priest.

The throng hissed in shock. Murmurs of *liar* and *insanity* resonated through the crowd.

I didn't see the guard's hand rise until the chain's loud clap echoed over the town center, bearing down on me. I jumped back, but too late. The sharp metal seared my shoulder.

I screamed. Someone called my name, the voice drowned out by the roaring in my ears. I flung my hand up to block another blow. I wished to be away, far away from the Golden King's guards.

The ring warmed. And suddenly I was airborne.

The ground blurred past as I flew backward, wind screeching through my ears. People scattered like startled birds as I sailed through the crowd and crashed into a vendor's tent two roads down from the guards. I landed hard on my back, bursting past fruit baskets. Apricots and grapes rolled away all around me.

The distant crowd became an entity, their fear morphing into rising anger.

"Magic," someone screamed.

"Where did she go?" another yelled.

Pounding boots drew closer and Zakaya loomed over me, with Lana close behind.

"Magic, Satya?" Zakaya hissed. "You've sealed your fate. I can't protect you, even if I wanted to."

Through tears of pain and rage, I hissed, "I'm not asking you to."

"Are you dense?" Lana shouted at her brother, shoving past to extend a hand. "This is your betrothed."

I grabbed Lana's hand and jumped to my feet. "I'm sorry, Lana."

She wrapped her arms around me, putting a lifetime of love in her embrace, and whispered, "Run."

I met Zakaya's horrified gaze.

Then I turned my back to him and grasped the tent's rear flap. Focusing on the ring, I made a wish.

And ran.

****

The ring pulsed with power, boosting me forward.

I sprinted through the town's back roads, feet barely touching the ground. My hood flew off, hair blowing behind me, but I couldn't stop. My right shoulder throbbed where the chain had singed it, each pulse matching my heartbeat as I raced past houses and through neighbors' gardens. Wind swelled as I cut through a narrow alley toward my street. Gasping, I flew up the crooked steps to our bookshop's door, my wounded shoulder banging against the doorframe.

Zakaya and his father surely had told them where I lived by now. That bitter thought was hard to swallow.

My trembling hands fought the stubborn lock, but before I could twist it, the door creaked open on its own.

Someone was already here.

The darkened bookshop swam before me. Bookshelves and display tables morphed into swaying silhouettes. Or maybe I was the one swaying.

My travel pack with the Spool lay hidden in a stack of rugs beneath a corner table. I couldn't leave without that satchel. Slipping into our shop's familiar gloom, I pulled the door shut with a barely audible click.

A shadow shifted at the open entrance to our private quarters. I grabbed the nearest makeshift weapon: an idle shelf Baba had meant to repair weeks ago. Clutching it, I crept past the cluttered, dusty bookshelves. My heart rammed relentlessly against my ribs as I neared the stack of rugs that hid my travel pack.

"Satya?"

I stiffened at the familiar voice. The shelf slipped from my grip and thumped onto the threadbare rug. The shadow moved into the muted light of a corner glowrock.

"Master Raman." My gaze locked on my former schoolmaster, the closest advisor to the Regent. The man Baba had lately clashed with. But also the only other person I knew whose name began with "Ra-."

What was he doing here? How had he gotten in?

As if reading my thoughts, he raised his hand, a rusty key dangling between his fingers. "Your father entrusted this to me years ago, after the raid."

"Why would he do that?" I asked, voice trembling.

"He wanted assurance his texts and notes would remain safe during his travels," Raman said. "I'm going to help you, Satya. But you must trust me."

I stumbled back against a display table, rattling its

contents. Something crashed to the floor. Clay shards scattered at my feet. I eyed Raman's hunched, frail form, calculating how far I could outrun him.

He leaned heavily on a bookcase, gripping his walking stick with shaking hands. That's when I noticed the large pack slung over his shoulder.

"There is so much you don't know, Satya," he said, dark eyes glistening beneath bushy brows. "I asked, *begged* your father to tell you the truth after the massacre. I knew you were in trouble when I saw that ring earlier today. It was inevitable. I can help you."

I shook with uncertainty. Could I trust him? In truth, I had no one else to turn to.

"Where's your father, child?" he asked in a quiet voice.

I barked the words out like a curse. "He's dead."

Raman closed his eyes.

Faint shouts echoed from the distance.

"I have to leave," I said, my voice hollow.

Raman's staff tap-tapped against the floor as he made his way to the door. "A darkness is spreading," he said, his words hushed and rapid. "We must stop its progress before it engulfs us all." Cracking the door open, he peered outside, then swiftly shut it. "I'm coming with you."

The rhythmic clang of armor and the muffled thud of footsteps drew closer. I dropped to my knees, grabbed my pack from under the display table, and slung it over my shoulder. Stepping outside with Raman, I locked the door, and we hurried down the deserted street. Shouts echoed a block behind us. A door slammed.

"Go, go," Raman whispered, hobbling faster, his walking stick clinking in rhythm.

We swerved into an empty alley, rushing through yards. Most people were still at the market, or what remained of it. I prayed the guards wouldn't harm anyone.

"Use the ring," Raman gasped.

"Would it work for both of us?" I asked, taking his arm when he stumbled.

"Yes."

With the ring, each time I'd wished for something, it somehow happened. Wishing to exit the palace unseen. Wishing to escape the Monster-King. Wishing to flee the pursuing guards.

Now, I wished for us to be far away from Mosatti.

The ring burned. Wind whisked by as I clung to Raman, packs thudding, our legs carrying us swiftly through the town as the sky darkened and the crescent moon raced across the stars at an impossible speed. Houses blurred. We flew up the hill to the outskirts, past the guarded gates, and up the steep hill toward the forest's edge.

Safely within the trees, our progress slowed and we came to a jarring stop. Raman doubled over, gasping.

"Are you all right?" I panted.

"I just...I just need a moment."

Behind us, Mosatti glinted in a silver halo, its rooftops like blades in the moonlight. I allowed myself to feel the agony of losing my family, my home and my life here. Of losing Zakaya.

Then I hardened my heart and turned my back to the scene below.

"We must keep moving," Raman said, pulling himself up with his walking stick.

A knife twisted in my chest as I turned my back to

Mosatti, and the only home I'd ever known.

My father's voice echoed in my head, *"Be equipped. Be observant. Be quick."*

My eyes burned. *Always, Baba.*

Chapter 9

Beware the rustling leaves' soft sigh,
the woods have ears, your words can fly.
~ Sop henian Folksong

For hours, we navigated a forgotten trail obscured by thorny brambles and serpentine roots. The woods pulsed with chirruping crickets, croaking frogs, and the faint sound of a gurgling stream. A coyote howled, answered by another. Soon a chorus of howls filled the night. Every sound needled my spine and scalp.

Raman charted our course using the stars. Despite his limp and a sagging gait, he clutched his walking stick with a trembling hand and maintained a deliberate pace. Since our escape we'd barely exchanged more than a few words.

Shoving aside a branch, I glanced back for any sign of pursuit. My mind conjured all kinds of dangers. Wild animals and mud-slicked slopes. Tiny demon-mice that herded unsuspecting thieves into danger. A beast with a crown.

"Where are we going?" I asked, my voice shaky with fatigue.

"I have an old friend who might help us," Raman said.

Us. I still didn't understand why my old schoolmaster would risk himself to aid a dead friend's daughter. But I felt too numb to ask and did not want to seem ungrateful, so I kept my silence. The darkness was nearly complete when Raman rubbed two glowrocks together and passed one to me. Soft light illuminated our surroundings, casting our twin shadows behind us. I couldn't shake the eerie feeling of being followed.

"How far is your friend?" My voice fell flat against the thick woods.

Raman released a heavy, exhausted breath. "We'll travel north as far as we can to throw off any pursuers. Then we'll cut east to the twin peaks of Massisa where I last saw her."

Mount Massisa, the legendary seat of the gods. I stared blindly ahead. At least he had a plan. Without the map of hidden temples, my own plans were fuzzy, at best. Would Raman have it? He was clearly the "Ra-" Baba had wanted me to talk to. I considered asking, but the darkness closed in like the walls of a tomb. I wasn't ready yet to disclose why I needed such a map, so I pressed my lips together and said nothing.

Raman often paused, muttering and gesturing with his walking stick. The glimmering hope of finding a Sacred and saving my family remained a faint beacon in the distance. All other thoughts I locked deep in my mind's dungeons.

"Maybe I can use the ring again…" I trailed off when Raman shook his head.

"I'm afraid these stiff knees cannot handle another sprint so soon."

I stole a glance at Raman, trying to gauge his intentions. No, I wouldn't reveal my plans to him until I understood his reasons for coming. Raman continued to mumble, sweeping his staff behind and around us.

"Is that a spell?" I asked.

"To cover our tracks," he said. "It won't mask our scent if they use hounds, but it's better than no spell at all."

Raman, our Regent's advisor, wielded forbidden magic?

A faint splash echoed in the distance, reminding me how close we still were to the Eugetz River. A wild animal? Or the Aurean guards? A rustle in the tree branches above had my heart racing until I spotted a dove preening pale feathers against the chill. The dove glanced down when we passed beneath it, its dark eyes catching the glowrock's gleam as it pinned us with its gaze.

"Doves are often used as spies," my father once told me.

I edged closer to Raman. "Could your spell divert a wild creature with keen senses?"

Raman glanced at me, mid-spell. "What creature?"

I wet my lips. I had to tell him. He deserved to know what we may have to face. Would he regret helping me then? "Before I left the palace, I...I saw the King."

I expected confusion, or indifference. Instead, his eyes filled with resignation. "There is no spell for such a creature, I'm afraid."

I stopped walking. "You *know* what he is?"

"I know what he's become," Raman said grimly. "This is, however, a story for later, when it is safe to rest." His gaze settled on the dove flitting from branch to branch, keeping pace with us. His tone darkened. "The woods have ears."

****

Complete darkness had swallowed the forest when

Raman collapsed heavily onto a massive tree stump, his breaths labored and uneven.

I dropped my pack and sank to my knees beside him. "Master Raman, are you all right?"

He met my gaze with weary eyes. "I will be fine."

"Maybe we should rest for the night."

"A wise idea," he said with a grunt. "I knew this day would come, and that the journey would not be easy. Still, it's been quite some time since I had to make such a hasty escape. And I was much younger then."

I raised my brows. "You've helped a fugitive escape before?"

"Many years ago," he said, grunting. "And *I* was the fugitive."

I waited for him to explain, but those few words seemed to have drained him. That comment alone made me realize how little I knew about my old schoolmaster.

I removed two apples from my pack, the ones Baba and I had taken to Vosk but never ate. My vision blurred as I silently handed one to Raman.

He retrieved a crusty loaf and feta from his own pack to share. "I bought these at the market this evening."

This evening. An eternity had come and gone since I'd watched the dance, pressed against Zakaya. Fragmented images assaulted my mind. Zakaya's betrayal, the Enlightener, the guard's chain. During our journey, the ache in my shoulder had gradually intensified. Now, as I finished the meager meal, it became unbearable. Blood seeped through the silver cape's seams. Inhaling sharply, I raised a glowrock and gingerly peeled back the torn fabrics of my cape and tunic to assess the damage.

My shoulder was unrecognizable. Skin flayed,

discolored, with a wound as large as my palm oozing blood. My stomach roiled, the food I'd swallowed rising to choke me.

Raman winced. "Allow me to help you with that." He fished out a bottle of hazel-balm and sheer strips of whisperweave cloth from his bag.

"You came equipped," I said weakly.

"When you have survived as long as I have," Raman said, cutting a strip of whisperweave with a sharp knife. "And seen all that I have seen, it is best to always be prepared for…unexpected journeys."

I frowned. *That's not cryptic at all.*

As he reached for my shoulder, his hand paused, worry etched on his face.

I tensed. "Will I survive?"

He chuckled. "The wound is not deep, but it's bleeding quite a bit. It will likely scar."

"A scar is the least of my worries," I muttered.

As Raman carefully cleaned my wound, I gritted my teeth.

"Be careful with the Gate-Ring, Satya," he said.

I glanced down at the stolen ring. "Gate-Ring…is it dangerous?"

"Magic always carries risks. It depends on how it is used," he said. "I am quite familiar with this ring and its powers of translocation."

My jaw dropped. "You've used it? When?"

"When your parents and I were Sacreds in the Legion of Garni…many years ago."

I slowly turned to face him, my mouth slackening. "You're a Sacred?" A Sacred! He'd been *right there* all along and I had no clue. A spark of hope sent a thrill through me. Could Raman wield the Weaver's Spool to revive my family?

But something didn't make sense. If my parents had been in this legion Raman spoke of, Baba would have known. He wouldn't have needed a map of hidden temples to find a Sacred when he and Raman were Sacreds themselves. How could I ask Raman about his abilities without revealing I had the Spool?

Raman's next words doused my sizzling plan.

"I cannot perform spirit-healing," he said. "The Legion's Sacreds preserved god-relics, but only human vessels of the gods, such as a Light Weaver, can wield them properly with the right shielding ritual…brace yourself, this may hurt."

A sharp jab shot through my shoulder. I groaned.

"Sorry. I need to stop the bleeding." Raman removed more whisperweave from his pack and pressed it onto my wound. I had to grit my teeth. "A Light Weaver has a unique bond with the gods."

A memory of my mother's rituals flashed in my mind's eye. "My mother used certain tools for healing. So she was…"

"A Light Weaver," he said. His hands were gentle as he applied hazel-balm to my torn skin and flesh.

I continued to gape. "I don't understand."

"She aided those who were about to pass, correct?"

"Yes."

"And she healed their spirits, guiding them into the afterlife."

I nodded.

"That's what a Light Weaver does," he said. "Only those who can channel the godforce have such an ability. Light Weaving tools are more than sacred. Their power flows directly from the gods to their vessels." He met my shocked gaze, his eyes knowing.

Frozen, I watched as Raman continued to apply hazel-balm to my wound. My mother wove beautiful tapestries, using her loom for healing. Yet she had never mentioned being a god-vessel.

"Without a proper ritual," Raman said, "the godforce surges through the relic and into the wielder with uncontrolled power. It funnels Luminous energy of pure light and the Eclipse energy of change and transformation. Without the proper balance and shielding, the energies clash and the wielder risks losing themselves in them. Your father would do the shielding rituals with her."

I jolted. "My father was a Light Weaver too?"

He shook his head. "No. He was a Sacred. Same as myself and Mona, the friend we're on our way to find. Don't you know why Sacreds are called warrior-healers?"

Still in shock, I shrugged my good shoulder. "You wield swords?" Though I'd never seen my mother wield even a pin to harm another.

He chuckled. "Not quite. Sacreds are shields. We fight the darkness while a god-vessel invites the light."

I pressed my lips together in frustration. *Goddess, there is so much I don't know.* "But this ring helped me escape without a ritual..." I paused, a new realization dawning on me. With everything that happened, I hadn't really thought too deeply about it until now. "I arrived on day three of Nurazard."

Raman's brows furrowed. "What do you mean?"

"Baba and I reached Vosk on day one of Nurazard. It took us three days, traveling partly by wagon. When I escaped the palace, I ran nonstop until I arrived home…on day three." I shook my head. "How could I have taken a three-day journey overnight while running nonstop? That's physically impossible…"

Raman's eyes narrowed in thought. "Yes, and hence, the danger. This ring is unlike any other god-relic. It draws from the godforce directly, weakening and aging its wielder. It rushes you from place to place in less than *half* the time, forcing your body to move with unnatural speed. Your conscious mind feels as if it's only been a few hours, depending on your travel distance. But days of your life pass in the blink of an eye. Months…" He fell silent.

"Did that happen to you?"

Raman's brows knitted. "I've lost years, Satya. *Years.* In the Legion, there was always a pressing matter. My body could not endure the constant movement through space and time. During the purge of all god-relics, right before the massacre, the Aurean guards confiscated the Gate-Ring." He released a mirthless laugh. "I surrendered it willingly."

I stared at the Gate-Ring with fresh eyes. This relic had taken days of my life already. Days I would never remember. "So this was your ring?"

"It belonged to the Legion." Raman's hands paused as he turned his furrowed gaze on me. "Still does, Satya."

I swallowed hard, unsettled by his tone. Would he demand I surrender the one relic that had helped me so far? But despite his warnings, we clearly still needed it. And he clearly had no intention of ever wielding it himself again.

I wrapped a hand protectively over the Ring, relieved I hadn't mentioned the Weaver's Spool hidden in my pack. "How does it even work?"

Raman's eyes drew inward. "The Gate-Ring is a conduit with a temporal distortion force. A reality-weaver, of a sort. Anyone can use a sacred relic with proper training, purity of intention, and unwavering focus."

My mind whirled with questions and possibilities. Proper training? *No.* Purity of intention? *Doubtful.* I hated the King, the Enlightener. I wanted to bring back the dead. And unwavering focus? Maybe. I was my father's daughter, after all. "But…how is it *I* can use it?"

Raman's hands paused. "When I saw you wearing the ring at the market, that is precisely what puzzled me. It defies my understanding of such relics. It takes years to master such complete focus," Raman said as he applied more hazel-balm to my wound. "Like your remarkably talented mother."

My mother's graceful weaving lingered vividly in my mind, though I couldn't recall her using a ring or a spool. Her abilities had been tied to her loom, and she'd been a master at it.

A master who refused to tell her own daughter the truth. I clenched my jaw. So much had been purposely kept from me…by my own *parents.*

Raman continued, seeming oblivious to my simmering emotions. "When the Legion of Garni was decimated thirty years ago, your parents and I were among the few survivors." He paused, meeting my shocked gaze. "Have your parents never spoken of the Legion?"

I shook my head. *They hadn't trusted me enough. Obviously.*

I vaguely registered Raman securing whisperweave on my shoulder. The cool breeze transformed into a roar in my ears. Maybe my parents kept me in the dark for a reason. And maybe this life I'd blindly thrown myself into held dangers I couldn't imagine. But I was here now, my family's only hope.

When Raman finished, I carefully slipped my torn tunic back over my shoulder and met his grim gaze. "Master Raman, I need to know…I need to know *everything*."

Chapter 10

Oh weaver, weave echoes of history's thread,
Unweave the truth the living past has bred.
~ Sophenian Folksong

The glowrocks illuminated the contours of Raman's weathered face as his story unfolded. His voice transported me back to the circular chamber of Mosatti Academy within the Masters Hall, with its wall-length windows framing a lush, green courtyard.

Before the massacre five years ago, another horrific one occurred three decades prior—an event shrouded in secrecy and disguised as a triumph for Sophene. A masked truth, carefully veiled. A purging. The Sacreds of the Ar-Haya Highlands were obliterated, the temples of the old gods left in ruins, ancient god-relics stolen or destroyed.

An army sent from East Oturmink had arrived, led by a general named Ahri-Luys.

Ahri-Luys had a strange affinity with certain creatures, an odd talent to entice and command them. He used them to steer his victims into the hands of his brutal forces. His army decimated temple after temple, village after village, picking out and executing satrap leaders and high-ranking officials in towns and villages all over the Highlands.

"In forty days, all the temples were gone," Raman

said. "Forty days of terror wiped away most of what we had built over centuries, a millennia. Survivors arrived at our remote Temple of Garni. They brought with them god-relics they'd managed to salvage, along with tales of swift and brutal battles."

Raman paused, his gaze far away. "We sent out scouts, but they never returned. Survivors crowded into Garni, the last remaining stronghold in the Ar-Haya Highlands."

I sat still, my shoulder pain long forgotten. The forest sounds around me merged with the terrified screams of the victims in the visions Raman's story painted in my mind.

"We pieced together the truth," Raman continued. "Ahri-Luys, who carried the flag of a little-known kingdom, Oturmink, sought to obliterate evil. He claimed that the Highlands harbored users of dark magic."

My jaw throbbed from the constant pressure of my clenched teeth. "Sacreds don't use dark magic."

Raman grunted, though I couldn't tell whether he agreed with my statement.

"We banded together," Raman said. "Formed a legion."

"The Legion of Garni," I whispered.

"We knew, days before they arrived, that Ahri-Luys's army would march on the temple. Despite survivors' warnings, we were unprepared for the dark methods he employed." Raman's hand shook as he gripped his staff. "Garni was a stronghold, built to withstand centuries of brutal wars and natural disasters. Little did we know that Garni would be our last stand against this evil sorcerer who defied all we knew of the godforce."

Raman grew silent, his eyes shining, jaw quivering.

I glanced away from his pained profile, giving him a moment. An iron fist clamped around my heart, squeezing, squeezing.

After a time, Raman cleared his throat and nodded, as if reaching a decision. "Perhaps it would be clearer if I showed you."

Puzzled, I watched him retrieve a roll of cloth from his pack. With great care, he unfurled a square tapestry spanning the size of four texts when laid out. Twigs crunched as he flattened the corners. "This is one of the *korks* I managed to save."

I brushed the soft cloth, clearly the lifelike handiwork of a Sacred. "Kork?"

He nodded. "These light-woven *korks* are rare, especially now."

Raman raised his glowrock over the silky cloth. At the tapestry's heart rose an imposing stone temple from snowy hills, bathed in the light of a rising or setting sun. Snow-draped steps led to a terrace where massive pillars supported a weathered tiled roof. Figures in pale robes stood on the platform, eyes fixed on the surrounding woods.

"The Temple of Garni. The Legion's final stronghold," Raman said. "Do you recognize your mother's work?"

My chest constricted with the weight of an erased history my own parents had been part of. "My mother made this?"

"I've kept this one hidden for decades," Raman said, his eyes studying the kork. "This is what your father and I argued about, what tested our friendship. I wanted him to tell you the truth, to see if perhaps you…" He paused, squinting his eyes as if battling with his own thoughts. "Suffice it to say that your father and I disagreed on how to best safeguard and continue to track down the sacred relics."

My mouth slackened in surprise. Even when my mother lived, Baba had relentlessly chased one elusive artifact after another, claiming they were for certain well-paying patrons. My mother had taken Baba's relic-pursuing missions in stride, and now I understood why. They were both harboring and safeguarding the Sacreds' relics.

In recent months Baba's and Raman's muffled angry voices had echoed from behind the closed doors of my father's workshop. I had assumed their disagreements meant Baba did not trust Raman. But the old me had hardly been interested in their quarrels. I'd been too absorbed in my own life and my plans with Zakaya.

That all seemed so unimportant now, and yet, at the same time, so *significant*.

"Your father changed after he lost your mother and brother," Raman said. "He became unfocused, almost…"

"Obsessed," I finished in a whisper.

Baba had been fixated with locating the Weaver's Spool, with finding a way to reunite our family. I knew it was wrong. I *knew* it, and yet I hadn't stopped him. Instead, I'd *helped* him. Look where that had gotten him. And me.

And now, I planned to finish what he'd started. What did that say about me?

Raman nodded. "Obsessed. Now there's a word for

the ages. His foolish, single-minded, *eshi* ideas pushed him into death's grip and nearly…" He went still. Lifting his hand, he gestured for me to stay quiet, and surveyed the shadowy woods.

The forest hummed around us in a symphony of sounds.

I strained my ears, and there. A noise in the distance that seemed out of sync with the forest's harmony. Was that the sound of leaves rustling in the breeze, or a moving mob? The screech of a night owl, or a woman's scream?

I shivered, trying not to think of the possibilities.

Raman murmured an incantation, then said in a lowered voice, "Whatever that was, it's far away." He motioned to the kork. "This depicts but a fleeting moment of a catastrophic event. For years before the second purge, I traversed this tapestry's paths, searching for ways to defeat this evil plague."

"Traversed?"

"The Ring, Satya." Raman pointed at my hand. "*That* ring. It allows the wearer to roam light-woven tapestries the same way it speeds you through time and space."

The moment Raman uttered the words, I knew what I had to do. "Show me."

****

For the next hour, Raman explained the rules governing the ancient magic, the dangers of navigating the tapestry, and the methods of entering and exiting safely. He emphasized the importance of pure, undistracted focus when wielding the godforce without losing oneself within it. I nearly laughed. My thoughts were a tangled mess, but I didn't tell him that. I wanted, *needed*, to see my parents again. That singular need consumed me. I didn't tell him that either.

"Satya, this is a bloody battle," Raman repeated for the fifth time. "It may be triggering. Are you certain…?"

"My parents are there," I reminded him. "Maybe I can help with your search for clues."

As I opened my mouth to begin the spell, Raman gripped my arm. "Remember, if Ahri-Luys senses your presence, he may trap you within the kork. His physical form might be absent from the kork, but his essence lingers. Be careful."

My chest tightened with a blend of dread and a desperate need to see my youthful parents. "I will."

Recalling Raman's earlier transference lesson, I focused on the temple grounds just as I would visualize a destination when using the Ring to travel. "Woven light, strings of gold, grant me passage to times of old."

The Ring grew warm. The dark woods shifted, swerved, warped.

A spectrum of threads rose from the cloth, each dazzling strand undulating to its own unseen rhythm. The Ring brightened, its azurite core a beacon pulling the rainbow of strings inward. With a whoosh, light-strands burst forth, synchronizing and seaming together into the silhouettes of hills, forests, and a massive structure.

The abrupt shift from dark to light left me squinting, unsteady. A fierce wind whistled past and brushed my skin, yet I felt nothing.

"You will not feel the chill of winter," Raman had explained. *"For your body is not truly there."*

As my vision adjusted, I gaped at the brilliant vista before me. The Temple of Garni, bathed in rosy dusk, towered over the snow-blanketed landscape. Ancient stone pillars four stories tall supported the colossal structure. A dozen broad steps ascended to the terrace where clusters of pale-robed Sacreds stood, arms raised, palms upturned, their droning chants filling the air.

"They will neither see nor hear you," Raman had said.

It felt like a lucid dream. Somewhere within this recorded history were my youthful parents from three decades ago. An intense yearning to find them gripped me. But as I stepped toward the temple, a strange noise from the woods made me pause. It began as the *hush* of rustling leaves, rapidly growing into the pattering of raindrops on tiled roofs. A dark swarm skittered from the bare thicket over the snow-covered rise.

Jaws stretched wide, dagger-sharp fangs bared, the swarm advanced with purpose. *Demon-mice.*

I opened my mouth to scream, but no sound emerged. Before I could move, the tiny creatures swerved around and *through* me. I shuddered at the eerie sensation of wind passing through my corporeal form as they skittered past and up the temple steps.

The robed figures screamed but maintained their stances, increasing the droning volume and frantic pace of their chants. Some fell, slaughtered mid-chant, completing their sacred words with their dying breaths. Blood splattered across the icy tiles.

The rodents gnawed through the heavy temple doors. Within moments, more robed figures emerged, fleeing the gnashing teeth and raking claws. A wiry, sunken-cheeked youth barreled through the horde, wielding a palm-sized carnelian sphere. Brilliant light burst from the relic, searing the rodents' eyes. I instantly recognized that slumping gait.

Baba.

My youthful father's eyes widened in horror at something behind me. I spun around to see stealthy figures emerging from the woods. Soldiers garbed in night-dark uniforms emblazoned with the crimson emblem I'd only read about in texts: three stars encircling a blood-red mountain, the Oturmink insignia.

A high-pitched yell shattered the stillness. The invaders charged toward the temple.

A swarm of green-clad Sophenian warriors burst from behind the stronghold's walls to face the onslaught. I bolted for the temple steps, but the Oturmink forces were swifter. The two armies collided in a cacophony of clashing steel. Swords met in screeching arcs, daggers flashed like lightning. Something frigid pierced my abdomen. Gasping, I glanced down to find a curved blade protruding from my gut, skewering the emerald-garbed warrior behind me.

Pure terror speared my chest. *This isn't real...this isn't real...*

Arrows rained down on the temple terrace as more demon-mice swarmed their prey in droves. One by one, the Sacreds crumpled to the stones. I lost sight of my father in the chaos.

The remaining Sacreds maintained their droning vigil. Bolts of blinding light erupted from their upraised palms. Dozens of dark-clad soldiers collapsed around me, howling. I recoiled, my insubstantial form passing through the fallen like wind.

More and more invaders poured from the woods, their guttural war cries shaking the air, the ground. The Sophenian forces began to retreat, outnumbered at least ten to one.

Paralyzed, I stood unmoving amid the raging battle: the bestial roars, the droning chants, the agonizing screams. My mind couldn't grasp that this was merely a shadow play, a piece of history woven into this kork's threads.

My vision blurred. This was a mistake. I shouldn't have come. I should have asked Raman to recount the tale instead. It was so much easier to pretend this was a story, something that had happened decades ago and had nothing to do with me.

But it had *everything* to do with me. My parents endured this horror. I came with a purpose. Returning now felt wrong. As if I'd given up, that I'd let my parents down.

My parents survived this, I reminded myself. I had to see this through, to find them before they escaped. Squaring my shoulders, I spun toward the temple steps.

That's when I saw her.

A solitary pale-robed figure stood between the terrace's pillars, somehow untouched by the swarming demon-mice. Dark hair billowed behind her like a river of silk as radiant light poured from her upraised hands

Before my mind caught up, I was already sprinting, soaring past the chaos through knee-deep drifts, my spirit-form vaulting over the fallen, until I halted mere handspans from her.

For a breath, it was like facing a mirror.

My youthful mother's face was my own. Hair the rich color of earth, honeyed eyes, high cheekbones and pointy chin. Even the dimple on her right cheek.

This was the woman whose tender lullabies had soothed my restless nights, whose loving embraces banished winter's chill, whose genuine laughter crinkled her eyes, and her sorrows drew straight from her heart and into the depths of her gaze. Her light extinguished far too soon.

Mama.

The weight of that single word reverberated through me.

I inhaled the chill air mixed with the scents of crisp snow and coppery blood. *This isn't real. It's a memory. My mother's memory.*

I blinked, trying to clear my head to focus. *Clues, I'm here for clues.*

Mama's unfocused eyes locked on the treeline bordering the snowy field. The object in her hand caught my attention. What I had first taken as pure light, emitted from her palms, was brilliant energy emanating from the relic in her grip. The relic my father had sacrificed his life for. The Weaver's Spool.

This close, I could see the woven strands of power coiling and twisting between the relic's disks, braiding into the blinding shaft of light that lanced out across the battlefield.

The ringing clash of steel and anguished screams faded into the background as a new sound reached my ears. Her voice.

She sang a haunting melody, the same ethereal tune emanating from the glass-enclosed cabinet where I'd found the Spool. A spell.

"Weavers of Light
empower this fight.
The past and future
must come together
to end our plight."

Ghostly apparitions unfurled from the Spool's

radiant core, multiplying and swelling in size as they drifted over the battlefield.

She repeated the spell over and over in her sing-song voice. *"...The past and future must come together..."*

The spectral forms flitted between the fighting figures. Even in the freezing air, sweat glistened on my mother's brow as her voice rose in desperation above the screams. *"The past and future must come together..."*

It was clear from her horror-struck gaze that whatever she aimed to achieve was failing. Tears brimmed in her resigned eyes as her voice rose to a scream. *"To end our plight..."*

"What does it mean?" I shouted, but my words thudded against an invisible wall.

My mind reeled. What was she trying to accomplish with this spell? How could summoning Weavers from the past and the future aid in this battle?

A sudden thought tore a gasp from me. *Unless...those from the past are brought back to life.*

I stared at the Weaver's Spool, the legendary resurrection stone clutched in her trembling hands.

In life, I'd seen my mother use other relics. A silver spoon for ailing infants, a ritual dagger for the elderly, a smoky quartz pillar to ease a soul's journey into the afterlife. But I'd never witnessed her utter this spell or use this relic.

Something was important about this battle. Something Raman had missed. But what?

Were those *spirits* rising from the Spool's center?

Scanning the battle from my elevated perch, I tracked the demon-mice continuing to herd clusters of Sacreds from the temple's interior. That's when I noticed what I'd missed. Inky shadows wafted amidst the fighting figures. And as each shadow fused with a dark-clad Oturmink soldier, a jagged milky-yellow frost crystallized over their blades and shields, granting them advantage over the Sophenian warriors and Sacreds.

The pale, indistinct spirits rising in wisps from my mother's Spool drifted above the battle, casting a soft glow over the fallen. But the heavier, shadowy entities flowed from the direction of the woods. There, a tall figure stood at the treeline, dark shadows slithering from an object clutched in his upraised fists. His eyes were shut, lips moving. Ahri-Luys.

He's casting a spell.

He turned, facing my mother. Facing *me*. A sense of recognition prickled my scalp, and just as I placed the tall figure, my mother's gaze snapped to me.

She whispered, "Beware the shadows."

An icy tremor needled its way up my spine. *She's speaking directly to me.*

My surroundings darkened. Ahri-Luys's voice rose over the battle's din. I didn't need to understand his words to know that this was a dark spell. He'd seen me.

A churning cloud of roiling shadows massed above the clustered soldiers and hurtled toward me. A trap.

With a final, lingering glance at my mother, I visualized the forest where Raman and I sat. Just as the swirling vortex reached me, the snow-swept terrace scene dissolved. The sounds of battle faded. Everything vanished until all that remained was my mother's disembodied head suspended like a pale moon against a midnight void, whispering…

"Beware…the shadows…"

Shadows…shadows…shadows.

Fractured visions flickered through the blackness:

Ahri-Luys's dark silhouette, the gnashing jaws of the demon-mice, my mother's anguished features.

The Spool's light winked out.

Then…stillness.

Reality shifted, inflated, and rearranged itself in stuttering waves. The damp woodland scents, the rough bark against my back, the dim star-flecked canopy overhead. I felt as though I'd been plunged fully clothed into icy depths and forcibly expelled, leaving my body too heavy for my legs.

The forest sounds sharpened with agonizing slowness as I crumpled bonelessly to the hard ground.

My mother's woven tapestry lay open at my feet.

Chapter 11

Better the bitter tonic of truth than the honeyed poison of lies.

~ Ar-Haya Highlands Proverb

"Deep breaths." Raman's voice cut through the fog. "Easy now."

Other sounds returned. The night serenade of crickets and frogs, leaves whispering overhead. Distant howls.

"Traveling the threads of a *kork* can be disorienting," Raman said.

"That is a *highlandic* understatement." I inhaled deeply, once, twice, before I could speak again. "Why didn't you tell me that Ahri-Luys is the Enlightener?"

Raman's knowing gaze settled on me. "I needed to confirm my own perceptions weren't distorted. You saw him as well?"

"Yes. Didn't you?"

"The general remained an obscure figure to me," Raman admitted. "No matter how often I ventured through the kork, he eluded me. Always one step ahead, and I could never quite get close enough to discern his features. Although I had my suspicions about his true identity, everything fell into place five years ago."

"Ahri-Luys, a general in the Oturmink army…" I whispered. "Now, a royal priest for the Aurean Golden

King? How does that make sense?"

Raman released a heavy sigh. "Truth often doesn't. First, tell me what you saw."

Raman listened without comment as I recounted my experience, his gaze fixed on the darkened woods. When I finished, he remained silent, but I could almost see his mind working out the variations between my account, his own experiences during the actual battle, and his journeys within the kork.

After a few moments, he said, "I've often wondered if my involvement in the battle tainted what I was shown in the kork. Now I believe I'm right. Shadowy figures, you say?"

I nodded. "They seemed to be helping the enemy soldiers. And the mice…"

Raman visibly shuddered. "Those sharp-toothed creatures, with their venomous fangs, I remember well." He paused. "What was Ahri-Luys, or rather the Enlightener, doing when the shadows emerged?"

"A spell, I think," I said. "First, I saw my mother using the Weaver's Spool, sending ghostly apparitions over the battle…"

"Aiding the spirits of the dead."

A lump constricted my throat. My impression had been wrong. I thought she was strengthening our soldiers, but in reality, her duties as a Light Weaver were to ease the passing of spirits into the afterlife. My mother's anguished cries were not of frustration at her futile efforts, but of heartbreak over watching her friends perish. "She chanted a spell, over and over…" I repeated the haunting words.

Raman's brows knitted. "I've never heard that invocation. That isn't the spell for aiding souls."

A crawling chill prickled my spine. "But she spoke directly to me…warned me about the shadows."

Disbelief stretched his weathered face. "Impossible."

"I know what I saw." My skull bristled with unease. Maybe my mother had woven an intentional message into the kork, one Raman had missed.

"The ring's continual use could be distorting your perceptions," Raman said. "You should stop using it."

I clenched my jaw. I hated that he made me question my own senses.

Raman shifted in his seat, tugging his walking stick closer. "Tell me what the Enlightener was doing."

His dismissive attitude stung. But my understanding of the Ring was limited, so I dropped the matter. Swallowing hard, I pushed off the unforgiving ground, palms caked in congealed soil, and settled beside Raman on the fallen tree trunk. "You mean, you want me to tell you another tale that may be warped by the Gate-Ring?" I couldn't keep the sarcasm from my words.

He sent me a sidelong glance. "I will attempt to capture the truth."

"I told you the truth," I snapped.

He sighed. "Your determination is convincing."

My mouth twitched. "The shadow-figures responded to his commands…"

I related the strange battle still vivid in my mind, the transformation of the Oturmink weapons as they grew sharper and more brutal with each touch of the shadows.

Raman's forehead creased. "I've had decades to ponder Ahri-Luys's motives and often wondered if this had been his plan all along."

"His plan?"

"After the final battle at Garni, Ahri-Luys paved the way for the Aureans to conquer Sophene without any resistance…and then he disappeared."

"Disappeared?"

"As far as the rest of the kingdom believed, the Aurean army defeated the Oturminks and 'saved' Sophene, along with the Ar-Haya Highlands. But I suspect Ahri-Luys depleted his powers during that battle." Raman exhaled heavily. "Such unbalanced, unshielded magic over an entire army extracts a brutal cost. It must have drained him, sapping his lifeforce until he became a withered husk."

"You think he channeled pure Eclipse energy?" Maybe that was the sinister shadow-magic I witnessed.

"Perhaps. He likely needed years to replenish his strength before infiltrating the Aurean monarchy." Raman scoffed, as if to himself. "What better path for a sorcerer to seize leadership in one of the most formidable kingdoms in all the Highlands?"

"He weakened Sophene and made it easy for the Aureans to seize control," I whispered, the horror of it sinking in. "He conquered the conqueror."

"Precisely." Raman's jaw tightened. "Sophene had no leaders left, no influential governing bodies. Ahri-Luys knew he could never defeat the Aureans, even with his immense power. So he manipulated a minor kingdom into seizing Sophene, fully aware that Oturmink couldn't maintain control. He *wanted* the Aureans to stroll in and take it. If only for him to eventually infiltrate the mind of the ill and weakened Golden King."

A throbbing pain pummeled the backs of my eyes. I kneaded my temples to ease the pressure, my mind whirling with Raman's core-shaking revelations.

Everything I knew of history had been twisted into lies.

Teachings glorified the Golden King's supposed triumph over our 'enemies,' a victory that 'ended our struggles.' But our schoolmasters glossed over his oppressive rules and unfair tariffs, as if we remained blind to the harsh reality surrounding us. Only the Aurean sun god Solvictus could be worshipped, while our own temples lay in ruins or repurposed.

Sophene was now governed by Aurean-appointed Regents. Years before I was born, Mosatti's previous Regent—a cruel leader from Vosk—was murdered by his own servant. That's when Zakaya's father took over the post. One of few Sophenians allowed such power. It struck me now, the difficult position Zakaya's father must be in, torn between loyalty to our people and allegiance to the Golden King.

What he must have been thinking when the Aurean soldiers had shown up in our town, ready to kill. *Goddess, I led them straight to Mosatti.*

Dread twisted my gut. "How can one man have so much influence over an entire army, over a powerful king?"

"Power alone isn't enough to accomplish such a feat. It takes a cunning mind." Raman squinted into the darkness, fascination and horror edging his voice. "During the attack on Garni, I remained within the temple, salvaging sacred relics until those infernal creatures appeared. The surviving Sacreds dispersed to protect the Legion. While your parents journeyed to Mosatti, I ventured to the Aurean city of Vosk and joined their academy. Ten years ago, I became a royal tutor. An advantageous role that kept me informed of the kingdom's affairs."

I raised my brows. *A spy?* I couldn't imagine my old schoolmaster taking on such a risky role. "Did the King know you were from the Legion of Garni?"

Raman barked out a laugh. "Certainly not. I may as well have handed him my own severed head. I was there for one purpose. To teach the royal youth the language of their conquered territory."

Heat surged through me. No wonder the crowned monster had spoken to me in my native tongue.

"Then five years ago," Raman said, "a royal priest arrived from East Paysha, and quickly snaked into the King's confidence. I didn't recognize him until it was too late."

"The Enlightener." I whispered. "Ahri-Luys?"

"He'd changed. Those strange eyes…" Raman's gaze drew inward. "Crown Prince Andreas became the Enlightener's charge. When the King fell ill, the Enlightener seized control. Overnight, the palace grew unsafe. I'd planned to flee, and then the crown prince was killed."

I sucked in a breath.

"An accident." Raman scoffed. "That's what they told everyone. 'The prince is healing,' they insisted. But that was no accident. They claimed that one of the royal horses had caught the wild sickness, threw the prince right off his back. But it was no ordinary horse."

I gasped. "The horse was *turned*?"

Raman nodded. "Magic of that kind does strange things to animals."

"Poor horse." My voice caught.

"The Enlightener performed a ritual and turned the crown prince into the monster you saw."

"What happened to the King?"

Raman's voice darkened. "He became the dev-prince's first victim. I witnessed the whole dreadful event from a hidden vestibule behind the prince's rooms. Still see it every time I close my eyes."

"Dev? As in the evil creatures in children's tales?"

"Devs are quite real," he said. "Soulless puppets, empty shells filled with something dark."

I shivered. *Goddess*.

Raman squinted his eyes into angry slits. "When Ahri-Luys first led his army to destroy the old temples, his abilities were limited to mice and rats, seemingly the only animals that could withstand such magic. The sinister power required to affect a human…" He adjusted his seat. "The repercussions are detrimental not only to the kingdom, but to all of humanity."

I swallowed hard against the weight of his words, chest constricting with unwelcome sympathy for the old king. The horror he witnessed as his son transformed. And it was the last thing he saw. The thought that devs were real, maybe living among us… I didn't think I could ever sleep again.

My body begged for sleep, but I couldn't get my mother's haunting face out of my head. In life, her subtle magic had infused everything. Crafting intricate tapestries, saving lives. Mama's talents had been respected and revered throughout Sophene and the Ar-Haya Highlands.

But everything changed five years ago. People began to view Sacreds with suspicion and fear, betraying them to the King's guards. Neighbor turned on neighbor, friend against friend. I didn't know which of Mama's numerous patrons gave away her skills and location, but a betrayal is a betrayal. None of that mattered anymore.

"The Mosatti massacre..." My throat constricted around the words, my hands fisting my cloak. "Was there no warning? My parents, *everyone*, could have been prepared, maybe spared..."

"Satya," Raman said, his own voice shaky. "The very night the crown prince turned, I fled to Mosatti to warn the Regent, but I arrived too late. The King was dead, the crown prince was the new King, and the Enlightener had already sent Aurean soldiers to do his bidding."

"The Regent *knows*?" My voice rose with rage.

Raman stared into the thicket for a long moment before he said, "After the massacre, the Enlightener accused him of harboring illegal magic users. Loyalties were questioned, his family threatened."

"He could have told the other satrapies, gathered allies..." A flush crept up my neck and cheeks. Anger. Betrayal. Had Zakaya known? I'd always accepted that, to him, I would be second to the role he was born into. His loyalty to his father, to Mosatti, was admirable. But would he have warned me if he'd known the truth about the King? I didn't know. And that *not knowing* about the boy I'd planned to marry—it *hurt*. "*You* could have told us." This time, I did not hide the accusation in my tone.

Raman's eyes softened. "Would it have mattered, Satya? By then, the Enlightener and his puppet-king were far away, a distant nightmare. The dev in the young King only emerged during feedings. No one else saw that side, and if they did, they disappeared." He released a long, slow breath. "If I spread such news, it would only create a mass hysteria the Golden King would deny, then send his 'priest' to take care of those spreading 'lies.' "

"Did my father know?" My voice was childlike,

small. The idea that my father knowingly led me into that monster's den…

Raman met my horrified gaze. "Sacreds don't keep things from each other," he said softly. "But he was focused on his plan to revive his wife and son. He didn't believe me." He sighed. "I have lived and relived those last few days before the Enlightener turned the prince into a monster, and I have tried to find clues, *any* clues of the Enlightener's ability to turn humans into devs. In hindsight, the clues are *everywhere*. I will live with that burden for the rest of my days."

I glanced away, chest constricting, eyes burning.

After a moment, Raman said, "you've endured immeasurable horrors in your young life, Satya. Our people have suffered for centuries at the hands of those who see us as beneath them. Our own leaders, well, I suppose they've done the best they're capable of."

A howl split the night, closer than before. I waited for the chorus, but it never came. All that I'd learned swirled in my mind: the Ring, Garni's battle, who and what Ahri-Luys became. It twisted around my mind in a storm of fear and confusion.

Raman chanted another spell.

"Should we keep moving?" I whispered.

He shook his head. "I've placed a protection spell around us. Whoever, or *what*ever, may be following us cannot detect us. At least for tonight."

Raman's account of the Monster-King's transformation played and replayed in my mind until a horrible thought occurred to me. If the Enlightener used the Weaver's Spool to turn the crown prince into *that*, would the same happen if I tried to revive my family?

What if my desperate desire to save them was already a dead cause?

Chapter 12

Beware the whispers of hasty desire,
An impulsive spark can start quite a fire.
                    ~ Ar-Haya Highlands Proverb

I offered to take the first watch.

The kork's battle scene replayed in my mind: my mother guiding spirits using the Weaver's Spool, shadow-phantoms emerging from the Enlightener's spell.

I suddenly understood what Raman meant by the clash of Luminous and Eclipse energies. Did the Enlightener channel one such force, while my mother wielded the other? Raman had emphasized the importance of achieving the right balance, but what *was* the right balance?

I glanced back at Raman's sleeping form, the steady rise and fall of his chest. Despite my growing trust, I couldn't tell him the truth. He wouldn't understand the extent of my father's and my fixation with the Weaver's Spool.

My father had given his life for that relic. I needed to learn how to unlock its power. My mother had done it…

I'd used the Gate-Ring without a ritual. Maybe the Spool wouldn't need one either.

After another quick glance at Raman, I slipped the

Spool out of my pack. It sat in my palm, just an ordinary stone. But as I held my glowrock closer, its wavering light penetrated the Spool's translucent depths, revealing vivid blue veins shot through with threads of sapphire and emerald, and faint flecks of obsidian. The *arevakhach* symbol adorned each disk. This most sacred of emblems represented eternity and everlasting celestial lifetimes.

Wait. I recognized this crystal. Azurite, from the mountains of Massisa, seat of the gods. The very place we were headed. This piece rivaled the one said to be encased at the tip of the Golden King's throne, arguably the most valuable gemstone in the Highlands. The wealth it could bring was *astronomical.*

I swatted that thought like a fly drawn to rotting fruit. I needed this Spool for a specific purpose, and it wasn't for riches.

My mother had unleashed the Spool's power during that pivotal battle decades ago. Maybe…maybe I could try too.

I bit my lip, my grip tightening. But what if I somehow corrupted its magic? This relic should be handled by a Sacred, not a seventeen-year-old fugitive. My hands shook with the need to do *something.* I should wait until I could think clearly, until I had a solid plan. Maybe I could trust Raman, tell him the truth. And maybe this Sacred friend of his would know how to use this relic.

Or I could go, search for that *eshi* map myself. Baba said to talk to "Ra-" but he never said "Ra-" had the map. A wave of exhaustion poured over me, the pain in my shoulder like a woodpecker's persistent peck.

Tomorrow. Tomorrow I'll decide.

I reached for my pack to return the Spool before Raman woke and saw it, when my fingers pressed against one of the engravings. A jolting surge of energy shot through my palm, making me gasp. A pulsing radiance surged through the Spool, heating the relic. I stared transfixed at the roiling energy within the now-spinning disks.

Without warning, a raging windstorm exploded through the forest, whipping my hair and cloak into a frenzy. A piercing screech tore over the sound of the lashing winds. The darkness around me moved. Inky, skeletal shadow-shapes oozed out from between tree trunks and undergrowth. My mother's voice echoed in my head. *Beware the shadows.*

The Spool's smooth surface rapidly grew scorching hot, fusing into my palms and fingers. My scream joined the chorus of the keening shadow-wraiths.

"Release the Spool, Satya!" Raman's voice pierced through the chaos.

More screeches reverberated through the air, resonating into my skull. I couldn't stop screaming. All around me, cackles and cries drowned my ears in discordance. Ghostly talons grazed my arms, pinched and scratched my flesh, yanked at my hair until my scalp burned.

Raman squatted before me, hands over mine. Sweat beaded on his forehead, his hands trembling as his spell rose over the cacophony.

"Conduit strong, seize the reins.
Essence untainted, mold and restrain.
Luminous and Eclipse unite.
In balance, harmonize the light."

Raman roared the last words, *"With my words of*

ancient lore, I seal the door forevermore."

Oh, the shadows did not like that spell. Like unruly children, they mocked, nipped, jerked, until pain lanced through every part of me. I lowered my head to the ground, my outstretched arms aching. Raman's firm hands remained atop mine and over the pulsating relic. He repeated the spell twice more, and finally, finally the shadow-wraiths dissolved into the night.

Our harsh breaths broke through the sudden, deafening silence.

Our hands sprang apart, the Spool thumping to the ground between us.

Raman's horrorstruck eyes met mine. "Satya, what have you done?"

Chapter 13

Beware the veil when dawn cracks the sky,
For in the dawning dark nightmares lie.
~ Aurean Children's Rhyme

The forest settled, stilled. Not a leaf stirred.

Raman's horrified gaze pinned me.

I rose, my ears throbbing to the rhythm of my racing heart. I couldn't bear the weight of his silence any longer. "What in the *highlands* just happened?"

Hands trembling, Raman hoisted himself up on his walking stick. "You, Satya, are as stubborn as the day you barged into Mosatti Academy's halls of learning."

"I…" I trailed off, caught between defense and regret.

"You have the Spool," Raman accused, his voice sharp. "You had it all along, and yet you kept it hidden. With your father gone, I assumed you had failed to acquire it."

"What…what happened just now?"

"What happened, Satya, is that you unwittingly opened a portal into the spirit realm."

I gaped. "Did…did you close it?" My question sounded foolish even to my own ears.

Raman arched an eyebrow, his fiery gaze still boring into me. "Yes, but at great cost."

I waited for him to explain, but he wasn't done

admonishing me as if I were an errant child. "Of all the reckless, thoughtless things to do."

Heat flushed my cheeks with shame, anger. "Maybe if *someone* had bothered to enlighten me, *taught* me about all this, I wouldn't be so oblivious."

Brushing off my outburst, Raman said, "Do you know what you have done?"

"I'm sure you're going to tell me," I snapped.

"You've called up a beacon, a shining signal into the forsaken dark skies above, for the Enlightener to find our trail."

My mouth slackened. The Spool lay on the ground between us, now just a lump of stone mocking me. As the weight of the situation sank in, my hot anger dissolved into chilling dread. "Goddess."

"You should hope that whichever goddess you're praying to will help us," Raman snapped. He began to gather his belongings, shoving healing supplies and water flask into his pack.

For three breaths I watched his furious movements in a frozen haze. Snapping out of the daze, I began collecting my own belongings. My shoulder throbbed as I bent to retrieve the Spool.

"The Weaver's Spool is a gateway for Luminous and Eclipse energies," Raman said, his voice tinged with irritation as he tightly cinched his pack. "Both forces carry the essence of the gods. And both forces can be used for light-weaving or shadow work. Think, for a moment, what that means."

Always the teacher, Raman never spelled out the obvious. This I remembered well.

"It called forth spirits from the other side of the veil," I murmured. "But you closed the gateway, didn't you?"

"Too late," Raman snapped. "I closed it *too late*. Sealing such a gateway requires two Sacreds, Satya. One as a conduit, the other as a shield. I performed the ritual alone, shouldering the roles of both. We are fortunate I succeeded."

He extended his palm to me, nodding to the Spool. "Hand it over, Satya."

My heart sank. I wrapped my quivering fingers around the Spool's base. "I'm sorry, but…"

"Unfortunately, your apology won't prevent the Enlightener from tracking us now. I cannot trust you with this relic…" He stopped mid-sentence, squinting into the dense woods.

Then I heard it. A distant rustle like the increasing patter of rain.

I'd heard that sound before. In the kork. Right before the demon-mice attack.

"Use the ring," Raman barked. "Now!"

We'd barely snatched up our packs when a horde of razor-toothed creatures burst from the thicket. They scurried out from between shrubs, their unnaturally long fangs gleaming in the dim light.

I clutched Raman's shoulder, my mind racing to recall a familiar place that wouldn't divert us from our course. The image of Tarin, a small village Baba and I had visited two years ago flashed before me. I anchored myself to it.

The forest contorted and twisted, spiraling into a vortex of entwined trees, massive boulders, and a canvas of starlit skies. A jarring tune grated through the air, the sound like iron rubbing against a stone wheel.

One breath. Two.

We collapsed in a heap of packs, cloaks and blankets.

I struggled to orient myself in the encompassing darkness. "Master Raman?"

He lay motionless beside me, a soft snore escaping his lips. I pressed my ear to his chest and exhaled in relief at the steady rhythm of his heartbeat.

Covering him with a blanket, I slumped to the ground.

Miraculously, the Spool had survived the journey. I slipped it into my waist pouch and surrendered to the oblivion of sleep.

****

I lie sprawled on our bookshop's threadbare rug, blood pooling from my shoulder wound. A boy's silhouette looms over me, backlit by blazing sunlight from the open doorway. The unmistakable golden helmet of the Aurean guards crowns his head.

His eyes are like the smoky grays and fading blues of twilight.

With a gentle hold, he pulls me away from the King's rampaging men, rescuing me from the carnage. Caral's limp hand slips from mine...

Distant thunder rumbled, jolting me awake at dawn.

I remained supine, the dream vivid as if it had happened days, not years, ago. Swallowing hard, I blinked away the lingering images. It had been over a year since I'd last dreamt of the boy who'd saved me during the Mosatti massacre. For months after, I'd believed that an Aurean soldier had rescued me. But that made no sense. A Sophene warrior seemed more likely. Maybe even Zakaya. Though Zakaya had never confirmed nor denied it, as he'd blocked out his own memories of that tragic day.

The recurring dream clung to me as I struggled to orient myself to our new surroundings. Thinner woods, prominent low brush. Beside me, Raman grunted, hefting himself up with his staff. Overnight, clouds had rolled in, draping everything in a dense layer of dew. Moisture seeped into my clothes, weighing them down. The only sounds were the hushed whispers of leaves and the distant cry of an eagle. But no hum of a bustling village.

I sat up, worry clawing at me. We were supposed to be in Tarin. Where had the Ring brought us? My attention abruptly shifted to a strange warmth prickling my left hand. On my finger, the Gate-Ring flashed bright. My entire hand glowed as if I'd dipped it in moonlight. In three blinks, the light faded.

"Master Raman, I…" I turned to Raman, intending to ask about it.

He glanced up from folding his blanket, his face contorted with a mixture of pain and restrained anger. Remorse and shame flooded me for my actions last night, so instead I said, "I'm truly sorry."

Avoiding my gaze, Raman stuffed his blanket into his pack. "I know."

The weight of his disapproval lingered as we packed in strained silence. During our meager meal of apples and cheese, Raman's hoarse voice broke the quiet. "Good decision, bringing us here. We're not far from Tarin. From there, it's a day's walk to Mount Massisa."

The heaviness in my chest lifted slightly. Even after all these years, his praise filled me with warmth.

"I focused on Tarin," I said. "But maybe it's best we didn't end up in the heart of town."

"The Gate-Ring holds sentient godforce," Raman said. "It can sense caution in the hidden crevices of your mind more keenly than you."

I tucked away that information to consider later. Shouldering our packs, we trudged through the woods, drizzle beading our faces and cloaks. This morning, the pang of loss was an embedded blade in my chest, twisting a little deeper with each step. Baba's death, Zakaya's betrayal, the night's horrors all replayed in my thoughts like a zoetrope of nightmares. As if to match my mood, the sky erupted, unleashing torrential rain. Hoods lowered, we slogged onward through the downpour.

Raman spoke for the first time since leaving our makeshift camp. "What happened to your father?"

Rain flowed in rivers down my face as I poured out details of that night in the King's treasure gallery. Baba's selfless sacrifice, the harrowing chase through labyrinthine tunnels, demon-mice nipping at my heels. The Enlightener's bone-chilling sorcery trapping souls within massive tapestries. The King's monstrous act and my desperate escape using the Gate-Ring.

Raman listened without interrupting. Finally, he pointed at my heavy satchel and said, "The Weaver's Spool is dangerous, Satya. I should…"

I shook my head before he finished. "I'm keeping it, for now." I didn't reveal the Spool now hid in the pouch around my waist. "I won't use it again without the proper training."

We both stopped, turned to face each other. If he insisted on taking the Spool, I could run. But leaving my elderly schoolmaster alone in the woods was not an option. Where would I even go?

"I want to understand how my mother wielded it," I said, swiping raindrops from my face. "Maybe you're right, and she was aiding the fallen. But *maybe* she preserved lives, too."

"You believe you can bring back your family," he interjected.

My mouth slackened in surprise. He'd guessed. But Raman knew of Baba's obsession, probably the reason they argued so often. Baba's fixation on using the Spool to reunite our family consumed him, transforming him into someone Raman couldn't trust. But how could I relinquish the one precious relic my father sacrificed everything for?

"Please trust me, Master Raman," I pleaded, blinking rain from my eyes.

For a long moment, Raman stared into the woods, as if battling his thoughts. Then he shook his head and resumed his wobbly stride. I watched his hunched back. I could follow, or I could take my own path.

But again, where would I *go*?

I hated that my only option was to blindly follow my schoolmaster in the hopes of…what? He'd never allow a Sacred to aid me in my quest. It was obvious from his tone and his stiff, angry strides, that he'd likely block my efforts. But what choice did I have? With a sigh, I started walking again and caught up to him.

"The Enlightener purged the Highlands of magical relics and their wielders *twice*," Raman snapped. "He will never stop hunting you."

With those haunting words ringing in my head, we continued our trek in silence, drenched by the rain seeping through our clothes.

****

By late afternoon, the rain dwindled to a gentle drizzle, then stopped altogether.

Raindrops slipped from leaves and branches like jewels, creating a rhythmic percussion on the forest floor. The parting clouds bled crimson and amber sunrays, casting longer and longer shadows across the forest floor. The air carried a crisp, earthy scent, faintly sweet.

The farther we drew from Mosatti, the more my predicament unraveled me like a frayed thread in a threadbare tapestry. Mama used to say that rain cleansed even the heaviest of burdens. But as I trudged beside Raman in my clinging, waterlogged clothes, the weight in my chest only grew heavier. The path's spongy earth gave way to firm ground. Massisa's distant peaks loomed closer, their summits touched by the setting sun's blush. Moss-covered rocks, slick with rain, lined our path, occasionally giving way to groves of unripe mulberry trees. I plucked a handful of tart mulberries to add to our dwindling stash of sustenance.

We had neared the village of Tarin when we heard the shout.

I immediately ducked. Crouching beside me, Raman mumbled a spell and gestured toward the west. We were on an abandoned trail on elevated ground, and I slid down a slope to peer at the valley below through a thicket of shrubs.

Tarin lay below, overrun by Aurean soldiers in their maroon uniforms and metallic war armor. Nestled between hills, the town's main road snaked through a handful of cottages and two farm structures, many of them marred by soot. Doors hung open or lay fallen, unhinged. Lifeless bodies dotted the road.

At the town's periphery, a line of horse-drawn carriages and wagons stood waiting. Groups of people crowded around them, their bodies contorted at odd angles, their movements strange and uncoordinated.

"It has begun," Raman whispered from behind.

A chilling realization gripped me. "Did…did I lead the Enlightener here?"

Raman's silence unnerved me and a suffocating mass settled in my chest as if the weight of the world had found its dwelling. My experimentations with the Spool had sent a beacon to the Enlightener. I'd wanted to escape, but I'd led him here instead. And now all these people were dead.

"After all these years, the Enlightener and his growing army are on the move again," Raman murmured, horror lacing his voice.

"*Growing* army?"

"The bodies he takes," Raman pointed, tone heavy. "They will join his horde of devs."

An army of the dead. Ice filled my veins. Amidst the silent procession marching east out of town, I spotted a stumbling figure. A tall, dark-haired boy in a torn, muddied bejeweled tunic.

"Zakaya," I croaked.

Raman clasped my arm, urging me to remain silent.

At first, I feared Zakaya had joined their pursuit to track me, but it soon became clear that he was a prisoner. Pushed and prodded by a maroon-clad guard, he stumbled and limped forward.

Eyes burning, I nearly called his name, nearly sprang from my hiding spot. But Raman's grip tightened. I swallowed hard. Zakaya was in danger because of *me*. They would hurt him, maybe kill him, to punish

Sophene. I sat frozen, torn. Thinking. *Thinking.*

"I'm going to give them what I took," I said in a harsh whisper, starting to rise.

Raman yanked me back. "Surrendering yourself will not change anything, Satya. It will only make matters worse."

"I need to do something!" I hissed. "I can't just leave him like that. He'll die."

"Satya, listen," Raman whispered. "Do you honestly believe the Enlightener will release you and Zakaya unscathed if you return the Spool? That he holds the Mosatti Regent's son hostage just for a few relics? This is part of something larger."

I gnawed on my lip, a metallic tang filling my mouth.

Raman pressed on, "We'll help him, Satya. But not like this. Once we find Mona, we will devise a plan together. If you act now, you will get us killed."

My lips trembled. He was right. What could I do in the face of so many soldiers and a powerful sorcerer? I hunkered down to gain a better vantage point between the shrubs. From the lead wagon, a tall bald figure emerged, his white cape fluttering behind him. The Enlightener. Another figure followed, yellow curls ruffling in the wind. The King…and he appeared almost human. My hand fisted in my cloak.

Raman stiffened. "Eshi."

The Enlightener crouched, nostrils flaring as he sniffed the air. His head snapped up with predatory focus. For a sickening moment, his gaze seemed to penetrate the foliage behind which Raman and I huddled like cornered prey. A snarl curled the royal priest's lip as he rose in one lithe motion, pale cloak billowing.

I clutched a hand over my thundering heart.

Raman's knuckles whitened on his staff. "Satya, use the Ring."

I swallowed hard. "W-what should I focus on?"

Raman gestured toward the distant mountains. "The first plateau beneath Mount Massisa, just south of the Spitaki Range. Can you picture it?"

I nodded, my gaze fixed on the figures below. Where were the Enlightener and Monster-King? A snarl from behind answered my thoughts.

I whipped around. The Enlightener stood on the incline above us, his towering silhouette backlit by the late afternoon sun. Those unearthly eyes locked on me. Another figure climbed up behind him, yellow curls bouncing with his lopsided gait. The Monster-King.

His face contorted mid-stride, flesh rippling. His mouth distended inhumanly wide, fangs sprouting from the corners.

I screamed.

Raman stepped between me and the King, staff raised in a trembling defensive arc. "Now, Satya!"

Terror froze me, locked my mind. But Raman's rasping command unstuck some core part of me. I envisioned the twin peaks. The Gate-Ring grew hot.

Just as the world upended around us, the Monster-King pounced.

Chapter 14

Dwell too long in shadow's lair,
And you'll find your true self is no longer there.
~ Sophenian Children's Rhyme

The crowned monster's distorted face vanished into a swirling vortex.

Walls of pressure crushed me from all sides, constricting my lungs. The world inverted, spun. The beast's snarls faded to a rustling breeze across grasses.

Our feet propelled us forward as tangled thorns, boulders, warped trees flashed by in slow motion, like pushing against the sea's deep currents. The sun raced across the sky, the warped world streaming past in streaks of grays and browns until distant forms gradually took shape. The twin peaks grew larger. Darkness swallowed the sky as the moon and stars soared by with trailing tails. Then, the world abruptly stilled.

I stumbled to my knees, chest heaving, frozen with shock and disorientation. We'd traveled mere moments, yet our day had vanished in a few dozen breaths. The night surrounded us, cool and still.

Raman's hands slipped from my arm as he crumpled to the ground. His eyes remained closed, his breathing labored. "That was quite...quite the journey."

I offered him a hand. He leaned on me, body trembling as he reached for his staff and struggled to stand. Our only light came from the crescent moon and pale glowrocks we each carried. As I moved to brighten them, Raman stopped me.

"Don't," he said. "Danger may lurk in the dark, but it also hides us."

The mountain peaks loomed above us like dark sentinels against the midnight sky. "Please don't say we have to climb up there." The whistling breeze swallowed my hushed words.

Raman released a shaky breath. "Only…only part of the way." When he saw my stricken look, he added, "But not tonight."

I couldn't agree more. Exhaustion weighed down my shoulders, my back. I craved the oblivion of sleep.

"Your arm." Raman's concerned tone pierced my fatigue. He held a glowrock over my wrist.

I'd been ignoring the stinging in my shoulder, but a new pain now demanded my attention. Blood oozed from a gash on my wrist.

"Satya, that is a bite," Raman said, fear roughening his voice.

I jolted, eyes widening on the wound. He may as well have told me I'd sprouted two heads. These things couldn't happen. Not now. Not when I still had so much I needed to do.

No, no, no…

"I thought the thorns scraped me," I whispered, my voice trembling. The King's fangs must have grazed me as we escaped. My lungs compressed. "Will I…will I…become like him?"

Raman's silence made my knees wobble. Nausea rose up to choke me. I'd hoped for reassurance, not the dark look he cast my way. I had thought things could not get any worse, and now...they were much, much worse.

How could I possibly sleep knowing I might wake up like that crowned creature? "How long do I have?" Goddess, was that childlike plea my own voice?

Raman pressed his lips into a grim line. "Apply some hazel-balm. It may slow the infection."

May slow it? I hated that answer *so* much.

"We need to find Mona *now*," I ground out.

Raman shook his head. "Not in the dark. The terrain is too narrow and steep. We'll set out at first light."

My chest rose and fell in panicked heaves, as if I'd been sprinting for days. I glanced up at the looming mountain, jaw clenched so tightly it ached. Dark ledges rose above in a labyrinth of sharp crags and narrow ridges. If the King's bite didn't kill me, a misstep in this treacherous terrain certainly would. Quivering with frustration and fear, I sank defeated to the ground and faced the silent woods below. I could almost feel Raman's eyes boring into my back.

"Didn't the King change right away?" I mumbled in a shaky voice.

"Yes, but his transformation was the result of a ritual. I would presume a bite such as yours takes longer."

Presume? "That's not reassuring."

A distant howl sliced through the night, sending a shiver like ants crawling over my scalp. The Monster-King's sharp fangs wavered in my mind's eye. Hands trembling, I pulled out the salve and whisperweave cloth from Raman's pack and applied a thick layer of hazel-balm over the wound. The double layer of oozing bites on my wrist had begun to blister, releasing a nose-pinching sour scent. I gritted my teeth against the rising panic and wrapped the thin cloth tightly, my mind racing. Thinking. Thinking…

The concept of devs was a myth, a cautionary tale to keep unruly children in line.

"Watch out, or a dev will come for you!" It had been a common threat, one I'd dismissed as nothing more than a child's tale. Now, I sat on the verge of becoming the very creature children were warned about. Would Baba's notes hold answers or a solution?

With trembling hands, I retrieved my father's texts from my pack. Raman had hinted that my father possessed knowledge about devs. With a glowrock held over them, I flipped through the pages. Page after page, I searched and searched. My father's notes were a chaotic mess, the desperate ramblings of someone who'd lost his grip on reality. Nonsensical phrases popped out: Light Weaver, night sea, sleeping sun.

Nothing about devs.

I had naively followed Baba in his quest. What if he'd been wrong about the Spool, about resurrection, about everything? I shoved the texts back into my pack and dropped my head into my hands, fisting my fingers in my matted hair. *Goddess, how will I ever sleep?*

A dissonant melody scraped against my skull, promising sweet oblivion. Then a whisper, *"Embrace the shadows."* That voice. It was everywhere. I wanted to escape my own skin. *"Sleep…"*

I began to tremble, my teeth chattering uncontrollably. I clamped my palms over my ears, but the voice persisted. In my peripheral vision, the darkness moved.

Raman's words reached me in faint echoes. "Love…compassion…overcome this…"

I shook my head, trying to clear the thickening fog.

"...Luminous and Eclipse energies..." Raman continued, his voice a desperate plea. "...balance required..."

I strained to hear, but that melody was a maddening counterpoint to his words.

Raman suddenly sat before me, his eyes filled with urgency. When had he moved?

"I have been contemplating this for hours," he said.

Hours? Time seemed to bend and stretch, morphing into an endless loop of whispers and chilling shadows.

"The Crown Prince," he continued. "...succumbed quickly...Enlightener's influence. But you, Satya, have known love...your parents, Zakaya..."

Love? The word swam in my mind...nonsensical, foreign.

A prickling warmth returned to my fingertips. A spark of clarity pierced my mind. Through the swirling fog, a single image materialized: Zakaya's face, twisted in betrayal.

"Not love," I rasped, my voice thick and unfamiliar. "Only hate." The word echoed in the vast emptiness of my skull, *hate...hate...hate.* It tasted right, a bitter truth lodged in my throat.

Raman's brows furrowed. "Sometimes, those who have wronged us suffer as much as, if not more than, we do."

I forced my heavy lids to stay open. Raman sat before me on the rocky ledge, his face etched with fear. The wind whispered through the valley, carrying away the faint melody.

"Maybe *wronged* is too mild a word for what happened at the market," I snapped, my mouth twisting into a frown. Why had my disjointed thoughts led me *there*, to that single moment of Zakaya's betrayal, when there were so many others who had wronged me: the Enlightener, the Golden King,…Baba…

In the glowrocks' dim light, Raman's eyes filled with a thousand unspoken emotions. "There she is. My determined student with a strong sense of justice—and single-minded determination."

"There is no justice in any of it," I rasped.

Raman now openly stared into my eyes. "Do you remember when you were perhaps nine, or ten, the day of your fifth-year examinations?"

I fought against my heavy eyelids as the memory resurfaced through the fog. "I refused to take them."

He nodded, a hint of a smile playing on his lips. "And do you recall why?"

"Why does it matter?" I snapped.

He raised an eyebrow, patiently waiting for my answer.

"Because…because it was an unfair examination."

"Unfair for whom?"

"For Zakaya," I mumbled, a lump forming in my throat…raw, painful…as if I'd swallowed sand. "He'd been sick and missed three of our history lessons."

Raman offered a sad smile. "As always, you are precise. Do you remember what you said to me that day?"

As if it were yesterday. A persistent wind rose, whipping at my hood, my hair. It carried with it an earthy, spicy scent of the mountains. I inhaled deeply, needing to erase the metallic tang of fear rising up my throat.

When I didn't respond, Raman answered for me,

"You said that it was important for our future leader to know his history because…"

"…he will grow up to take care of us all," I finished.

That day Zakaya and I became friends. It would be years before that friendship blossomed into something more. But on that day, after our lessons, he approached me and said, "Satya, I will always take care of my people."

I understood what Master Raman was trying to tell me. Duty had shaped Zakaya since birth. In truth, I couldn't blame his betrayal. He'd only done what he'd been raised to do. Protect his people. Except he no longer considered me one of his people.

I glanced down at the wound on my wrist, the skin around the whisperweave bandage turning bruise-like. If Zakaya could see me now, he wouldn't even consider me a *person*.

Thoughts of Zakaya became my anchor, keeping me from drowning. I clung to these memories despite the agonizing pain they unleashed. Pain meant I could still feel. That I remained connected to *me*.

My whole body vibrated like the strings of a lyre. I grasped my hand over the ring, anchoring myself to the here and now. To thoughts of Zakaya. I envisioned him as a child, the Regent's privileged son, born to live on a pedestal, adored by all, many girls vying for his attention as we grew up. When he directed his gaze toward me, a mere merchant's daughter, it felt as if I'd been plucked from the shadows and brought into the warm glow of the sun. Goddess, that feeling…I still remembered it.

A rush of power spiraled from the soles of my feet, climbing higher and higher, flooding my entire being.

My mind conjured the curve of Zakaya's smile, the

comforting solidity of his chest as we hugged. But then his betrayed eyes at Nurazard flashed before me and I wanted to slam my fist against his face. Why had I ever thought we could make it work?

Zakaya's mother had always been kind, but his father's cold disapproval of my inferior status stung. Maybe a part of Zakaya felt the same, though he never voiced it. The way he often looked at me, a small, knowing smile playing on his lips, a secret language we both understood but never spoke. I hadn't realized until now how much that bothered me.

My vision blurred with a gritty film. I blinked repeatedly, the dry air of this elevation offering no relief. A thick, viscous fluid clung to my lashes.

Raman's breath hitched.

I frantically wiped at my eyes, but wound up smearing the thick mucus over my face. "No, no, no…" I croaked. My vision blurred behind a renewed wave of thick tears.

"Satya…" Raman's usually steady voice cracked with fear.

"This can't happen," I sputtered. "I'm…I'm not ready. I need to figure out how to fix this."

"Satya," his voice softened.

I clung onto my thoughts of Zakaya, the only thing anchoring me to myself. "I never…" I coughed as I tried to speak. "I never told you Zakaya betrayed me at the market…you weren't there…"

"No, I wasn't," Raman interrupted gently. "I'd left to prepare for this journey. But I've known you both since childhood. Your strengths, weaknesses…" He paused, his voice filled with a mixture of sadness and understanding. "…and your loyalties."

I clung to his words, even as the film regrew over my vision. The vortex within me continued to spiral, but something shifted. A flicker of my own will, intertwined with the Gate-Ring's energy, wrestled me back, pulling me from the brink.

Raman was right. Zakaya was raised with unwavering loyalty to his people. And me? Where had my loyalties been these past few years? I'd been consumed with the singular desire to bring my family back. I had no right to judge Zakaya. We'd both placed other priorities above our bond. Swallowing the lump in my throat, I faced the harsh truth. I had lost him.

We lost each other, a silent voice whispered in my head.

Worse, I was on the verge of losing myself.

****

Night fell, a black cloak veiling my eyes. I spent an eternity beneath a jagged overhang, shivering from the frigid temperatures and a growing fever.

My thoughts were like scattered leaves whipped in a gale. Nonsensical images, echoes, and fragrances swirled in a chaotic dance within me, along with an ever-shifting kaleidoscope of emotions. Peace and fear, joy and grief, love and hate. The Ring remained an unyielding anchor, its warmth persistently tugging me back to reality, back to myself.

The bite-wounds were relentless daggers stabbing at my wrist. I drifted in and out of sleep. Each time I surfaced, Raman remained an unwavering presence beside me. He talked and talked. His words a soothing hum I couldn't make sense of, yet the only sound that kept me grounded.

I awoke with a gasp to the first rays of dawn piercing

the darkness. The remnants of a nightmare clung to my foggy mind—a monstrous serpent-dragon chasing me through endless, exitless corridors. Blinking through a film of exhaustion, I fought to accept what my muddled thoughts refused. *I'm turning into a dev.*

The fever's fiery grip had loosened. On my pinky, the Gate-Ring blazed, its light pulsing against my flesh like a trapped heartbeat. I sat up, captivated by the strange energy flooding my finger. Was the Ring's magic slowing my dev transformation?

Raman slumped against the mountain wall, snoring softly. The poor man had kept vigil all night. As the sky slowly lightened, the Ring's glow faded. I gingerly unwrapped the whisperweave cloth from my throbbing wrist. Bile rose at the sight. The inflamed, oozing wound reeked of nose-pinching decay.

Raman stirred, and I quickly rewrapped my wrist, pulling my sleeve down before he could see.

"Satya," he gasped, as if rising for air. "How do you feel?"

"As good as anyone about to turn into a monster," I mumbled.

A ghost of a smile touched his lips. "You have retained your spirited attitude. A good sign."

Unable to eat, I offered Raman the last crushed mulberries. Then we began our painstaking climb. Using the Ring wasn't an option. Raman could barely walk. He couldn't even hold a conversation. And I could hardly focus on the path, let alone visualize a destination I'd never been to…that even Raman hadn't been to.

With each step, I pushed away the discordant voice that promised relief and oblivion. Twice we stopped for short breaks, and finished the last of our water.

Raman wavered beside me, leaning heavily on his wobbling staff. How ridiculous we were, the two of us embarking on this perilous journey together. Raman, a Sacred-in-hiding, a former *spy*. And I, on the brink of losing my humanity.

"We make a great traveling pair," I spoke into the silence, a burst of hysterical laughter bubbling out.

Raman sent me a side-glance, but said nothing.

For hours we climbed over boulders and steep inclines. As dawn blended into late morning, my fever rose again. My ears throbbed and face heated despite the chill. The restless darkness within me stirred with my body's rising heat. In the recesses of my mind, the discordant melody was a relentless disharmony of jarring notes. I focused on the Gate-Ring's consistent warmth and the rhythmic tap-tapping of Raman's staff. If we didn't find Mona today, we were in deep, *deep* trouble.

When we paused again, the sun blazed directly overhead, a pale yellow orb without warmth. Rolling hills of woodland stretched into the horizon. The mournful wind mirrored my inner havoc. The path had narrowed, plummeting sharply to our left. Eyes fixed ahead, I forced each step, one hand gripping Raman's elbow, the other grasping the mountain walls. Raman wheezed in the thinning air. We'd only climbed partway, but the temperature had noticeably dropped. My shivers increased. I didn't want to dwell on what that meant.

A gray-white dove perched on a ledge above. I blinked through watery vision, convinced I'd seen it before.

Raman followed my gaze. "I believe Mona settled nearby, if memory serves."

I swayed, grasping the rough wall. "What exactly

are we looking for?"

Raman shook his head and muttered, "With Mona, it is always a riddle."

My gaze locked on the dove. My vision blurred, the single bird morphing into two, then three, then back to one again. "Could she be tracking us through the eyes of an animal?"

"Perhaps," Raman muttered, sitting heavily on a nearby boulder. "She might be using a relic to monitor activity on this mountain…or to remain invisible. Let's take another break."

The exposed ledge offered little shelter. I didn't savor the idea of spending a night here. What if I, *as Satya*, never woke in the morning? The thought sent a fresh wave of tremors through me. "How will we find her?"

"We cannot," Raman said calmly. "We wait for her to find *us*."

Exhaustion and despair overwhelmed me as I slumped beside him, dropping my pack. "But she doesn't even know we're looking for her."

Raman grunted. "Mona always knows when someone is looking for her."

I shivered uncontrollably, drifting in and out of sleep beside him. Raman remained a silent sentry, lips pressed with worry.

The relentless ache in my shoulder and the throb of my wrist created a discordant rhythm, like conflicting heartbeats. Each time I surfaced, Raman's unwavering gaze met mine. I finally grew irritated and snapped at him to stop staring. All the while, the dove watched over us from its perch.

As the sky shifted from a fiery azure to a deep

indigo, a mixture of terror and resignation warred within me. Every time I dozed off, Raman shook me awake. After the third time, I finally understood. The dev could emerge when I was at my most vulnerable. In my sleep.

Raman, in his kindness, was allowing me short bursts of rest.

I'd dozed off again when a sudden, piercing screech tore over the mountain.

My eyes snapped open, heart pounding. Shadows writhed on the mountain face above.

I tried to scramble to my feet, but a wave of dizziness crashed over me and I landed unceremoniously on my backside. "Master Raman, there's something…"

Cries filled the air as a dozen lean figures dropped from the ledges above, scattering soil and pebbles in their wake. Men with bushy hair, woolen vests, and gleaming daggers surrounded us.

Raman gripped my arm. "Satya, hide your eyes."

Chapter 15

The way is dark, the road is long,
I'll come find you, if you whisper this song.
                    ~ Sophenian Children's Rhyme

A shadow fell before me.

Gritting my teeth against a flare of pain, I hoisted myself up using the rock face as support and slung my pack over my shoulder. I squinted through gritty lashes as a tall, broad-shouldered man with dark curls and a scowl as sharp as a dagger emerged from the shadows.

"Ovek?" he barked.

Raman raised his palm in a gesture of peace. "Enker."

"Voch, ovek?" the man repeated, suspicion lacing his deep voice.

I ducked my head, letting my matted hair fall over my face to shield my burning, itchy eyes.

Raman tightened his grip on his staff. "Yas Anahitahi hamara."

The man turned to his companions and unleashed a string of harsh words in their native tongue.

Raman and I exchanged a worried glance. Who were these people? The Ar-Haya Highlands boasted a tapestry of settlements, from bustling villages to warrior tribes, and even the occasional band of roamers. We'd chosen less-traveled paths to avoid an unwanted encounter. But fate, it seemed, had other plans.

A rough hand clamped down on my wounded shoulder, sending a jolt of searing pain through me. I yelped, struggling in vain against the man's iron grip as he dragged me away from Raman. Sweat beaded on my brow despite the cold mountain air.

My vision blurred at the edges. "Master Raman!"

Raman followed, his staff thudding against the earth. His words flew out in rapid bursts, clearly struggling to make himself understood. My captor's grip loosened. He turned to the leader, their exchange a heated volley of harsh syllables. Finally, my shoulder was released. The warrior remained beside me as we resumed the trek. I was apparently no longer a prisoner, though we obviously had no choice but to follow.

My legs buckled, threatening to give way beneath me. I stumbled toward Raman and grasped his arm. Despite my rising panic, a chilling disconnect settled over me. As if a part of me had numbed to the darkness tugging at my will. This darkness, the dev-worm within me, whispered promises of oblivion.

"The Ring…I can use it," I whispered to Raman, my words slurred.

"Not in your current condition," Raman murmured. "Too risky."

He was right. I could hardly maintain my balance, let alone concentrate on using the Ring. "What did they say to you?"

"They believed I'm offering you as a blind sacrifice to the dragon in the mountain."

I sputtered. "*What?*"

"Rest assured," Raman said. "I clarified the misunderstanding."

"What did you tell them?"

"I explained that you, my granddaughter, have lost your sight. We seek the blessing of the goddess Anahit at her mountain altar in the hopes of restoring your vision. They claim a serpent dragon guards the altar."

My jaw dropped. "There really is a dragon in the mountain?"

"They firmly believe so."

Bandits and dragons, altars of goddesses, ancient tribes…this new reality had become a fantastical arras woven from whispers of legend. "Where are they taking us?"

"I informed them we're friends with the lady of the mountain," Raman said.

"Lady of the…you mean Mona."

He grunted. "I can only hope they know who she is. This *is* where I last saw her."

How can he be so calm about this? "Who are these people?"

"The Azzi," Raman said. "They revere various deities, including the serpent-dragon. They offer a yearly sacrifice in its honor."

My steps faltered. The man behind us prodded my back, urging me onward.

"Please don't say it's *human* sacrifice?" I whispered, stumbling forward.

"I've heard it's usually goats, chickens, or an occasional horse," Raman said. "The Azzis are a splinter group of the southern Scytha warriors, known for clinging to ancient customs. Only the gods know how *this* group's traditions have evolved."

Time stretched on as we followed the path around the mountain. The Azzis scaled ledges with the agility of mountain goats, uncaring of the steep inclines. But they kept Raman and me on more even trails, though in my fevered state, every barrier became a massive obstacle. A rock, a tree root, a pebble.

With each unsteady step, the dev-worm clawed at my sanity until I couldn't decide which fate terrified me more: being sacrificed to the fabled dragon in the mountain, or succumbing to the relentless dev-voice on the verge of consuming me.

****

The sun dipped below the jagged peaks, casting long, skeletal shadows across our path. The chirping of birds had dwindled to an occasional mournful call, replaced by the eerie rustling of unseen creatures in the gathering darkness.

I stole fleeting moments when no eyes were on me to glimpse the path ahead. My fevered body and blurred vision betrayed me with each stumble, obscuring the trail's dips and rises until it felt as though I walked over the uneven depths of the sea. Each precarious step threatened to pull me down, down, down.

Embrace the shadows. That voice. It resonated everywhere. It whispered from the shrubs, echoed from the soaring falcons, resonated from the stones of the mountain itself.

Raman and I leaned on each other until it was unclear who supported whom. At times, an unnatural force seemed to dictate my every step, as if an unseen hand controlled my movements. The Gate-Ring's searing heat jolted me back to myself repeatedly, keeping me from succumbing to the shadow-whispers.

The Azzis led us through a mountain crag and into its depths. Rough-hewn steps carved into the rock descended into inky blackness. We followed the narrow passage in single file, glowrocks casting an eerie, flickering dance of shadows on rough stone walls. The air grew stale and thick, heavy with the scents of damp earth and something metallic.

Just when it seemed we'd plunged into a dragon's lair, we surfaced onto a jutting ledge. To my left, the cliff face plunged over a hundred handspans to a foamy river snaking through a vast ravine, its banks dotted with willows. Caves, carved into the rock face in honeycomb patterns, glowed in the warm light of torches and glowrocks. Figures bundled in woolen vests and cloaks teemed around the riverbank, casting nets into the water or tending to cooking fires. Laughter and chatter drifted upward.

Homes. Life.

The scent of roasted meat wafted in the air. A conflicting mix of hunger and nausea churned in my stomach.

Dozens of figures swooped down from the ledges, clinging to vines as they navigated the treacherous mountain paths with practiced ease. The mountain walls and forest guarding these cliffs veiled this hidden village. If I hadn't been led here, I'd have missed it entirely.

Perched on a set of ledges that rose like a staircase toward her, a woman draped in a silvery cloak sat upon a rocky platform that oddly resembled a throne.

"Mona?" I whispered.

Raman nodded with obvious relief. My hand tightened around my pack strap. All my hopes hinged on this woman helping us, helping *me*. Assuming she could heal me, how would she react to my plan for the Weaver's Spool?

The tall Azzi leader, a stark silhouette against the dying light, strode to the edge, motioning to us to follow. The world shrank to the rough rock wall beneath my trembling fingers as we descended a sloping ledge toward the bustling village. Raman's staff thumped rhythmically behind me. We reached a wobbly wooden bridge, its planks groaning beneath our combined weight while we crossed the river.

Mona remained motionless as we approached, her hands folded on her lap. Raman had led me to believe that they were friends, but the look she sent us was far from friendly.

The villagers eyed us with suspicion as we stopped a dozen paces from the Sacred. Mona's cloak fluttered softly in the cool breeze, the sound like the flapping of a baby bird's wings. She sat upon an altar of obsidian, its surface a mirror reflecting the flickering glowrocks, torches, and cooking fires. Her makeshift throne gave the odd impression that she sat among the constellations.

My head throbbed, the dev-worm's voice a constant hiss in my feverish mind. Raman's arm supported me, keeping me from collapsing. A pale form swooped down from the trees, its wings catching the fading light, and landed on Mona's shoulder. A dove.

Was this the same dove who'd been shadowing us for days?

"Mona." The tenor of Raman's voice reverberated across the ravine, clear of the pain and fatigue he betrayed in his trembling arm. "Is this necessary?"

Mona ignored him, her gaze shifting to me. Hoping the dark hid my dev-eyes, I stole a glance at her before dropping my gaze to the ground. Dark curls framed a heart-shaped face. She looked to be about my mother's age, had my mother still lived. The fairness of her skin ruled out Sophenian descent, but her wide-set dark eyes and prominent hawk nose hinted at a northern lineage, maybe Asyneed. I frowned. The Asyneeds were known for their animosity toward the southern kingdoms.

"You brought me a charge?" Mona spoke the royal language, her voice a deep rumble with harsh r's and abrupt vowels.

"She's *my* charge," Raman countered in the same tongue. "But we need your help."

Mona barked a disbelieving laugh. "My help? After all dzis time, the Legion seeks *my* help?"

Her sharp tone set our captors on edge. They shuffled closer to Raman and me, daggers gripped.

"Perhaps you can assure your people that we pose no threat," Raman suggested.

Mona snapped out a few sharp words and the Azzi leader barked right back.

"What are they saying?" I whispered to Raman.

"Not sure," Raman muttered. "They're speaking too fast."

Following the heated exchange, the warriors behind us retreated, lowering their weapons.

"You were saying about dze Legion?" Mona said.

"The Legion did not send me, Mona," Raman clarified. "I haven't seen or heard from them in quite some time, perhaps longer than you."

"Then why are you here?" she snapped. "And who is dzis girl?"

Raman placed a hand over mine in the crook of his arm, and squeezed for reassurance. "Satya is under my protection and we need access to the Legion. Quickly, if possible."

"Access?" Mona's tone rose with disbelief. "Do you mean dze transport crystal?"

"Yes."

I stole a glance at Mona, hope and anticipation warring within me. How was this transport crystal different from the Ring?

Mona studied her nails. "I'm afraid dze crystal doesn't, ah, work anymore."

Raman's hand tightened on mine. "You were tasked with keeping it functional."

Mona leaned back with a pout. "I was tasked with keeping it *hidden*. Really, Raman, must you belittle me so in front of my people?"

"What have you done to the transport crystal?" A hard edge crept into Raman's voice, the familiar tone he used to command unruly students.

"It's heez fault," Mona snapped, waving at the darkness behind her.

Now, I openly stared. The shadows behind Mona shifted. A tall, hooded form cloaked in dull gray leaned against the cavern's rough wall. As he shifted into the light, a metallic jiggle echoed through the ravine. A thick chain, glinting faintly in the fading light, snaked from his right wrist and looped around Mona's left.

A prisoner? Or if he wasn't a prisoner, then why the chains?

"Is that…?" Raman sputtered. "Mona, what have you done to the boy? You were supposed to *protect* him."

"Dze *boy*?" Mona snapped. "He's no longer a *boy*. He tried to run. I had to use some unconventional methods with dze god-relics to keep him here." Her voice crackled with rising anger that accentuated her harsh accent. "I'm afraid it drained any magic from dze transport crystal."

Raman glared at Mona, trembling with fury. "Sacred relics are not to be used without proper rituals."

Mona shrugged. "It was an emergency. And proper rituals require time and people, Raman. Do I look like *people* to you? I am but *one* Sacred."

For a tense moment the two Sacreds locked eyes, neither yielding.

Then Raman turned his gaze to the hooded figure. "Rei, are you all right?"

A long pause followed, filled only by the crackling fires and the occasional coo of the dove on Mona's shoulder. Then a deep voice drawled from beneath the hood. "Couldn't be better. I go where she goes. She made sure of that."

That accent. Crisp as the winter breeze, and just as frosty. The same brogue as those from the Golden King's city of Vosk.

"It was for your own protection," Mona snapped back. "You know what they'd do if you returned."

Returned where? Vosk? Who was this man from the King's city that both Sacreds were set on protecting? A member of the King's guard…or a hidden royal?

The hooded man's fierce words cut through the ravine. "I'd rather die free than live as a slave to a witch."

I clenched my jaw. *And he speaks like an entitled ass.*

"You were never supposed to be *chained*," Raman said, his tone dark.

Mona huffed in exasperation, flinging her hands up in the air and cried out, "I am *not* a witch, and he is *not* a slave." She leaned forward, making the dove flutter its wings. Lowering her voice to a harsh whisper, she said, "And he's certainly not pleasant company. I don't want to be chained to him either, but…"

"But you cannot undo the spell," Raman said.

Mona's lips thinned into a stubborn line. "It seems the binding spell took the spellcaster crystal's power too. Enough about us and our woes. Tell me about dzis girl. Zzatya, is it?"

My name on her tongue buzzed like a swarm of bees, and the snap in her tone was their sting. Clearly, she was changing the subject, but I could feel the weight of everyone's eyes on me. This woman had already damaged two artifacts. How could she possibly help me? All the hope and anticipation I'd clung to morphed into a dense, leaden weight in the pit of my stomach.

"It's Satya," I said, pushing the words past parched lips.

"Why are you his charge?" Mona said. "What brought you here? And why in the name of the gods and goddesses does he need to take you to the Legion of Garni, when they won't even emerge from hiding for Rei here?"

Before I could respond, Raman said, "She's Varta's daughter."

My chest tightening at the mention of my mother.

"Oh. *Oh!*" Mona stood so suddenly the dove on her shoulder took flight with a flurry of gray-white wings. She marched down from the rocky outcropping. The clunking chain rattled as the tall hooded figure—Rei-from-Vosk—trailed behind her.

Mona stopped abruptly before me. For a few quiet and uncomfortable moments, I watched the hem of Mona's gray dress fluttering beneath her cloak. She reached out and brushed her fingertips against the end of my unruly hair, and said the last thing I expected.

"You have her hair," she murmured, almost to herself. "Smooth as silk. I always envied that about her…"

Mona's simple statement sent a jolt through me. This woman held a connection to my mother's past. A thousand questions swirled in my feverish mind, but my sluggish thoughts refused to formulate even one.

"Before you ask," Mona said to me, "your modzer hated me."

I cleared my throat and stared at the ground, curious for the story buried beneath Mona's careless statement. I became aware of the Ring warming my finger, keeping the darkness caged.

Behind Mona, the hooded figure remained a silent shadow, though I could feel the prickle of his gaze.

"Where is your father?" Mona said, apparently a master at abruptly changing a topic.

My throat tightened. "He's dead."

"Oh," Mona said. "I see the situation more clearly now."

A soft coo echoed from the dove on her lofty perch high above us.

"It is best that Satya and I stay out of view," Raman said, his voice urgent.

Mona closed her eyes, her face creased in concentration. "Tatu says you're being hunted." Her eyes snapped open. "Tatu says the Golden King himself pursues you."

I cast a glance at the dove high up on the trees. *Tatu knows a lot, doesn't she.*

Before I could stammer out a half-truth, Raman cut

in, "Mona, allow me to explain…"

"Why is the King after you?" Mona asked me, ignoring Raman.

Because I stole from him.

The Monster-King's words echoed in my head: *"Weaver of light. Weaver of souls. Come to tame the monster, have you?"*

Mona raised her glowrock, bathing my face and arm in light. My cloak sleeve had risen. The whisperweave cloth had fallen during our haphazard trek over the mountain paths, revealing the dev-king's oozing fang wounds.

It happened quickly. Mona barked orders. Rough hands seized my arms. They yanked me away from Raman and the village, dragging me down a narrow path that snaked around the river by the base of the hill.

"Wait," I screamed, my voice weak, hoarse. "Please listen."

My pleas were met with chilling silence. We rounded the bend. The sounds of village life faded behind us. We reached the village's edge and kept walking. A growing throng of Azzi warriors followed behind us, faces grim in the flickering light of torches and glowrocks.

Raman's voice, laced with urgency, reached my ears from somewhere behind. The rhythmic clinking of the chain that bound Mona to Rei echoed as they followed in our wake.

The path snaked around a rocky bend by the river and opened, exposing an imposing structure. The mountain face yawned open, revealing a deep, jagged gash that resembled a lightning bolt's scar. The narrow gap pulsed with an otherworldly energy, tugging at the dev-voice festering within me. I tried to envision the forest above the village, the base of the twin mountains, but the Gate-Ring continued to pulse, a searing ember against my skin. *Why isn't it working?*

Raman's voice rose over the clamor. "It happened nearly two days ago, and she is *fighting* it."

"The timing is irrelevant," Mona snapped. "Tatu saw that sheez ill, not bitten! I wondered about her eyes…but now the bites?"

A guttural growl erupted from the cavern's depths. The Azzis were convinced a dragon inhabited the mountain. I now almost believed it.

I wedged my heels into the hardened ground, but the men shoving me were far stronger. My knees buckled, but they kept dragging me toward the cavern's gaping maw.

"Mona," Raman yelled. "Let us discuss this…"

Mona swerved around to face Raman. "Discuss what? Your *charge* has brought a battle upon our heads." Her eyes reflected fear and a haunting familiarity with dev transformations. She marched toward me and stared into my eyes. "Sheez hiding *secrets*. Perhaps dze serpent-dragon will make you speak, little *sut*."

Sut. A liar, a false one.

The cavern entrance was a yawning mouth, ready to devour. Another deep growl rumbled from its depths, sending a swarm of spiders crawling over my skin.

Embrace the shadows.

"Let me go," I screamed as they dragged me bodily toward the cavern.

The Azzis began a haunting chant, gradually rising in volume and resonating through the deep ravine. The air crackled with the fluttering of wings as swallows burst from canopies above, soaring into the darkened sky. A booming drumbeat joined the escalating chants. The rapid tempo hammered against my ribs, each beat a physical blow that resonated through my bones and skull.

Terror clawed its way up my throat. "No!"

My voice and Raman's protests were drowned by the Azzis' rising chants.

The cavern's entrance beckoned, its phantom energy drawing me closer, closer.

The gaping maw seemed to expand. Within its inky depths, impenetrable darkness concealed unknown horrors, fueling my imagination with visions of serpent-dragons and dev kings. The Azzis chanted furiously, matching the drum's rapid tempo.

Maybe their ways hadn't changed after all. Maybe they still sacrificed maidens, especially ones who led danger to them.

Fingers dug into my arms, dragged me forward. My pack slipped from my shoulders and tumbled down the rocky path toward the river. I twisted and fought, but to no avail. I could no longer see Raman. I could no longer see anyone through the yellow film of my vision and the brightness of glowrocks held to my face.

We were now five arm-lengths from the murky opening. Another ear-splitting growl erupted from the cavern entrance, ripping a scream from my throat. Three arm-lengths. One.

A final shove sent me tumbling forward. My scream trapped in my throat as I plummeted through the cavern's gaping maw.

Chapter 16

When serpents coil a twisted snare,
May courage stand against despair.
                    ~ Sophenian Folksong

The cavern's mouth swallowed me whole with a bone-chilling rip.

I fell to my knees on damp, hard ground.

The world outside vanished behind an impenetrable veil. Ahead lay only shadows, behind me, a dense and oppressive darkness. A nose-pinching scent of decay clawed at my nostrils, scraping my throat. My ears clogged with a thunderous rhythm. My own heartbeat or the pulse of the mountain's rumored inhabitant?

Abruptly, the pulsing ceased.

Deafening silence.

A distant sound of dripping water resounded from the cavern's depths.

Drip. Plunk. Drip. Plunk.

I tried to use the Gate-Ring's translocation powers, to envision being somewhere outside the cavern. Nothing changed. Maybe the Ring held no power here, yet it continued to heat my finger the way it had for the past day.

A soft glow appeared ahead, as if a door had cracked open, releasing a circle of light.

My father's words echoed in my mind. *Be equipped.*

Be observant. Be quick.

I dug into my belt-pouch for Baba's dagger and my fingers grazed the Spool. Energy radiated up my arm. The Gate-Ring grew warmer in response. Maybe a mortal weapon would be useless here. But a relic of the gods...

I pushed past the guilt prickling at my conscience for concealing the Spool from Raman. But if I hadn't stowed it in my belt-pouch, it would now be lying useless in my pack at the river's edge. I withdrew the Spool, vividly recalling my last encounter with it when spirits of the dead had tried to rip me apart. But I'd seen how my mother had aided the battle in the kork. There had to be more to this god-relic than ushering the dead to the beyond.

This place. It wasn't of this world. I could feel it in the air around me, in the godforce coursing through the two relics. A strange calm enveloped me, and with it, clarity.

There must be a way out.

The floor felt gritty and solid beneath my boots. With the Spool poised before me, I stumbled toward the distant light. Each step resounded through the chamber like a pulse. As the pale glow expanded from the cavern's rear, a jagged silhouette took shape. Wooden spires rose to a peak, intermingling with the cavern's obsidian boulders. Luminescent veins resembling expanding tree roots continuously intertwined and merged until they became one with the living stone. As if the mountain itself slowly consumed the wooden structure.

I gasped. *This is an ancient temple.*

As I neared the beckoning light, the dev within me

thrashed. Sweat beaded on my forehead. Swaying shadows cast by ancient columns came into shape. Beyond them, a vast pool stretched out, spanning at least ten men across.

A chill snaked down my spine. *Not an escape.*

The light originated from the water itself. Liquid droplets plummeted from the cavern ceiling like tears, marring the pool's mirror stillness into webs of ripples. *Drip. Plunk. Drip. Plunk.*

A low snarl rose over the sound of dripping water, raising the hairs on my arms. I nearly dropped the Spool. The beastly growl zigzagged off the walls as if a monster hid in every crevice.

A gravelly voice hissed, "Ah, fresh *sss*ustenance."

Barely a whisper, each word ricocheted from different directions as if the creature was continuously moving. I gripped the Spool tighter, my legs weakening.

"Who are you?" I called out, my own voice echoing.

"The question is*ss*, who are *you*?" The last guttural word bounced around the cavern. *You…you…you.*

My body tensed against the tremors that threatened to consume me. It took me a moment to realize he spoke in Sophenian. *My* language. If I could keep him talking, distract him, maybe he wouldn't rush to…*eat* me. "S-Satya."

His snarl vibrated from the ground into the soles of my torn boots. "This is not what I as*ss*ked."

Thoughts raced through my mind, envisioning ways this shadow-creature might consume me. Would I become its meal, or be cast into the molten lakes deep in the pits of this mountain?

Anger at my old schoolmaster mingled with my terror. Why had Raman brought me here only for Mona to sacrifice me to this beast? How could I best a beast I could not see?

"Show yourself," I demanded.

A high-pitched grating sound screeched across the cavern walls, fading quickly. The sudden silence pressed down on me. A prickle of awareness skittered down my spine as I sensed a presence behind me. Harsh breaths tickled my ears. The hairs on the back of my neck stood alert.

"I'm here, there, everywhere," he growled, each word echoing around the chamber. The creature's breath reeked. "I dwell in the shadows of your rage, in the darkness of your fears, in the depths of your desssperation."

I spun around to face…empty space. A rage unlike anything I'd ever felt prickled my scalp, made me lightheaded. A riddle?

"Who finds refuge in shadows, afraid of the light?" I retorted, my voice hoarse but steady. "Who resides beside a refreshing pool yet knows not the notion of bathing?"

A snarling laugh ricocheted around the cavern walls. "You like riddlesss?"

"I don't care for riddles," I retorted. A lie. I loved riddles under *normal* circumstances.

"A shame," the beast snarled, his voice resounding from every corner. "I relish riddles, especially with a mind as sharp as yoursss." A shuffling sound traveled over the wall. Then a low snarl, "You have been chosen by Ahriman, the Archdemon of Despair and Chaosss." He made a sucking sound, as if savoring the thought of a feast.

With each word he uttered, the oozing bites on my

wrist throbbed, glowing in sickly hues. Had the Monster-King marked me for this purpose? To be hunted by the Archdemon of Despair and Chaos?

The dev within me growled.

"Who are you?" I asked again, my voice steady despite the fear bubbling up to choke me. I needed to keep him talking, to gather information, maybe find a way to escape. If I could only understand his role in the myths and legends, I could discover a key to my freedom.

The creature's icy breath caressed my neck. I swallowed hard, whirling around and finding…nothing there.

"I am Vishap," he hissed, elongating his name in a bone-chilling stretch. *Vishaaaaaap.*

A cold dread crawled over my scalp as realization dawned on me. Vishap, the serpent-dragon, the guardian of the gates to the Underworld. The beast who had terrorized dozens of villages in the Highlands over a thousand years ago. Defeated by Vahagn, the Dragon Reaper, and banished to the Underworld. His depictions littered Baba's texts, copied from markings on ancient cavern walls. A serpent longer than five men, scales as sharp as daggers, incisors that could break through stone.

But the texts had said nothing about this creature's ability to speak.

Back at our shop we had a statue of Vahagn slaying this very beast. But Vahagn was a powerful warrior-god. Who was *I*?

The tightness in my chest constricted my lungs. The beast's putrid stench, the gripping fear, my rising fever, the dev within clawing for release… Too much. This felt *too much.*

But even in this state of *too much*, I knew that every word I uttered now would have consequences.

"What does Ahriman want from me?" I asked, my voice steady despite the cold tremors zigzagging over my skin.

The creature ignored my question, asking one of his own. "Can you feel it? That sensation lurking within the depths of your being?"

He means the dev-worm. "I feel nothing but your horrid stench."

The beast hissed, "Then, answer this…what quietly resides in shadows deep, and hides unseen for secrets keep. Elusive and grim, the fragments dim?"

"I *said*, I don't like riddles," I snapped, clenching my teeth.

But the answer came unbidden, slowly rising to the surface. *Memories.*

A sudden surge of visions overwhelmed me. Images of betrayal, violence, and loss flooded my mind, replaying moments that had shaped my life…in reverse.

The Azzis tossing me into this cavern.

Raman leading me to this mess.

The king's guard whipping me with a chain.

Zakaya's betrayal at the market.

Back…back…back…

Demon-mice chasing me through a maze of tunnels.

A dagger in Baba's heart.

My father dragging me into a double-life of thievery.

The memories continued to surge backwards, to the massacre five years ago…

The king's guards barging through our town, tearing people from their homes, killing anyone they deemed dangerous. Anyone using forbidden relics and magic.

Baba had been on one of his merchant quests when it happened. When they'd come to our shop, my mother had stood at the door, refusing to let them in. "It's me you want," she'd said in her calm voice. "Leave them be."

She'd gone down first, a dagger slitting her throat, and they'd pushed her body aside and barged in. I'd tried to protect Caral, a dagger going straight through my shoulder. Then Caral lay lifeless beside me.

They'd left me for dead.

The fire simmering beneath the surface for so long now roared to life, igniting the dev-worm within me.

Vishap hissed, "Rage, *rage!*" His voice taunted me, stoking the flames of my anger. The raging storm turned inward, consuming me from within. The fire within rose to an inferno.

The dead bodies in Tarin. The Enlightener collecting them for his dev army.

I felt the weight of my mistakes, the guilt for the lives I'd inadvertently cost.

Who are you? Vishap had asked.

Who am I but a selfish girl drowning in a sea of errors?

Who am I but a mere mortal attempting to play games with a god?

My breathing became labored, my chest constricting as fury overpowered me. The fang marks crackled and blistered, releasing waves of heat and an acrid scent. I coughed and sputtered. Blood spewed from my mouth.

I collapsed to my knees, my snarls merging with the guttural growls reverberating across the cavern. Thick mucus slipped from my eyes. The dev-worm within me roared to life.

Vishap slithered through the shadows before me. "Let it rise, let the anger *feed* you."

A primal hunger surged through me. The thirst for blood, for death.

Ahriman. Ahriman. Ahriman. The creature repeatedly chanted that name.

Visions of my past twisted and warped, melding with my memories. The emptiness in my father's eyes, his desperate plea for me to bring them back from the dead. This was my purpose. This was my *choice*.

The serpent dragon's voice pierced through the darkness. "Who are you?" His words bounced around the cavern. *You…you…you.*

The darkness beckoned, promising strength, liberation. It extinguished the light of the Spool, the Ring. It left me with a choice.

My choice, a choice to wield the darkness that consumed me.

Glorious, *glorious* rage.

The dev within lashed out. A primal roar tore from my throat, shredding at my vocal cords, my eardrums. I screamed again as sharp fangs pierced the edges of my gums, blood spurting down my chin.

A deep voice resonated around me, as if the rocks themselves were speaking.

"Welcome, Weaver of Darkness."

Chapter 17

"I dwell in the shadows of your rage, in the darkness of your fears, in the depths of your desperation."
~ *The Vishap's Riddle*

My dev-worm unfurled like a serpent shedding skin.

Shadow-tendrils coiled through my thoughts with sinister grace, twisting and distorting them until my own mind became a labyrinth I could no longer navigate. Until every part of me pulsed with a consuming rage and an insatiable hunger to conquer, to destroy, to *hurt*.

"Weaver of Darkne*sss*..." Vishap's words slithered through the air. "Chosen by Ahriman, Archdemon of Despair and Chao*sss*."

Iridescent purple scales shimmered in the unearthly light. A sinuous tail whipped past, sharp edges gleaming like upward-pointing blades. The serpent-dragon weaved through the shadows, revealing glimpses of his immense form. "Your anger fuel*sss* you, empower*sss* you. Your rage nourishes Ahriman."

My mind ripped in two. A part of me clung desperately to the flickering flame of *me*, but a larger part desired the seductive abyss offering oblivion.

Two paths, the fortune teller had foretold.

I sensed a presence behind me. I spun around and came face to face with Vishap.

The dragon's head loomed seven times larger than a

human's. Eyes of molten lava, maw dripping with slime, dagger-sharp teeth, each capable of piercing my skull with ease.

"It i*sss* time," he snarled. A stone cup materialized on the ground between us. "Drink, and you will draw from Ahriman's strength. Drink and you will have all that you desire, to return your loved ones back from death. *Drink*."

Wispy shadows spiraled upwards from the Spool, twisting and weaving into shapes. And there they stood, my parents and brother. Their arms reached out through the vision. A lump rose up my throat, ending in another snarl from my lips. "You-you can do that?"

"Ahriman is all-powerful," Vishap said. "Drink and it will be done."

I reached for the cup with trembling hands. Never in my life had I yearned for the darkness, for the hollow power that Vishap dangled before me. But if it meant reviving my family, wouldn't I sacrifice everything I had? My life, my very spirit?

My hand stilled. *My spirit.*

I recalled the dead noblewoman's essence trapped in a violent kork, the ugliness of the Enlightener's manipulation, the Monster-King's acts. Was this Ahriman's twisted bargain? To reunite me with a hollow shell of my family? To transform into a creature of the dark with eyes of mucus-yellow and a heart veiled in shadow?

I lifted the cup under my nose, and nearly dropped it. A metallic scent assaulted my senses. Blood.

Strangely, a part of me—the part that belonged to the oozing fang marks and the dev-worm within—craved it. But the flicker of my clinging essence recoiled in disgust.

"Remember what they did to you," Vishap growled. "The guards, your friends, your betrothed. Even your own father. Drink, and you will wield Ahriman's powers."

My fangs nipped at my mouth as another snarl escaped my lips. A metallic tang filled my mouth. The vision of my family merged back into the shadows.

"Drink!" Vishap hissed, his tone now tinged with desperation.

The Gate-Ring and the Weaver's Spool pulsed with a blinding blue brilliance, the heat surging over my skin. My reality shifted.

A melody slipped through my mind's shadow-walls, echoing with forgotten truths and untapped strength. The familiar notes unraveled the knots in my chest, loosening my clenched jaw. Like a fragile flame defying the darkest hour of night, a sliver of *me* clawed through the walls of darkness and fought back to the surface.

The *me* who believed in good.

The *me* who demanded justice.

The *me* I'd forgotten.

The melody grew sharp, bold. It emerged from the chaotic debris of my thoughts and surfaced to the forefront of my awareness. With deliberate yet painful jabs, threads of clarity rose from the wreckage like honed blades rising through dense earth.

The persistent tune wove its way from the maze of my thoughts, lifting more memories to the surface. But with each joyful memory, another rose to counter it.

Zakaya's soft smile…the betrayal in his eyes.

Lana's infectious laugh…her horror at my actions.

A boy with stormy eyes the color of the twilight sky

rescuing me from the clutches of death...the helmet of the conquering kingdom adorning his head.

For a fleeting moment, the threat faded. I fixated instead on the moments of joys and hardships, loves and trials, strengths and vulnerabilities, mistakes and unwavering resilience.

Within these flashes, the duality of the godforce pulsed with the rhythm of creation, plaiting the fabric of lives, of our world. Light and shadow. Shadow and light. Without one, the other could not exist. I tucked that realization to the back of my mind to reflect on later.

Amidst the surging tune, a woman's voice emerged, her words echoing through the corridors of my mind. S*h-shadows...shadows,   d-darkness...darkness,   release, beware...*

That voice. Its timbre, the familiar resonance. It struck a chord within me, as if singing the lost *me* back into being. Her words rearranged and intertwined with the melody, gaining clarity and purpose, coalescing into coherent phrases, *"Beware the shadows. Release the darkness."*

I clung onto the tune, humming it softly.

The Spool's disks sprang to life, spinning and gaining momentum. Threads of vibrant light rose from the Gate-Ring and laced around the Spool. Like master weavers, the two relics fused their azurite-threads, creating a radiant vision before me.

At first the image wavered, but it gradually sharpened into focus.

Mama's skilled hands weave threads of light into a tapestry, guiding souls to the afterlife. Her presence is a gentle force as she teaches me her art of healing. The softness of the silken cloth, the brilliance and warmth radiating from the threads, the lingering scent of patchouli oil. All interlace with the soothing hum of her voice.

Mama's smile, her eyes, every gentle feature exuded boundless love that bathed my mind and heart in warmth.

"Mama," I whispered.

The vision blurred and another took its place, then another. Vivid memories, brimming with the long-suppressed warmth and joy of my childhood, emerged. Each carried a collage of images, sounds, scents, sensations, *emotions*.

The Spool, a humming conduit, channeled the essence of my past into the present. Its energy chipped at my charred heart, balmed over my searing skin. Murky tears clouded my vision as my mother's voice cleared a path in the turmoil, continuously reweaving the strands of my memories. One word, one note at a time.

Her melody swelled, stirring *me* awake. The *me* tucked within the crevices. The *me* bent low and compressed to take up minimal space.

Now that *me* unfolded, rose tall, and faced the dev-worm.

There *she* stood in my mind's eye, a dark shadow wearing my face crafted from the Monster-King's bites. For three heartbeats, I locked gazes with mucus-yellow eyes.

The Satya-dev snarled.

I opened my fanged jaws and propelled my voice through strained vocal cords, joining my mother's tune with a soft hum. First one note, then another. A broken symphony followed.

The Satya-dev lunged. And just as *her* shadow-claws pierced my chest, *she* froze, angling her head.

Listened. One breath. Two.

Dark wisps rose from her head and vanished in a swirl of shadow-flakes. Threads of smoke writhed into the Spool.

Vishap's voice rose. "I sense the fury simmering within you. Embrace it."

Shadow-strands slithered through the Spool and Gate-Ring, rippling and distorting the radiant tapestry before me. The shadows coalesced, each vision morphing into scenes ripped from my past. I stood paralyzed, a bystander in my own memories. The more I witnessed, the more I realized something felt off. Zakaya's betrayal, the enraged townspeople, Master Raman's retreat, Lana doing nothing. These weren't my true memories.

Now, fully aware, I saw and sensed Vishap's manipulation. *He's toying with me.*

Lana *had* done something. She'd tried to help me.

Yes, Zakaya had betrayed me, but he'd been torn between his duty as the Regent's son and his love for me. Master Raman hadn't abandoned me at the festival; he'd gone to pack for our escape. Once again, the tapestry darkened, unveiling my father's indifference after the massacre, leaving me to grieve alone.

In the ethereal expanse, I heard the desperation in my father's voice. The pain of loss etched on his face as he immersed himself in his books and texts. His search for the Spool, all that research, had been his escape. Why hadn't I realized that before? He'd suffered and mourned in his own way; had tried to do right in his own way. I hadn't realized I'd been clinging to that anger until this moment.

This creature was twisting my memories until all I

saw were the jagged edges of events. All of it ripped from context, a distortion of the truth.

It was all about perception. Selective focus.

The blisters on my wrist throbbed. The Ring seared my finger, the Spool my palm, each vying for my attention. Through murk-filled eyes, I watched the visions play out, grounding myself in the reality I knew to be true. Maybe Vishap thought these twisted memories would amplify my rage, but instead they highlighted how much those closest to me had cared.

"Satya," my mother's voice echoed across the years from the vision. "Don't let anger sever the bonds of friendship. Let it go."

The memory surged back, a moment from years ago. How old had I been? Eleven? Twelve? A forgotten argument with Lana, the cause lost to time. It took days to quell my youthful rage, until Lana forced me to confront it. Ashamed, I'd been just as much at fault over a simple misunderstanding. But that brought mutual forgiveness, our bond reforged.

Now, that lesson resurfaced. *Forgiveness.*

More memories unearthed, each a study in compassion and forgiveness. Through the Spool, my mother's spirit wove a counterpoint to Vishap's venomous whispers. The serpent-dragon's guttural voice echoed through the cavern, chanting the Archdemon of Despair and Chaos's name, and reminding me of the awful things others had done to me.

And for every vile word, I countered silently in my heart.

"Your betrothed betrayed you…" *I forgive you, Zakaya.*

"Your own father led you into danger…" *I forgive*

you, Baba.

"Your people scorned you…" *I forgive you, Mosatti.*
I forgive. I forgive. I forgive.
Please…forgive me too.

White-hot energy erupted from my core. It pulsed through my veins, chasing away hate, rage, and despair with a wave of exhilarating warmth. A tangible force sprouted in my chest. It bloomed, blossomed, flourished, turning to the light like a dahlia facing the sun.

Hope. As real as the dryness in my mouth. As frantic as the hammering of my heart.

The lingering threads of the dev-worm recoiled and retreated to the hidden crevices of my mind. My fangs slipped from my gums and fell to the ground with two distinct thuds.

"…and your father…" Vishap was saying.

"My father always wanted what's best for me," I snapped, my voice resounding around the cavern. "*Always.*"

A pause.

A guttural snarl.

The temple-cavern blurred, its living walls dissolving beneath a shroud of thick haze. Emerging from within the fog, Vishap's head appeared, his formidable maw parting to emit a venomous hiss. "Ahriman grows restle*ssss*."

Pale blue light pulsed from the Spool and the Gate-Ring, luminous spectral fingers reaching out. The dense fog thinned and dissipated, revealing the cavernous space. Behind Vishap, the pool shimmered, its surface rippling with reflections that danced across the obsidian columns. Was this another illusion, or had the pool grown larger, and closer to the cavern's edge?

The azure water shimmered as if a globe of blue light resided within its depths. Vishap recoiled with a hiss, retreating from the water's edge. Was the pool toxic to him? If he evaded it, it was exactly where I needed to be. I took a step toward the water.

Vishap's tail lashed out, dagger-sharp scales scraping the ground, blocking my path.

Jaw set, I clutched the brilliant Spool before me and took another determined step forward.

His gaze met mine. "We seek what can destroy us. We yearn what others desire. In the end, it is all about the victory."

My senses sharpened. The world snapped into focus. "You speak in riddles."

"You *think* in riddles," Vishap snarled, his sour stench clogging my nose. "Do you accept Ahriman's bargain?"

Think in riddles? He *was* in my head, manipulating me even now.

I clung to the Spool in one hand, the blood-filled cup in the other. One, a Sacreds' tool, the other a shadowed promise.

Vishap was offering me a bargain. That meant I had a choice.

Shadow and light. Luminous and Eclipse. The devworm stirred within, but did I detect a waning of its energy? I inhaled a putrid breath. Tightening my grip on the Spool, I let the stone cup slip from my grasp.

It vanished before it met the ground.

For a heartbeat, I gaped at the ground where the blood should have spilled. The cup wasn't real. It never had been.

If it wasn't real, then…

My gaze flicked to Vishap, this creature of the Underworld, Ahriman's agent. A master manipulator. "I *reject* his offer."

Vishap reared on hind legs, towering over me. His massive form obscured the pool as he unleashed a thunderous roar that shook the cavern. I ducked against his fiery spittle raining over my skin.

Agonizing pain pierced my eardrums. I screamed.

The dev-worm within writhed, its viscous presence straining to burst out. But I sealed my lips before its roar could respond to Vishap, denying it a voice.

Shadow-serpents erupted from the serpent-dragon, swirling around Vishap in a rapidly multiplying storm. Dozens became hundreds slinking over his body, enshrouding him. The shadow-veiled serpent-dragon expanded tenfold.

I stumbled back until my spine hit the cavern's rough wall. Before me stood not Vishap, but a creature made of shifting shadow-serpents.

"You will now answer to Ahriman," the creature boomed, deep voice echoing through the cavern. Gone was the hissing voice of the dragon, the lighthearted banter of riddles. This creature came from a much darker place.

Ahriman. Angra Mainyu, the destructive spirit. This creature was evil by *choice*. One did not bargain with such darkness. One ran.

"You dare reject the Archdemon of Despair and Chaos?" it roared.

I whimpered as the colossal form neared, its tempest of hissing shadow-serpents extending slimy tongues to brush my skin.

Breathing ragged, I was about to close my eyes

against the onslaught when I glimpsed something out of place. Delicate light tendrils floated above the Spool, connecting to the Gate-Ring and merging with the massive image before me.

Image. That's all this was.

Vishap was wielding my own tools against me!

This serpent-storm couldn't be Ahriman. If Ahriman were present, I'd already be dead, my spirit sucked into his realm. No, this was another deception, like the visions earlier.

You want to play? Oh, I will play.

They say a drowning person clings to straws. In my desperation, I clung onto my straw. This idea could work. It *had* to work.

Sweat beads clung to my skin as I stared at the nightmarish creature before me. Slowly, I removed my brother's small tapestry from my belt-pouch. The living realm my mother had encapsulated in woven light-threads. Within it, Anahit, Goddess of Healing, joined Nar and Tsovian, the twin-deities of the sea, and Vahagn, the mighty Dragon Reaper. I focused on Vahagn, his form vivid and commanding as he wielded his sword over a defeated dragon.

Caral's nightmares had been trapped and vanquished within these delicate threads. Maybe it would do the same for me.

I conjured a vivid image of Vishap pinned beneath Vahagn's sword, praying that my mother's woven magic would be enough.

My mother's spell from the battle-kork rose to my lips. "Weavers of Light, empower this fight. The past and future must come together to end our plight."

Threads of light as thick as luminous ribbons glided

from the Spool and the Gate-Ring, encircling the rolling serpent-storm before me. The fake-Ahriman's shadow-serpents abruptly halted their slithering dance. Then, one by one, they fizzled and vanished.

As the shadows dissipated, they unveiled Vishap, restored to his normal size. I continued to chant the spell as the persistent light tendrils from the relics relentlessly assaulted Vishap. The serpent-dragon shrank further and further.

The once-imposing creature rapidly diminished in size. "What have you done?" His growl turned feeble, resembling that of a young wolf pup. He now stood no larger than a donkey.

"Didn't you say that, in the end, it is all about the victory?" I said, my voice brittle.

"I thought you said you despise riddles," he snapped in a tiny voice, his body now barely the size of a goat.

"I lied," I said, looming over him. "I *adore* riddles."

Vishap's tiny eyes blinked once, twice. Then, with a resounding pop, he burst into smoke. The final tendrils of his essence whisked into the kork.

Chapter 18

Even in the darkest night,
A falling star will find its light.
                    ~ Ar-Haya Highlands Proverb

Vishap's furious pup-growls faded with a dying hiss, the putrid scent of decay dissipating with him. An invigorating petrichor aroma of damp earth and rain filled the air.

I blinked. Blinked again. No more murk clouded my vision. My limbs weakened with relief, but my relief was short-lived as the Spool's disks continued to spin and hum.

How did one turn off a god-relic?

I tucked the light-woven tapestry—now Vishap's prison—into my belt-pouch. Pebbles crunched underfoot as I drew closer to the water's edge. Radiant ribbons of mist spiraled outward from the Spool's whirring disks, faster and faster, until the cavern washed in a shimmering, honey-sweet haze.

My grip tightened on the Spool. Mama's spell banished Vishap, but what other forces had I unleashed? Crouching, I swiped a hand through the steadily thickening fog, half-expecting a lurking creature to bite it off. The mist parted briefly, offering a glimpse of the gleaming pool before the haze reclaimed it.

The dense, shimmery fog continued to rise from the

Spool, spreading and coalescing into storm clouds filled with trapped starlight. As it ascended higher, it slowly unveiled a transformed space.

The cavern had expanded while Vishap shrank. Azurite crystals jutted from the now-distant walls and towering ceiling. The pool had grown into a lake at the cavern's heart.

Iridescent clouds continued to swirl and dance as they molded into distinct figures and bodies. The otherworldly forms of countless ghostly women, varying in age and size. Hands joined as if in a celestial line-dance, they filled every path and crevice, even hovering over the water's still surface.

A chant resonated from the assembly of spirits, "Daughter of light...daughter of light...daughter of light." Their ethereal chorus echoed off the cavern walls. *Light...light...light.*

I stood, clutching the Spool tightly. Had I accidentally unleashed spirits from its portal again? But unlike the violent forest apparitions, these spirits emanated gentleness. One glided toward me with ethereal grace, ghost-hair billowing in a luminous halo caught in an unearthly breeze. She paused a mere handspan away.

My heart stuttered. "Mama?" I breathed.

But as her features sharpened, I realized this ancient woman carried a haunting resemblance. The same almond-shaped eyes and delicate pointy chin. The same dimple on the right of her mouth, the exact one my mother and I shared.

"You summoned?" the spirit asked.

"I...summoned?" I repeated in a hush.

A smaller spirit-figure detached herself from the

spectral assembly. A child, barely ten, her gauzy form shimmering as she approached. Her features mirrored the ancient one's. And *mine*.

I blinked repeatedly. Real or illusion?

The child's radiant smile seemed *very* real. Our gazes locked, stirring a spark of recognition within me. Those vivid blue endless-sky eyes held a truth I could almost grasp.

Before I could process the implications, the elderly spirit spoke again. "We are Light Weavers of the past and future. Some among us are your ancestors." She glanced fondly at the child, "And others, your descendants."

The child extended her small hand toward me, fingers hovering over the Spool. "It is not yet your time," she whispered softly, her words carrying a wisdom far beyond her youthful appearance. "And it is not my time, either. For me to exist in your world, you must endure and survive what lies ahead."

"You have summoned us to your aid." The elderly spirit's voice carried into the vastness. *Aid…aid…aid.* Her arms extended to encompass the myriad of spirits surrounding the cavern. "And we have heeded your call. We offer you passage to that which you seek."

"What I seek…" How could they know what I sought when I no longer knew it myself?

The elderly spirit brushed a feathery caress on my cheek. Radiant light emanated from the center of her chest, surging into me. My heart quickened, as if ascending toward a precipice I couldn't see beyond.

"Oh, dear child," she said. "Your path ahead is veiled in questions and draped in shadows. The determination and strength you displayed against the

Archdemon of Despair and Chaos will be pivotal in the choices ahead…along with some divine guidance."

"Divine guidance…?" I whispered, my voice fragile.

Goddess, was I going to repeat every word she said? They all must think me ignorant, oblivious. But the energy pouring through the Spool and now encompassing the entire cavern filled my chest with an intoxicating power, making it hard to catch my breath, let alone speak.

The elderly spirit spread her arms, and ribbons of light burst from her fingertips, unfurling into a radiant sphere encompassing all. The child's eyes widened at the display in innocent wonder. Although I had just met the spirit-child, overwhelming love washed over me.

The spirits' voices joined together in a harmonious chorus: "Strands of light, threads of power, merge together in the final hour."

"Remember this spell," the child whispered.

Before I could grasp the significance of their words, both specters rested breezy hands on my shoulders. Their touch surged potent energy through me, the past and future infusing the present. I felt a profound connection to all the spirits that surrounded me, as if our essences were intertwining. Their brilliance intensified until all I could see were their ghostly halos.

Their voices resonated from every direction, "Daughter of light, welcome into our midst."

A surge of clarity filled me, and I knew what I sought. To return to my world. Master the god-relics. Save my family.

The spirits' glowing forms converged into a mesmerizing tapestry of interlocking threads, but the child lingered, whispering, "She's waiting for you."

Then with a resounding *whoosh*, she joined the ethereal circle spiraling into the godforce whipping through the Spool.

"Who?" I asked, my voice echoing into the vastness. Alone again.

The Spool's whirling disks slowed, still emitting faint multi-hued wisps. I lifted the god-relic to my eye level, half-expecting to glimpse the ethereal assembly within its disks. Had my mother been among them? But if her spirit dwelled with that gathering, she would have revealed herself. I was sure of it. No, she remained trapped within the Enlightener's kork, alongside countless Sophenian souls he'd ensnared.

"Facing your own truths is painful," a woman's voice chimed delicately. "But it is an obligatory path to healing."

I whipped around. The cavern's brilliant azurites illuminated the massive lake that reached the far walls, its still surface mirroring the azurite-studded ceiling above. Roughly ten boat-lengths into the glassy water sat a woman upon a golden boat, her aura so brilliant I squinted my eyes to adjust.

Who is she? Was this yet another trial? My mind raced, sifting through the fragments of knowledge I'd gleaned from Baba's texts, trying to place her among the pantheon of forgotten deities. Was this a benevolent figure offering aid, or a celestial power with motives as murky as Vishap's?

As I neared the water's edge, her features grew more distinct. Lustrous hair, the color of rich earth, cascaded down to her waist. Her joyful dark eyes locked onto mine. A gleaming plate rested in her lap, its radiance matching the sparkling adornments on her fingers. A ring on every finger, but one. Each ring featured a light-refracting crystal in various hues. As my gaze fixated on them, an inexplicable compulsion drove me to count again. Nine rings. Somehow, that detail felt significant.

"Who are you?" she asked.

It was the same question Vishap had posed earlier, but from her, it carried a different weight, as if it held the key to my fate.

"Satya Lumian," I stammered.

"Tell me, Satya Lumian…" Echoes of my name rang through the air in a strange vibration of tinkling bells and distant promises. "How does a young mortal like yourself remain tethered to Ahriman's darkness without succumbing to its allure? Boldly wielding the gods' tools as if they belong to you? Capturing the interest of celestial beings who *vouch* for you? And now, you have garnered the attention of a goddess."

She *was* a goddess. Well, according to her. "I…"

"You have called on the spirits of past and future Light Weavers," she continued, not waiting for my response. "By releasing the Cup of Shadows, you have proven your worth. To them *and* to me. I ask again, who are you?"

As her words trailed off, the plate radiated with blinding light. Her energy pulsed through the air, fusing with that of the Weaver's Spool and the Gate-Ring. The combined godforce of the three relics collided with a resounding hum, glimmering ribbons weaving together as gossamer light particles spiraled around me. My wrist stung. The fang marks blazed, fizzed, melted. Air tunneled through my ears and nose in a disorienting rush until the sensation subsided.

My arm pain receded. Vanished.

Who am I?

These mystical artifacts responded to my touch, my thoughts. Vishap had tried to convince me that I wielded darkness. But he was wrong. Deep within, I had always walked in the light.

Raman's words echoed through my mind. *My student, with a strong sense of justice.*

The voices of the ethereal Light Weavers resounded in my head, "*Daughter of light, welcome into our midst.*"

"I'm…" I sputtered, hope swelling. "Am I a Light Weaver?"

"Are you still unsure of *who* you are?" she asked.

Her melodic words danced through the air, filling my spirit with newfound confidence. Doubt melted away, replaced by a growing sense of purpose.

In my mind's eye, I saw my youthful mother amidst the chaos of battle. Her hair whipping, robes swirling as she clutched the Spool, guiding the spirits of her friends to the afterlife. Could I do that? Was I strong enough to embrace my destiny as a guardian of harmony in a world teetering on the edge of darkness?

Same as my mother did?

Yes, an inner voice vowed. I was her daughter, shaped for this purpose long before I understood what it meant.

"I am a Light Weaver," I said, my voice firm with conviction.

The goddess smiled, unleashing another brilliant beam from her plate, enveloping me in a halo of light. I gaped at my glowing form, clutching the humming Spool tighter as power flooded my veins, my entire body vibrating with it. I could feel the weight of responsibility settling upon my shoulders, but somehow it did not feel overwhelming. It felt *right*.

"You have impressed me," the goddess said. "You must walk the light, yet wield the shadows. It is a balance I think you are beginning to understand."

Her hands splayed upon the golden plate, her rings blazing so brightly I squinted. Strands of light poured forth from the Gate-Ring into the Spool. I inhaled a cleansing breath, released it. My lungs felt renewed, full of this new, intense energy.

"I claim you as my vessel, Satya Lumian," the goddess announced. "You are my Agent of Dawn, *Light Weaver*."

Again, I tried to recall my knowledge of the gods. Was she Tsovinar, the sea goddess, or Astlik, the love and star goddess? Many gods and goddesses had been lost to living memory, thanks to the Enlightener's purges.

"Who are you?" I whispered.

Through the brilliant halo, I saw her lips stretch into a smile. Then in a voice so powerful it resonated over and *through* the space around me, she spoke into my head. *"I am She, bringer of dawn, riser of the sleeping sun. Come, you must know your pantheon of the gods."*

Bringer of dawn...riser of the sleeping sun. Words from my father's notes crystallized. "You're Ayg...Goddess of Dawn."

She laughed, the sound like tinkling bells and the mighty roar of crashing waves, the unrelenting flow of molten lava and the swift rush of the wind...all woven into one euphonious melody.

As her laughter faded, I strained my ears for its echoes.

"Why are you helping me?" I cringed at how ungrateful I must sound.

Ayg's golden vessel drifted back, ripples cascading over the still water. "The gods are at war. Our most powerful one is trapped. The realms of mortals and gods are linked intimately. Let's just say, I see potential in you."

Her cryptic words confused me. What did a war between gods have to do with mortals? And what potential could she possibly see in me, a mere girl, that could help with a war between *deities*?

"The absence of light creates the void," Ayg continued. "The light of dawn illuminates the path for those who hide in the shadows. It brings hope to the lost and guides trapped souls out of their prisons of darkness. Satya, the tools within your grasp will aid you in this work. They are your connection to my immense power."

Her fingers curved over her glowing plate, drawing my attention to her nine glittering rings. My eyes fell on my own ring. "The tools…"

"The tenth ring," Ayg said. "I have bestowed its power upon you."

As she spoke, the Gate-Ring continued to radiate in soft blue, and her words finally sank in. *This is Ayg's ring!*

"Without the power of the gods flowing through them," Ayg explained. "Mortals may utilize sacred relics, but with deadly risks. As my vessel, your command of these tools is still limited, though enhanced enough to enable you to fulfill your duties in the mortal realm."

Duties? A sudden burst of heat surged through my veins. My arms glimmered as if molten sunrays flowed beneath my skin. "I-I'm glowing."

"Thanks to the spirits of past and future Light Weavers, the godforce is strong within you," Ayg said. "But be warned, Satya. Ahriman's shadow clings to you, just beyond my reach."

Clawing fear pierced my chest. The otherworldly eyes of the Enlightener and Monster-King flickered in my mind. I brushed my fingers over my glowing skin. "But can't you do something?" My voice escaped in a thin plea.

"No. However, *you* must do something." Ayg's voice grew solemn. "To sever Ahriman's grip on your realm, and release our trapped kin, you must vanquish his vessel in your world."

"His vessel…the Enlightener?"

"Ahriman's ears are sharp. Thus, my words are veiled. Heed the night's truth to tell the story of dawn."

I blew out a frustrated breath. The gods loved their riddles.

The cavern walls rumbled, the ground shook. Water splashed at my feet, cascading waves darkening the pebbles on shore. I stumbled, trying to balance myself on the shaky ground.

Ayg angled her golden plate upward. "Daughter of Light, observe."

A beam of light erupted from her plate, piercing the cavern ceiling and illuminating hordes of sharp blue crystals. The cavern ceiling rumbled, cracked, split. Glittering gems plummeted into the lake and scattered, but not one fell on me.

The ceiling opened outward, a doorway into the night sky.

"*Always follow the light*," she spoke directly into my

head.

The ceiling gaped wider, unveiling an impossibly large full moon that drenched the cavern in its ethereal glow. A movement in the sky snagged my eye. A winged creature, its form graceful against the velvety expanse, arced toward the fractured ceiling.

As it surged closer and grew larger, I gasped. A magnificent horse with a shimmery coat of moonlight soared through the cavern's gap. Feathered wings, vast as a cottage roof, sliced the air with a deafening whoosh. My hair whipped into my face, momentarily blinding me, as the stunning beast landed with a soft thud before me, releasing a melodic whinny.

"Satya," Ayg's voice boomed over the tides. "Daughter of Dawn, agent of the rising sun, I give you passage upon my steed. You must now return to the realm of the living."

My heart hammered against my ribs as I reached out, a hesitant touch against the horse's warm, silky neck. At my caress, the creature dipped her head, her dark eyes gleaming with an otherworldly intelligence. With a gentle whicker, she lowered her front knees, inviting me to climb on.

Gripping the steed's thick, white mane, I hauled myself onto her back. She rose and unfurled her majestic wings. I held onto her mane, the still-glowing Spool gripped tight. With a powerful push of her hind legs, we were airborne. We hurtled past the rugged cavern walls, through the jagged ceiling, and into the vast expanse of darkness above.

The wind roared in my ears, my long hair trailed behind me, and my tunic billowed and danced with the rhythmic beat of the horse's wings.

"Always follow the light," Ayg's voice tinkled into my mind. *"Daughter of Dawn."*

Above us the massive sphere grew impossibly larger, and my father's notes appeared before me with sudden clarity.

I was wrong. Not the moon. But the sun.

And not the night sky. *This* was the sun's nighttime voyage. The Night Sea of legend.

And we were falling,

...falling,

......falling

.........toward the sleeping sun.

Chapter 19

"Heed the night's truth to tell the story of dawn."
~ Ayg's Riddle

Pebbles dug into my back like tiny fingertips as other sensations slowly filtered in…the relentless roar of rushing water, cool mist prickling my face, my soaked clothes and hair clinging to me.

Disjointed visions flitted through the darkness behind my leaden eyelids. A monstrous serpent-dragon with blades for teeth. The cavern's vaulted ceiling unfurling like a blossoming flower. A goddess with a golden plate trailing bolts of light.

There's something…something important I'm forgetting.

A jolt of panic surged through me. My hands curled at my sides, meeting mud and slick pebbles.

The Spool! Just as memory crashed back in relentless waves, a woman's thick, accented voice reached my ears. "She's either dead…or she's beat dze curse."

I forced my lids open. I lay on a rocky riverbank, the cavern's maw radiating dark energy across the path. Warriors in rough-spun wool and daggers glinting in the morning light surrounded me. One warrior crouched beside me, his cream tunic plastered to broad shoulders. His face slowly sharpened into focus: an angular chin, furrowed brows, sun-kissed brown hair damp and clinging to his forehead. His steady gaze, the blue-gray of dusk after a summer storm, held mine, sending a jolt through me. A memory flickered, but before I could grasp it, a wave of nausea washed it away.

"She's quite alive and quite uncursed," he said, offering me his hand.

That accent. Cool, crisp. It was *him*, the hooded figure from the Aurean Kingdom, the one chained to Mona.

This close, he seemed younger than I expected, maybe not much older than me. A slightly crooked nose and a deep gash on his chin hinted at a past skirmish. Something flashed in his eyes, something I couldn't read.

Heat crept up my cheeks. I had no business gawking like a fool at *anyone* from the Aurean Kingdom. My stomach agreed as another surge of nausea crashed over me. The world tilted. I rolled over and emptied my meager rations onto the cold, damp ground. As the wave subsided, I turned back, drained and humiliated.

Raman pushed through the circle of warriors, his face etched with relief. "Satya, thank the gods!"

The Aurean warrior rose and retreated a pace.

Mona lifted her waterlogged skirt slightly off the ground, making the chain between herself and the Aurean warrior clink. "Lovely morning for a swim, no?"

Her skirt clung damply to her legs, as if she too had ventured into the water. Who in their right mind went swimming fully dressed? A shiver coursed through me, a reminder of my own soggy state. Well, *me*, apparently.

Raman leaned over me, deep creases furrowing his brow. "How do you feel, Satya?"

"I...I feel...heavy," the words scraped out as if

gravel coated my throat.

Raman tightened his lips, nodding toward the Aurean warrior. "If not for Rei, you would have drowned."

Rei. Through weighted eyelids, my sluggish gaze found him again, but his narrowed eyes were now locked on Mona.

"See? Sheez not dead," Mona snapped, irritation sharpening her tone, as if resuming an argument. She jangled her blue-eyed beaded bracelet at Rei. "You can stop piercing me with dze evil eye."

Rei's jaw flexed, water droplets clinging to his bronzed skin. "You claimed that cavern isn't a portal."

"It is *not* the type of portal we can use," Mona insisted. "As I have said before…"

"Then explain how she entered last night and ended up in the river this morning," Rei ground out.

Hours? It had felt like days, weeks…a moon-cycle. Which reminded me how I'd ended up there in the first place. "I did not *enter* the cavern. I was shoved."

"My people don't ask questions when a dev-bitten is involved," Mona said. "And you, Varta's daughter, were hiding your eyes and your bites."

As I took Raman's offered hand and pulled myself up, I noticed an object on the river's edge a few handspans away, beside my abandoned satchel. "My pouch!"

"You wouldn't let go of it," Rei said, his brow furrowed, casting shadows over his guarded eyes.

"Thanks," I mumbled, stubbornly avoiding his gaze. Rescuing me didn't erase where he clearly came from.

Picking up the pouch with shaky hands, I brushed my fingers over the stiff, wet leather. Was the Spool inside or did I lose it? For now, I had no choice but to trust Raman to keep my secret. Given her history with god-relics, goddess only knew what Mona's reaction would be.

Mona's voice, sharp as a crow's caw, snapped me from my thoughts. "On a related note, you're welcome and congratulations."

"What…why?"

"You, daughter of Varta," she said, a hint of grudging respect in her voice, "Are the only one to ever return from Dragon's Maw."

The portal-cavern's entrance pulsed with tangible energy, its ghostly tendrils crawling over my skin. Within me, the writhing shadow responded to its lure. The words of the goddess stirred in my memory. *Ahriman's shadow clings to you.*

Panic surged through me, the burden of this secret threatening to consume me. I stumbled back until water squished into my soggy boots at the riverbank. "Dragon's Maw…"

"It's where we've been sending the afflicted," Mona said. "It's the cave of healing or slaying, depending on…"

I narrowed my eyes. "*Slaying?*"

"Depending on the afflicted," Mona snapped, leaning forward. "Your eyes…dzey are ringed."

"W-what?"

"Ringed, Zzatya," she repeated. "There are golden rings around your pupils. Same color as a dev's eyes, except less thick, and more…shine." She frowned and mumbled to herself. "*That*, I have not yet seen."

"You've seen other devs?" Raman said, his voice dark.

Mona sighed heavily. "Unfortunately."

Mona's words sank in. My hand flew to my face, brushing against my skin, terror clawing at me. There were others like the Monster-King. And my eyes were ringed, similar to a dev's. Was the Archdemon of Despair and Chaos leering out at the world through my gaze? Darkness bloomed at the edges of my vision. The dev-worm coiled around my heart, squeezing, squeezing…

Mona's voice drifted through my fog. "Let us get you some dry clothes and warm tea to drink."

Her words sparked more fragments of memory. *"Drink, and you will draw from Ahriman's strength. Drink!"*

The Gate-Ring grew warmer, snapping me out of my head. I became aware of everyone's curious stares. Heat flooded my cheeks as I turned to Mona. "Why did you have me thrown in there?"

Mona flung her hand at my arm. "Why eez everyone so angry? I *helped* you."

Only then did I truly register the change. The agonizing pain in my wrist…gone. The oozing fang wounds had healed into a pair of crescent-shaped scars.

****

Mona led us along the winding river path, three warriors trailing at a short distance behind. Rei followed with Raman's travel pack slung over one shoulder. The chain binding him to Mona clinked along the ground, a softly glowing relic that seemed to shift fluidly with their movements.

"Where do you live now?" Raman asked Mona.

"It's a surprise," Mona teased, casting a sly glance at him as we rounded a bend.

The bustling village unfolded before us, bathed in morning sunlight. Lush vegetation draped terraced mountain walls dotted with cavern entrances. Woven grass-ropes, knotted vine bridges, and corded ladders crisscrossed the precarious heights where Azzis of all ages maneuvered with graceful ease. I snapped my gaping mouth shut when I caught Mona smirking at me.

The air hung heavy with woodsmoke. Villagers tended to sweet-smelling stew pots over fire pits while others cast nets into the rushing river. Children bounced on the thick boughs of a mulberry tree, raining purple berries onto woolen blankets below as others collected the bounty. A giggling boy darted past until an older girl yanked him back, her eyes widening as she met my gaze.

"Visitors are clearly a rare sight," Mona said with a wry smile.

Unease prickled my skin as the Azzis gave us a wide berth, casting wary looks at Raman and me. With my sodden pack thwacking against my back, our squelching boots, and the jangling chain, we made quite the musical ensemble. The lively village fell silent as more and more gazes turned our way. Hoisting my increasingly weighty pack higher, I felt the villagers' heavy scrutiny. Raman's reassuring nod did little to calm my racing heart.

I sighed with relief as we rounded another bend, leaving the bustling heart of the village behind. The air buzzed with the low hum of conversation and the clatter of metal from an open cavern smithy. One man rhythmically hammered a dagger, his reverberating rings punctuating the clatter as others crafted swords, daggers, and spears. A seasoned artisan hunched over, meticulously sculpting a bronze-copper disk into a shield.

My merchant's eye instinctively assessed the superior craftsmanship, impressed by the Azzis' advanced metallurgy skills. An older craftsman with a graying beard glanced up at Mona and thumped his fist to his chest. I'd noticed the Azzis exchange the same gesture during our journey here, in what I assumed was a sign of respect. Mona acknowledged him with a brief nod. The man's gaze flicked to me, brow furrowing slightly before he returned to his work.

A weight pressed on my chest. My mother had once garnered such respect. But since the massacre, I'd become invisible, even to myself. While I assisted my father in managing the shop, an ever-widening chasm of isolation had taken root. I kept secrets from everyone. From Zakaya and Lana. From Baba. While I shared my father's goals in reviving our family, his fixation on finding the Spool had consumed him. As for me, I'd drifted, lost, in the currents of my own bottomless grief.

A lump lodged in my throat. I glanced at the crescent moons carved into my wrist and wondered if the goddess had also bestowed me with heightened self-reflection.

Mona's voice jolted me out of my thoughts. "Here we are."

We'd reached a small hut nestled at the foot of the caves. The structure's weathered wood bore the scars of time, its size no larger than my modest sleeping quarters back home. The rounded doorway clung to stone hinges, while the rooftop seamlessly merged with the mountain's natural overhang.

"Dze temple of Anahit," Mona announced with flourish, shooting Raman a grin. "I told you I'd find it."

Raman made a sputtering sound. "After a thousand years…it still stands and survived the purges.

Incredible."

A thousand years? I studied the structure with fresh eyes. A surge of hope shot through me. Could this be one of the temples Baba had hoped to find? Maybe it was even marked on the elusive map I hadn't been able to acquire. I stole a glance at Mona, my hands tightening over my belt pouch. A sliver of unease wormed its way in. As a Sacred, she might claim to know how to wield the Spool, but she might ruin it the same way she'd done the other relics.

As we entered, the three warriors who'd been trailing us quietly dispersed. The village sounds faded, replaced by an enveloping serenity.

The dev-worm within me hissed, sending a thread of pain through my skull. As the Gate-Ring warmed my finger, the slithering shadow writhed deeper into the recesses of my mind. A wave of melancholy gripped me. A profound sense of *karot*. As if a fragment of my past had been erased, leaving behind an insatiable yearning for something I could not remember.

Rei's eyes briefly met mine. Curiosity flickered in his pale eyes before he glanced away, leaving me flustered. Unwelcome heat flooded my cheeks. I couldn't deny it, at least to myself, that I was curious about him.

An archway led into a softly lit cavern. On a waist-high wooden table, a child-sized statue of the goddess Anahit guarded the entrance, its aged bronze tinted green. Her lifelike eyes radiated the wisdom of the revered healer, goddess of fertility and water. My merchant's eye recognized the statue's potential value, but my lingering *karot* refused to reduce it to mere riches.

A wide-rimmed bowl of water filled with dried herbs sat before the sculpture, infusing the air with the subtle scent of mint, wild oregano and rose petals. Mona dipped a finger into the bowl, then touched her brow, heart, and the pulses at her neck and wrists, softly murmuring a chant.

Whispers bounced off the chamber walls before settling into silence. A protection spell. One that stirred memories of my mother's rituals. The pang of karot swelled, a mix of loss and longing. I swallowed against the tightness in my throat.

Mona beckoned us through the archway into a sparsely furnished cavern that unexpectedly had a lived-in feel. To the left, four stone benches surrounded a circular wooden table atop a faded rug. A warm breeze drifted from a dark passageway at the back, where the temple's timeworn wooden structure seamlessly merged with the mountain rock. The gentle murmur of cascading water echoed from deep within.

"The alcove with the statue is the only remaining piece of Anahit's temple," Mona explained while gathering clothes from a nearby basket. "The rest is our home."

In a far alcove, a stack of folded blankets and two straw mattresses lay about three arm-lengths apart. Presumably Rei's and Mona's sleeping quarters. How must it feel to be bound to someone you didn't get along with? In *every* situation? *Goddess, they both must be miserable.*

Rei deposited Raman's travel-pack in a corner with a thud, the slithering chain lengthening and shortening with his and Mona's movements. I couldn't help but feel a twinge of sympathy for this man from the Golden

King's city. He didn't act with the entitled air of a pampered royal. Maybe he'd been a former royal guard ostracized for defying the Monster-King's growing corruption? His lean, toned physique hinted at a warrior's training, though how he maintained such a build while magically chained to Mona, I couldn't imagine. But why would the Sacreds go to such lengths to protect a mere guard?

It's not my concern. I had my own demons to slay, and he clearly had his. I frankly did not care enough to ask about his identity, especially since our paths would never cross again after we parted. Feeling Rei's eyes on me, I quickly averted my gaze, warmth creeping up my cheeks. I'd obviously been staring at him for far too long. Again.

Grunting, Raman lowered himself onto a stone bench by the table, his hands on his knees.

I rushed to his side. "Master Raman, are you all right?"

He waved me off. "Go change out of those wet clothes before you catch a chill. Don't worry about me."

I hefted my pack higher, but Mona's words stopped me. "Leave it. I'll give you a change of clothing datz much warmer than what you've likely packed."

She handed Raman a thick woolen blanket, which he draped around his shivering form over his cloak. Mona was right. The few thin outfits I'd packed wouldn't withstand the chilling altitude here, even with layering.

Leaving my travel pack behind, I followed Rei and Mona through the dimly lit stone corridor into the mountain's heart. The distant murmur of flowing water grew louder, echoing through the gradually brightening passageway. As we ventured deeper into the mountain, a balmy warmth enveloped me. Sensation gradually returned to my numb fingers, toes, and ears, causing them to tingle back to life.

Mona cast a glance back at me. "Dzis mountain is an ancient volcano. The deeper we go, the warmer it is. Feels nice, no?"

"It does," I said, savoring the warmth permeating my bones.

The sloping path opened into a sun-dappled oasis. A cavernous ceiling honeycombed with holes filtered golden light onto an emerald pool large enough for a dozen bathers. Steam wafted from mossy boulders encircling the water's edge, the humid air heavy with the earthy, mineral-rich aroma. Multiple cascading waterfalls fed the pool with gentle murmurs before flowing out on the other side. Warm air moistened my skin as I stepped inside, brushing against featherlight fern fronds lining the walls.

Rei lingered at the entrance, a tall shadow at the tunnel's mouth.

"Here," Mona said, placing a stack of clothes on a dry moss-covered boulder. "These are for you. If you lay your damp things out, they'll be dry by morning."

"Thank you," I said. "But what about you…?"

"We'll change elsewhere," Mona said with a wry smile. Leaning closer, she wrinkled her nose and whispered, "After days of travel, I am sure you will appreciate a bath, no?"

They walked away, leaving me slack-jawed. I raised my collar and took a hesitant sniff. Dear goddess, the nose-pinching sulphurous reek of Dragon's Maw clung to me, enough to make a dev faint.

As soon as their footfalls faded, I ripped the belt-pouch from my waist, fingers trembling as I tore at the clasp. And there, nestled amidst my travel tools, lay the Weaver's Spool, untouched and unharmed. My knees grew weak with relief. How in the world had it survived? *None of this makes sense.*

Maybe the dev-bites on my wrist had healed, but wasn't this proof that at least part of my experience in Dragon's Maw might have been an illusion? I'd used the Spool, had held it in my grip until I'd been given passage back to the realm of the living...

A dream? But what about the healed wound? I brushed my fingers over the scarred bites. No, it was real. All of it. It had to be. I glanced around. We were clearly in one of the ancient temples Baba had hoped to find. With Mona, a Sacred. This place held power. I could feel it reverberating around me, vibrating into my very bones.

Maybe I could ask Mona to show me how to use the Weaver's Spool. There *had* to be a safe way to bring my family back. What good was the godforce to me if I couldn't?

Chapter 20

A crescent moon has a shadowed space,
The full truth hides in its hidden face.
~ Sophenian Folksong

The hot spring water was a welcome shock after days spent on the bone-chilling mountain paths. With each brush of moss against my skin and hair, a layer of exhaustion and grime scrubbed away. I left my damp clothes on the sun-dappled rocks to dry and pulled on Mona's moss-green woolen dress. Welcome warmth embraced my bones as I plaited my wet hair into a thick braid down my back and headed down the corridor. The rhythmic squish-squish of my still-damp boots echoed in the silence as I approached the main cavern.

The dev-worm's presence still lingered, a chilling whisper at the periphery of my senses. But the Gate-Ring pulsed with a reassuring warmth whenever the shadows within me stirred. A flicker of hope ignited within me. Maybe Ahriman's connection had weakened now that Ayg chose me as her vessel. I'd outsmarted Vishap. Maybe I could overcome the dev-worm too.

My steps grew heavy at the entrance to the cavern's living quarters. Wrapping my hand around my belt-pouch, I wondered again how much I could trust the others.

I can't choose my allies.

Same as my parents, Raman and Mona were Legion of Garni Sacreds. Though I knew nothing of the Legion, I trusted Raman, and he appeared to trust Mona. She might hold the key to my mother's Light Weaving skills. I needed to be honest about the Spool, Vishap, the Goddess of Dawn…even if the others thought me mad.

I inhaled deeply to steady my nerves and entered the living quarters. Mona and Rei hadn't returned. Raman slept on a straw mattress, his soft snores rumbling through the space. Two Azzi youths sat bathed in the hearth's warm glow. The girl, who looked to be near my age, brewed a sweet-smelling mixture over the fire, while the boy, just a child, created a poultice from the concoction.

The girl looked up and smiled, patting the spot beside her. "Please join us. Mistress Mona said we can stay."

"Your Sophenian is perfect," I said, taking a seat on the soft cushion. "I'm Satya."

"I know who you are," she said, while continuing to stir the brew. "My father, Tavid, is also from Mosatti, like you. He discovered this village years ago as a scout and decided to stay when he met my mother." A small smile played on her features. "He taught me Sophenian."

I returned her smile. "That's a really sweet story, uh…"

"I'm Pari," she said, scooping another handful of herbs inside a whisperweave cloth for the boy to start a new poultice. "And this is my brother, Azad."

Azad stared at my eyes for a long moment, then quickly dropped his gaze.

"Our mother and grandmother are the village healers," Pari said. "They're teaching us their skills.

When Sacred Mona told us about your shoulder, we wanted to help."

The throb in my shoulder had eased to a dull ache. With everything that happened, I'd stopped paying attention to it. Now that I *was* paying attention, my wound throbbed anew. "Thank you, but I'm fine…"

"The bandages are soaked and need replacing." Pari shifted beside me, and Azad handed her a poultice. She nodded toward my shoulder. "May I?"

Slipping off the cloak, I lowered the dress collar to bare my shoulder. As Pari removed the bloodied whisperweave, Azad's eyes widened at the sight of my open wound.

Pari sucked in a breath. "It looks painful."

"My shoulder has its own heartbeat." I pressed my lips together when she began to treat the broken skin. "How did you know I'm from Mosatti?"

"You have the same accent as my father," Pari said. "And the whole village knows about you by now."

My stomach tightened. Did they know that I'd stolen from the Golden King? That he'd transformed into a monster? That I'd betrayed my entire town, or that the Enlightener might at this very moment be tracking me using my knife? I couldn't lie to these people. Not after what happened in Tarin. "There's an evil sorcerer on my trail."

Pari's brow furrowed in concentration as she worked on my shoulder. "There have been signs of darkness approaching for months. My father said so. Surely this sorcerer and his army have grander plans than chasing one person."

The thought of the Enlightener's undead army ravaging this peaceful village and turning the Azzis into devs sent a shudder through me.

"Even if they are following you," Pari continued, her voice firm, "This is a village of warriors. We are all trained to defend ourselves."

"This sorcerer and the King's army...they're dangerous," I said.

Pari met my gaze, her eyes sparkling with quiet strength. "The Azzis believe fate is a tapestry woven only by the gods." Her gaze lingered on the faint pulse of light emanating from the Gate-Ring, a silent question in her eyes. Despite Pari's kindness, I wasn't ready to relive the horrors of Dragon's Maw with someone I barely knew. So I stared silently into the fire as Pari finished wrapping my shoulder and smoothed back the fabric of my sleeve.

"Thank you both," I said, then turned to the young boy. "Do you speak Sophenian too?"

When he didn't respond, Pari said, "Azad doesn't speak at all."

A pang of sympathy squeezed my heart. "Oh."

With a warm smile, Pari signed to Azad. He grinned and replied in kind. Pari chuckled. "He says you're *very* beautiful."

The tension in my shoulders eased for the first time in days, and a genuine laugh bubbled up from my chest.

The sound of shuffling drew my attention to the back entrance as Mona and Rei emerged from the tunnels. Rei had changed into a loose pale tunic and gray pants, the common Azzi village attire I'd seen on the other men. His gaze traveled over my face, his eyes wide with...appreciation? No one, not even Zakaya, had ever looked at me that way. An unwelcome warmth spread through me.

I suddenly became acutely aware of him. Undeniably handsome, possibly the most attractive man I'd ever seen. Guilt gnawed at me for such thoughts, as if I'd somehow betrayed Zakaya. Rei stirred a confusing flutter in my stomach. It wasn't just his demeanor or speech, though his refined manners and clipped accent amplified his allure. What captivated me was the way his piercing blue-gray gaze seemed to see right through me. I had the strange sense of knowing him from somewhere, at some time.

But that was ridiculous. Not only was Rei a stranger—his crisp accent betrayed him as being from Vosk, the Aurean King's golden city!

Shocked at my thoughts, I shoved the feelings aside and dropped my gaze from his.

Piercing blue-gray gaze? Refined manners? Am I daft?

He might be attractive, and he might be gallant, but I couldn't forget how his countrymen had *gallantly* invaded Sophene, swords dripping with innocent blood.

Mona, now in a fresh gray gown, inspected me. "Good, the dress fits."

As I thanked her, Pari and Azad gathered their things to leave. Azad turned to Rei, thumping a fist to his own chest. With a small smile, Rei returned the gesture. That smile…a revelation, a glimpse of warmth that cracked his stoic warrior façade. If I thought him handsome before, this unguarded expression…goddess help me.

After the siblings left, Mona brewed fragrant tea and laid out a simple breakfast of dried apricots, raisins, sunflower seeds, crumbled feta, and warm lavash flatbreads. As Rei filled our brass mugs with honeyed rose tea, the rich aromas awoke a ravenous hunger in me after days of deprivation. Raman joined us, but his plate remained barely touched.

"Master Raman, aren't you hungry?" I asked.

He offered me a weary smile. "I can only manage small portions for now. I'll be fine."

I gnawed at my lip. Since leaving Mosatti, he'd grown paler and frailer by the day. Our relationship, too, had shifted. The stern schoolmaster had transformed into a trusted mentor, even a friend. And we faced this predicament because of me. Goddess, this newfound honesty with myself *hurt*.

I met Mona's analyzing gaze across the table. "Why didn't my mother like you?"

I bit my lip again. The words had tumbled out unbidden.

Mona's eyebrow arched as she sipped her tea, letting the silence linger before replying. "I tried to steal your father from her."

Baba? With this woman? The very idea felt ridiculous. Scowling, all I could utter was, "What?"

Mona shrugged. "Well, it didn't work, did it?"

The quiet stretched again until Mona leaned forward, her tone turning serious. "Look, Satya Lumian. All of dzat is irrelevant to the present. If we're to work together through dzis mess you've created, I need to know…how did you escape Dragon's Maw?"

The flickering firelight danced across everyone's faces. Mona's arched brow dared me to lie. Rei remained unreadable despite the flames glinting in his now storm-colored eyes. But Raman's gaze held a silent plea brimming with faith I still couldn't fathom, but trusted. Secrets weighed me down until they became a physical weight that threatened to crush me.

Mutely, I retrieved the Weaver's Spool from my belt-pouch and placed it on the rough-hewn table with a soft thud. Somehow, the relic felt heavier, sturdier.

Mona's sharp inhale sliced the silence. "Where and how did you get that?"

"It's a long story," I said.

Before I could begin, Mona turned to Raman, her tone tinged with disbelief. "You entrusted her with a sacred relic?"

"We faced a far greater threat," Raman explained. "Once we cleared a few misunderstandings, the relic was safe in Satya's pack, until…it wasn't." He glanced at me, raising his own brows expectantly.

Mona persisted, "Well it is obvious the Spool and Ring were under Yanik and Varta's protection, and now their daughter has them. Why were dzey entrusted with such precious god-relics, while I was left with the ones incredibly difficult to control?" She raised her arms and let them fall in exasperation, causing the chain to jangle between her and Rei.

The truth about the relics slammed into me. The Wall Splitter and the others hidden in plain sight all these years in our shop. My father had kept their origins secret, leading me to believe he'd acquired them on his mysterious journeys. These were god-relics, entrusted to my parents by the Legion for safekeeping.

A bitter mix of grief and betrayal twisted in my gut. But alongside it, a new understanding. My parents had concealed the truth about these dangerous artifacts in an effort to shield me from the perilous world of ancient relics and their hidden powers. They couldn't have known that this dark world would find me anyway.

"The Spool and the Gate-Ring were not in my father's possession," I clarified. "I found them at the King's palace."

Rei's hand, clamped around his mug of tea, froze in midair. A flicker of surprise crossed his features before an unreadable mask settled back in place. He took a deliberate sip, his twilight eyes unwavering from mine.

Mona's palm smacked the table, making me jump. "They do *not* belong to dzat wretched king. But how do you...?"

"I stole them," I interrupted, meeting her gaze head-on.

"Satya, tell us what happened," Raman said, his voice laced with sincerity. "I trust them. You can too. They deserve to know, so that we can forge a path forward."

I swallowed, meeting his trusting eyes, and nodded.

The words tumbled out in a torrent I could no longer contain as I unburdened my story. "After the Mosatti massacre, my father planned to resurrect my mother and brother using the Weaver's Spool..."

Detached, I recounted each twist and turn as if narrating someone else's journey: thieving in the Golden King's Gallery of Treasures, Baba's tragic death, the heinous acts of the Enlightener and the Monster-King, the relentless chase by the demon-mice, my escape from the palace, and my subsequent flight from Mosatti with Raman's aid.

At some point, Raman's hand reached out to grip mine in silent support. Rei's jaw clenched tight as I spoke. Mona's eyes couldn't get any wider as I spared no detail and described the kork's epic battle, Mama's strange spell, even my grave error involving the Spool, the events that unfolded in Tarin, the king's venomous bite…culminating with my experiences in Dragon's Maw: Vishap's trials, the Circle of Light Weavers, Ayg's pronouncement.

A heavy silence settled in the room. Rei's gaze had not left my face the entire time I'd spoken, his brows furrowed. A flicker of something crossed his eyes, a complex emotion too quick for me to decipher. Being from Vosk, he surely held a connection to the palace. He *had* to know what unfolded within its walls. Yet, throughout my story detailing horrors and betrayals, his expression remained measured, devoid of the outrage or disgust I would have expected. Instead, the hard lines of his face softened almost imperceptibly, leaving behind an unreadable mask that both intrigued and unsettled me.

"Returning someone from the dead is…" Mona's voice faltered, unable to complete her sentence.

"Blasphemy," I supplied. "I know."

"And yet you intend to proceed with such a dark act anyway?" Mona slammed her hand on the table, the sound echoing in the tense silence. "Satya, your mother would be horrified."

"I know," I repeated, my voice barely a whisper. "But I'd rather she be horrified in life than silent in death."

Mona pressed her lips together. Raman and Rei hadn't said a word. While Raman knew most of my story, he hadn't known I was determined to still follow through with my father's plan to resurrect my family. Disbelief and disappointment masked his features, and in that moment, I saw not my mentor or friend but my old schoolmaster.

"Well," Mona said. "How is dzat for honesty?" She

leaned forward, pointing at the Spool "May I?" But she wasn't asking for my permission. Her eyes were on Raman.

I gritted my teeth, though it made sense for the Sacreds to place their trust in each other above all else. Mona might have known my parents, trusted them. But she barely knew *me*.

When Raman inclined his head, Mona cautiously reached for the Weaver's Spool. Her fingers brushed against the intricate carvings, her eyes narrowed in concentration as she mumbled a low incantation. A flicker of frustration crossed her face. "It doesn't work."

"It clearly did for me," I countered, extending my hand for the Spool. "It's how I escaped Dragon's Maw."

Mona scoffed, tightening her grip on the Spool. "Sheer luck! You have no idea what forces you're dealing with, the potential for disaster these relics hold."

"Disaster?" I bristled, my voice rising a notch. "I'm only trying to bring my family back." My voice broke at the final word. I blinked away the burn in my eyes.

Raman's voice boomed, silencing Mona and me. "You will do no such thing."

"But," I began, then stopped at the look Raman sent me. I knew that look. The one that conveyed, *You still have much to learn.*

Raman turned to Mona. "Ayg has chosen her, healed her…for a purpose."

Mona threw her hands up in exasperation. "Chosen? Chosen for what? To unleash chaos with these artifacts? She doesn't even understand how they work."

Raman met her gaze with quiet determination. "She will learn. We will help her learn."

My eyes flitted between the two Sacreds. "Hello?

I'm right here…"

The tense silence stretched. Finally, Mona let out a defeated sigh. "Fine," she snapped, thumping the Spool on the table with a force that rattled the cups, making me cringe. "But heed this, Varta's daughter. You will not use this god-relic on your own. Ayg might have chosen you as her vessel, but years of training are needed to control such power."

Years? Goddess, I didn't have years. I wanted my family back *now*. But if it was up to Raman, I couldn't use the Spool for that, regardless. Then what purpose would my training serve? Why had Ayg bestowed her godforce if I couldn't use it to help those I cherished most?

With a heavy heart, I retrieved the Spool and replaced it in my belt pouch, next to the folded tapestry where I'd imprisoned Vishap. Sudden unease settled in my gut. Was I truly in control of these powerful relics, or were they controlling me? I remembered Ayg's cryptic words about the Spool's exclusivity to her vessels, and how Vishap had turned my own tools against me. The dev-worm pulled at my thoughts, my tongue, trying to stop me from admitting its existence. For that alone I needed to be truthful—I couldn't keep fighting this darkness on my own. I might as well tell them *all* of it.

"There's something else," I said.

Mona raised a brow.

Placing my hand over the crescent moons on my wrist, I mustered courage to share one final, chilling truth. "Ayg chose me as her vessel, but I'm still tethered to the Archdemon of Despair and Chaos."

As I spoke, the dev-worm's now-familiar

malevolent energy slithered through my mind, as if patiently biding its time. Clenching my trembling fists, I pictured Ahriman's grip strengthening, overshadowing even Ayg. I clearly saw the Monster King, his bloody fangs, sharp claws. The thought of becoming such a creature of darkness sent a fresh wave of terror through me.

"To break free," I continued into the heavy silence, "I must sever Ahriman's hold from the Enlightener."

Mona gasped, searching my gaze as if waiting for the Archdemon of Despair and Chaos to pop out of my ringed pupils. Raman and Rei were also staring, their expressions a blend of pity, worry and horror.

I huffed out in irritation and snapped, "I'm not a dev."

My words rang with frustration, but my trembling voice betrayed my fear. I was so tired of being scared. Straightening my spine, I said, "Ahriman's hold began the moment the Golden King bit me. This Gate-Ring has kept the infection at bay...for now."

"And to be rid of it?" Mona asked.

"I only need to figure out how to defeat the Enlightener's army," I said. "Should be as easy as wresting honey from a nest of angry hornets."

Raman and Mona exchanged a weighty glance. Raman placed a hand on my arm. "We will help you, Satya. You are a goddess vessel. I trust your strength. You should too."

Throughout my tale Rei had been a silent listener, his eyes drawing inward. Now, his determined gaze met mine. "Then that's what we'll do. We will prepare for the Enlightener's inevitable attack," he said, leaning forward with an air of quiet command. "Gather more weapons, ready our warriors. We cannot afford to be caught off guard."

I studied Rei more closely, intrigued by his self-assured tone, as if he was accustomed to issuing orders. Something in his determined eyes stirred my grudging respect. This man might be from the Aurean Kingdom, but we shared an enemy. If he was willing to fight this battle, I'd be foolish to refuse his help. Besides, I wasn't naïve enough to think this was just about me.

Mona waved her hand in the air, the chain between them clattering. "And how, exactly, do you propose to accomplish that?"

I glanced at the chain, my thoughts spinning. I couldn't face the Enlightener and the crowned monster alone. *I didn't choose my allies. They chose me.* "Maybe I can help with that."

"How?" Rei and Mona asked in unison, a desperate hope clinging to their voices.

I fished the needle-thin silver tool from my pouch and held it up to them as it glinted in the firelight. "This is a Wall Splitter."

Mona gasped. "That was your father's! I cannot believe it survived two raids."

"The King's army confiscated most of the items in our shop, but this remained hidden. I'm not sure if it will work…" I glanced at Raman.

Raman studied the tool. "Perhaps."

"What does it do?" Rei asked, his clipped voice genuinely curious.

"I've only seen my father use it a few times to break through stone walls," I began, but a twinge of guilt stopped me. I'd been on the verge of revealing years of questionable missions. "May I try?"

When both Mona and Rei nodded, I stood and pointed at the shackle that bound them. "Hold up the chain between you as far as it will stretch."

"Wait," Mona said, as they both rose to their feet. "Rei, if this works you must promise me something."

Rei didn't break eye contact with me as he told Mona, "I will not run."

"Oh, good," Mona said, twisting her mouth in a sardonic grin. "I have never heard dzat before." She exchanged a secret look with Raman. "All right, Satya. Let's see what dzis thing can do."

"You may want to close your eyes," I warned.

With a steady hand, I pressed the silver needle into the chain's central link. A jolt of energy sparked from the tool as it grazed the enchanted metal. The room pulsed with an otherworldly thrum, the air thick with a tang of ozone. The Wall Splitter flared, a blinding beacon that forced me to clamp my eyelids shut. A deafening crack echoed through the chamber.

My eyes snapped open at Mona's gasp. The chain lay in two severed halves at our feet, the broken ends glowing with an eerie luminescence. The shackles, loosened by the break, hung limply from their wrists. Mona yanked hers off and dropped it to the floor as if it burned her. Rei's movements were more deliberate as he removed his own chain. Mona massaged her wrist, a purple bruise visible where the chain had chafed her skin. A similar bruise marred Rei's wrist.

As the chain's two halves rattled together, a jolt of energy surged through the air. Then, with a snap, they seamlessly rejoined, becoming whole once more.

Rei met my gaze. One side of his mouth lifted in an almost-smile.

"I never want to see that thing again for as long as I live," Mona said, her voice heavy with relief as she inspected her freed wrist.

But her words were lost in the rising storm within me. A single, chilling whisper echoed, *Embrace the shadows.*

I stiffened. I'd successfully used three god-relics, when Mona had ruined several and couldn't activate the Spool. The Sacreds were willing to train me. The mere thought of it made my stomach flutter with delicious anticipation, with a reckless plan.

As I tucked the Wall Splitter into my belt pouch, my fingers brushed the Spool. The hairs on my arms prickled to attention.

The voice, cold and seductive, continued to whisper, *"You don't need the Sacreds to resurrect your family. You are the one with the godforce. Do it yourself."*

Chapter 21

Stitch by stitch, the wound will mend,
A healing thread with a gentle hand.
~ Sophenian Children's Rhyme

The sun-dappled oasis greeted us with the sound of cascading waters.

Rei, finally free of the enchanted chain, had left to consult with the Azzi elders about safeguarding the village. He'd been gone for hours, leaving the Legion's two Sacreds and myself to begin my training.

"It's more private here," Mona said, as we settled on the moss-covered boulders farthest from the rippling pool. "We'll begin with a simple healing exercise."

For hours, every detail of my encounters with Vishap, the circle of Light Weavers, and Ayg was scrutinized, analyzed, and carefully documented in Mona's journal.

The slithering whispers in my head remained a chilling secret. They turned my thoughts to ash, leaving nothing but choking silence when I attempted to voice them aloud. But instead of fear, the emotion that should have overwhelmed me, a thrilling anticipation bubbled within.

"The godforce is yours to use at your will," the dev-worm hissed. *"All you need to do is embrace the shadows."*

In response to each slithering whisper, the Gate-Ring grew hot in warning. But my traitorous thoughts clung to the whispered promises.

The basic knowledge the Sacreds had taught me so far felt oddly familiar, like a half-remembered dream. Years spent observing my mother's seemingly mundane healing rituals now held hidden meaning. A pang of regret and bitterness shot through me. Why hadn't my parents included me in the Sacreds' world? My mother could have, *should* have, at least taught me the fundamentals.

"*They kept you in the dark*," the dev-worm offered.

Mona's words sliced through the chilling whispers in my head. "…and as a goddess-vessel, you exist on the threshold between worlds. Ours, and that of the gods. You must master the sacred balance."

I recalled Raman's ramblings during our journey here. "You mean the balance between Luminous and Eclipse energies."

Mona turned to Raman. "You *have* been teaching her."

"Not enough," Raman admitted. "Our journey here consumed all our attention. Satya, you need to channel your inner student. Become the sponge I know you to be."

Sponge. The word echoed in my mind, a stark reminder of a different time. Back when I'd brimmed with hope for a radiant future. When my challenges involved school assignments and yearning for Zakaya to notice me.

Who was I now? A desperate and lonely fugitive consumed by a single purpose. Here I sat, learning the craft my mother had devoted her life to but had deliberately kept hidden from me.

"She betrayed you," the dev-worm jeered.

To keep me safe, I countered, pushing against the torrent of doubt the whispers unleashed. A bead of sweat traced a path down my neck.

Raman's voice cut through my spiraling thoughts. "…light-weaving primarily relies on the Luminous energy," he explained. "But to truly heal someone, you must also tap into the Eclipse to discern the threads of disease, illness or emotional pain."

Mona added, "And be mindful of the chosen medium. Each woven cloth has its own unique energy. Select one that resonates with the spirit of the person you are healing."

"The key is to tap into their innate compassion for themselves," Raman said. "Healing can only occur if the person genuinely desires it on a deeper level."

"Deeper levels…deeper desires…a delicious hunger…" A tremor ran through me.

"Satya," Raman said, brows furrowed with worry. "Are you feeling all right?"

No, I'm not all right. A dev-worm has taken permanent residence in my head! "I'm fine."

Mona's gaze sharpened. "Your ringed pupils…dzey are glowing."

The dev-worm writhed within me. *"Ask them. Ask them how to resurrect a mortal."*

"I'm fine," I repeated, my voice harsher than I'd meant. Before reason could intervene, I blurted, "What if the person's body is long buried but their spirit has been trapped? Can they be brought back to life?"

Mona's jaw dropped. "We cannot call back departed spirits. That requires the use of pure Eclipse Energy. It borders on dark magic."

"*Ahriman offers such power…*" the dev-worm taunted.

I ground my teeth. "The Enlightener has trapped countless Sophenian souls," I said, my voice choked with emotion. "He's done this to my family."

"Let us first focus on aiding the living, Satya," Raman said, his voice heavy with sympathy. "Once the Enlightener is dealt with, we can explore the possibility of saving the trapped spirits."

A suffocating pressure constricted my chest. He was right. They were both right. Yet the shadow-voice was…so compelling, so *convincing*.

"Let's put theory into practice," Mona said, pointing at the stack of rugs on the floor that Pari had gathered for us. The rugs varied in size, ranging from five to ten handspans wide.

With some effort, I shoved the dev-worm's tempting whispers into the dark recesses of my mind. "All right," I said, my voice firm. "Who am I healing?"

"Me," Raman said with a tired sigh. "These past few days have drained me of all energy."

"You trust me to…heal you?" I raised my brows.

Mona leaned closer. "Healing extends beyond the physical, dear. Yepo, the Azzi's head healer, has taken care of that for Raman. Never underestimate the power of healing the spirit. When someone's essence is healed, the body often follows."

A wave of karot, stronger than before, washed over me. My mother had often repeated those same words to me. A warmth bloomed in my chest, pushing against the dev-worm's icy tendrils. I nodded, feeling a little more confident, and spread the rugs on the mossy ground before Raman.

His hands trembled as he set aside his staff and pointed to one of the smaller rugs. "This one," he said, his voice tinged with a hint of a smile.

The miniature rug was a colorful display of flowers and leaves. Cheerful. Peaceful. I picked it up and handed it to Raman.

"It reminds me of my grandmother's garden," he murmured, his fingers tracing the fabric. A nostalgic glimmer flickered in his eyes. Resting his palms on the intricately woven tapestry, he met my gaze with a silent nod.

I settled into a comfortable cross-legged position across from him. Mona took her place beside me, her hand reaching out to gently touch mine over the Weaver's Spool.

"My shielding spell will maintain control over the Eclipse forces," Mona said. "Focus on the Luminous energy for now. Remember to prioritize the individual's overall well-being, not the specific ailment."

A tendril of worry snaked through me. How would Mona's shielding spell interact with the festering dev-worm burrowed within me? Any darkness clinging to me could taint Raman's healing. A silent snicker reverberated through my head. I ground my teeth. *Go away.*

Drawing in a deep breath, I reviewed the Sacreds' teachings from earlier today. To create a pure conduit for healing, I needed to uplift my own energy by summoning an anchoring memory. I searched my mind for a cherished moment and, immediately, memories of Nurazard from years ago surfaced. My family, vibrant and alive. Caral, his face smeared with chocolate. Mama with a radiant smile, her tapestries a splash of color against our market tent. Baba's hearty laugh as he bartered with customers. Lana and I, giggling conspirators, sneaking cookies from the Regent's tent.

Warmth blossomed within my chest. The Weaver's Spool pulsed, and the Luminous energy thrumming with renewed vigor. As the spell formed on my lips, I channeled the brilliance around me. For a glorious heartbeat, the dev-worm's oppressive presence vanished. A wave of relief settled, an uncorrupted wholeness I hadn't felt in what felt like an eternity.

Mona's voice dipped to a murmured chant, the words of her shielding spell weaving a protective barrier. "Luminous and Eclipse unite. In balance, harmonize the light."

My inner dev-worm thrashed, writhed, then settled. Mona's hand shook over mine as she absorbed tendrils of Eclipse forces rising from Raman and from me.

Through the veil of Luminous godforce, I glimpsed glittering silver strands rising from Mona and to the distant form of her dove, Tatu. But then, shadowy strands of ailments swirled around Raman. A delicate strand of light extended from the glowing relics and connected with Raman's chest. Raman's breath hitched and his eyes fluttered shut.

"By Ayg's grace and my deep connection," I sang the words of the spell, my voice steady. "I weave these threads, the spirit's protection. With light and love, I mend what's torn. Restoring health, the spirit reborn."

As I chanted, a gentle warmth bloomed in my hands. Vibrant energy pulsed within me, a surging river coursing from the soles of my feet to the crown of my head and back again. The smoky threads of Eclipse energy intertwined with the luminous halo now surrounding Raman, creating a mesmerizing dance of light and darkness.

Mona leaned in and murmured, "Stay rooted in the Luminous energy, Satya. Draw upon his essence while you coax out the shadows of illness."

I tightened my grip on the Spool, anchoring myself in Nurazard's cheerful memories. "Master Raman, journey back to your grandmother's garden. Recall the vibrant health that once pulsed through you, your natural state of being."

As I spoke, smoky tendrils separated from Raman's body. These shadowy strands intermingled with the Luminous energy swirling around and through the relics, and connected with the rug's threads in his lap. With each infusion of Raman's essence, the tapestry's petals and leaves pulsed with renewed life, their hues deepening.

A genuine smile lit up Raman's face, and a single tear traced a glistening path down his lined cheek. "I...I..." he stammered. "I can feel it. The sun's warmth on my face. Playing 'jumping the nest' with my sisters. The cool breeze in my hair as I race through the tall grass, my body light and free. I'm nearly flying...the sweet scent of lavender from the garden..."

The aroma of lavender teased my nostrils.

"I'm leaping," Raman said, his voice infused with innocent joy. "Bounding, dashing. Joyful. So...joyful."

The tapestry pulsed with vibrant energy, as if it were breathing. Leaves and flower petals swirled in the air before us. The shadow of a child danced in their midst, as if the essence of Raman's spirit intwined with the rug's threads, merging his past and present. A child's giggle echoed in the air. Smoky tendrils still twirled around the spirit-child.

"Focus, Satya," Mona whispered. "Dze Eclipse energy is like quicksand. Do not allow it to pull you under. Hold onto your anchor memory."

Gritting my teeth, I wrestled with my own mind. The warmth of the Gate-Ring and the Spool were a distant, faint comfort against the chilling whispers slithering through my thoughts.

"*Let it go,*" the dev-worm hissed, its voice seductive. "*Let the darkness flow.*"

With a surge of defiance, I grasped onto the Nurazard memory, anchoring myself against the treacherous current. Warmth bloomed in my palms, pushing back the shadows. I whispered the spell's final words, each syllable infused with determination. "Forces of light and shadow, by your energies this healing is blessed. Illuminating paths where spirits find rest. Ayg, I thank you for your grace in this sacred space."

I visualized the light purifying Raman's spirit. The Weaver's Spool pulsed like a frantic heartbeat. A flicker of pain crossed Raman's features. One heartbeat. Two. Then a radiant smile bloomed across his lips, lifting his bird-nest beard.

With a shaky laugh, he stood. "I feel…I feel as if I can run for leagues." His eyes shone with the illumination of the sunrays streaming through the cavern ceiling. "Satya, I have not felt this well since your mother's healing rituals. Thank you, my child. *Thank you.*"

A lump formed in my throat, a mix of relief and lingering worry.

"Indeed, Raman," Mona said, beaming. "Dzis

goddess-vessel *is* remarkably adept at absorbing instruction."

****

That night, as we settled onto the newly prepared straw mattresses tucked into a cavern alcove, Rei returned. His silhouette was stark against the flickering firelight in the outer chamber. He hunched intently over a dagger, a constant companion that never left his side.

"*He's not what he seems,*" the dev-worm sneered.

Leaning closer to Raman, I nodded toward Rei and whispered, "Who is he? He's obviously from Vosk. But *who* is he? I need to know, if I'm to put my trust in him."

Raman's eyes slid toward Rei's bent head. "He saved your life, Satya, at the river," he said gently. "If you trust me, please know that you can trust him as well."

The dev-worm hissed. Ignoring it, I released a frustrated breath at his cryptic answer. "How can you say that?" I hadn't meant for my voice to be so harsh, for it to rise. "How can you trust a man from the one place, the one kingdom, that has *devastated* us?" I lowered my voice. "Please, I need to know. Was he in the old King's guard? Did he once work for the Enlightener? Is he a member of the Aurean royal family?"

Raman's brow furrowed and his gaze grew uneasy. "I am afraid I cannot answer that. The truth is more complicated than you may think. While I want to be honest with you, it is not my place to reveal his identity."

Raman's gaze darted past me again. I turned to see Rei glancing our way. When our eyes met, his lips tightened and he dropped his gaze back to his dagger. A warm flush crept up my cheeks. He'd obviously heard us.

Raman's ambiguous response had, at least, revealed a part of the truth. Rei clearly held significance to the Legion, regardless of what role he may have played in the massacre that had destroyed my life.

That night, sleep eluded me like a wraith dancing just beyond my grasp. Raman kept vigilant watch, his steady presence a safeguard against any stirring of my connection to Ahriman. When unconsciousness finally claimed me, I plummeted into a twisted realm of hissing serpentine shadows.

A giant silhouette roared and thrashed, straining against unseen bonds.

Ayg's gentle voice whispered through darkened chambers, *"Heed the night's truth to tell the story of dawn."*

Her riddle hung like a massive, chained doorway in the air before writhing tendrils slithered like worms, choking out the goddess's words.

A raspy growl cut across the gloom. *"You cannot hold me off for long, sweet Satya."*

A chorus of sinister whispers echoed, *"Sssatya, Sssatya, Sssatya…"*

My heart thundered like stampeding boars as I whipped around, finding myself adrift in a heaving ocean of sulfurous shadow-forms. Sickly yellow eyes bore into me from every angle, unblinking, inescapable.

"Summon the light all you want, little weaver…" the gravelly voice reverberated from everywhere and nowhere.

"Leave me alone!" My scream echoed into the abyss, swallowed by the sea of scales and fangs.

The growling laughter rose again. *"You are bound to me forever."*

215

A thousand sibilant whispers mocked in return,
"Forever...forever...forever..."

Chapter 22

*Little whispers, secrets keep, tucked away in dreams
and sleep.*
*Some you share with open arms, but hidden ones
hold many charms.*

~ Sophenian Children's Rhyme

Over the following weeks, we settled into a routine
in the healing cavern's outer chamber. Yepo, the head-
healer and Pari's grandmother, guided the healings.
Across the cavernous space, Pari and her mother, Tereza,
tended to people's injuries by a massive hearth.
Meanwhile, I delved deeper into my training with the
two Sacreds in one of the open alcoves. A vibrant
tapestry of rugs, each a potential canvas for light-
weaving rituals, surrounded us. Our rhythmic chants
resonated through the cavern's heart, drawing curious
glances our way.

The incessant clang of weaponry from the Azzis'
training outside echoed into the healing cavern, a stark
counterpoint to the steady stream of those seeking
healing. Battered bodies with dagger slashes and
fractured bones arrived alongside weary souls bearing
the invisible scars of turmoil. Those with wounds that
transcended the physical—a hollowness in their eyes, a
lingering ache that no poultice could soothe, what Mona
termed as 'spirit wounds'—were directed to me and the

Sacreds.

"All physical wounds have their roots in the spirit," Raman explained. "Find its shadow's root, and the wound will heal."

But finding the shadow's root proved to be a formidable challenge. With many patients, I struggled to pinpoint where the shadows hid, especially since my own dev-worm incessantly pricked at me, attempting to manipulate the very shadows I tried to untangle from others.

In some, the Eclipse was strong, and it took longer to harmonize their inner Luminous forces. In a few cases, particularly among the warriors, none of the tapestry depictions resonated with their experiences, and I had to make a choice for them. I began to understand that all they truly desired was peace, and a woven cloth featuring nothing but the serene expanse of sky and meadow served that purpose.

Time blurred. Faces and names melted into a haze of fleeting encounters. Mona and Raman alternated their roles as translator and shield, while Yepo guided a diverse array of people my way. Warriors, the elderly, children, and even a few animals. Vagrik, a black, floppy-eared dog grieved for his late master. Healing Vagrik proved simplest, as his thoughts were pure and uncomplicated.

"Doesn't Vagrık mean 'little tiger'?" I murmured, ruffling the dog's ears. "You really are a little brave tiger, aren't you?" The dog's entire body leaned into my touch. After his recovery, he settled beside me, his soft snores creating a comforting rhythm.

Azad, Pari's brother, watched with a mix of wonder and awe as we performed healing after healing. While assisting with the poultices, his wide-eyed gaze often shifted to the halo of light enveloping Mona, Raman, and me during our rituals. Every time I caught a glimpse of Azad, my heart constricted. Although they looked nothing alike, his innocence and charm reminded me of my little brother, Caral. I forced my gaze away, lest I allow my own grief to disrupt the healings.

Yepo glided gracefully between the main chamber and the inner alcoves, tending to patients at various stages of recovery. Her flowing woolen robe swept the rug-covered floors as she moved, her neatly braided silver hair cascading down her back like a river of moonlight.

The interactions between Yepo, Tereza, and Pari flowed in a harmonious dance among the three generations of women. A yearning, sharp and familiar, bloomed in my chest. A desire for that intangible sense of belonging and connection that had eluded me for so, so long. A reminder that, for many, this was the norm. Family, love, acceptance.

Burying feelings of loss and nostalgic *karot*, I dove into honing my craft. With each healing, my proficiency blossomed, and the godforce grew more fluid, potent. Whenever the Eclipse energy threatened to overpower the Luminous, I drew more from Ayg's godforce to balance the two, pushing Eclipse's shadows into the earth to be transcended and transformed.

During a healing ritual, Tatu landed on Mona's shoulder as she shielded. The bird's shadow flickered like smoke in my periphery, glittering silver threads connecting her not just to Mona but to something beyond this world's veil. When Raman shielded, no such ethereal tethers bound him, only a protective barrier controlling the pure Eclipse energies, preventing them from overwhelming the ritual. The dev-worm railed against their defenses, thrashing and hissing until spent.

After the first week, the rituals became easier. Yet unease knotted my gut. My inner dev-worm gave up fighting, and instead observed my actions with cold, calculating silence. I tried not to dwell on what that could mean. Instead, I channeled my focus into each patient's healing, while neglecting my own.

Light-weaving proved astonishingly intimate. Even without shared language, the ethereal tapestries revealed glimpses into a patient's essence. Their deepest hopes, the loves that fueled them, the shadows of hate and fear that lingered. Those with the greatest challenges were the hardest to mend, and a few walked away disappointed.

Pari also possessed a gift that surpassed traditional methods. Her touch identified the source of pain and its origin, reaching beyond herbs and brews.

"Her lineage has always been attuned to these abilities," Mona whispered during a break. "Pari's mother and grandmother and I are guiding her growth."

By the end of the third week, I was mentally and physically exhausted. My knees ached from kneeling, my back threatened to collapse. I slumped back on my heels as my last patient for the day, Souren, left the alcove. The young well-muscled warrior had arrived with a storm cloud hanging over him—heavy eyes, slumped shoulders, burdened by pre-battle anxieties and nightmares. He now walked off with a newfound lightness.

A satisfied smile tugged at my lips. Healing Souren hadn't been difficult. His Luminous energy was strong with much love in his heart. He pined for a girl whose hands possessed a healing touch, though his yearning glances seemed to miss their mark as Pari offered him little more than a passing acknowledgment.

Ah, young love, I mused. *It's never rational.*

Memories of Zakaya and the aftermath of his betrayal quickly sobered me. Frowning at the crescent moons on my wrist, I spoke my thoughts aloud, "I still need to learn how to heal a dev-bite."

"Let's hope it does not come to dzat," Mona said.

Raman and I exchanged dark looks. After witnessing the horrors in Tarin, we both knew it *would* come to that. The question was, how soon.

That evening, as I headed back to our quarters, I noticed Rei climbing up a braided vine to the tip of a cliff above the ravine, his arms rippling with lean muscle. He gracefully swung down from the cliff, moving with the agility of an Azzi warrior. As he landed at the river's edge, Vagrik, the black floppy-eared dog I'd healed, darted in front of him. I hadn't even realized the pup was following me. I swiftly grabbed the dog and jumped out of the way. Rei's attempt to avoid the collision led to a tumble and a splash, leaving him drenched by the river's edge.

I held the dog close and called out to Rei, "Are you all right?"

"I'm fine," he said, standing up stiffly, one hand pressed against his arm. His face flushed, clearly embarrassed that I'd witnessed his tumble.

I recalled my conversation with Raman a few weeks ago, one Rei had clearly overheard. Heat crept up my neck at the memory. Since then, Rei and I had barely exchanged more than a few terse words, both of us consumed by our individual training.

Vagrik wriggled in my arms, and I gently released him. Shaking off his wet fur, the pup settled at my feet, tongue hanging out and gaze fixed on me. Rei gave me a curt nod, then strode purposefully toward his Azzi trainers. Gripping a braided vine, he hauled himself up the cliff face, determination etched in every line of his body despite his bruised arm.

For the past few weeks, I'd caught glimpses of him busily preparing for the impending battle. He returned to the temple late each night, just to sleep, his days consumed by practice. I watched from afar as he honed his skills. The fluidity of his sword and dagger skills betrayed a warrior's background, though the spear still gave him trouble. Now it seemed he was determined to master the vines with the same competence as the Azzis.

For a few moments, I studied his agile movements, that focused determination…

Then I firmly turned away. *Really, Satya? Agile movements and determination? Ugh.*

I stormed back into the temple, my mind a chaotic mess of thoughts and emotions I was too exhausted to untangle.

Vagrik, my silent shadow, trailed after me.

****

That night I fell into a fitful sleep, tormented by the dev-worm's sinister whispers.

I dreamt that the dev-worm wafted like smoke from my body and transformed into a writhing mass of serpents that bit at my hands, arms, neck. Their venomous tongues left behind a slimy residue of darkness.

I jolted awake with a scream, my Gate-Ring ablaze. I sat for a few long moments, hand gripped to my chest.

My heart raced as I caught my breath. Despite the terror of the nightmare, I found solace in the knowledge that Ayg's power, channeled through the Gate-Ring, continuously combatted Ahriman's grip. Even Raman had stopped holding vigil at my side as I slept. Vagrik, who had quietly nestled at my feet, sat up abruptly. His ears were pressed flat against his head, his dark eyes wide and glistening in the ruddy, pale light of a single glowrock illuminating the entire chamber.

"Sorry I woke you," I whispered to the dog and gently stroked his little head. He gave my palm a small lick, then curled into a ball and promptly fell back asleep.

I gave up trying to sleep and rose. Slipping into my shabby boots, I wrapped my cloak around my shoulders and padded through the dimly lit temple, passing by the stoic statue of Anahit.

Outside, enveloping darkness greeted me. The shadows of a dozen Azzi guards stood watch at strategic positions—the bridge, the water's edge, and the cliffs above. Settling on a boulder by the temple's doorway, I closed my eyes and sucked the cool night air into my lungs, trying to shake off the nightmare.

A shuffling sound beside me jolted me from my thoughts, and my eyes snapped open.

Rei stood on the other side of the doorway, his gaze fixed on the ravine's dark expanse. "Couldn't sleep either?" he asked, his deep voice breaking the quiet.

"No."

An awkward silence stretched between us. I'd noticed that he'd moved his cot as far from Mona as he could manage. Had my scream woken him too?

"I'm not your enemy," Rei said, his low voice interrupting my thoughts.

I shot him a sidelong glance. "Aren't you?"

Rei didn't respond for a few moments, his gaze returning to the ledges above the ravine. "I may be from Vosk. And I may have ties to the palace, as you've guessed. But those people, they are not my brethren. Never were." He trailed off, his jaw clenching.

Remnants of my haunting nightmare, combined with unwelcome emotions tangled within me, increasing my irritation. My words tumbled out with a hint of bitterness. "You're from the Golden King's city, the kingdom that *conquered* ours." I shook my head. "You may think that does not make me your enemy, but it will forever make you mine."

The air grew heavy with the weight of my angry words, a tense silence settling between us. I turned away, determined to create distance between myself and this man from the Aurean Kingdom, someone I had no right to feel anything for but disdain. But as I passed him at the temple's doorway, I caught a flash of hurt in Rei's expression before he averted his gaze and glared into the night.

****

Murmurs and a gentle glow stirred me from sleep.

From my corner, the open doorway beyond Anahit's statue revealed a world cloaked in twilight. I'd fallen asleep again without the haunting remnants of additional nightmares.

Tossing off the wool blanket, I found a radiant aura cocooning my body. Despite the exhaustive daily healing rituals that left me drained, Ayg's now-familiar essence surged through me with renewed vigor each morning since I'd arrived. I closed my eyes, taking a moment to savor the divine warmth.

When I rose, the others had already gathered around the small table, breaking their fast. Crisp morning air wafted from the open doorway. The dark forest surrounding the ravine teemed with birdsong, harmonizing with the river's gentle gurgles.

I greeted the others with a soft, "Good light," as I took the empty seat beside Raman. Raman's smile was broader. His eyes held an extra spark since his healing, warming my heart each time I noticed it.

Rei kept his gaze fixed on his food as he ate, his head bowed. His ever-present dagger lay on the table beside him, its intricate swirls gleaming in the soft light. A symbol on the hilt caught my attention. A diamond-shaped eye swallowing the sun. The Aurean sigil that adorned the doors, walls and tapestries of the Golden King's palace. If I needed confirmation of where his loyalty lay, there it was.

Memories of our brief conversation last night flooded back, a rush of heat surging over my neck and cheeks. I had every right to distrust this man, given his association with the Aurean Kingdom. Yet he had never personally done me any harm.

As if sensing my attention, Rei glanced up, and our eyes locked. I didn't know what to do with my hands, my gaze. Clearing my throat, I smoothed down my skirts and shifted my attention to the spread of foods on the table. Pomegranate seeds, dried apricots, almonds and goat cheese were arranged in a bowl beside a stack of steaming lavash. I reached for the bread, spread it with goat cheese, and took a satisfying bite.

My mind drifted back to my conversation with Rei last night. "*I may have ties to the palace…but those people are not my brethren.*"

"Ties to the palace" implied a connection to the royal family.

"Not my brethren"…what did that even mean? A distant relative of the royal family? Maybe an ostracized cousin? The Aurean royals were notoriously secretive. I wasn't even sure how many children the old King had. And why would the Sacreds protect a royal? None of this made sense.

An insistent scratch on my shin drew my attention downward. Vagrik gazed up at me, his wide eyes and lolling tongue a clear plea for food. I scooped a generous dollop of goat cheese from my sandwich and offered it to him. As he licked it off my fingers, my mind drifted until a commotion at the temple entrance shattered our peace.

A cluster of Azzi warriors, led by the towering Kev who had guided Raman and me here, poured into the chamber.

"Evil man camp…other side of mountain," Kev boomed in broken Sophenian.

Mona rose as a blur of wings landed on her shoulder. A silent exchange passed between Mona and her familiar before Tatu soared back outside. Mona launched into a rapid exchange with the Azzis, their guttural tongue crackling back and forth in a heated conversation.

Mona tensed, her eyes widening as she turned to face us. "Kev says that the Enlightener and his army have been sighted nearby. They're escorting the son of a Sophene leader."

Bread still halfway to my mouth, I gasped. "Zakaya."

"We cannot help him yet, Satya," Raman said.

"I have to do something!" My voice trembled with

urgency. "It's my fault they've imprisoned him. He could die. I can't just sit idle and watch it happen."

"We are not sitting idle," Mona snapped. "The Azzis have been preparing for battle since your arrival! Scouts have been dispatched to secure the safety of this village."

Kev's voice rose as he jabbed an accusing finger at me, making it clear who he blamed for this mess. With a glare, he stomped off with his men in tow.

I dropped my half-eaten wrap back into my bowl and offered it to Vagrik, shivering with a cold mix of shame, guilt and dread. The Enlightener could be using my knife to track me. Had I unwittingly brought those monsters to the borders of this peaceful village?

I barely registered the ongoing conversation until Mona's sharp voice broke through the fog. "...makes no sense."

"You can't stop me," Rei retorted. "I *need* to go."

Raman said, his voice a warning, "Mona, it isn't your place..."

Mona's eyes thinned to slits. "My *place*? You vant me to know my *place*?" She threw up her hands, accent growing stronger, harsher in anger. "How about I kept him safe for years, Ram. That was my *place*!" She turned to me. "Vat do you think, Zzatya!"

Caught off guard, I stammered, "What...?"

Mona rolled her eyes and gestured toward Rei, who stood hovering over the table. "Dzis one insists on spying."

"Spying?"

"I'm assembling a scouting group to spy on the Enlightener's camp," Rei said, meeting my gaze. "To find out what their plans are, maybe locate your...man."

I gritted my teeth. Zakaya was *not* my man. Not

anymore. But that wasn't his concern. I stood so forcefully my seat cushion flipped backward, startling Vagrik. "I'm going too."

Mona gasped, hands flying to grasp her hair. "Now dzis one wants to go? You youths, so impatient. You think you're invincible."

"I'm going," Rei ground through clenched teeth. "You can't stop me." He paused, meeting my gaze. "But Satya, you shouldn't come. It *is* too dangerous."

I raised my brows, annoyed for noticing that it was the first time he'd said my name. Even with his clipped accent, elongated vowels caressed it…Saaa-tee-yaa. My name on his tongue sounded…important. I tramped down on that idiotic feeling and waved a hand at the open doorway. "I had an altercation with a dragon and survived."

A faint smile flickered at the corner of Rei's lips, but quickly vanished. "We need to get close, assess the situation. And determine if we need to evacuate the village or prepare to fight. If you're captured, they can use your abilities against you. Against all of us."

I bit my lip, furious at him for telling me what I could or could not do. Maybe more furious at myself for noticing him so much. But what if he was right? Could the Enlightener exploit my connection to Ayg, devastate this village? Destroy what little hope I had left of saving my family?

"Satya." Raman placed a gentle hand on my arm. "They'll determine the gravity of the situation, see what can be done for Zakaya. Once we have more information, we can plan accordingly."

Rei nodded, securing his dagger's scabbard at his waist with a loud click of finality.

A surge of determination rose within me. I'd vanquished Vishap. Ayg's godforce coursed through me. Yet they treated me like a fragile child.

"I choose to go," I said firmly to Raman. "It's *my* decision, not yours." I turned to Rei, glaring. "And certainly not yours."

Tatu's squawk interrupted our conversation as she landed on Mona's shoulder again in a flutter of wings.

"Goddess," Mona cried with alarm. "Kev had already dispatched scouts before they came to alert us, but," She left her sentence hanging as a sound reached us.

A distinctive growl.

Heart thundering, I rushed outside with the others.

Figures burst from the trees above. Four men hauled two others, half-carrying and half-dragging them toward the bridge. As they stumbled closer, my gaze sharpened on the injured men. One bore deep scrapes along his neck, discolored blood oozing from a jagged wound.

The unmistakable mark of fangs.

But the wounds on the second man sent a jolt of terror through me. He thrashed and snarled; his crimson-soaked vest torn to reveal gaping gashes carved into his torso. His head snapped up, revealing mud-yellow eyes.

My stomach caved. This man was no longer human. He'd transformed into a creature of darkness, same as the Monster-King.

A *dev*.

Chapter 23

A fledgling flame may sputter low,
But practice fans the light's warm glow.
~ Ar-Haya Highlands Proverb

A crowd quickly gathered outside the healers'
cavern, anxious voices rising into a roar of commotion.

"Nerses," Kev's urgent voice cut through the
clamor, as he and another warrior half-dragged, half-
carried the man with the gash on his torso. Kev grunted
with the effort of restraining him, the muscles in his neck
cording with strain. Nerses, clearly afflicted with the
more serious wound, made deep guttural sounds, more
animal than human. His eyes, wide and unblinking, had
already glazed over with a sickly yellow film.

Pari stumbled alongside the other victim with the
visible dev-bites marring his neck. "Baba," she wept,
voice cracking with anguish, her petite frame buffeted by
the jostling bodies.

Bile burned my throat as I lingered on the cavern's
threshold, arm wrapped uselessly around Azad's thin
shoulders. His complexion ashen, the boy went rigid
against me. I felt rooted, horrified yet unable to tear my
gaze away from the transforming devs.

Yepo's commanding voice cut through the
commotion as she barked terse orders with steely calm.
Pari's father was deposited on a rough pallet, his matted

curls spilling across the thin padding. His bulging eyes were already glazing over in that telltale sickly yellow sheen. Tereza, his wife, dropped to her knees beside him with a muffled sob, cradling his lolling head.

Azad's trembling arms wrapped around my waist. I gently stroking his hair, wishing I could shield his young eyes from the unfolding horror. The thought that there were more creatures like the Monster King chilled my blood, twisting my gut into knots.

It took four warriors, including Rei, to wrestle the growling Nerses onto the cot and pin him down. Their hands and forearms were sheathed in thick leathers as they strained against his thrashing. Dagger-sharp incisors erupted from the corners of his mouth in a spray of blackened spittle and blood. The gathered villagers recoiled with a collective hiss.

Mona's voice drifted from behind me. "You were just saying about learning to heal dev bites?" Her tone was deceptively mild as she looked at me expectantly.

As if her words had severed some trance binding me to the spot, I gently disentangled myself from Azad, my gaze on Nerses.

Yepo and Kev argued in terse bursts of Azzian, their voices escalating with urgency. While I didn't understand the words, they clearly disagreed about what should be done.

As I drew closer to Nerses's thrashing form, the dev-worm within me uncoiled with a violent jerk. "It's hard to believe that the Enlightener has this much power," I murmured, hearing the horrified awe in my voice. I hadn't meant to sound so impressed.

Mona trailed after me, her expression grim. "What is harder to fathom is dze absurdity of their debate when there's only one merciful choice. That poor man's spirit is quickly being snuffed out, and soon his essence will be utterly lost, beyond anyone's reach."

I glanced over my shoulder at her, jaw clenched. "You mean they'll take him to Dragon's Maw?"

Mona shrugged. "It's the only conceivable path."

My stomach tightened. As the first rays of dawn kissed the tree lines above and cast long shadows across the ravine, the crescent moons on my wrist emitted a faint, reassuring glow. Maybe the others doubted my readiness for this ritual…but I'd brought this battle to their doorstep. I had to try. I owed them that much.

I removed the Weaver's Spool from my belt pouch, its disks already sparking with raw power. My voice rose over the commotion, making many heads turn my way. "Wait."

Raman pushed through the jostling crowd, his staff tap-tapping as he quickly approached. "Satya, you are not ready. This might be beyond your capabilities…"

Mona interrupted, "Do you really want to wait until the situation worsens and she's had *no* practice?" Her comment cut through Raman's objection like a well-honed blade. Raman's brows drew together, but he clamped his lips into a thin line, eyes filled with worry.

Yepo shouted something harsh in Azzian, gesturing for me to stay back. Kev, Rei and two other burly Azzis strained with grunts of exertion, fighting to subdue Nerses's wildly thrashing form. The dev's snarls resonated across the ravine. With each violent convulsion, his jaw bones cracked audibly, his mouth distending unnaturally.

I locked eyes with Yepo. I wanted, needed, to try healing these devs, but not against her wishes. Her gaze betrayed her internal conflict as she met Kev's resigned eyes. I waited until she finally dipped her chin in a subtle nod.

Immediately, I dropped to my knees beside Nerses. The Weaver's Spool pulsed with a familiar warmth, but this time it felt sluggish, almost hesitant. As I held it over Nerses's wildly writhing body, an ear-splitting howl erupted from his throat, cutting through me like a serrated blade.

Deep within, that dark and primal part of me connected to the Archdemon of Despair and Chaos, stirred in response. My inner dev-worm. It coiled and twisted, scraping at my nerves like jagged fingernails. Sweat slicked my brow as I locked gazes with Nerses's mucus-yellow eyes. I latched onto my anchor memory, on my family's joyous day at Nurazard all those years ago, recalling my mother's pleased smile as she showcased her work…

A sliver of Luminous energy crackled through the Ring and Spool, heating the relics. I drew a shaky breath, steadying myself as I prepared to unleash the healing spell. But then Nerses twisted with inhuman strength. One arm tore free from his restraints, the movement so fast I barely registered it. His hand shot out, clamping onto my wrist in a bone-crushing grip.

His face contorted into a monstrous snarl, the muscles cording along his jaw in grotesque undulations as his maw cracked wider…wider. Blood-caked fangs, each longer than my fingers, gleamed hungrily in the morning light. I yanked and twisted, but his vise-grip dragged my hand agonizingly closer to those nightmarish fangs.

An abrupt stillness settled over me, as if I'd been

submerged in waters that swallowed all sound and coherent thought. That dark thing within me leaned in toward the gaping maw, drawn like a moth to a flame. A soft, rumbling snarl built in my own throat as my dev-worm unfurled, grinning.

Cries of alarm resounded from somewhere far away. Mona's voice cut through the gel-like boundaries engulfing my senses, "Satya, hurry."

I stared, transfixed by those blood-soaked fangs. So, so close. No, not like a moth to a flame. More like a fly caught in a spiderweb. I shook off the darkness and a sudden, searing wave of warmth pulsed from the Gate-Ring anew, its power cutting through my mind like a miniature sun crashing into the night. With a gasping hiss of protest, the dev-worm recoiled.

Rei's gloved hand clamped around my wrist, yanking me free from Nerses's grasp. I gaped at my freed hand with a mixture of disbelief and horror. For a nightmarish moment, I'd *craved* the raw power coursing through the dev, envisioned those fangs sinking into my flesh. A prickling wave of icy revulsion stung my skin.

"Satya, focus," Mona's command cracked like a whip. Her hand clamped on my arm, ready to initiate the shielding ritual. She clearly hadn't seen my reaction, what I'd done...*almost* done. How could I heal a dev when my own inner-darkness craved its foul energies?

Sweat poured down my back as shame and doubt assailed me, but I clamped it down. *Daughter of Light. I'm a Daughter of Light, accepted among the circle of past and future Light Weavers. A chosen vessel. Ayg chose me for this purpose. I can do this. I must do this.*

I grasped for my anchor memory again. Images flickered in my mind. My parents' warm smiles, Caral's infectious laughter, Lana's glee as we shared stolen sweets. The Gate-Ring and Spool responded with a surge of heat.

Just as a tapestry of visions flickered above Nerses, he tore free from his restraints and lunged, sharp claws aimed for my throat. The warriors wrestled his wildly thrashing limbs back to the ground.

"You're going to get bitten," Rei's shout cut through the turmoil.

"I have to try," I gasped out, my voice tight with determination. "Please help me."

Without waiting for his response, I raised the Spool determinedly over Nerses's thrashing form once more.

Something in my gaze must have convinced Rei, for he nodded and barked urgent orders in Azzian. In a swift motion, he grappled the dev, twisting its arm and pinning it down.

My eyes widened. "Rei, don't…"

"Do what you need to do," he cut in, voice taut with effort.

I nodded, pushing aside visions of how catastrophically this could end. Rei could get hurt, bitten. But I couldn't dwell on that now.

A tense silence fell, broken by the guttural growls of the transforming devs.

Gripping the Spool tight, I plunged deeper into my memories. Rei's steady presence anchored me as I searched inward. There—a precious gem. A rare healing vigil with my mother. A family friend had crossed the veil, and the quiet beauty of my mother's incantation had struck me even as a child, filling me with such awe that I'd committed it to memory. Now it resonated with remarkable clarity. This memory, steeped in love and loss, became my new anchor.

Mona's silver-threaded shielding spell enveloped my conduit energy. Together, we waded into the heart of the shadowy storm emerging from Nerses's chest.

My voice rose above the snarls and chaos. "Soul enshrouded, consumed by night, through these threads so bright, follow the light…"

The Weaver's Spool hummed in my grasp. A radiant glow pulsed from its core, a stream of blue light reaching out and latching onto the Gate-Ring. The Spool's soft luminescence bathed Nerses, and his eyes fluttered closed as if in surrender.

Above him, a mirage of misty forms and whispers flickered into existence. Then a sound like a massive sail caught in a gust, the rhythmic *fwap-fwap* of wings beating the air. From the sky's vast expanse, a majestic, otherworldly steed descended gracefully toward the now-motionless man.

An ethereal spirit-child hovered over Nerses's body. Weightlessly, the boy rose and settled onto the spectral horse's back. With a powerful flap of its wings, the luminous steed vanished into the vibrant canvas of dawn, carrying Nerses's spirit with it.

"What in the goddess's name was that?" Pari gasped, her glistening eyes fixated on the sky. "Did anyone else see the bright light? It just vanished."

"Nerses's spirit," Raman murmured from behind me. "Satya, you just performed a soul transfer. You guided him into the afterlife."

"Without training," Mona added, a stunned tremor in her voice. "You *are* your mother's daughter."

"That spell," Raman added. "*That* was the spell your mother sang during that battle."

For an endless breath, I stared transfixed at the sky, skin prickling. How had the spell come to me at just the right moment? I hadn't recalled my mother's incantation in years. My gaze fell on the Spool. It had been my mother's tool. Did it store the spells within?

And while the others witnessed the soul's light abandoning the body, I'd been shown the full journey. The spirit-steed's mane had streamed like banners of pale fire, wings outstretched across the clouds as it carried Nerses's essence into the ether.

A hush fell as the warriors hesitantly loosened their grips on Nerses's lifeless body.

In that silence, a distant roar echoed in my ears, a muffled bellow that seeped like ice into my bones. My vision tunneled, darkening at the edges.

I stood in a black void. In the far distance, a colossal, indistinct shape writhed and thrashed, each lumbering movement accompanied by that ominous rumble.

A grating voice reverberated across the gloom, *"There is no escape from the shadow chains." Chains…chains…chains.*

Before me, a sinuous shadow-form peeled itself from my own body. A twisted mirror image…my face, my eyes, my shape. But its cruel grin was not my own.

I opened my mouth to scream, when Pari's panicked cry cut through the vision, "Satya, careful!"

The tunnel swirled into a vortex and vanished. Reality slammed back into focus.

Nerses stared at me with eyes turned to sickly yellow pools, pupils shrunk to pinpricks. A guttural growl rumbled from his throat, gnarled claws extended from his fingers. A jolt of terror shot through me.

The warriors tightened their grips on his thrashing

form. But the newly transformed dev lunged, claws aimed at my chest. I leaped back with a strangled cry. The air erupted in shouts and curses. A burly villager, his face contorted with exertion, managed to collar the dev with a heavy braided vine. Three others hoisted Nerses off the ground and dragged him, snarling and thrashing, down the village path toward Dragon's Maw.

Paralyzed, my gaze fell on Pari's father. He'd be next. Unless I could repeat the soul ritual and save his spirit. A heavy weight settled in my chest. What use was my ability if I could only usher souls to the afterlife, leaving their bodies as empty vessels for the Archdemon of Despair and Chaos? Maybe if I'd physically touched Nerses, I could have helped him. But how could I do that safely?

A hand on my arm interrupted my spiraling thoughts. Pari stood before me, eyes red and swollen. "Please, Satya, help my father. Please, *try*."

Her plea broke my heart, piercing through my uncertainty. I stared at the growling man on the cot. He wasn't as far gone as Nerses, but he wasn't far behind. I needed to get close enough to touch him.

Gloves. I needed the same elbow-length bladesmith gloves the others used. Biting my lip, I considered the tools I recalled seeing at the bladesmith's. Maybe…maybe I could try again. "I'll be right back."

Pushing through the gathered crowd, I sprinted down the path toward the bladesmith, my heart pounding in sync with the rhythmic thud of my boots. The soil yielded beneath my feet, releasing the aroma of damp earth mingled with wild thyme, sage, and oregano that grew along the riverbank. These scents, potent and grounding, cleared my head enough for a glimmer of a plan to take shape.

Clanging greeted me in the bladesmith's cavern. The grizzled foreman glanced up as I burst in.

"Gloves," I blurted. "And a shield." I searched for the word "please" in their vocabulary, and added, "Khentrem."

He squinted, then barked a curt order, jerking his chin toward the distant Dragon's Maw. His message was clear. That's where he'd send me if he could. Without another word, he stomped into the cavern, dismissing me entirely.

Frantic, I scanned the chaos of tools and weapons, finally spotting a discarded leather glove which I snatched up. A round unfinished shield lay in a corner, elaborate designs etched halfway around its surface. Its center held a slit meant for the yet-to-be-attached shield spike. Perfect for aligning the Gate-Ring.

I bolted back to the healers with the shield and glove clutched tight. The men now wrestled Pari's father, whose once-human eyes glowed sickly yellow. Growls escaped his throat.

"Baba, wake up!" Pari cried, voice heavy with tears. Souren, the young warrior who secretly had a crush on Pari, held her back, his arm around her shoulders.

Slipping the thick glove over my right hand, I leaned over the writhing man. My shoulder grazed Rei's as he pinned the man's flailing limb. With my ungloved hand, I positioned the shield before me, gripping the interior handle to align the Gate-Ring with the center gap.

Mona placed a firm hand on my shoulder, offering to be my shield again.

"What's his name?" I asked.

"Tavid," Pari choked out.

"Tavid," I repeated gently. "Can you hear me?"

Tavid's body convulsed. A jagged incisor erupted as blood and froth spewed from his mouth. A sharp metallic scent stung my nostrils.

With my gloved hand, I hovered the Weaver's Spool over the bite wounds on his neck. When I opened my mouth to sing the same spell as before, my mother's healing spell poured from my lips instead, as if the Spool knew which spell was needed. So I sang the incantation and called back his spirit, envisioning his healed body. Mona joined in with the now familiar shielding chant.

Tavid stilled. Light poured from the Ring, luminous threads churning from the Spool to interweave into a shimmering tapestry suspended above him. Ethereal forms emerged. Pari, Azad, their mother, their faces radiant with love. The kaleidoscope of memories pulsed with a seamless fusion of cherished impressions. Tavid's childhood in Mosatti's narrow streets, serene lakeside swims with his parents and siblings, the Azzi ravine, his beautiful wife, his daughter's birth, his son's.

Darkness slithered like oil, staining the sunlit visions. The shadow-forms congealed into a malevolent presence hovering before me. I gasped, my spell disrupted. Mona's grip on my hand tightened. Sweat beaded my brow as I channeled all my energy through the relics.

Within that roiling entity, the same horrifying vision from before flickered. The cavernous tunnel, the writhing shadow-giant at the end, its low reverberating roars.

"Embrace the shadows," a voice hissed into my head.

I envisioned my mother on that battleground,

focused on her spell despite the chaos and horror raging around her. A strange calm settled over me, the kind of calm where all options narrow down to a single choice. Trust. Surrender.

I surrendered to the healing spell.

Mona's shielding chant faded to a distant hum. A radiant sphere expanded from the thrumming Spool, encompassing the entire gathered crowd. The encroaching shadow recoiled with a guttural howl, shriveling, as a spirit-form made of pure light coalesced before me. It radiated warmth, peace, love. The essence of Tavid's soul.

My voice rose, no longer a spell-song but a battle cry rending the air as I completed the ritual, "…through dawn's embrace, with the goddess as my guide, shadows depart, restore the light!"

Tavid's spirit whisked into his prone body, suffusing him like warm water through a sponge. His resounding roar echoed across the village as the luminous sphere burst in a celestial downpour of star-specks around us and fizzed into the earth.

Tavid's eyes flew open, his irises warm brown once more. Whoops of joy erupted as Pari flung herself into her father's arms. Tavid's wife and son joined the jubilant tangle of arms as he sat up.

I hadn't realized I'd slumped against Rei until his supportive arm slipped from my shoulders, leaving me swaying. Flustered, I stowed the Spool back into my pouch.

Yepo approached, clasping my shoulder. "Shnorha," she murmured, one of the few Azzian words I'd learned. *Thank you.*

Rei's gaze remained fixed on me, a mix of awe and

curiosity in those twilight-depths. His gentle grip found my elbow, steadying me as nausea and lightheadedness made the world tilt. The crowd fell into an eerie hush, every eye on Tavid and me.

I'd healed a man, had guided his spirit back into his body. But that warm feeling of accomplishment curdled as I recalled the lurid visions bleeding into the ritual. That massive, undulating shadow-thing at the end of the lightless tunnel…could it be the Archdemon of Despair and Chaos himself piercing through?

Ayg's words echoed in my head. *"…Ahriman's shadow clings to you, just beyond my reach."* The thought turned my blood into icy rivers.

And the shadow-entity who had tried to slither its way into the healing tapestry? Was that my very own dev-worm straining for release? What if these sinister entities continued to haunt me each time I attempted to wield the godforce…until I was too weak to fight them?

And if they could disrupt the most sacred rituals…what hope did I have to master this power? What hope did any of us have to resist this overwhelming darkness?

Then my eyes found Pari and her joyous, reunited family. For now, at least, the forces of darkness had been banished into the void.

As the hushed crowd dispersed and Rei released my arm, I fervently hoped this would be the last dev I would ever have to heal. But my inner darkness laughed at that thought.

Such hope was as fruitless as a honeybee searching for nectar in a sea of embers.

Chapter 24

Sharp Weapons Cannot Kill the Dead
~ Azzi War Chant

That afternoon, Kev's scouts returned with a chilling report. The Enlightener had infected most of his growing forces, morphing them into devs like the Monster King. Savage, vicious, hungry.

Even more disturbing, he'd amassed a macabre collection of wagons overflowing with slaughtered innocents, systematically reanimating the lifeless bodies into soulless foot soldiers for his legion. It wouldn't be long before his dev scouts stumbled upon the hidden paths to the Azzi village.

Kev ordered an immediate evacuation. The most vulnerable villagers would take shelter in underground caverns a day's trek away, while every able fighter remained behind to defend the village and its sacred caves. Families with their children in tow ascended the mountain, laden packs over their shoulders. Some carried infants nestled in back slings. Their loyal animal companions—dogs, cats, and even donkeys—kept pace at their feet.

Kev would soon follow, along with a group of his most seasoned warriors, to escort those fleeing to the cavern shelters.

The village, now mostly empty, consisted of over a

hundred battle-ready fighters. All day I'd gnawed my lip with worry. Would their strength and skills be enough to withstand the Enlightener's forces—against an army of the dead? A grim realization struck me: if any of them were bitten, they would turn against their own. The mere thought left my heart frozen with dread.

The village transformed rapidly. Climbing ropes were pulled up and hidden, braided bridges across cavern entrances taken down. Log barriers ringed the ravine, sharpened stakes slicked with poisonous oils lined the riverbank. I wondered if such toxins would even be effective. Devs were, after all, already *dead*.

Not dead, I reminded myself. *Soulless bodies.*

After healing Tavid, I could no longer dismiss the devs as mere monsters. They were once innocent victims, their souls now waiting to be freed. That healing had changed everything for me. The idea that devs *could* be healed upended my perceptions about the godforce and its potential.

A dog barked nearby. My ears prickled. Vagrik? The stubborn pup had made Anahit's temple his home, constantly underfoot. Earlier, Pari and her parents had bid a tearful goodbye to Azad before sending him to safety with other evacuees, while the healers stayed behind. I had tried to send Vagrik with him, but the loyal dog refused to leave my side. He now lay curled at the temple's entrance, studying me as I worked on the defenses.

"Shouldn't we all flee?" I asked Raman as we bound thorny, crimson vines around the wooden barricades fortifying the bridge's entrance. The pungent tendrils, contrasting starkly against the earthy logs and smelling like vomit, were secured into the blockades at every possible gateway.

"It's part of a broader strategy," Raman explained. "Rei's idea is to impede the advance of the Enlightener's forces by erecting defenses in every town and village. The collective resistance will restrict the army's movements, making them less challenging to overcome."

Rei's ability to see the larger picture surprised me. That the village leaders and the Sacreds agreed with him was not only startling but telling. *Who are you, Rei?*

As the sun dipped below the mountain peaks, elongating shadows through the ravine, the barricades neared completion. The rhythmic clangs of the bladesmiths echoed as they forged an arsenal. Daggers, swords, spears, and shields took shape.

The once-peaceful haven had become a stronghold.

Before his planned departure, Kev assembled a group of us at the bladesmith quarters. The bustling workspace had fallen silent as we gathered around a large stone table. Spread across it lay a meticulously crafted map of the Highlands, etched onto a thin leather parchment.

Hampo, the grizzled head-bladesmith who had shooed me away that morning, stood beside me, focused on the map. He had nodded to me when I first approached, his deep frown almost welcoming. Almost.

Their voices echoed within the bladesmiths' cavernous ceiling as Kev and the others struggled to formulate a plan everyone could agree upon. Beside me, Mona translated in whispers as the discussion unfolded. So far, every conceivable strategy had been examined and dismissed.

Attacking the Enlightener's camp with all the Azzi

warriors? Too risky. It would leave the village vulnerable. Sending small groups of Azzi fighters to repeatedly engage the enemy and then retreat? Again, too risky. They could be pursued and the paths to the village could be discovered. Deploying small groups of Azzi fighters throughout the surrounding forests to guard the various entrances into the village? This would leave the village half-empty.

Risky. Risky. Risky.

Emotions intensified, voices flared. Hampo slammed his fist onto the stone table. Vagrik, who had remained quietly at my feet, began to bark and howl, contributing to the escalating chaos.

Mona continued to translate, her animated interpretations matching the fervor of the discussion. "And dzey want to place sling-shooters in the trees, build more barricades at every entrance, including the bridge," she added, slapping her palm on the stone table with a wince. "All dzat will take time…" She continued her sentence in Azzian, her arms flailing.

No single plan had gained unanimous approval so far. Finally, Rei, speaking in a low voice, managed to hush the others and offered several suggestions. Kev, Hampo and the others exchanged frowns and meaningful glances, eventually nodding their agreement.

"What did Rei propose?" I whispered to Mona.

"He sayz we lead devs to Dragon's Maw, and keep all other village entrances blocked," she said. "We position dze most skilled sling-shooters in the trees, station the best fighters at the bridge's end to force the devs to funnel in from there. We'll lead them straight into the portal cavern, one small group at a time."

Across from me, Rei's finger traced the mountain

path, sketching an invisible route from the Azzi village to Yerezum, the nearest town. The line curved around a mountain and led eastward toward the coast of the Kaspatir Sea. He threw a brief glance my way before returning his focus to the map. He surprised me by speaking in Sophenian. "Kev, you're sending your people to the underground tunnels of Odzar Valley." He nodded at the unmarked spot on the map where his finger rested. "Yerezum isn't far. Their Regent needs to be informed of the situation. He can relay the message to other towns and villages. If everyone acts as we are, we can keep the Enlightener's horde out of populated areas."

Kev nodded, his eyes narrowing as he studied the map and continued in Sophenian. "Tonight, I guide my people through caves of Odzar Valley. When they safe, I send message to warn Yerezum." He met each of our gazes, his frown deepening. "I trust all you to protect my village."

Rei responded with a solemn nod, while Hampo thumped his chest and uttered something in Azzian that made everyone laugh, easing the palpable tension. I had no idea what he said, but the others sent me small smiles.

I flushed. "What?"

Mona leaned closer and whispered, "He sayz the devs will take one look at our beautiful Light Weaver and transform back on their own."

I rolled my eyes. Rei met my gaze, an almost-smile tugging at one side of his lips.

Goddess, why is it so hot in here?

As soon as Kev departed with a group of Azzi warriors, Rei and Hampo engaged in a hushed debate. Rei finally raised his gaze and locked eyes with me, his expression filled with solemn determination. "A few of us will be heading to the Enlightener's camp tonight to assess the situation, to gauge the threat we're facing."

Zakaya! It had been weeks since I'd seen him dragged along like a prisoner. I couldn't be too late to save him. If he'd turned, I could heal him. "I'm coming with you."

To my surprise, Rei didn't argue. His gaze flicked to the Ring on my finger, a silent request.

I nodded in acknowledgement. "I'll use the Ring to transport us."

Our gazes locked, and I glimpsed the internal conflict warring within him. Finally, he dipped his head in agreement. "We'll walk to the camp, stay at a safe distance. Only a few of us will approach for observation, without revealing ourselves. Your help might be crucial on the return trip, depending on what awaits us."

"What about Zakaya?" I asked, rubbing my chest where a persistent knot had taken residence.

"I still think *dzat* is a bad idea," Mona insisted. "Saving one can endanger many…"

Before I could retort, Rei's clipped voice cut in. "The Mosatti Regent's son being held captive has far-reaching repercussions for the entire kingdom. It could spark a rebellion we're not prepared for."

Spoken like a true leader. Who are you, Rei? I studied him again—his rigid posture, his focused gaze, his eyes that shone with strength and intelligence.

Raman chimed in with a huff of agreement. "The Mosatti Regent's position is precarious, to say the least. He's the only Sophenian in such a role since the previous Regent's assassination. Sophenians see him as a beacon of hope for the kingdom, the one to pave the way for more Sophenian leaders." He stroked his thick beard, his eyes glued to the map. "But if something were to happen to his son, it would be seen as an act of war initiated by the Aureans, a sign of further oppression."

A heavy silence hung in the air, thick with the weight of our decision. We had different reasons for wanting to rescue Zakaya, but the urgency was undeniable. We debated how to extract him, but a simple "sneak him out" plan felt inadequate. Ultimately, the *how* would depend on what awaited us. The gnawing fear of failure tightened the knot in my chest.

"So, we rescue dzis boy," Mona said, one brow arched. "Then what? Exposing ourselves risks the village's location. He'll unleash those nightmarish rodents."

I grimaced, remembering the Enlightener's vicious tiny-soldiers herding me through the palace, and how they'd devoured the Sacreds during the Legion's final stand.

"I have an idea," I said, a plan forming in my mind. "Kev set traps and smoke diversions for the mice, but..."

"Burnt rosemary and sage," Mona interjected, nodding. "Dzey hate the smell,"

"But these are no ordinary vermin," I countered. "He'll send them first to weaken us. We can't wait for them to come to us."

Rei's brow furrowed. "You're suggesting we draw them out?"

"Exactly," I said. "Mona, what relic do you use to control Tatu?"

"No relics," she said. "Tatu is a spirit animal, connected to me through the goddess Anahit."

I recalled the difference between Mona's silvery shielding threads and Raman's shimmering, colorless ones. During our rituals, especially the recent ones, I'd glimpsed something through Mona's energy, something large and ominous that possibly tethered her to Tatu. "How does your connection work?"

She shrugged. "I ask her to show me things, but I don't always want to see through her eyes. Sometimes I block her visions to give us both a break, so she can fly around and be a bird for a while."

An idea sparked. "Maybe we can combine our abilities."

Mona frowned. "Meaning?"

I swallowed, acknowledging the risks, but I couldn't think of a better option. "After we spy on the Enlightener's camp and gauge the situation, I'll open the spirit-portal with the Spool. Then, you can link me to the mice through Anahit's power. I think…I think I can find the Enlightener's connection to the vermin. Together, maybe we can sever his control, the same way you block Tatu's visions."

The chamber grew silent as everyone absorbed the plan. Outside, the ravine remained eerily quiet, save for the rushing river.

"There's a flaw in dzis plan," Mona said finally. "We cannot attempt this until he uses the connection with the mice. And by then, it might be too late."

"Unless," Raman interjected, brows knitted, "we set traps far enough and loud enough to warn us of their approach."

All eyes turned to me. I took a slow, measured breath. "We'll need to link to him quickly. We won't have much time."

Rei studied me for a long moment, lips pursed in contemplation. "I'll make sure the traps are set tonight, before we head out."

A knot of apprehension tightened in my stomach. Tonight.

Tonight, we would decide Zakaya's fate. Then trick a powerful sorcerer to divert his demon-horde, and possibly face an army of devs.

"Easy as stealing honey from beehives," I muttered, repeating one of Baba's favorite phrases. Mostly to reassure myself.

My comment earned doubtful looks and raised brows. Except for Rei's half-grin.

I turned away before my betraying lips responded to that smile.

****

Evening shadows settled over the ravine. Torches flickered to life and glowrocks illuminated workspaces: the bladesmiths' forge, the healer's quarters, the temple. The rest of the dwellings remained eerily dark and deserted.

I waited by the bridge for the others to join me. The river rushed and danced with the current's rhythm, sloshing over rocks and boulders. Its soothing sound harmonized with the periodic clinks of metal as the last of the barriers were erected around the village limits. Warriors moved about, some with cautious strides, their alert eyes scanning the thickets above, while others bustled with hurried steps to gather weapons or go to their posts.

Mona and I had convinced Raman to remain behind tonight. Though he didn't appear thrilled with the decision, he'd finally agreed to assist Yepo in preparing the healing quarters.

My entire body quivered with anticipation. I reached

for the cold hilt of Baba's dagger to steady myself. With trembling fingers and clammy palms, I busied myself by imitating the fluid motions of the skilled warriors. My attempts at parries and strikes felt awkward as I tried to mimic the precision and skill I'd observed from afar while Rei and the others had trained.

I didn't notice Rei's approach until his clipped voice pierced through my concentration. "That's a good hammer grip."

Whirling around to face him, I stumbled, nearly losing my balance with my dagger pointed at him. Feeling foolish, I quickly lowered the weapon and muttered, "Thanks."

"In that position, you'll be able to strike a dev's chest," he said. "But you'll need to get close enough."

"I know," I said. "But I'm not trying to kill or hurt them."

His gaze locked with mine. "You've said that before."

"Because I mean it," I said, trying not to sound defensive.

"I understand."

"Do you?" *Why am I challenging him?*

"I do," he said, taking a step closer. "You can't kill them with a dagger anyway, only slow them down. You need to ward them off if their razor-sharp teeth get too close to you."

"Obviously." I barely stopped myself from rolling my eyes.

He gave me that almost-smile and my heart stilled.

"Yes, obviously," he said, imitating me. "Except you can't do that with a hammer hold."

"How am I supposed to hold it, then?" I asked,

genuinely wanting to know.

"Turn the dagger point to face up, instead of down."

I promptly switched the hilt to follow Rei's guidance. His hand came to rest gently on my wrist, adjusting my position so that the dagger slipped farther away from my body. The blade brushed against the leather scale-armor on his chest with a faint whisper. "See how this grip can protect you?"

Pursing my lips, I nodded, trying to focus on the lesson despite the unsettling effect of his proximity. His pale eyes reflected the golden-orange hues of the setting sun, distracting me. My heart hammered, my cheeks grew warm. I quickly lowered my weapon before I accidentally hurt either of us.

"Good," he said, nodding with approval, seeming completely clueless to the effect he had on me. "Practice that stance every chance you get until it becomes second nature. It could save your life. And if any of those creatures…"

"People," I corrected.

"Right. If any of the infected people get too close, you ward them off by keeping them away from your arms, hands, face. And never turn your back on them."

"That is obvious too," I said.

He dropped his hands and stepped back. "You don't like me."

I busied myself with placing my dagger back in its sheath, and tried to keep my voice neutral. "What makes you say that?"

"It's a guess," he said, his tone even.

"Maybe it's because of how your kind has treated my people," I said, unable to meet his eyes.

"My kind…"

"The Aurean barbarians— Excuse me, the crowned monster's soldiers," I spat, glaring at him.

"Ah, right," he said, his tone calm, cool. "Soldiers."

"Weren't you?" I said, my grip tightening on the dagger's sheath. "A royal soldier for the Golden King?"

He looked away and mumbled, "Soldier...maybe that's what I've become."

My frown deepened. *All right, he's obviously not a soldier.*

Before any more could be said, the soft crunch of pebbles interrupted our exchange. Mona and Hampo approached us, accompanied by a half-dozen Azzi warriors who would be joining us on tonight's mission.

All thoughts of Rei's identity vanished. My heart rammed against my chest with resounding thumps. It was time.

Chapter 25

Not all fangs gleam in the night,
Some monsters like to hide in plain sight.
~ Aurean Children's Rhyme

Night fell like a suffocating cloak.

Beneath the looming elms, gnarled branches reached out like skeletal claws as our weary procession weaved through the dense undergrowth.

Hampo and three others scouted ahead to secure our path. The thick canopy obscured the moon and stars, plunging us into near-darkness as we ascended the mountainous path. We didn't dare light any of our glowrocks lest we be discovered. The uneven ground crunched beneath our boots, their rhythmic *chuf-chuffing* harmonizing with the nocturnal chorus of insects. An owl's hoot pierced the night, making me jump.

I'd opted to wear form-fitting pants and loose shirt, typically worn by Mosatti boys. My waist-length cloak, and the shield strapped to my back, made it easier to travel this way. Easier to run.

Mona moved with grace beside me, Tatu perched on her shoulder. Her split travel skirts allowed her to stride freely, the knee-length fur cloak swaying with each step. Leaning in, she whispered, "I must know…is it true? Do dze men of Mosatti leap over fires to woo their women? Did your betrothed perform such a daring feat for you?

Is that the reason for this grand rescue?"

Rei grunted from behind, muttering something about archaic traditions.

"That is a tradition," I said. "But Zakaya never did that. And not because it's an *archaic* tradition." I glanced back at Rei over my shoulder. Though the dark hid his features, I could almost imagine the curve of his lips in that almost-smile.

I did not tell them that Zakaya had jumped over fires for other girls before me, and that it had been a foolish fantasy of mine for him to do the same for me. I'd seen countless boys do the fire jump for the girls they adored. But Zakaya and I had been friends long before we'd fallen in love. To him, it had probably seemed pointless to repeat a romantic gesture he'd already performed multiple times for others. I pushed away such thoughts. None of that mattered now.

We all grew silent after that, trekking along the uncharted paths above the valley where the Enlightener's army had set up camp. Tatu flew ahead, periodically returning to Mona to update her on our direction.

As we neared the enemy camp, the gibbous moon hung above us, its ethereal glow seeping through the gnarled elm branches. A faint scent of smoke teased my nostrils.

Emerging from the shadows, Hampo and his men joined us, their movements so soundless I hadn't heard them approach. With the grace of seasoned hunters, they swung from braided vines and descended from the surrounding tree branches, their agile landings mimicking the gentle rustling of leaves in the wind.

At Hampo's silent signal, our group stopped at a precipice concealed by juniper and hawthorn bushes. A sprawling encampment stretched across the valley below. Weathered tents, yellowed by time and grime, dotted the expanse. Soldiers gathered around scattered firepits, while additional guards walked about the camp, their movements stilted and awkward, as if unaccustomed to moving.

"Devs," I whispered.

Rei nodded, his gaze scanning the camp. "At least a few hundred," he said, then turned to Hampo, murmuring in Azzian. Hampo's eyes darkened.

"What is it?" I asked.

"Dev creatures…some from Azzi," Hampo said in broken Sophenian, his shoulders slumped.

My chest tightened. I could only imagine how he must be feeling seeing friends, neighbors, maybe family, altered drastically into those *things*.

Goddess, a few hundred! More than double the warriors we'd left behind to protect the village.

Mona hissed, "Some have completed the transformation, and some are in the midst of the process."

Dread constricted my lungs. "How can you tell the difference?"

Her gaze sharpened, scanning the scattered figures below. She pointed toward a group wandering aimlessly, their movements disjointed. "Those there. Their spirits still struggle against the Enlightener's hold. But see those?" She pointed to the cluster at the far side of the camp.

A shudder coursed through me as my gaze landed on the group of a few dozen figures. They moved with an eerie grace, fluid and deadly, as they brandished their double-edged daggers that glinted in the dim firelight.

Their unnatural speed and uncanny prowess revealed the chilling truth. These men and women, once free-willed, now danced as marionettes, their every action dictated by the Enlightener…and by extension, the Archdemon of Despair and Chaos.

Soon, once the new devs succumbed, their bodies would become equally lethal. A sudden harrowing thought pierced my mind. I shivered, envisioning Zakaya, my once-beloved betrothed, moving with lethal grace, wielding a double-edged dagger against *me*.

A surge of terror gripped me anew. How could we possibly confront hundreds—or more—of these abominations, who were possibly more dangerous than the king's formidable golden army?

Except, these were once-good souls twisted into hollow creatures of darkness.

"We have to save them," I whispered.

Rei's gaze shifted to me, his eyes veiled in shadow. "You can't save them all, Light Weaver," he murmured, his words laden with an unspoken burden.

There was a deeper meaning woven into his words, an undercurrent of personal experience.

"We have to try," I said, gritting my teeth.

Rei's gaze lingered on me, his expression guarded.

Before he could reply, a tortured scream rent the air, slicing through the camp's confines.

"Zakaya," I gasped, my voice catching in my throat. My entire body trembled with the need to move, to do *something*. I leaned forward, my feet teetering at the edge of the precipice. Loose soil cascaded into the undergrowth below, mimicking the gentle patter of rain.

Rei's hand whipped out and grasped my arm, tugging me back.

"We wait...that could have been anyone," Rei whispered, his voice gentle.

Be equipped. Be observant. Be quick. Baba's voice reverberated through my skull, reminding me that I'd been trained by the finest thief in the Highlands. Rei's unwavering gaze remained fixed on me. Swallowing the lumps in my throat, I nodded.

The ceaseless screams continued.

That's Zakaya. I'm sure of it. I knew that voice, had heard it for years. During play when we were younger, calling to his friends, to me, over distances at the market, at the academy. His voice was imprinted in my ears. My whole body trembled with rage, with sorrow. With *guilt*.

Our cliffside vigil stretched in tense silence, only the faint scraping of Rei meticulously sharpening his blade disrupting the stillness. Tatu's silent form darted over the enemy tents before veering off. Seconds later, the dove alighted on Mona's shoulder.

"Your beau is in the third tent from the left," Mona murmured, mouth twisting on the final words. "The large one."

My breath seized in my chest as I followed her gaze. The imposing tent stood out not just by its size, but by the fresh sheepskins adorning it, materials favored by the Golden King's elite. The screams had stopped, replaced by a haunting silence. Visions of Zakaya suffering unspeakable torments within those flapping walls gripped me.

"We'll save him," Rei murmured, his tone hardening with determination.

I swallowed hard, giving a firm nod. We *had* to save the Regent's son. I didn't want to think about the ramifications if he died, or worse, became a dev. My own horror and guilt aside, it would be catastrophic. The Regent would go straight to the other satrapies for help. The Enlightener would take advantage of the storm. But my tumultuous thoughts kept circling back to a more visceral fear. *Am I too late to save the man I once loved?*

"The guards will eventually sleep," Rei went on, gaze still locked on the camp's perimeter. Something haunted his voice when he added, "Even those…creatures."

My hand strayed toward the Gate-Ring, pulse fluttering with nerves. "I can transport us straight into that tent. But I'm not sure how many the Ring can handle at once."

Mona snorted. "Dzat is a relic of the gods. She can move an entire army."

She. Mona's use of the pronoun reminded me that this Ring wasn't merely a tool. It was a living embodiment of the divine, my personal connection to Ayg's power. The weight of that truth, the immense responsibility it carried, made my shoulders droop.

Movement in the camp's center caught my attention as a tall figure emerged from Zakaya's prison tent. His bald head glowed in the firepits' flickering flames.

The Enlightener.

He unfurled a massive tapestry, then withdrew an object that leaked oily tendrils of darkness across the cloth. A noxious stench, a blend of sulfur and charred trash, permeated the air. The Enlightener shouted a command. A nearby dev came forward, her movements disjointed. She appeared so young, maybe younger than me. Poor girl. Had she been taken from Tarin, or maybe from Azzi?

The Enlightener raised the relic, unleashing a

dissonant chant that assaulted my ears, making me grind my teeth. Smoke lifted from the tapestry in sickening coils and wormed its way down the throat of the young girl standing obediently before him. Her head snapped backward at an unnatural angle, jaw gaping skyward, as she inhaled the noxious fumes. For endless heartbeats she remained frozen in that grotesque, straining pose, tendons stretched taut as if her very neck would snap.

Then it happened. A meaty crunch reverberated through the air as her body crumpled. She convulsed and writhed, limbs contorting until her movements stilled with unnerving abruptness.

My fingers strayed toward the Weaver's Spool, the urge to race down and intercede almost overpowering. But then a soft luminescence began leaking from the girl's slackened form, coalescing into ethereal tendrils that seeped into the Enlightener's tapestry.

At the Enlightener's barked command, the dev-girl rose rigidly to her feet, movements disturbingly unnatural as she joined a group of others. My mother used to guide souls of the dead into tapestries if their spirit needed healing before moving on. But the Enlightener's spells twisted this sacred purpose into something darker, evil. I suddenly understood what he was doing.

"He's trapped her soul," I murmured, more to myself than anyone else. "That's how he controls them."

Rei angled his head toward me.

I gestured to the horrific scene below. "When a dev bites someone, it turns the victim into another mindless slave with only one purpose. To spread the affliction to others. But the Enlightener can manipulate them by trapping their souls into that kork."

"May the gods and goddesses protect us," Mona muttered.

"That's what I'm counting on," I said with more conviction than I felt.

Inky thunderheads had gathered overhead, swallowing the moon's feeble light as the Enlightener's perverse rite dragged on. Dev-thralls unloaded lifeless bodies from wagons stationed at the camp's edges. One by one, the Enlightener reanimated each soulless corpse, adding them to his grotesque puppet-legion.

I shuddered, hugging myself tightly as Hampo murmured from behind us, "We go now...when he distracted."

Terror turned my legs to oak as I forced myself upright, fumbling with the shield across my back. Every snapped twig, every rustled leaf had my nerves tautly wound like a lyre's strings.

Rei's steady hand found my shoulder in the dark. "Ready?" His rugged profile was merely a silhouette against the night, but I longed for a glimpse of those storm-tossed eyes.

Clearing my tightened throat, I gave a small nod. "Ready."

We formed a tight circle with Mona and the six Azzi warriors. My outstretched hand signaled the others to link, creating a towering stack of joined hands—Rei's calloused palm resting over mine, then Mona's, down to the final warrior. Unexpectedly, Rei's fingers wrapped around my hand, giving me a reassuring squeeze. Our eyes met in the dark, his reflecting the Ring's pale radiance and holding...something more.

Hampo cleared his throat pointedly, nodding to me to proceed.

I envisioned the Enlightener's imposing tent with Zakaya inside, his once-kingly attire tattered, skin glistening with feverish sweat. That haunting image had tormented my waking thoughts for weeks.

The world blurred into a vortex, howling winds lashing our faces. We streaked through the foliage in a disorienting rush, bypassing slumbering devs and prowling sentries. The massive tent rapidly ballooned toward us. With a final lurching heave, we tumbled through the open flaps into the dim, cavernous interior.

Rei and the Azzis leapt into action, steel flashing as they deftly disarmed and subdued the three dev guards with herb-soaked kerchiefs. In the corner, a figure lay curled and motionless save for his ragged breaths. His once-regal Nurazard finery hung in muddied rags, deep gashes scoring his arm and shoulder. The amulet of Vahagn the Dragon Reaper, which I'd given him, hung loose from his neck, as if in mockery to the gods for his current state.

I fell to my knees beside him, bile burning my throat as his eyes snapped open, his once-rich brown irises now sickeningly veiled in milky film.

"Zakaya..." I choked out, voice cracking like shattered glass.

A guttural sound rumbled from deep within his throat. I jerked back, swinging the shield from my back as a barrier between us.

Mona laid a steadying hand on my arm. "Careful, Satya."

Rei turned to us, his knuckles pale from the death grip around the hilt of his bloodied dagger. His rasping breaths matched the rise and fall of his chest. Behind him, the bodies of fallen devs littered the floor, surrounded by Azzi warriors.

"Not dead," Rei rasped at my stricken look. "Just…temporarily indisposed."

I managed a numb nod as complicated emotions welled up. Gratitude that he'd truly heard my wish to save these people. Yet my battered heart coiled with grief and guilt over the man I had once loved.

"He's…" I gestured helplessly at Zakaya's unnatural state, unable to give voice to the obvious.

Hampo's indrawn breath hissed through clenched teeth at the pitiable sight, but Rei's jaw only tightened, his stoic expression betraying no surprise. A hollow numbness filled me. I'd expected this, had steeled myself for it. And yet a tiny glimmer of hope had lingered that maybe Zakaya had been spared. The Enlightener clearly had a special purpose for Zakaya, the same way he was manipulating the Monster King.

Mona's voice cut through my turmoil. "You can still heal him, Satya. But we need to leave *now*."

My heart twisted anew. *Am I already too late?*

As Rei and Hampo bent down to lift Zakaya between them, the tent flaps flew open.

Two devs stormed inside in a blurred frenzy. Blades clashed as the Azzi met the attack. A tall figure loomed at the entrance.

The Enlightener's bald pate glowed bloody in the sputtering glowrocks' luminescence.

My hands froze in midair, a handspan away from the dagger at my belt.

"You…" His terrifying gaze locked onto mine. "You are the Light Weaver."

Rei immediately stepped between us. "Remember me?" His voice scraped like rusted blades.

I stole a glimpse around Rei's legs.

The Enlightener's face, wide-eyed, filled with stark recognition. "You're alive," he breathed.

"Surprise," Rei growled.

I caught Mona's eye and gestured for her to draw nearer. She nodded, her hand tightening on my shoulder, her other hand on Zakaya's trembling arm. With the two new devs temporarily subdued, Hampo and the other Azzis swiftly caught on and shuffled closer, forging an interconnected chain linked by subtle touches of hands, elbows, shoulders.

But Rei had taken several steps too far, advancing on the Enlightener, dagger raised.

The Enlightener's gaze met mine. "What are you doing…?"

Tightening my grip on the shield, I pressed it into Zakaya's trembling chest and channeled all my energy into envisioning the Azzi healing cavern. A surge of energy whipped through the tent, warping its boundaries. I thrust out my free hand toward Rei as our physical forms dispersed into ethereal shadows. But I couldn't tell if I'd connected to him in time.

We slipped through the camp like smoke in the wind. Firepits and prowling devs smeared past in a blur as we arrowed up the treacherous mountain paths at blinding speed. The inky shroud of night bled into the steel grays of a storm-swollen dawn. The unmistakable growl of Zakaya's dev-voice rent the air like claws dragged across bone, merging with the fading echoes of the living dead.

Chapter 26

Though unseen scars may mar the soul,
The spirit's strength can make them whole.
                              ~ Sophenian Folksong

We crashed in a tangled heap outside the healers' cavern entrance. Around me, the others scrambled to their feet in the driving rain.

My knees thudded to the ground beside Zakaya's convulsing form. I held the shield between us— somehow I'd kept my grip on it through our journey— and aligned the Gate-Ring with its center hole to initiate the ritual.

"Mona! Raman!" My voice ricocheted into the cavern, drowned by a thunderclap.

Mona rose, her eyes darting around in panic as rivulets of water streamed down her face. She gripped Hampo's arm. "Where's Rei? Where are the others?"

A horrible thickness settled over my chest. *Oh, no...*

Mona shouted urgent orders to the cluster of Azzis, and they immediately sprinted back toward the bridge, with Mona and Tatu in tow.

"Mona, wait," I called out, but they were already too far away. Why didn't they wait for me to use the Ring?

I glanced up at the thicket, hands trembling as a surge of dread flooded me. I'd tried to snag onto Rei's tunic during the translocation and thought my fingers had at least brushed the fabric. But if I'd missed, if they were still trapped inside that cursed camp…

Zakaya's guttural growl shattered that terrifying thought, his mucus-veiled eyes pinning me with an intense, unwavering focus. I released a shuddering breath. I couldn't abandon him, not like this.

"I'm here, I'm here," Raman's voice cut through the chaos around us as he appeared at my side.

I drew out the Weaver's Spool from my pouch, but in my haste it slipped from my rain-slickened grip and splashed into the mud. I snatched it back up, smearing its surface with grime as my fingers trembled violently.

Raman's steady hand rested over my wrist. "Satya, you will help him. But first, take a deep, calming breath."

I managed a jerky nod and inhaled deeply through my nose, the familiar scents of rain and forest filling my lungs. As I exhaled, I felt my trembling jaw still, the rigid tension seep from my shoulders. *I can do this…I must.*

Yepo emerged from the healers' quarters carrying a poultice, her hood pulled low against the ferocious downpour that rendered her ash-gray cloak a saturated black. Her eyes widened in dismay at Zakaya's shivering form. She kneeled at his other side and gently applied the poultice to his feverish brow with a gloved hand before giving me a solemn nod to begin.

Swallowing hard, I tuned out the surrounding cacophony of warriors' shouts and stomping boots as they prepared for battle. I forced thoughts of Rei's uncertain fate from my mind, directing all my focus on Zakaya. My knees sank into the moist soil, mud seeping through the thick fabric of my pants, but I barely registered the discomfort.

Rain and sweat mingled on Zakaya's ashen skin.

Gasping growls escaped his lips, flecks of foam gathering at the corners of his mouth. He shivered uncontrollably while Yepo maintained the poultice firmly against his brow, her other hand gripping his shoulder to still his violent tremors.

He's been newly bitten, I realized with a sickening lurch.

I couldn't begin to imagine—didn't *want* to imagine—the horrors Zakaya had witnessed these past endless weeks. Surrounded by the horde of the dead as he awaited this horrible fate. And the Enlightener had waited, made him watch. *Goddess*.

Icy dread gripped me. What if I failed? What if the darkness consumed Zakaya, forcing me to cast him into the abyss of Dragon's Maw, lost forever?

And it would be my fault.

I gripped the mud-slicked Spool in a white-knuckled grasp and sent a silent plea to Ayg.

A warm surge of energy spiraled from my heart into the crescent moons on my wrist, as if the goddess heard my entreaty. The power continued to curl through the Gate-Ring and into my fingers, surging outward until it enveloped our small group in a radiant pool of light.

"Luminous and Eclipse unite," Raman began. "In balance, harmonize the light…"

My incantation intertwined with Raman's shielding chant, our words harmonizing with the glowing threads extending from the Ring and Spool. The luminous strands connected, transforming the Spool into an incandescent orb as bright as a full moon.

An ethereal tapestry materialized in the rain-spattered air before us. Scenes of Zakaya celebrating Nurazard with his family, surrounded by the adoring, joyful faces of the Mosatti's townsfolk. A diverse gathering of his friends, from nobles to farmhands. Undoubtedly, he loved his family and his friends. And he clearly cared deeply for his people. But, amidst this mural of meaningful memories, one significant element was noticeably absent.

Me.

Even as a veil of sadness draped over me, I wasn't surprised. Our bitter parting had undoubtedly severed whatever affection Zakaya once held for me. He had claimed he loved me, but his love had been conditioned upon me fitting into his world.

Did I ever fit into his world?

My chest tightened at this realization. *This isn't about me. I'm not trying to make Zakaya love me. I want to save his life.*

"Focus on these happy memories," I murmured.

Zakaya stilled, pupils darting feverishly beneath his now-closed lids. I couldn't tell if he sensed me or even grasped his reality anymore. But I continued to hum, hoping, praying that he wasn't yet lost to the dev-curse.

Shadow-tendrils slithered through the visions, tainting and warping Zakaya's memories. Oily blots of darkness riddled the swirling images, carving voids like ruined patches in a tapestry. They twisted into razor-sharp shadow-daggers that lashed out, tearing at my sleeves and shredding through the cloth, drawing blood. I gritted my teeth through the pain and continuously repeated the spell.

Raman's rhythmic chant harmonized with the intensifying downpour, encircling us in a protective shield. A brilliant bubble of energy radiated from the relics, pushing back the darkness. But it wasn't enough.

One ropy shadow-tentacle latched onto a luminous thread, dragging me toward its void.

My inner dev-worm burst alive, a thrashing serpent with fangs of steel. Searing lacerations pierced my arms, black smoke wisped from my skin. Rain lashed my face as the incantation tore from my lips in panicked screams, the melody forgotten.

Then he appeared.

In my darkening periphery, the massive shadow-beast roared at the end of the lightless tunnel. He thrashed against invisible bindings, and raged and raged and raged.

"Begone," I screamed, my voice hoarse. "Transmute…transform…"

A guttural whisper slithered through my mind. *"You may deceive others with your half-learned spells, but you can never deceive yourself…"*

An inhuman bellow erupted from Zakaya's throat, echoing my own defiant scream.

Raman slumped heavily against me, chanting faintly as his energy waned. Ayg's power flowed through the relics as I screamed the healing words again and again, until vibrant hues of crimson, viridian, and azure swirled into the incandescent sphere, chasing the shadows.

Rain pelted the luminous barrier in sheets, transforming each drop into a glimmering star in the maelstrom. The shadow-blobs convulsed under the spell's onslaught…until at last, one by one, each dissolved into the thirsty earth with anguished hisses. My inner dev-worm's cruel laughter echoed, then faded with the last fizzing shadow.

Goddess…how many more devs could I heal before the darkness dragged me under?

Zakaya gasped as if tasting air for the first time in an eternity, his chest rising and falling with obvious effort. The foam rimming his lips thinned to clear spittle and dribbled down his quivering chin.

Thunder boomed overhead, snapping me from my daze. Drenched hair clung to my skull, my cloak soaked through. My arms were a mess of stinging cuts and scrapes.

Spent tears traced tracks through the rain and grime on my cheeks. But my gaze remained fixed on Zakaya's dirt-stained, torn shirt clinging to his skin, watching the rise and fall of his chest. "Wake up, wake up," I murmured.

Raman squeezed my hand in comfort.

With agonizing slowness, Zakaya's eyelids fluttered open, his dark pupils struggling to focus. Fresh tears warmed my eyes.

Zakaya stared at me in confusion, blinking rapidly against the downpour.

"Za-Zakaya…" I choked on his name.

"Satya?" he rasped.

I had done this to him. My actions had nearly cost him his soul. He should be home in Mosatti with his family, not clinging to life because of me. A sob caught in my throat.

Zakaya tried to rise, but his shoulder buckled and he fell back with a cry.

"Don't rush to sit up," I urged. "Wait until you're ready."

The nicks on my skin had bled into my clothes, darkening the brown fabric, but I barely registered the stinging pain. I longed to collapse into the muddy puddles and surrender to the sleep tugging at me.

Tereza, Pari's mother, appeared beside me, her gentle hand on my arm. "We prepare cot for him. Go rest."

Zakaya looked at me wearily, lips pressed together. Yepo, who had quietly left a moment ago, returned with steaming concoctions and handed one to me and another to Zakaya.

"Zakaya..." I whispered.

Ignoring me, he slowly sat up, body trembling. With unsteady hands, he brought the cup to his mouth and downed the entire concoction in three gulps, some spilling onto his soaked shirt. Wiping his mouth, he fixed me with an icy glare. "I have nothing to say to you," he croaked, his voice harsh, unforgiving.

I swallowed, my throat constricting. A heavy weight settled in my chest. *I saved your life!* I wanted to scream, eyes brimming.

I could almost hear his accusing voice counter, *It's all your fault in the first place.*

With trembling hands I slipped the Spool back into my pouch and rose on shaky legs, gripping the cup tightly. Zakaya struggled to his feet. Though every part of me wanted to help him, the look in his eyes made it clear that he wouldn't welcome it. Tereza and Yepo ushered him into the healers' cavern, supporting him under his arms until he collapsed onto a cot in the outer room. Immediately, he turned his back to us all.

Lightning flashed across the ravine as a low rumble of thunder rolled through. I hesitated at the entrance, my knees buckling with fatigue, and debated whether to sit vigil at his side or give him the space he clearly needed.

"Give him time," Raman murmured, his voice barely audible above the pounding rain.

Heart heavy, I downed the brew and left without a word. I had known Zakaya's feelings for me had plunged into a very dark place, that he'd reject me. But Goddess, the way he'd looked at me…as if I was his most hated enemy…

But a more pressing problem gnawed at me as I returned to the temple. I scanned the treeline above, desperate for any sign of Mona, Rei, or the others. I refused to accept the worst. Using the Ring in my drained state, with no clue where they could be? Not a good idea.

My gut twisted. That guttural voice and cruel laughter still echoed in my mind from the ritual. I couldn't get the massive, roaring giant out of my head.

Could it be Ahriman, the Archdemon of Despair and Chaos himself building a tunnel into the mortal realm?

Through me?

Chapter 27

Streams once joined in what used to be,
Sometimes part ways, eternally free.
                    ~ Ar-Haya Highlands Proverb

I awoke to midday sunlight spilling through the temple's open doorway, my mud-caked clothes clinging uncomfortably. Strange dreams had plagued my brief slumber. The goddess's cryptic words echoed hauntingly, *"Heed the night's truth to tell the story of dawn."*

What did that even mean? Sitting up, I shook my head to clear the voices—the goddess, the raging giant, the dark whispers.

After I'd healed Zakaya in the early hours of dawn, I collapsed from sheer exhaustion. Right before I fell asleep, Mona had returned with the grim news that Rei and some Azzis had been left behind at the Enlightener's camp. That worry alone had given me nightmares. Visions of Rei transformed into a creature of such nightmares, or Rei tortured, Rei dead.

My chest squeezed. I couldn't believe I'd fallen asleep.

"I think I hear something." Mona's voice pulled me from my groggy daze. She stood at the temple's entrance, her gaze fixed outside.

I tossed off the covers and joined her at the door on

wobbly legs, hastily pulling on my boots. The morning rain had finally abated, leaving behind a crisp, earthy scent. Mona's silent vigil broke my heart. Rei was her charge, and from what I could tell during the past few weeks, he was like a son to her. She'd be devastated if something happened to him.

I should have gone with them. Guilt and fear twisted my gut into a tight knot. I should have ensured Rei and the others were linked before activating the Ring.

I could almost hear Baba's voice echoing in my ears. *Should've. Could've. Would've. What can you do now, Satya jan?*

Mona's back straightened as sounds of shuffling and distant commotion reached us. She grasped my arm just as a small group of figures burst through the thicket. Rei, flanked by three Azzi warriors, supported three others between them.

"Thank the Goddess!" Mona gasped.

The tightness in my chest loosened a little at the sight of Rei, seemingly unharmed, though I couldn't say the same for a few of the others. I snatched my shield and waist pouch, hurrying with Mona to meet them by the healing cavern.

"What happened?" I called out to Rei as we neared, my breaths still catching up to my racing heart.

"We had some complications," Rei said briskly. He and the others carefully lowered the growling warriors at the river's edge near the healing cavern.

Complications! This was more than a complication. They'd had to fight off the devs because of my carelessness. It was a wonder they all made it out of there alive, and a miracle that some of them were still unbitten.

"Mona, I need the shielding spell," I called out,

trying to keep the panic from my voice.

"Right here," Mona said, her voice clipped with stress as she knelt beside me. "No need to yell."

While Rei and the others held down the devs' writhing bodies, I performed the now-familiar ritual where they'd collapsed. Brilliant godforce spiraled through me and the relics before arcing out, bathing each dev in cleansing light. After the first dev's spirit returned and his body healed, I was struck by how the goddess used me not only as a conduit for her powers but as a filter to heal the afflicteds' mortal bodies.

But when I moved on to the second dev, the shadows emerging from him thickened into viscous tendrils that prodded and pierced through Mona's shield, stinging my skin like a swarm of hornets.

A seductive whisper caressed my mind. *"Give in…let me take the pain…"*

"Yessss…" my inner dev hissed. I wanted, *needed*, to surrender to that velvety darkness.

"No," I screamed, fighting against the hungering part that dwelled within me.

When I didn't succumb, the voice grew guttural, its words oozing like toxic sludge. *"Deceive them all you want, little Light Weaver. You're a mere puppet sipping at powers beyond you. Your feeble attempts will never break your chains to the Archdemon of Despair and Chaos."*

I gritted my teeth, jaw clenched until it ached. The third man's shadows coiled thickest of all, inkier than a cavern's depths. They hissed and sputtered, lashing out with needled tendrils to pierce my arms. A bolt of pain speared up my right arm as one mercilessly stabbed the back of my hand, warm blood pooling. I hissed, infusing more godforce into the shadows until they fizzed and burst into the soil in an acrid plume.

The dev-worm within me thrashed, straining against my weakened control to burst free. Its voice balled up in the back of my throat and rose into a snarl from my mouth. My eyes watered, burned.

Suddenly, I was watching through *its* eyes—the Satya-dev that dwelled within. I hovered in that void-like tunnel with slithering shadows for walls. At the far end, bathed in ashen light, a towering, indistinct giant roared. His thunderous, deafening bellow shook the tunnel. I stood frozen in place, unable to cover my ears, to move.

"*Look*," the same raspy voice hissed into my ear, its rank breath ghosting along my neck. "*Watch and see...*"

"*Who is the roaring giant?*" I asked.

The voice responded to my thoughts. "*Do you feel him reaching for you? Do you crave such power? It can be yoursss...*"

Every instinct screamed for me to run, but in this realm I was not in control of my movements, *it* was.

In the distance, as if from a great chasm, a voice called my name. "*Satya!*"

The darkness closed in. The roaring, thrashing giant seemed to move closer.

Air. I need air. I can't breathe. I can't...

****

I gasped awake, slumped against Mona. The third man I'd struggled to heal blinked slowly awake. I stared at his dark eyes, free of the mucus-yellow. No fangs. No snarls escaping his throat. But...I'd been in a shadow-realm seeing through my inner-dev's vision...how was this man healed?

"Satya, you fainted..." Mona threw a hand up in

exasperation.

I'd obviously not been out for too long or Mona and the others wouldn't be so calm.

"How long was I out?" I pulled away from Mona, sitting up straighter. Every muscle screamed in protest.

"A few brief moments, but…he almost didn't make it." Mona nodded toward the third man now rising to his feet, rubbing his head.

A few brief moments? It had felt like an eternity trapped in that suffocating void-tunnel. My legs trembled under the shield's weight as I stayed hunched over, drawing in lungfuls of mineral-tinged river spray. Sweat poured down my back, clothes clinging clammy and chilled against my skin as I shivered. I felt as if I'd run for leagues.

The once-transforming devs had risen, eyes clear of the sickly yellow, the mucus sloughed away. My bloodied fingers trembled, one hand bone-white around the shield's inner handle, the other clutching the Spool in a death grip.

For those few moments, I'd seen through my inner-dev's gaze. She'd shown me her direct link to Ahriman…at the void-tunnel's end. And that raspy voice that had spoken to me still brought chills to my spine.

I blinked, trying to clear my head. Had my mother felt this way? Exhausted and weakened by the powers coursing through her, desperate to save everyone, yet cursing the limitations of her conduit abilities? Had she also battled the same darkness and voices that now haunted me? I blinked. She couldn't have because she hadn't been bitten. I was.

But despite the exhaustion that tugged at the edges of my consciousness, and the looming shadows' persistent threat, the godforce had still reached the devs through me…had healed them wholly.

Gradually, I became aware of the silence, broken only by the gushing river. Rei stood a few paces away amidst the Azzis, concern etching his face as his eyes drifted over my bloodstained arms and hands. I tucked the Spool into my belt pouch and adjusted the shield across my back, absently trying to wipe the crimson stains from my tunic and cloak. Then I froze. Zakaya, now clad in the loose black pants and pale linen tunic of the Azzis, leaned against the stone archway of the healers' cavern beside Raman, gaping at me.

My knees threatened to buckle as I rose. Rei stepped forward, but Zakaya was already at my side, hand on my elbow. His eyes raked over my muddied boys' attire, then back to my face.

"That's how you healed me?" he asked, his tone incredulous.

I nodded, digging my heels into the squelchy soil to keep steady.

"You're…you're a Light Weaver?" Zakaya's hand slipped from my arm as he took a step back.

"Yes."

"But…how could that be?"

"She's a chosen goddess-vessel," Raman said from behind us and stepped to my side.

"Everyone said you were dead." Zakaya's voice erupted in shock, his eyes locked onto Raman. "That Satya…that she'd killed you and…"

"*What*?" My voice came out in a shocked shrill. They thought I'd murdered my former schoolmaster?

Zakaya's gaze remained on Raman, his eyes wide with disbelief. "But you're alive."

Raman made a choking sound, his beard wobbling with a chuckle. "Quite."

Zakaya ran his hand over his matted hair. "I don't understand."

"Zakaya," I said, "there is so much I need to tell you."

He pressed his lips together, his gaze returning to me. And waited.

So I told him.

Everything.

****

The entire time I spoke, Zakaya's unwavering gaze remained locked on me. I started with the thieving at the palace…the Spool, relics, demon-mice, and the Monster-King. I told him about Raman's and my escape from Mosatti, the devastation at Tarin, getting bitten, and all that I'd experienced in Dragon's Maw. And finally, our spy-and-rescue mission at the Enlightener's camp.

Rei leaned at the entrance, absently scraping his dagger hilt while I spoke. His gaze frequently darted to the tree lines above, his jaw locked tight as if wrestling some inner conflict.

When I finished, Zakaya huffed out a long breath. "I need to return. Warn my father."

Raman nodded. "Yes."

Zakaya leaned forward, eyes hardening. "Both of you could be viewed as traitors, regardless. You stole from the King." He pointed an accusing finger at me, then turned to Raman. "And you helped her escape."

My inner-dev hissed with a guttural voice that sounded disturbingly like my own. *"How many times will you accept being second to his responsibilities before you've had enough?"*

My cheeks heated, fists clenched. "And you brought those murdering guards to my door," I snapped.

Rei cleared his throat. When I shot him a look, he quickly averted his eyes back to his dagger. Right. I was referring to the Golden King's guards. Probably his *friends*.

"I had no choice," Zakaya said.

"There's always a choice," Satya-dev snarled.

I gritted my teeth. "I am—*was*—your betrothed. *Of course* you had a choice. You could have *listened*. I would have told you what I'd witnessed at the palace."

Zakaya sighed, his next words shocking me into silence. "I'm sorry." When he looked at me again, the anger had left his eyes. "I had to, Satya. You must know how it would have seemed if I, the Regent's son, helped you escape?"

"You mean the Regent who turned a blind eye to Aurean tyranny?" I said tightly. "Who allowed the Golden King to erase our history, claim our crafts, ban our worship? Who failed to warn his own people before the massacre? The only Sophenian Regent who could have made a difference and chose not to…" I fisted my hands. *"That* Regent?"

Rei's hand paused on his dagger. For a long moment no one spoke as I stood there fuming. Satya-dev's snarl reverberated in my ears.

Finally, Zakaya's soft voice filled the silence. "Yes, that Regent."

Mona released an annoyed huff. Raman pressed his lips together, studying Zakaya with an unreadable gaze.

Zakaya paused, seeming to gather his thoughts, then said, "There is much my father kept from my family, from me…but that's no excuse, I know. I promise, he doesn't know about the current dev infestation. The Enlightener, he…" His voice broke and he cleared his throat. "He plans to spread his undead swarm through the larger towns one at a time, including Mosatti. Do you think that had my father known this plan, he'd have done nothing?" He shook his head. "My father's actions may seem cowardly, but he's done his best to protect his people."

"To protect his people, or protect himself?" Satyadev hissed in my ear.

I glanced away, my hands clutching my belt pouch so tight I could feel every tool within it. His words reminded me of the horrors he must have witnessed at the Enlightener's camp, and how much bigger our current problem was than his betrayal—than both our betrayals.

For a long moment, neither one of us could hold the other's gaze.

"There's much work to be done," Mona's voice cut through the silence, reminding us all that we had a village to defend.

"A moment," Zakaya said, frowning at me. "I need a moment with Satya. Alone."

****

The once-bustling village had grown eerily silent as Zakaya and I walked farther down the gurgling river, the damp earth squelching beneath our feet. As we stopped at the water's edge, an invisible chasm seemed to separate us. So much remained unsaid between us, but time was not on our side.

I cleared my throat, arms wrapped around my middle. "How do you feel?"

Zakaya shrugged, his hands buried in his pockets.

With a casual kick, he sent a pebble skimming across the water, the splash causing a nearby toad to dart away. "I feel as if…I'll never sleep again."

My heart squeezed with sympathy. Having personally experienced a dev bite, I could imagine his inner turmoil. I'd told Zakaya everything. Except for the dev-worm lurking within me. Did Zakaya also feel such a stirring within himself?

His gaze briefly flickered to me, then he quickly looked away. "Your eyes," his voice trailed off, his lips pressed together.

I frowned, all too aware of my once honey-colored pupils now permanently ringed in gold, brighter at dawn—according to Mona. With a yellow hue so similar to a dev's sickly gaze I feared what the change might mean. I traced the crescent moons on my wrist, the faint tingling centering me in Ayg's power. "I'm not a dev, Zakaya."

Zakaya shook his head. "I'm just…I'm trying to understand what it means."

I rubbed at the nicks and cuts on my arms and hands, remnants of the rituals. Goddess, they itched until I wanted to scrape my skin off raw. But my eyes? I hadn't even begun to process that unsettling change. "So am I."

His throat visibly bobbed as he swallowed and met my burning eyes. "I need to warn my father, Mosatti…" He trailed off. I could tell he wanted to say more, but he shook his head as if fighting an internal battle. "About whatever is happening here in the Highlands."

"Of course," I said, voice tight. "You're the Regent's son. It's your duty."

He frowned at the gurgling water. "Satya, I—I should have helped you when the guards…" His voice broke and he cleared his throat.

My shoulder had mostly healed, with a scar that would remain with me forever. A lingering ache remained where the chain had whipped me. Yes, he should have helped me. Should have listened to me. But he hadn't. He hadn't because of who he was, because of what he represented…because of what my actions had cost him.

"I understand why you did it…I'm sorry too…" My voice trailed off.

Zakaya angled his head away from me, facing the river. His shoulders drooped and I thought I heard a muffled sniffle.

My eyes stung. We'd caused so much damage, my father and I. Never considering the consequences of our single-minded path. We'd been so selfish. But I couldn't be angry at a father who was no longer among the living. After the massacre, his grief had taken him to a very dark place. I should have helped him, but I'd been grieving too. We had both drifted, disconnected from everyone. And now, although I'd finally found a path to cling to, that disconnect from those I once cared about broadened into a chasm I couldn't bridge.

Zakaya turned and drew closer to me. He pulled his hands out of his pockets, holding out a small object in his palm. The betrothal ring. The one I'd tossed back at him during Nurazard.

My hands trembled, torn between the urge to reach for the ring and the knowledge that accepting it would be a lie. A part of me longed to pretend that we could fix this fissure between us, but Ayg's energy coursing through me made it impossible to deceive myself. Or Zakaya.

This was not all right. What I had done was not all right. What *he* had done was not all right. The pain we had caused each other… None of it was all right.

Zakaya continued to hold out the ring, a subtle tremor in his fingers. "I want you to come with me. Now that I know the truth, I will speak with my father, clear your name. We can't trust a king who's become…*that*." He nodded toward the trees in the general direction of the Enlightener's camp.

I met his red-rimmed eyes, my hands fisted at my sides. "Only moments ago, you called me a traitor…"

"I was angry," he said, his words soft and tinged with regret. "…in shock, actually…"

For a long moment we locked gazes, his filled with regret. What did he see in my gold-ringed eyes? Anger. Betrayal. Regret. Love?

Could I go back to the way things were? Was that what he was proposing? No, I couldn't do it. Even if Zakaya cleared my name, how could I return knowing what I knew now? My skill as a Light Weaver was desperately needed here. I couldn't turn my back on the Azzis. On Mona and Raman. On Rei.

On my family.

"Zakaya, I can't go back with you," I finally said, my heart aching with the weight of my decision.

His fingers closed over the ring and he dropped his hand. "Why not? You don't need to hide anymore. Not after I tell my father what you've faced. What we're all facing…"

"I'm not hiding, not anymore." With the decision to stay, my mind raced with a slowly-forming plan. A crazy, impossible plan. It went beyond leading the Enlightener away. Beyond vanquishing him. I hadn't thought past all that. Until now.

Once we vanquished the Enlightener, I could help Raman and Mona rebuild the Legion. If they'd have me. We'd find other Sacreds, recruit more. Teach them. Together, we could heal the Highlands, keep the darkness at bay, and protect the villages and towns. Like my parents, I'd been unknowingly crawling toward this path all along.

But the lurking darkness within me, the seething dev-worm, that had to be dealt with first.

"Then why stay?" Zakaya's voice rose with confusion, his brow furrowed. "What am I missing?"

"I'm a Light Weaver." The truth of that statement settled over me like a mantle.

"I know!" Zakaya said. "It's the reason I want you to come…" His mouth snapped closed.

And there was the truth of it. The realization stung like a slap. He wanted me to return to Mosatti because of what I could do, not because we were betrothed. *Formerly* betrothed. And the betrothal ring was just a…a what? A consolation?

"I can't," I said, pressing my lips together.

Zakaya pushed the ring back into his pocket with force. "You hope to fight the Enlightener and his army singlehandedly with a spool? Satya, you'll need an army of your own! You're not a soldier. You'll get killed…or worse."

I shrugged, conveying courage I didn't feel. "It's a *magic* spool," I muttered.

He stared at me as if I'd grown an extra dev head to go along with my strange eyes.

"No, I'm not a soldier," I snapped, raising my own voice. "I am a Light Weaver." I was surprised at my firm tone, my confidence. "And it is *my* duty to see this through. Wherever it may lead me."

Zakaya stepped closer and took my fists in his hands, calmly straightening my fingers. His red-rimmed eyes overflowed; two tears slipped down his face. "Satya, we can start again, you and I," he said, his voice hoarse. "We'll overcome this. I don't want to say goodbye. Not like this."

The tapestry of his memories flashed before me. Moments that meant the most to him. I couldn't forget that *I'd* been missing. Maybe he still cared about me, but I couldn't ask him to put me above all else. It wouldn't be fair to the Regent's son. And there, right *there*, was the crux of why we couldn't be together.

It wouldn't matter what I'd become. A Light Weaver. A Sacred. In the eyes of his family and everyone in Mosatti, I would forever be a merchant's daughter. A thief. A fugitive.

"I'm sorry," I whispered, my eyes burning. "There's no overcoming this, Zakaya. There's no starting over. Too much has happened."

His throat bobbed a few times as he swallowed. "We're never going to be all right, are we—you and I?" he said, voice low with hurt.

I felt the pulse in his hands, the warmth of his touch, and his deeply buried regret. Yet I knew the truth. And his red-rimmed eyes confirmed that he did too.

"Our paths have strayed," I said, my voice firm. "You have your own duty, as I do mine. We both need to be at peace with that."

Zakaya sniffled and dropped my hands, turning his gaze to the rushing river. He nodded once, then again more firmly. Without another word he turned his back to me and strode off.

My heart shattered as I watched him walk away, mourning the innocent love we had once shared. But what good was that love if it splintered at the first major hurdle?

****

I stayed by the river for a few moments to gather myself. The late afternoon sun painted flickering gemlike crests on the water's surface. Behind me, the village stood still, warriors watchful at the river's edges, the bridge, the ledges above and hidden in the trees. So deceptively peaceful. Like the calm before a tempest.

I felt a presence behind me and turned to see Hampo standing a few paces away, his open palms cradling a war dagger. The bladesmith had approached with hardly a sound or scuff of his boots. How much of my discussion with Zakaya had he heard? Did it truly matter?

My eyes widened as he raised the weapon. Then he turned it, hilt first, and handed it to me. Clearing his throat, he said in gruff Sophenian, "For you."

I gazed at the dagger, at the Azzian inscription written on its hilt. Raman had told me its meaning: *Honor in life, honor in death.* And I understood the weight of this gesture. This was a profound sign of respect, especially from him. Though I lacked combat skills, I couldn't refuse such a valuable gift. I might need to protect myself. I *would* need to protect myself. That thought alone stilled my breath. "Shnorha," I whispered.

His lips thinned with a hint of a smile. Then he turned and left.

Despite losing Zakaya, my heart expanded beyond my chest. This precious gift, from one of the most esteemed members of their society, proved one thing. The Azzis now considered me one of their own.

Chapter 28

Tiny paws, like a gentle breeze
Listen close to the stirring of the trees.
                          ~ Azzi Children's Rhyme

Zakaya left shortly after we spoke. Without a word of goodbye.

Two Azzi warriors would guide him back to the forests near Mosatti, after which he'd make his way home. I watched as he crossed the bridge, climbed the narrow ledges leading out of the ravine, and disappeared into the dense thicket. He did not look back once. Even as my chest constricted, I knew it was better this way.

Soon after, scouts returned with dire news. The dev army was on the move. And they were slowly advancing in our direction.

All afternoon, the sounds of pounding ricocheted across the ravine as more barricades were built. I helped Pari and her family reinforce the main entrance to the healers' cavern where we would need to gather the injured. Dusk descended quickly. Birdsong twittered to near silence, and even the river's rush muted. The forest loomed over us, casting long shadows over the ravine. Azzi warriors took up strategic positions by the river's edge, guarding the bridge and the ledges above. Watchful. Waiting.

I stood alone at the bridge's narrow entrance,

surveying the eerily still village, when Rei approached and leaned silently against the scuffed wooden railing beside me, his features obscured in shadow.

The words tumbled out before I could stop them. "How does it feel to be on the opposing side of a conflict?"

For a long moment, Rei said nothing, gaze fixed on the forest above. Finally, he murmured, "I am not your enemy here, Satya."

I fidgeted with my belt pouch clasp. What had I called his people during our conversation weeks ago? *Aurean barbarians*. Which implied how I felt about Rei, by extension, though I now realized how rudely unfair that was. Since I'd arrived here, Rei had shown me nothing but respect and kindness. And yet I still couldn't trust him.

Though a part of me wanted to.

"Does it truly matter?" I kept my tone carefully neutral. "We have bigger issues."

"Doesn't it?" he said, his voice clipped.

I glanced at him sharply. He almost sounded…hurt.

"We're on the same side," he continued, posture stiff.

"You never told me who you are," I blurted.

Rei's jaw tightened. "You never asked *me*."

My mouth slackened. He *was* hurt. True, I'd never asked him directly. Instead, I asked Raman, and Rei had clearly overheard. But he must surely understand my valid reasons for not trusting a man from Vosk. Someone who obviously held a significant position in the Aurean royalty or army. The same brutal force who'd slaughtered my family.

I clenched my fists, forcing my mind away from

those memories. "In truth," I admitted, my voice steady despite my inner turmoil, "at the moment, I'd rather not know."

He stiffened. "Fine, then *I* have a question." Glancing at my arms, he lowered his voice. "Are you going to tell the others what happened during your dev healings?"

He'd seen the creeping shadows slicing into my skin. Mona and Raman hadn't mentioned my fainting spell again, so even as my shields, they hadn't sensed how dangerously real the darkness became during the harrowing rituals. But Rei had clearly watched me closely enough to notice what was happening to *me*.

I shook my head. "I'm not planning on sharing those…complications."

Rei's brows furrowed. "Why not?"

"Because they have enough weighing on them already," I said, hugging myself.

Rei pressed his lips together but didn't respond.

Anxious to change the topic, I said, "I'm sorry you were left behind when we escaped the Enlightener's camp. How did you get out? It all happened so fast…"

"You did what you had to, to save your…Zakaya," he said, no judgment in his tone.

"He's not my Zakaya," I snapped, then frowned at my own sharp tone. "But how *did* you escape?"

Rei cleared his throat. "Hampo had slipped me a bottle of the same oils we used on the cloths to incapacitate the devs. When the Enlightener left us in the tent to be dealt with, we covered our noses and I spilled the entire bottle around us. It knocked out the devs long enough for us to flee."

I stole a sidelong glance at his stiff profile. "I'm

sorry you were left behind when I used the Gate-Ring."

Rei's gaze softened. "You got the others to safety. You couldn't have known we hadn't linked in time."

I swallowed hard. "I tried to link with you…but you were too far, and…"

"Satya," he said warmly, "it's all right."

Our eyes locked, and I found myself struggling against…something…in his gaze. That half-smile again, and for a brief second, my treacherous lips responded.

I turned my attention back to the thicket above us, steadying my breath. And as we stood there, side by side, awaiting the army of the dead, it didn't escape me that while I might still hate the *Aurean barbarians*…I no longer hated Rei.

Maybe I never had.

****

Night had fallen when we heard it.

A distant crash resounded through the forest, then another. The traps.

Then the spine-shriveling growing hush of an approaching gale. Demon-mice.

"Here they come," I whispered, heart lurching painfully.

Rei's voice cut through the tension. "From which direction?"

Mona closed her eyes, communing with Tatu. "All around us. Everywhere. We have minutes."

I spun to face her, forcing down my fear. "Ready?"

She gave a determined nod. Gritting my teeth, I focused my intent through the Gate-Ring, reaching to fuse with the ethereal link between Mona and Tatu. In my mind's eye, Tatu's shadow-wings fluttered around a silvery tether. I knotted it with the godforce flowing from the Spool. Gold and silver merged into an incandescent cord, my connection to Mona's bond with her spirit animal.

Riding that connection, I expanded my sight, casting it into the roiling void until I hit a shadow wall. Sweat beaded my brow as I channeled more energy, but the barrier only thickened. My dev-worm writhed as a hoarse growl clawed its way out of my throat before I could contain it.

That thick barrier—It was my own tether to the darkness, to Ahriman. I could almost see my dev-worm straining to break out, its sharp claws scratching at the wall. I yelped, recoiling from the shadow-mass, fighting the visions the Satya-dev was trying to show me.

Mona's and Raman's distant hum echoed as my own spell thumped in my ears like stones. Straining, I channeled more power. Shadows slivered through the Spool, weaving into our linked gossamer braid like wisps of night threading daylight. Oily tendrils probed for a way through the tether. Panic tightened my chest. Was my dev-worm asserting itself after I'd expended so much energy?

Gritting my teeth, I sang the next part of the incantation, "Silver threads, like a winding stream, open this portal into realms unseen."

A strange, silky force rippled the atmosphere as the Spool's portal yawned open, light emanating from the relic. The portal's vastness drew nearer.

Together, the two Sacreds and I chanted, "Through this portal, realms entwine, our purpose clear, our wills aligned."

We fell silent, bracing for the impending onslaught. The trees stirred. The ground shivered.

The hush swelled steadily and erupted into a storm. Demon-mice darted through the woods' veil of darkness, claws tearing the forest floor, hisses growing louder as they neared, tiny yellow-mucus eyes fixed on the Spool's glowing portal.

Mona's grip tightened on my wrist. Raman and I murmured the spell to fuse with the Enlightener's hold on the demon-mice. Our incantation rang out, calling to the forces controlling them, "Merged energies, our spirits sing, through barriers of darkness, the godforce we bring!"

The first horde reached us. Tiny paws climbed my pants, claws pricking my skin. The others cursed and slashed at the tiny creatures with daggers.

Brilliant light burst from the Spool, painting the ravine in dazzling color. The surrounding darkness splintered into a glimmering cascade as the majestic elms trembled beneath the radiant godforce. Another surge of demon-mice emerged from the dense woods, advancing toward the ledges and into the ravine.

Rei cursed as more of the foul creatures swarmed us. The Azzi warriors braced themselves, daggers glinting. Mona gasped, drawing closer to me, but Raman stood his ground, staff raised before him like a weapon.

We can do this. We must do this.

Drawing on my link to Ayg, I channeled another surge of godforce. The army of mice abruptly froze. Those poised to attack, climbing limbs and perched upon the shrubs and trees, collapsed, leaving bloodied scrapes on everyone's limbs.

Just when I thought we'd killed them, the one before me rose on its haunches, beady-black eyes glancing around dazed. It blinked at me with normal mouse-eyes and tiny jaw, then scampered away. The rest scattered in disarray and vanished into the inky woods.

"It worked," I gasped.

"Of course it worked," Mona said with a grin.

Rei gently gripped my shoulders, eyes shadowed. "Are you all right?" His voice was soft, sending an unexpected shiver through me.

I nodded, momentarily distracted by his closeness, by his woodsy scent mingling with iron and mint. "Are you?"

"I'm fine."

I swallowed. There was something oddly familiar about him. I'd sensed it the moment we first met, but I'd been too furious at his existence here to notice. Before I could dwell on it, he withdrew, dropping his hands.

A skittering sound made us all whip around to see a small floppy-eared dog bounding toward us.

"Vagrik! What are you doing here?" The foolish pup must have followed our trail from the healing quarters.

I bent to scoop him up when a guttural growl split the night. Vagrik's body quivered as if struck by a bolt of lightning. Before I could pick him up, he turned tail and sprinted away, disappearing into the bushes by the river's edge.

"No…" I took a step to follow, but Rei's firm voice stopped me.

"Leave him," he said, his eyes focused on the tree lines. "That dog is a survivor. We have far bigger problems."

A sudden stillness descended over the ravine, as if the mountain itself held its breath. Another snarl pierced the silence. My shoulder brushed against Rei's side. His arm pressed against mine, dagger held ready. His free hand found mine, intertwining our fingers in silent support. I squeezed back. A multitude of growls resonated from the darkness. The hairs on the back of my neck rose.

"The devs," Rei whispered. "They're coming."

Chapter 29

In plainest sight, the answer lies,
A secret hid before your eyes.

~ Azzi Children's Game

The night erupted in a cacophony of roars.

In the gibbous moon's soft light, moving shadows emerged from dark corners, their forms barely distinguishable. Azzi warriors leapt to guard the village, spears leveled and daggers drawn. In the trees and on mountain ledges above, archers nocked arrows to bowstrings, ready to loose volleys.

Arrows hissed through the air, pinning some devs where they stalked or scrambled on all fours. Blades clashed with steely ring as devs poured into the ravine. The foul creatures moved with unnatural speed, swords and axes deflecting strikes and delivering vicious slashing blows. Arrows found their marks, but the devs did not fall easily, shrugging off wounds that would have been fatal to mortals. A warrior's anguished scream tore through the night as a dev's jagged blade punched through his chest, the creature's sharp teeth sinking into the Azzi's shoulder simultaneously.

These were the advanced devs. The lethal ones that moved with speed and strength. Piercing screams reverberated around us as more of our warriors fell victim to vicious bites and plunging blades. Mona's urgent motions guided us into an alcove across the bridge. For a few heartbeats, we watched in horrified silence as the brutal battle unfolded.

"I need to help them," Rei ground out through gritted teeth, pulling against Mona's grasp on his arm.

"You will!" Mona said. "But not like this. Don't make me use that chain on you again."

Rei's jaw ticked, but he turned to me, voice low with urgency. "Satya, please use the Ring. Take Mona and Raman to safety."

I gave him a firm nod. Yes, I would take the Sacreds to safety, but that didn't mean I'd abandon Rei and the others here while they put their lives at risk. I could help them.

Before Mona or Raman could object, I slipped the Spool back into my pouch and grasped their arms. I shot Rei one last look before the connection severed.

The world warped and we found ourselves standing within the barricaded healing cavern. Glowrocks bathed the healing quarters in gentle radiance. Gasps of surprise echoed through the chamber as the familiar faces of Yepo, Pari and her parents surrounded us with expressions of relief.

"Satya!" Pari cried, engulfing me in a hug. "You're safe, thank the goddess."

A knot of Azzi warriors waited alongside them, as if they knew this cavern would be their final stand. My eyes burned with the weight of responsibility for all these lives. This would *not* be their last stand.

Tatu flew in through the barricade, alighting on Mona's shoulder. Mona's eyes widened. "Tatu sayzz the devs have breached some home barriers."

Everyone fell silent as the truth sank in. It was only

a matter of time before they broke into the healing cavern.

My heart hammered as I pulled from Pari's embrace. "I'm going back."

"Satya, don't be rash," Raman warned. "We need a plan…"

"There's no time," I insisted. "Those devs are like wild creatures, worse than wild creatures. Rei may be doing something rash right now…"

Mona and Raman both opened their mouths to argue, but I cut them off. "I'm sorry."

I focused on the shadowy alcove where I'd left Rei. In a blink, I stood beside him in the concealed nook, relieved he hadn't yet joined the fray. He gripped a long branch, deftly whittling it into a makeshift spear. He visibly jumped when I appeared.

"Satya," he hissed. "What are you doing back here?"

"Where do you wish to go?" I extended my hand.

Rei's gaze shifted to the multiple dark forms descending into the ravine, their snarls and hisses echoing like sharp-toothed snakes. His jaw clenched as a bone-chilling war cry echoed through the night. More twisted figures emerged from the tree lines with unnaturally swift and jerky movements.

"There's something I must do," Rei said, his voice heavy.

I kept my hand out. "Then let me help."

"You don't understand," he snapped.

"You're right, I *don't*," I snapped back in a harsh whisper. "Take my hand. Just tell me where."

Rei's grip faltered on his dagger as he released a weary sigh. "There are things about me you don't know. I'll explain later. Please, Satya…*go*."

Our alcove abruptly darkened. Three dark silhouettes rose onto the ledge directly above us. Pale moonlight cast a silvery glow on mucus-filled eyes scanning the shadows where we hid.

I froze. Could devs see in the dark? I didn't want to find out. Gripping Rei's arm, I tried to focus my intent on the Ring. But panic scattered my thoughts. Fears for Vagrik and the people hidden in the healing cavern muddled my concentration. As the devs climbed down, I activated the Gate-Ring.

With a jarring lurch, we stood precariously on the edge of a cliff overlooking the roaring river, its churning waters partially obscured in the dark. The dank scents of earth and decay flooded my nostrils. Frigid spray lashed our faces, our clothes, rendering the rocks treacherously slick beneath our feet. Fear coiled in my gut as I spotted the lethal drop just beyond the cliff's edge.

A faint whimper caught my ear. Silvery moonlight cascaded over the slope below, revealing the huddled figure of a quivering Vagrik crouched behind a scraggly bush. The Ring must have sensed my frantic thoughts, transporting us to where I needed to be.

I bent low, straining to haul him up, but the pup slipped farther down the incline, beyond my reach. Dropping to my knees on the slick boulders, I extended my hand, fingertips barely grazing his snout. Ears flat, Vagrik stared up at me with enormous, terrified eyes, claws scrabbling in the loose dirt as pitiful whines escaped him. Snatching a long twig, I pushed it toward him. He grabbed it between his teeth.

"Vagrik, it'll be all right," I soothed.

Liar! My inner dev-worm cackled.

Ignoring the horrid voice, my gaze flicked to the

churning river below, torn between desperation to save the dog and the risks. The drop was no higher than five or six men. I could use the Ring, grab Vagrik on my way down, and with the Ring's help, maybe we could avoid the jutting rocks. I could link to Rei and maybe...

"Satya," Rei's voice held a terse warning.

I glanced over my shoulder at Rei's rigid back. Why wasn't he helping me?

His set shoulders, the rigid determination in his stance...it sparked a feeling, a memory that danced frustratingly out of reach. But there was no time to untangle it. There was a reason Rei hadn't helped. Three devs had closed in a dozen paces away.

The deformed trio advanced, eyes glinting in the pale moonlight. Rei edged back, angling his body to shield me, his makeshift spear pointed at the devs. His stance was rigid, eyes locked on the devs with pure horror.

One more step and I could lunge, grab his leg, activate the Ring.

I glanced frantically between Rei's taut profile, the devs, and poor whimpering Vagrik, whose paws slipped, dirt and pebbles raining down into the frothy water as the stick slipped from his mouth.

An ugly, grating laugh punched the night. I turned back to Rei just as one dev stepped forward, towering over the others, broader across the shoulders. His matted, dirt-encrusted yellow curls bounced as he mock-bowed. The Monster-King.

The other two devs held back, as if awaiting his command.

He'd changed even more. Less human, more a creature of darkness. Fangs as long as fingers jutted from his gaping maw. His eyes were now murky and soulless.

Rei muttered a horrified oath.

I came to another shocking realization, one that made my skull prickle.

Rei knew this abomination, this creature who had once been our King. He knew him *personally*. It was obvious from the naked terror in Rei's eyes, the visceral horror, the betrayal.

"Hello, brother mine," the Monster-King rasped in that gravely sing-song. "Weren't you supposed to be dead? And they say *I* can't be killed."

Chapter 30

From the same tree, two branches rise.
One seeks the sun, the other hides.

~ *Aurean Ballad*

I froze as the wall of secrets around Rei shattered.

All this time I'd hoped it wasn't true. Rei wasn't a royal guard. He was royalty. The younger prince.

"You're no brother of mine," Rei spat.

"Is that how you treat family now?" the Monster-King taunted, advancing toward Rei with a growl. "The wilds have changed you, have they?"

"Rei," I whispered, "take my hand."

The creature's gaze snapped to me, his mucus-filled eyes calculating. "Dear brother, you've brought a Light Weaver to tame me? How sweet." He took another step closer to Rei. "Has no one told you? Monsters. Cannot. Be tamed."

Vagrik unleashed a piercing shriek. The terrified dog's howls snapped Rei and me out of our stupor. Rei sprang forward, his fist meeting the creature-king's maw with a well-placed punch, and wrestled him to the ground.

I screamed. The other two devs descended upon Rei. I didn't think. I jumped forward, wrapped my hand around Rei's thrashing ankle, and envisioned Vagrik's precarious perch at the ledge. As soon as Rei pushed the three figures off him, I activated the Ring.

The Gate-Ring burned my finger, and suddenly we were teetering dangerously at the rocky ledge beside the dog. Rei threw out his hand and grabbed an overhanging root with one hand and my arm with the other. His spear plummeted into the river.

The Monster-King's head appeared over the cliff. Even in the darkness I could see his ghastly smile. Moonlight highlighted the glistening blood on his teeth. "Running off so soon?"

I gasped in terror. Whose blood was that?

The other two devs swung from low-hanging branches and roots as they descended toward us, their snarls mixed with the river's rush below.

I scooped up Vagrik, but my foot slipped on the loose gravel. Rei whipped out a hand to catch my fall, but my wet fingers slipped from his grip. A branch snapped.

And the three of us tumbled into the churning waters below.

Chapter 31

Darkened waters, shadows deep,
Beneath the currents, all secrets keep.
~ Ar-Haya Highlands Proverb

I sank like a rock.

The river's furious current seized me in an inky vortex, foamy arms tossing me in all directions until nausea and disorientation muddled any sense of up or down.

Panic clawed my burning chest as I kicked and struggled against the relentless torrent. Each time my head breached the surface, I gulped desperate lungfuls of air, only for the next swell to engulf me again. My heart thundered against my ribs, my limbs screamed with exertion.

The next time I surfaced, a terrified bark echoed over the river's roar.

Vagrik!

The tiny dog paddled ahead, paws struggling to keep his head above the maelstrom. Drawing strength from the pup's courage, I redoubled my efforts to stay afloat.

Where was Rei? I screamed his name, but the rapids' endless roar swallowed my cry.

Use the Ring, idiot!

I focused on the image of floating calmly on the water's surface. Power surged through the Ring. As if taking pity on me, the currents eased their assault, and I bobbed to the surface for the dozenth time. But this time I stayed there.

The waters encircling Vagrik and me became as still as a pond. The current, no longer intent on drowning us, gently guided us forward. I scanned the river's edges for Rei in the moonlit darkness, but I couldn't see beyond the foamy waves outside our circle of calm. A hulking shape gradually materialized ahead, a moss-covered boulder thrust up from the river's midst, just a few dozen strokes away.

As we neared the boulder, Vagrik's tiny paws paddled furiously until his claws found purchase on the slimy surface. With a yelp, he scrambled atop the rock's rounded crest and vigorously shook himself, his fur rippling in waves. Then he crouched down, his dark eyes fixed unblinkingly on me, as if willing me to join him.

Above the river's relentless roar, a chorus of inhuman growls resounded through the night air. I reached Vagrik and grabbed onto the boulder, just as the rapids resumed their violent dance around me.

A group of five or six devs scrambled in a loose pack over the craggy cliffs. They descended with unsettling swiftness as they pursued my course, their soulless eyes locked on me.

Could these monsters even swim? I should use the Ring to transport myself and Vagrik away from this deathtrap. But I couldn't—*wouldn't*—leave Rei behind again.

"Rei," I screamed, my voice cracking.

I'd activated the Ring as we'd fallen, but my hand had slipped from Rei's as we plunged. Both Vagrik and Rei had fallen without the Ring's protection.

Vagrik survived. Rei has to be all right.

Across the churning expanse, the Monster-King's towering shape materialized, loping between the other devs to the rocky ledge parallel to where Vagrik and I had found temporary refuge. His foul underlings fanned out in a loose formation, grotesque maws gaping unnaturally wide as they added their rumbling snarls to the river's dull roars. A few more twisted shapes slithered from the tree lines and joined the hunting pack.

The rock bit into my palms as I clung to it, frozen with terror. Vagrik released a deep, guttural growl from beside me.

"Rei!" My hoarse scream pierced the air.

Across the river, a motionless dark shape lay half-submerged in the shallows. The strengthening current tried to tear me from the rock with its grasping foam-fingers. Gripping tighter, I squinted at the prone figure. *Did he just move?*

The figure stirred and slowly sat up.

Rei! Thank the Goddess.

Our eyes met over the tumultuous waters.

"Satya, use the Ring!" Rei's shout barely carried over the river's roar and the devs' increasing growls.

One hand clinging to the slimy boulder, I pulled Vagrik against me with the other. The pup whimpered and squirmed, vainly trying to scramble back onto the rock.

Above, the Monster-King perched on a jutting outcrop, mucus-yellow eyes peering down. "There's no escape, my dear Light Weaver." His gravelly bellow cut through the rushing waves. "Just ask my brother."

At his signal, three devs broke ranks and scrambled down the rocks toward Rei.

"Rei, watch out!" I screamed.

The Monster-King sprang from his lofty perch, elongated limbs slicing the air as he plummeted in a perfect dive. His powerful strokes knifed through foam and current, straight toward Vagrik and me.

Rei staggered up, clutching his side.

The Monster-King's arms whipped through the waves, his ghastly face drawing nearer. I wouldn't use the Ring's magic to calm the waters again—instead, I'd use the river's current to help me.

One. Two. Three…

I waited for him to get further from Rei and as close to me as I dared. *Nine. Ten.*

As the crowned creature reached me, I pressed Vagrik close and released the boulder. An ear-splitting roar tore from the dev as his clawed hands slashed empty air.

But the surging current had already seized us, pushing us downstream and away from the King, the devs, from Rei.

With one arm wrapped around Vagrik's squirming body, I kicked hard to keep us both afloat as I focused on Rei, willing the Ring's magic to take us to him. We plunged under. The dizzying rush swept us upriver against the current, and seconds later we tumbled onto rough gravel at the river's edge. Curling protectively around the dog, I slammed into Rei with bone-jarring force. Vagrik squealed, but I didn't let go.

"Satya," Rei gasped, his voice a rough plea.

A dev dropped from the ledge directly above, growling low. I grasped Rei's hand, already visualizing the healing cavern as power built within the Gate-Ring.

The world fractured around us. My gaze snapped to

Rei's shoulder. His ragged shirt was soaked with blood seeping from an angry, jagged wound. Cold dread laced my veins. That wasn't an injury from the fall.

That was a bite.

Chapter 32

Whispers of a lullaby, a forgotten dream
Lost echoes linger in memory's stream.
                              ~ Sophenian Folksong

The world reformed into the softly lit sanctuary of the healing cavern, and into the heart of a crowded chamber. Immediately, Vagrik yelped and leapt from my arms.

Rei slumped to the ground beside me, gasping. The bitemark looked even worse from this angle. The oozing wound on his shoulder was quickly turning a sickly yellow, and his entire pallor had grayed.

"He's been bitten," I shouted, my voice panicked, as I fumbled for the Spool.

Mona dropped to her knees on the other side of Rei, her determined gaze locking with mine. "I'm ready."

With shaking fingers, I held up the shield and Spool above Rei's trembling body. Mona placed her palm over mine. Our voices merged in a harmonious chant. The Spool's azurite core flared, its ethereal threads interweaving with the Gate-Ring's to form a shimmering sphere of light above Rei.

Mona immediately began the shielding chant, "Luminous and Eclipse unite. In balance, harmonize the light."

"Soul enshrouded, consumed by night," I sang, my

voice steady despite my quivering nerves. "Through these threads of light, we seek to ignite…"

A surge of energy coursed through me, flowing into the Spool and Ring, weaving into a sphere of light above Rei. His body convulsed as ethereal specters took form within the radiant sphere, his memories and emotions unfolding before me.

In the vision, Rei's father, the former Golden King, stood tall and regal. His eyes filled with disapproval as he admonished his younger son Rei, the illegitimate child. A sharp contrast to the open pride he showed his older son, the legitimate heir to the throne.

In the next vision, a beautiful woman with dark hair and a kind smile read to a very young Rei. It was evident from the emotions of love emanating from Rei that this woman was his mother, the king's mistress.

The next scene was in the royal barn. Teen Rei's face lit with joy as his brother patiently showed him how to saddle a horse. They both looked carefree, happy.

The scene morphed as shadows wove into the ethereal scene above Rei's writhing body. Tendrils reached toward the relics, slashing my skin. I clamped my jaw against the pain and continued to build the light-sphere around us.

"Satya!" Raman's voice echoed from a distance.

Mona continued to chant, her voice rising in fear.

"*Satya*," the rasping voice hissed in my head. "*Satya, follow the shadows…*"

A guttural roar erupted and for a breath, there he was, the roaring giant. I gritted my teeth and continued to sing the spell. Dark shadows slithered through the tapestry, testing the brilliant sphere's boundaries.

Within the sphere, the young Rei watched in horror

as the Enlightener cast a spell over his entranced brother. In the next vision, the brothers argued, wrestling each other to the ground.

The scene shifted. Rei's memories conjured visions of Mosatti and the massacre five years ago and the ethereal form of the teenaged Rei, dressed as a royal guard, marching among the King's army that slaughtered innocents.

My heart stilled. He'd been there, had attacked and killed my people. I nearly dropped the Spool, nearly ended the spell.

But then, my own ethereal image emerged within his memories, a more striking version of myself at thirteen. Our bookshop, two guards, my dead mother. There I stood, fighting fiercely against the King's guards with a bookshelf as a weapon to protect my little brother. A dagger pierced my shoulder and I fell unconscious. Rei rushed in. The guards left, thinking me dead. But Rei knelt beside me, gently brushing hair from my neck to check my pulse. He sucked in his breath when I momentarily opened my eyes and blinked up at him.

Here, my own memories flooded my mind with images of a boy with eyes the blue-gray of twilight, the one who'd lingered in my dreams and memories. The boy who had rescued me during that deadly attack. My grip on the shield loosened, and my fingers trembled with the need to brush my fingers over his face. It had been Rei all along. Rei, the illegitimate prince, and now the only human heir to the Golden King's throne.

In theory, he was my enemy.

But in truth, he was the boy whose actions had saved my life, the boy I'd never forgotten.

Within the vision, Rei lifted me and hid me in my

father's workroom. Back outside our workshop, he pulled down his helmet and spoke with authority, thwarting every guard who sought to enter our bookshop. After barring the door so that the Aurean soldiers would think the building empty, he left and rushed in and out of various houses and shops, rescuing more victims.

Why would the King's own son, illegitimate or not, turn against his own father? It must have taken immense courage to defy the Golden King and stand against the Enlightener. How did he manage it? And why? These were questions only he could answer.

Once more, Rei's vision shifted, and I saw myself again, but this time more recently in the Azzi village. My long dark hair floated in waves as I practiced using the Spool with skill and grace. My voice echoed ethereally in Rei's mind. The scene continued with me helping Pari and her family prepare poultices, and then laughing with Azad. I hadn't realized he'd paid so much attention to me. Always gazing from afar, the same way I'd been studying him.

Warmth radiated from his vision. I could sense his emotions growing full with something akin to admiration for my strength, skills, and beauty. Was that truly how he saw me?

A wave of my own emotions tangled within me. Confusion, compassion, admiration. As I chanted, Rei's final memory grew into a radiant beacon above us: the moment when he and I had locked eyes by the bridge, right after we'd released the demon-mice from their dark prisons. His closeness had affected me, and it was clear from the emotions radiating from Rei that the impact had been mutual.

As our two images merged within the beacon, the

sphere burst into a million speckles of light and cascaded down upon us. It was then I realized that the shadow-tendrils were gone. They'd vanished with Rei's recent memories of me.

I hadn't realized I'd stopped singing until Mona removed her hand from mine, offering me a knowing smile. How much had she sensed?

I sat back on my heels, the revelation of our shared history leaving me with more questions than answers. But one thing was undeniably clear. I couldn't ignore the connection that Rei and I shared, regardless of the complications.

Rei gasped awake. As I met his gaze, I sensed a familiar emotion, a deep longing in his beautiful twilight-eyes. Did my own gaze reflect the same?

Gently, I pressed my hand to his chest. "You'll be all right," I whispered.

His eyes closed as he slipped into unconsciousness.

****

Raman helped Pari's father discreetly change Rei out of his dripping clothes.

Meanwhile, my teeth chattered as I changed out of my own soaking garments in a hidden alcove, with Vagrik settled beside me, his fur still damp. Someone had dried him, fed him. He now lay at my feet with his eyes half-closed, softly snoring.

I dressed in a clean, practical boy's outfit, then wrung out my drenched hair and braided it down my back. My scalp tingled with cold as I wrapped myself in Pari's cloak, sighing as warmth finally seeped into my bones.

I returned to the main chamber. Immediately, my gaze drifted to Rei's sleeping form in the far corner by the hearth, his shoulders twitching beneath the thin blanket.

For too long, I'd questioned my memories of that dreadful day. But tonight, the proof had revealed itself. The boy who'd saved my life had been living here with the Azzis all this time. I still couldn't fully grasp the magnitude of that truth, could not wrap my mind around the implications.

Would Rei realize just how many of his innermost thoughts and buried memories had been bared during the ritual? I shook my head in disbelief as flashes of the visions replayed in my mind. Images of a young Rei pretending to be an Aurean royal guard, secretly saving the very people his own tyrannical brother, under the influence of the Enlightener, had sentenced to death.

Raman and Mona were engaged in a hushed conversation when I approached. They both straightened when they saw me.

"Why didn't you tell me the truth about Rei?" I accused.

Mona threw up her hands. "We couldn't risk distracting you. We had, *have*, far more urgent matters."

"Satya," Raman added, "Rei did not want us to say anything because of…"

"The massacre?" I finished with a shake of my head. "But he saved my life back then, along with so many other Sophenians. I'm alive because of him! Why would he hide that?"

They both looked at me with confusion. Clearly, they had not known that part either. The visions I witnessed during the rituals were mine alone. Others only glimpsed lights and shadows. I tried wrapping my mind around the idea of Rei and me, but knew deep down it was an impossible dream.

There could never be "Rei and me."

Ever.

The thought cut through me, leaving an ache I didn't want to untangle. "Didn't either of you consider that I already guessed he's someone important from Vosk?" I said, rubbing my chest. "It was a matter of time before I learned the truth."

"You needed to stay focused…" Mona insisted, her voice apologetic.

"Well, wonderful then," I retorted, throwing up my hands. Fantastic. I was beginning to act just like Mona. "How is *shock* supposed to help me focus?"

Raman sighed, seeming to deflate. "You're right, we should have told you from the start. But again, it wasn't our place to share."

Tatu flew in through a gap in the barricades and landed on Mona's shoulder. They communed silently. I pushed aside my anger and hurt, reminding myself of the dire situation outside where Azzi warriors were dying or turning into devs.

Forget who Rei is. You're a Light Weaver. Only you can help these people now.

A crazy plan formed in my head. "I'm going back out there."

"Are you mad?" Mona cried.

"Maybe," I admitted, pushing down at the uncertainty creeping into my tone. "But I have a plan."

Raman's brows furrowed. "What are you thinking?"

Yepo and her family, along with a few other Azzis, grouped around us.

"You will not like it," I warned, inhaling deeply to steady my nerves.

As I explained my idea, a heavy silence fell over the group. I could feel the tension building, the resignation filling the eyes of every warrior as Mona translated, realizing this might be our best chance to confront the devs. The Enlightener wouldn't stop in this village. He'd move on to the next village, then the next, until he conquered the entire Ar-Haya Highlands, amassing an army to take over larger towns and cities, the entire kingdom. Zakaya had even confirmed that, based on what he'd heard and witnessed while imprisoned in that camp. I swallowed hard as the weight of my plan pressed down on my chest.

Finally, Raman said, "Satya, that is either the most reckless plan you have ever had, or the most brilliant."

"I'll take the latter," I said, my voice confident, despite nagging doubts. "Who's coming with me?"

Chapter 33

"The work is not short, the results are distant."
~ Ar-Haya Highlands Proverb

The Enlightener might be building an army of the dead, but we would rebuild our army of the *living*. At least, that was my desperate hope.

I took a few moments to center myself, tuning out the others debating over who would join me. The faint sounds of the battle raging outside, the clashes of steel, cries, and growls, reminded me of my purpose. Through a crevice in the cavern's ceiling, a cool breeze carried the fresh scents of recent rainfall and moist earth. The gentle trickle of water mingled with the rhythmic pounding of axes as our warriors labored to fortify the outer barriers, rebuilding behind the existing defenses that the devs had nearly torn through. The healing cavern had transformed into both sanctuary and fortress.

A sense of unreality gripped me as I played and replayed the plan in my mind. First, we'd rescue the survivors, including Hampo and a small group who, according to Tatu, had barricaded themselves inside the bladesmith quarters. But it was the next phase of my plan that triggered a roiling sense of dread in the pit of my stomach.

Tatu had returned with the grim news that the newly bitten were being herded across the bridge back toward the Enlightener's camp. The reasons were clear. Those poor people weren't yet under the Enlightener's full control. If we could intercept the freshly turned before they reached the Enlightener, stopping their transformation, it would increase the size of our defense. Tatu's visions confirmed that the dense thicket atop the hill was empty of devs. We'd transport a small team there, and perform the rituals one dev at a time.

Tavid, Pari's father and a man I'd saved earlier from the dev curse, approached alongside a youthful Azzi warrior. "Souren and I have gathered a group ready to accompany you," he said, solemn pride in his voice. "You saved me when I'd lost myself to this *infection*. I knew of your mother in the days serving Mosatti. She was a highly respected Sacred. It would be an honor to assist you in carrying on her legacy."

His words were a soothing balm over the turbulence in my heart, easing the pressure of doubt and fear, reminding me that my mother's noble work lived on through me. "Thank you."

Tavid called out to the others and warriors began to weave their way through the crowded cavern to join us. An expectant hush fell over the chamber, every eye fixed on our small knot with a weight of desperate hope and fear.

Like my mother before me, I was about to enter a deadly battle, with the god-relics as my weapons and my courage as my shield.

****

We arrived in the middle of the bladesmith quarters amidst snarls and hisses. The entrance had been barred with logs wrapped in sharp brambles and thorny vines. Hampo leaned against the wall by a stack of shields, his arm all bloodied.

"Hampo," I cried, rushing up to him. "Are you…"

"No bite," he gasped, clutching his arm and wincing. "Dagger wound."

I glanced through the gaps in the vines and my heart sank. Leading a massive group of devs, the same young girl whose soul the Enlightener had stolen at the camp gnashed her teeth and growled, determined to break through the barrier. Beyond them prowled the vicious devs wielding twin daggers. Cries and anguished screams resounded from outside. The coppery scent of blood overpowered the metallic smells of the bladesmiths' forges.

I turned to Hampo. "Are there other survivors out there, apart from everyone here?"

"Only us." Hampo's gaze swept over the handful of Azzi warriors with him, no more than a dozen, each bearing signs of pain and injury. I tried not to think about what that meant. The implications of what he said, that all other warriors had been killed or turned… *Goddess*.

Wordlessly, we all forged a link. In a blink, we tumbled back into the healing cavern, amidst chaos and yells. Tereza tended to Hampo's wounded arm while he barked terse orders to his warriors. A group of their most powerful fighters gathered around us, already connecting.

Amid the chaos, I quickly checked on Rei's sleeping form, relieved to see his shoulder bite no longer oozing with bile. His handsome features remained peaceful in sleep. Swallowing hard, I turned away. I needed to focus on the plan's critical next phase.

Mona appeared at my side, features set in grim determination. "I'm coming with you. You'll need a shield."

I nodded my thanks. I hated that she would come into the fray, but what choice did I have? She was right. I did need a shield, and Raman was not an option.

The Gate-Ring flared against my finger as two dozen of us blurred into streaks of motion. Our ethereal forms crossed the barricades, darted past snarling devs, raced over the bridge, and scaled the cliffside. With surprising agility, we landed within the shelter of a secluded copse of mature elms, their boughs veiling us from sight.

The interplay of branches framed the sprawling ravine below, a chilling display of shattered defenses in the light of scattered glowrocks. Bodies sprawled upon the ground, some lifeless. Others, clearly bitten and beginning to stir. An overwhelming horde of the dead clambered over one another, breaching entrances into dwellings. No one had yet spotted the Enlightener nor the Monster-King.

The warriors that accompanied me sprang back into the fray to capture the newly bitten. Within moments, we had our first dev. An Azzi elder with a gray beard and wild, dark eyes. With Mona chanting the shielding spell, I unleashed the Spool's energy to heal him.

Next, a younger man from another village. Some of the devs were young, a few mere children. Hampo and a knot of warriors surrounded us, forming a protective barrier with weapons at the ready as we continued the rituals, one dev after another. Before long we had a few dozen healed victims sprawled nearby and recovering.

Some stayed near us, trembling. Quite a few of those we healed were Azzi warriors who returned to the battle. But I could see the fear in their eyes too.

Pain lanced through my muscles in relentless tides, threatening to drown me beneath its crashing waves. But I couldn't afford to give in, to stop. With each healing, my inner-dev thrashed and struck out, desperate to burst free from my skin and merge with the inky shadows we extracted from the tormented devs. The ever-present shadow tunnel through Satya-dev's eyes flickered in and out of view, the writhing giant at its end merging with the trees and devs around us, creating a nightmarish ever-changing tapestry.

Whisper-thin cuts and piercings crisscrossed my hands and arms, beading ruby droplets of blood. Thick, ropey veins in an unsettling bluish hue mapped their way across the backs of my trembling hands, clusters of brown age-spots blossoming amidst the newly protruding veins. Even my bones ached with a grinding throb, and it became a monumental effort to keep the shield before me, to hold the Spool above each victim.

But I ignored it all and kept going with trembling arms, kept channeling, kept singing the healing spells, my voice so raw the words tore at my throat like thorny vines.

Mona raised a glowrock closer to my face and blinked. "Satya, you are aging before my eyes. And are those…clumps of white hair?"

Pursing my lips, I pushed that worry to the back of my mind. Raman had warned me about the consistent use of the Gate-Ring, but what choice did I have?

The sky gradually lightened. My shoulders sagged as if burdened by an unseen weight. I glanced down at the ravine and the invisible weight grew heavier. Despite our efforts, the number of devs seemed to be increasing. How was that possible?

Hampo and his men spoke in hushed tones nearby, trying to plan the best way to attack and regain the village.

As Mona and I completed another healing ritual, I let out a frustrated groan. "This is taking too long."

Mona's expression mirrored my fatigue. "It is nearly morning and they're not giving up. Are dzey multiplying?"

Hampo pointed at the village below. "They more and more!"

I followed his gaze across the ravine to the destroyed barricades. Groups of devs had scaled the braided vines, breaching the higher cliffside dwellings.

"I don't understand…" I whispered. Our efforts were clearly not working. It was like spitting on a raging fire and expecting to put it out.

Mona raised a hand to quiet us. "Do you feel that?"

My gaze roamed over the ravaged village and settled on the distant entrance to Dragon's Maw. The portal-cavern pulsed with a powerful energy, its tendrils reaching us even here.

Snarls and growls drew closer. The devs had noticed us. A large hunting pack was already crossing the bridge, headed in our direction.

"Yes, I feel it," I said, shoving down a surge of dread. "Let's get everyone to safety…link!"

****

Our large group arrived in the already crowded healing cavern. The healers immediately rushed to the injured.

Raman pushed his way through the crowd toward us. I blinked. He was now dressed as one of the Azzi warriors in loose woolen pants and a fur vest over leather scale-armor. It was odd seeing my former schoolmaster transformed into a warrior. I'd never seen Raman in anything but a robe. "What is happening out there?" he asked.

Mona and I quickly summarized the unfolding events for the assembled group: the devs multiplying, breaching barriers, the majority of the Azzi warriors falling victim to bites and conversions, and Dragon's Maw crackling with intensified energy.

Raman's brow furrowed, beard jutting as he pressed his lips into a tight line. I recognized that expression— the one that betrayed he could not think of a way out of this dire situation. Eyes growing sad, he touched my graying hair and flicked a glance to the Ring. We both knew I had no choice, so he made no comment. My fingers tightened over my belt pouch.

Amidst the rising clamor of voices, a deep timbre calling my name reached my ears. I swiveled around to find Rei navigating through the crowd, heading toward me. He looked pale, his gait slightly angled, favoring one side. His shoulder was wrapped in a fresh whisperweave bandage. As he approached, his concerned gaze locked onto the myriad cuts scoring my hands and forearms. "You're bleeding."

No mention of my aging skin and hair.

I glanced down at the streaks of crimson staining my sleeves and skin almost as if noticing them for the first time. With all that had happened, the stinging pain had retreated into the back of my awareness. "I'm fine."

"Satya," he said, his deep voice taking on a softness I hadn't heard from him before, as his blue-gray gaze held mine. "Thank you…for healing me."

The depth of gratitude and vulnerability in those

words filled my chest with warmth. "You're welcome."

A knot in my chest loosened at seeing him on his feet, his striking eyes clear of the dev infection. Clearing my throat, I added, "I'm just…really glad you're all right."

A faint half-smile tugged at a corner of his lips. "Me too."

Our gazes held for several heartbeats. His cheeks deepened in color as he likely wondered how much of his thoughts and memories I'd witnessed during the ritual. I wasn't sure what he saw in my expression, but his jaw clenched subtly and he was the first to break the connection.

So much lay unsaid between us. He, the boy with eyes mirroring a stormy twilight sky, the one who had pulled me from the clutches of death five years ago. Out of all the Sophenians he'd selflessly saved that day, somehow he remembered me. Goddess, we'd been children on the cusp of adulthood, and yet those memories still lingered within us both.

The raised voices around us had escalated into a heated debate, with Hampo, Yepo, Tavid, Mona and Raman all caught up in a fervent disagreement over our situation. I cleared my throat, shifting my focus back to the ongoing conversation.

"…and we cannot abandon the village," Mona exclaimed to Raman, then rattled off her argument with the Azzis.

"They want to abandon the village?" I asked.

"The healers want to stay and heal the devs," Mona said. "I told them you want that too, no?"

"Of course I want that too," I said firmly. The mere thought of giving up on those tormented souls, leaving them to the Enlightener's control, curdled my stomach.

"Good, because I said as much. But some feel we are fighting against a tide we cannot stop, while others want to fight to dze end…"

"We fight!" Souren, the young Azzi warrior, declared in Sophenian, his handsome face set in defiant lines. He stole a sidelong glance in my direction before he quickly looked away and pumped a fist in the air. "We strong."

Hampo shook his head, looking irritated. Yepo unleashed a string of commanding Azzian at Souren, emphasizing them with gestures directed at me. I caught a few words. The elderly healer, clearly a respected elder in this village, fervently championed my efforts over Souren's and the other warriors' battle skills. She sent me an approving nod before returning to her duties at the cavern's far end, where Tereza and Pari tended to groups of the injured.

"Yes, we are strong," I said, raising my voice to be heard over the cacophony. "But they're multiplying. The Enlightener must be creating new devs even as we undo his work."

Tavid nodded. "They're coming from that war camp." He repeated his words in Azzian for the others.

Rei's voice sliced through our conversation. "The Enlightener could be tapping a more potent energy source."

I turned to him, mouth agape. He was right. Dragon's Maw currently emanated an immense surge of power, more potent than anything I'd sensed before. Was the Enlightener somehow drawing from the cavern's energy? Was that even possible?

My fingers traced the Weaver's Spool's contours

over my belt pouch, the familiar shape grounding me. The lake chamber in Dragon's Maw was covered in countless azurites—the same crystal that created the Spool and Gate-Ring. This gem linked to the godforce. A conduit.

If I could reach the chamber where I met Ayg, maybe the azurites would amplify the godforce to simultaneously heal multiple devs.

My gaze fell to the Gate-Ring. Would it transport me there? "What if…"

Rei cast me a quizzical look.

The cacophony around us drowned my voice. "What if…" I repeated louder until the others hushed and turned their attention to me. "What if we use Dragon's Maw's energy against the Enlightener's army." My words drew puzzled frowns once Mona translated.

Raman's eyes narrowed in contemplation. "What are you proposing, Satya?"

"Rei might be right," I said. "The Enlightener could be tapping into the power of Dragon's Maw to continuously rebuild and strengthen his forces. All those lifeless bodies at his camp—he was turning them into devs." The oasis fell silent, besides the sounds of growls and clanging resonating from outside. I took another steadying breath. "Maybe that's why his war camp is on the other side of this mountain, close to Dragon's Maw."

"But how could he do that from a distance?" Mona said.

I shrugged. "I don't know. But I need to get closer to Dragon's Maw to see…" I explained the connection between the Spool, the Gate-Ring, and the azurite gems that covered the entire portal cavern. "Maybe I don't need to be inside the cavern, just closer to the entrance."

Tavid translated my plan to the Azzis, who then turned to me with a mix of astonishment and skepticism.

"Satya," Raman said, "even your mother never attempted anything of such magnitude."

"I have to try."

"She has a point," Rei said, a glint of respect in his gaze.

Mona leaned toward Raman. "Do you think the Gate-Ring could transport us to that crystal chamber inside the cavern?"

Raman stroked his beard. "Dragon's Maw is a portal, not a physical space in our reality. I'm not convinced it would work."

"But we can't be sure until we try," I said firmly. "Anyway, we might not even need to. Maybe just being near the entrance is enough if the Enlightener is using it from farther away."

The enormity of the plan stretched wider than the Massisa Mountains. Was this how my mother had felt during Ahri-Luys's devastation thirty years ago? She was near my age when she'd fought for her friends' lives. This thought alone strengthened my resolve.

Raman frowned. "Be careful, Satya. That cavern's energy isn't purely benevolent. I should accompany you…"

"You're needed here," I said. Even with Raman's limited magic, he'd been an immense help in maintaining the barricades. "Mona and I will be careful."

Mona chimed in, her tone light. "Indeed, dzis girl, she has some intriguing ideas…and eez a bit pushy with them, no?" She smiled to lighten her words.

Raman said gravely, "If the Enlightener learns of your actions, he'll use the same powerful godforce against you."

His words prickled my skin with warning, and an unwelcome premonition. Isn't that what Vishap tried to do? And he'd nearly succeeded.

I needed to do this fast before the Enlightener caught on. A vision of my youthful father aiding the fallen in the kork flashed before me. In this, I needed to channel his resourcefulness and courage. I needed to think like Baba.

Be equipped.

Be observant.

Be quick.

Chapter 34

"A crooked brother is worse than an enemy."
~ Ar-Haya Highlands Proverb

A torrential downpour drenched us in the concealed alcove beside Dragon's Maw. Our ragtag band—Rei, Mona, Hampo, Tavid, Souren, and three other Azzi warriors—huddled close, set to accompany me to the portal-cavern's entrance. Once there, I'd attempt to harness the cavern's energy. If that failed, I'd have no choice but to use the Ring to locate the azurite chamber within and transport all of us there. Then somehow…*somehow* figure out how to use all those crystals to connect to the devs. I tried not to dwell on the countless ways it could all go terribly, catastrophically wrong.

Flickering shadows from our dimly-lit glowrocks danced across the damp walls, illuminating the space just enough to guide our steps. Above the storm's roar, a mournful whimper reached my ears. I aimed my glowrock down to find a floppy-eared dog tugging at my pants.

I stifled an exasperated scream and whispered, "Vagrik! You foolish dog!"

The others exchanged worried looks.

"No time to return him." Mona's whisper carried an edge. "We have more pressing issues."

She was right. I gritted my teeth, ears straining against the eerie snarls merging with the storm's rumbles around the village bend.

"Stay here," I whispered to Vagrik. Ears pressed to his skull, the poor dog cowered in a corner.

Hampo and Rei led as we slipped along the alcove's edge, our squelching steps blending into the battering rain's rhythm. Sheets of rain pummeled the alcove's outer walls as rolls of thunder merged with the tangible energy emanating from the portal-cavern.

A deafening screech tore through the storm's cacophony. A lithe shadow swung down from an impossibly high ledge, landing a dozen paces before Dragon's Maw's entrance, blocking our path. I stumbled back. Mona collided into me with an alarmed yelp. Rainwater blurred my vision. Blinking it away, the tall figure's form came into focus.

The Monster-King.

In the dim light of our glowrocks, he looked nearly human, save for the mucus-yellow of his eyes betraying the fanged monster within. Had he been lurking on the ledges above, waiting for us with calculated patience? Unless…he was guarding the portal-cavern's entrance.

Our group brandished daggers. I tightened my grip on the Spool.

"Why, hello, little brother," the Monster-King crowed with a regal air. "Back so soon?"

"What do you want?" Rei hissed, raising his dagger.

"Is that a challenge?" the dev sneered, fangs glinting. "You wish to fight me for the crown, little brother?"

Rei's growl cut through the tension. "I don't give a damn about the crown. And you're *not* my brother."

The Monster-King threw back his head with a mocking laugh. "You cannot defeat Ahriman, foolish *brother*."

"What do you want?" Rei repeated, his dagger poised.

The dev-king's lips curled into a taunting grin, laughter lingering in his words. "Isn't it obvious? I want your charming heartmate's godforce...and *her*, upon reflection." His grin widened, eyes raking over me. "Such a pretty Light Weaver rightfully belongs to the Golden King. As for you, little brother, it's time you reclaimed your rightful place beside me. Tell me, why have you not joined us?" He tsked. "Ah...she healed you, didn't she."

Heartmate? Rightfully belongs? As if I were a commodity to be claimed. Was that what the royals taught their princes? A hiss slipped unbidden from my lips. Rei glanced back, shaking his head slightly, gesturing for me to stay behind him.

Tavid motioned to the others, subtly coordinating their positions. Their weapons poised, the Azzis formed a protective half-circle around Rei, Mona, and me.

Despite the sharp daggers leveled at him, the crowned dev's empty hands hung loosely at his sides, not a hint of fear in his mucus-colored eyes. He obviously knew mortal weapons could never vanquish a dev. A harsh lesson we'd learned from the Azzis' ill-fated battle.

I tightened my grip on the Spool, stepping up beside Rei.

Rei raised his dagger threateningly at his brother. "Get out of our way."

"No," the crowned dev spat out, his smile

evaporating. His jaw unhinged, elongating as fangs protruded from the corners of his mouth. The yellow of his pupils thickened, glistening in the glowrocks' pale light. His hands curled into claws, nails morphing into spiny blades that sliced through his own fingertips.

What stood before us was no longer a man, but a creature of the underworld.

Rei lunged, shoulders colliding into his brother's midsection with a grunt. Their forms blurred in a flurry of punches and kicks, fists and claws. Their two shadows struggled across the rain-slicked ground.

My clothes clung to me, loose tendrils of hair escaping my braid to form a soggy curtain across my face. Each raindrop prickled against my skin. I stood rooted, helpless, as each flash of lightning brought the scuffling figures into stark clarity.

Flash. Rei's hands locked around his brother's throat.

Flash. The crowned monster's gaping maw, fangs stained red.

Flash. Rei's bloodied fingers grasping for his dagger that had fallen onto the slick ground.

Thunder rumbled overhead, the sound like a stampede of wild boars. Whipping winds yanked at my clothes and hair as I considered my options. Using the cavern's energy from here was too risky with devs infesting the village. Or I could use the Gate-Ring to enter the cavern, but that meant abandoning Rei and the others to the dev-riddled village. Any moment, their scuffle would draw unwanted attention. The Azzi warriors edged closer to the battling brothers.

I locked gazes with Mona and nodded to the Spool. Understanding flickered in her gaze.

I sprinted forward, the rain lashing at my face, and crouched down a few arm-lengths from the fighting pair, waiting for an opportunity to get close enough to begin the ritual. Just a touch—an arm, shoulder, anything. Rei just needed to hold his brother still.

The other Azzis moved with precision, trying to capture the dev without harming Rei. They swirled around the dueling siblings, dodging the monster's snapping jaws. Despite his brother's formidable might, Rei's five-year ordeal seemed to have strengthened his determination. He wrestled the King to the ground, dagger at his throat.

"Maybe devs cannot be killed," Rei's voice dripped with raw emotion, "but let's see how you function without a head."

The King snarled, his efforts to bite thwarted by Rei's agile evasion and swift counterstrikes. Rei's blade found its way to his brother's throat again, only to abruptly freeze.

I stood poised with the Spool clutched tightly, ready to begin the ritual right here, right now. Mona's urgent footsteps closed the distance. She fell to her knees beside me, clutching my arm, her touch grounding me.

Rei's fingers trembled on the dagger's hilt, eyes glistening with barely contained horror. It dawned on me then. He couldn't do it. He might be able to kill a dev, but he could not kill his own brother.

Two Azzis wrenched Rei away, while Hampo and Souren restrained the snarling creature. I gripped the Spool tight and drew the shield from my back, ready to begin the ritual—and froze as a storm of memories swirled within me.

I was back in Mosatti five years ago—my screams

echoed off our shop's walls as that young guard—Rei—carried me from death. My mother's lifeless form on the steps, my little brother's at the threshold of our family quarters.

It was this man. This crowned monster, the Golden King, who had ordered those merciless killings. It didn't matter that the Enlightener had manipulated him, that he'd already been infected. It didn't matter that this creature was Rei's brother.

The dev-worm writhed within me, its snarls reverberating from the shadows of my mind. My rage rose and grew until my entire body trembled with an all-consuming fury I'd never known.

The Golden King was a monster. I would not, could not, heal such darkness. Let the Dragon's Maw's godforce judge his fate.

As the dev King aimed to sink his fangs into Souren's arm, I broke free from Mona's connection and surged forward in the downpour. The crowned dev tore free, pinning me with his gaze.

Rain and tears stung my eyes as I channeled the godforce through the Gate-Ring and Spool. The surge of power boosted my movements, and as the Monster-King closed in, I thrust my heel up, delivering a forceful kick to his abdomen.

Lightning flashed, casting a multi-hued glow where my foot met its mark.

The Monster-King hurtled into the portal's entrance, his furious roars swallowed by Dragon's Maw's dense energy.

The momentum of my kick threw me off balance. I teetered at the threshold. A small form darted to my side. Vagrik, drenched and furious, tugged at my pants. I stumbled back, falling.

Vagrik barked frantically at the cavern opening. The darkness unfurled wispy tentacles reaching for me. I rolled away. Vagrik's barks turned to panicked yelps as the fog-fingers coiled around him instead, dragging him toward the swirling void.

"Vagrik!" I lunged, but the shadows were too swift.

They slurped the pup into the abyss.

Chapter 35

"A mind misled is a barren land, a heart deceived is a bottomless pit."

~ *Ar-Haya Highlands Proverb*

"No!" I sprinted toward the cavern entrance, panic spearing my chest in rapid, agonizing jabs.

"Satya," Mona's voice cut through the haze as she caught my arm. "We cannot delay a moment longer."

Icy rain stung my face. My clothes clung to me in sodden layers. Rei stood rigid, his horror-struck gaze fixed on the cavern entrance. I took a step toward him, ready to apologize. I'd just hurled his brother into Dragon's Maw. What choice did I have? The warriors with us would have done the same. Rei must know that. But his stiff stance, the way he angled his body away from us all, did not invite conversation or apology.

Beyond the tree lines' silhouette, the faint lightening of the sky flickered at the edges of night. Dawn approached, when the godforce thrummed strongest within me. The sounds of clashing metal and feral snarls drew nearer. The battle had spread dangerously close to us. We couldn't linger here. I had no choice but to take everyone into the portal-cavern.

Swallowing hard, I centered my thoughts on the azurite pool within the cavern. Making sure to catch Rei's gaze, I called out, "Link."

As the others connected to me, our surroundings warped, twisted.

My heart plummeted, and continued to drop, drop, drop.

Raw power ripped through me, leaving a metallic tang on my tongue. I lost all sense of the others, of my own body. I shrank to a speck of dust in an endless void, falling, falling…

Then, the world slammed to an abrupt stop.

I tumbled onto damp pebbles, pain lancing through my knees. Whispers echoed like distant voices before fading to the steady *drip-drip-drip* of water plinks. The cavern's rich, rain-soaked scent enveloped me.

Disoriented, I scrambled to my feet, gaping. *It worked.*

The cavern chamber was as vast as I remembered, with a lake that extended to its far reaches. A pale blue hue emanated from azurite crystals blanketing the lofty ceiling and distant walls. A breathless laugh escaped me. "It worked, can you bel…" I spun around.

I was alone.

For a long moment, I stood frozen, waiting. Hoping. Nothing.

My knees weakened. Something had gone horribly wrong. Where were the others? Had the link scattered them elsewhere? Or were they even now facing their own trials in this realm of the gods?

"Mona! Rei! Hampo! Vagrik?" My shaky voice echoed back hauntingly, "…*rik…rik…rik.*"

I forced myself to breathe, to *think*. I could use the Gate-Ring to return, but I'd wind up in the midst of a losing battle. If the others were captured, their best chance of surviving depended on my success *here*.

I straightened my heavy shoulders. I'd come here with a purpose. I needed to focus on this mission, or every sacrifice, every failure, would be all I had left. *Goddess, please keep them safe.*

I studied the vast azurite display more closely. The crystals ranged in size and shape from delicate teardrop prisms to the size of pinecones with countless facets. Veins branched across each faceted gem, shadows flitting within them like living, breathing things.

During my last visit, I hadn't fully grasped this portal-cavern's true nature. Could only I, as Ayg's vessel, access it? Was that why Vishap had avoided it, why the others hadn't been allowed in? This is where I'd communed with the ethereal circle of Light Weavers…and with the Goddess of Dawn herself.

"Ayg?" My whisper resonated over the pool and distant walls.

The crystals softly chimed in response.

"Ayg!" I yelled. My voice carried over the shimmering clusters, zinging into each crystal and bouncing back. *…Ayg…Ayg…Agy.*

I crouched at the water's edge. The Spool and the Gate-Ring thrummed with power, resonating with the pulsing glow surrounding me. The water's glassy surface reflected the brilliant cerulean, revealing more dazzling gemstones on the lake floor.

"Ayg, if you can hear me, I need a shield." My plea rippled over the water, chiming back in an eerie chorus, *shield, shield, shield.*

As my voice faded, the azurites flickered to life. And I was suddenly surrounded by a multitude of reflections of *me.*

I blinked, and thousands of my own eyes blinked

back from each faceted surface. How did one go about activating an entire portal-cavern?

The crystals began to vibrate like thousands of tiny bells pealing in unison. My countless reflections morphed into a kaleidoscope of shifting expressions. Beaming smiles, furrowed frowns, features contorted in silent screams of rage. A shiver danced down my spine. Was this another test?

Then the myriad images blurred into a swirling vortex of color. Reds bled into blues, green into lavender, a relentless cycle of shifting hues. *Shifting hues…*

My jaw slackened. This was a message.

I thought back to the Sacreds' lessons, to my father's texts, but it was my mother's voice that echoed through my memories: *Color deciphers emotions. Rose for love, blue for grief, green for envy, lavender for fear, red for rage…*

Wait. The swirling colors weren't random. They reflected the turbulent emotions that defined me. The ones I kept hidden from everyone. Even from myself. The vivid hues continued to shift and swirl in a kaleidoscope of colors before gradually coalescing into the murky shade of mud. The color of suffocating, crippling guilt.

The air left my lungs in a whoosh. Guilt, my constant companion. Guilt for surviving when my family had perished. For my sometimes reckless impulsiveness. For rushing headlong into actions without considering consequences. How often had Raman warned me of that flaw? How often had my parents?

And now, guilt over the immense power Ayg had bestowed, a responsibility I wielded with the clumsy grace of a child. A gift, yes. But a terrifying one I felt woefully unprepared to hold. My eyes clouded. Is this what the goddess was trying to show me?

A subtle movement in my periphery froze me in place. Slowly turning, I found myself staring into a pair of mucus-yellow eyes. A darker, twisted mirror image of *me* crouched on the cavern floor, an ugly grin stretching across her colorless face. I remained still, frozen rigid with terror. This was my inner dev-worm. *Satya-dev*.

She'd appeared to me in this very cavern during Vishap's trial, then again during my healing rituals. But I had never seen her this clearly, this…solid. I jumped up and stumbled back, the hairs on my arms standing on end. This *was* another trial.

Satya-dev cocked her head and rose, ebony tendrils of hair swaying to an invisible wind. "Did you think you could escape me?" Her raspy voice prickled my skin. "We are bound, you and I."

I took another step back, icy fear coiling around my heart. *How…?*

Her unnerving smile stretched wider. "This is the source of your guilt, is it not? Your inability to fully unleash your power?" She tsked. "Such a disappointing vessel for a goddess."

I gripped the Spool so tightly my fingers stung. "You can't be real."

"Can't I?" She glided closer, a pool of inky darkness spreading from her feet. "I am as real as your fear, as real as your rage…I am your darkness personified. I am *you*."

My head shook in denial, but she pressed on. "I am the part that helped you survive after the massacre, nurturing that raging need for self-preservation."

"Self-pity," I whispered, my jaw clenching.

Her mirthless laugh grated like nails on stone. "Do

you know why I fight to escape during every ritual? Because it's the only time your godforce burns bright enough, and your tenuous control over me weakens enough, for me to break free." Her gaze roved over the cuts on my arms. "Pity you fight it. You have no idea how powerful I can make you."

"I don't need, nor want, that kind of power." Even as I said it, even as I convinced myself that it was true, my trembling hands betrayed me.

She brushed a clammy hand over my arm. An icy chill skittered across my skin. "Do you know what happens, dear Light Weaver, when rage, fear, guilt, hatred are kept bound and repressed?" She leaned in until her foul breath stung my nostrils. "That is how a Dark Weaver is born."

Her raspy words resounded across the cavern walls: *...born...born...born.*

I stared at this twisted mirror—my own face, so familiar yet so foreign. This was the darkness within me that I'd suppressed for so long its weight had become a bushel of jagged rocks lashed to my back. The weight of responsibility I'd recklessly shunned until it was too late. The weight of smoldering hatred for the Aurean soldiers, for their cruel King. The weight of selfish dreams indulged while my family could no longer dream in death.

The awful, gut-twisting guilt came crashing back in waves. That same unbearable weight now stood before me, wearing my face, but with a deadened, soulless heart.

"You made me into a victim," I whispered. "Took away my power."

She laughed her grating laugh. "No one can take

away your power. You did that all on your own."

Hot, ugly rage burst through my chest. How dare she judge me? How dare this wretched aspect of myself claim to know me! She represented the part I'd struggled to keep bound and leashed until she'd become my invisible, unshakable baggage.

"I hate you!" The scream ripped from my throat before my mind could fully form the thought. And as the raw words settled in the hollow of my heart, I stared into my own eyes reflected back in the Satya-dev's mucus-irises. My eyes widened in a sudden, horrified realization.

She nodded slowly, understanding filling her own soulless gaze. "That's what I thought."

With a final sickly wink, she dissolved into smoke and silence.

I crumpled to my knees atop the wet pebbles, clutching the Spool in a white-knuckled grip. All these years, I'd been so wrong. It wasn't just guilt that had piled onto the crushing weight I'd been carrying. It was this festering, unending hatred for who I'd become.

How could I ever be worthy as a goddess vessel?

I didn't know how long I sat there, maybe a few moments, maybe years. My breathing ragged, my heart frantic, my entire body trembling. Feeling lost, lost, lost.

Then a whispery caress brushed against my cheek, and Ayg's soothing, hazel-balm voice drifted into my mind. *"Lay down your Eclipse energies, love. You are safe here."*

Breathe. Breathe. Breathe.

Each inhalation was a conscious effort to release the crushing weight that sat like a boulder on my chest, my back. As I did, a new color flickered within the crystals.

Brilliant gold.

Gold, for courage. Gold for trust.

And I understood. My gold-ringed irises were not a mark of Ahriman but a reflection of the golden plate Ayg had held in her lap, the color that marked me as a Light Weaver.

With this realization, the swirling vortex of hues coalesced into a blinding flash of pure white light. A weightless peace descended over me. My shoulders relaxed. And I knew what I must do. It had to work. *It will work.*

I needed fate, or I had nothing.

Raman's teachings flitted through my thoughts: *The first step in a light-weaving ritual is to anchor yourself in an uplifting memory.*

The memory of the Nurazard festival of years ago that I'd previously used as my anchor dissolved, replaced by Rei's smile—twilight eyes crinkled at the corners, his lips stretched in a genuine expression that lit up and transformed his face. I anchored myself to that smile and began the spell-song. "By Ayg's grace and my deep connection, I weave these threads, the spirits' protection…"

Tendrils of light spiraled from the relics, weaving delicate patterns like the gossamer webs of massive spiders around me. They tethered me to each azure crystal until I sat in an iridescent cocoon.

As my spell thrummed within the sphere of light, the crystals changed. Each one now reflected a different face. Some familiar, some strangers.

A horrifying realization shattered my newfound peace. Each crystal pulsed with a trapped lifeforce, a prison crafted from the very godforce meant to protect.

The Enlightener had twisted this power, tethering mortals to these gleaming cages. This explained the rapid creation of devs. He must possess a tool or conduit to wield such pure Eclipse energy and to manipulate the portal from afar.

How much festering hate and rage could fuel such profound darkness? The Satya-dev's words sank deep into my mind: *Do you know what happens…when rage, fear, guilt, hatred are kept bound? That is how a Dark Weaver is born.*

I continued the spell, my mind whirling. Each crystal was tethered to a thread of mortal essence, stolen by the Enlightener to fuel his monstrous army. The sheer number was overwhelming. Days, maybe weeks, could melt away while I cleansed these souls one by one. The multitude of light-threads still linked me to all the crystals within this portal-cavern. My spell wove a connection to these trapped souls, but could I release them all at once?

I glanced down at the glowing Gate-Ring and an idea sprouted. The Ring worked differently when paired with the Spool. Together, these relics channeled the godforce to heal. But on its own, the Ring warped time and space, enabling rapid travel. Couldn't it achieve the opposite?

I paused mid-spell as a daring plan took root. The Ring had temporal shielding, a localized pocket that protected me and my companions during travel. Instead of accelerating time, maybe the Ring could slow it down. I huffed at my own audacity, wondering what the Sacreds would make of such a blasphemous use of the relics.

What did I have to lose?

Everything.

But doing nothing also left me with nothing.

Focusing on the Ring, I issued a silent plea: *Shield me from time's passage.*

An eerie silence descended. The rhythmic drip-drip of water ceased abruptly, droplets hanging suspended in midair like forgotten tears. The very air seemed to hold its breath.

Inhale. Exhale. And again.

I expelled a sigh of relief. I wasn't frozen in this time warp. The cavern was.

I met the frozen gazes of the spirits trapped within the crystals. With Rei's smile anchoring me, I began the healing chant anew. For the first time in my training, I was on my own, without a shielding spell for protection. If the Satya-dev wanted to lash out, I wouldn't be able to stop her. A battle raged within me.

This is going to be hard…

Do it anyway.

This may not work…

Do it anyway.

I may fail and be worse off…

Do it anyway.

Do it anyway.

Do it anyway.

My impulsive actions had always been a double-edged dagger. A heavy weight settled in my gut, a sense of giving something up. A sacrifice.

I knew what the Ring's constant use could do, felt it each time I'd used it during the past few days. It would age me. Had already started aging me. I could grow old rapidly and die right here on the threshold to the realm of the gods. Worse, without a shield, the dark energy could overwhelm me. Even thinking of it made the Satya-dev thrash.

Here I sat, at the precipice of another reckless act. But this time, it wasn't blind impulse. I'd weighed the options, the dangers, and the potential consequences. Deep within, I knew it was the only choice I had.

Straightening my spine, I let the spell's words flow from my lips. The Gate-Ring pulsed as strands of light arced outward, infusing the Spool before illuminating the shimmering cocoon enveloping me.

The cavern's azurites shimmered in response. As the final syllable left my lips, a kaleidoscope of color burst from the Spool. Blues, reds, greens, golds and pinks—a spectrum of all the trapped spirits' emotions cascaded over my silken bubble in dazzling waves.

Whispers of laughter twisted with cries of pain, screams of rage echoing alongside whimpers of agony and shouts of joy. These were their memories, their hopes, their fears. I wasn't here to judge but to restore their essence that had been so cruelly stolen.

The time-sphere held firm as I channeled the healing light, maybe one soul at a time, maybe hundreds. My perception was warped.

The air shimmered, carrying the scent of fresh rain and the sweetness of honey on my tongue. Each crystal pulsed with blinding white light as the trapped essence was freed, before returning to its natural azure hue. The shadows they cast writhed and dissolved, sucked into the earth to be transmuted and transformed into pure Luminous energy. An invisible shield contained the release. Maybe Ayg? I didn't know who or how, but I was grateful.

Time warped, bent. The relentless tapestry of

visions continued. Faces etched with age and youth, mothers, fathers, grandparents, children. I barely felt the pool's dampness seeping through my cloak and pants, the scrape of pebbles against my knees.

A different force hummed in the air, a power that resonated with neither light nor shadow. It was the thrumming heart of the portal itself, the godforce in its purest form. A harmonious blend that Raman had alluded to after I'd been bitten. This energy, both Luminous and Eclipse, yet somehow distinct, swirled around me like a cloud of whisperweave. Despite its subtle nature, this force permeated the entire cavern, washing over me in a wave of unimaginable comfort. Maybe *it* was my shield.

My vision clouded, or maybe I'd never stopped crying. But this time, it wasn't sadness, but awe at the profound presence that enveloped me. With renewed purpose, I continued channeling the healing light until each crystal returned to its azure glow. Until every last spirit was freed.

Until I no longer knew where I began and where I ended. It was done.

With a soft pop, my protective sphere dissolved, leaving me drained but filled with a strange, calming warmth. My hair, freed from its braids, flowed around me in a cloud of silver and white. I gasped at the implication but had no energy to consider what it meant.

I whispered to the Gate-Ring, "Return me to…" But my voice faded as the world around me dissolved into a whirling vortex. My head met the wet pebbles at the pool's shore.

I welcomed oblivion.

Chapter 36

"A crooked dagger cannot cut a straight line."
~ Azzi War Chant

Icy awareness jolted me awake.

My eyes flew open to the Azzi healing quarters' familiar stone walls. I lay sprawled atop the alcove's threadbare rug where I'd spent countless hours learning to weave the godforce, the Spool tight in my grip.

Dim light filtered through gauzy curtains draping the niche's entrance. How long had I been in Dragon's Maw?

I caught my reflection in a decorative wall mirror, and inhaled sharply. The woman staring back was a stranger with a river of silver hair. Her face, a roadmap of creases around the mouth, across the forehead, beneath the eyes. Mouth agape, I traced the unfamiliar grooves of my face with trembling fingers.

Raman had warned me about the Ring's price, how its frequent use would accelerate aging. A temporal-relic's curse. But I hadn't realized its consequence would be so swift, so starkly evident.

An eerie tomblike heaviness hung in the air. Stagnant. Cold. The oppressive weight pressed down on everything. Outside, not a sound stirred. No clash of steel, no guttural growls or bloodcurdling screams of battle. If I'd succeeded in freeing all those trapped spirits in the portal-cavern, then where were the shouts of joy? Cries of relief?

Across the room, a hearth held an impossibly still fire—the flames frozen mid-flicker. Cold dread coiled around my heart. Time remained frozen.

I stuffed the Spool into my pouch and scrambled to my feet, legs weak and protesting as if I'd run for days without rest. My back throbbed as I lunged for the alcove's curtain, parting it with trembling hands.

Daylight streamed in through the shattered barricades at the healing cavern's main entrance. The sanctuary I'd left bustling with brave survivors preparing for a final stand was now a frozen tableau of a battle reaching its horrifying end.

A tide of nausea welled up from the pit of my stomach as I crept around the petrified figures. Devs. Everywhere. A battle frozen in time, terror etched into every detail by a macabre hand. Some faces were recognizable, others forever strangers. These monstrous puppets, once decent mortals robbed of their lives, stood in mid-motion. Double-edged daggers gleamed in paralyzed hands, jaws gaped impossibly wide, frozen screams on contorted faces. They lurched menacingly toward petrified victims.

A wave of dizziness washed over me, threatening to buckle my knees. The Ring's faint hum pulsed against the suffocating stillness. If I used it to thaw the frozen river of time, wouldn't I unleash this carnage? Wouldn't it condemn the very people I'd fought to save? A sickening dread suffocated me. Where were the spirits I thought I'd freed? The ones trapped within the portal-cavern's crystals? Had that even been real?

Was this a consequence of wielding a power I barely

understood? The chilling reality behind Raman's warnings about the Ring's devastating cost? But Ayg had insisted that a god-vessel can use a relic safely within limits. There was something I was missing here. But what?

"Satya?" a strangled voice whispered from a back alcove.

I whirled around, my heart racing. In the dim light filtering from the darkest back corner, stood Raman. He held his staff before him, its broken tip spitting the faint blue light of a crystal.

I rushed to him and wrapped my arms around his frail form.

When we finally pulled back, his gaze dropped to my hair. "Oh, Satya..." he stammered, his eyes filled with a sorrowful understanding. He reached out a hand to my face, then dropped it. "Your beautiful face," he murmured, his voice heavy with heartache.

I swallowed hard, forcing down the surge of emotions threatening to engulf me. Now wasn't the time for self-pity. Not with so much at stake.

He frowned, his gaze flickering to the Ring on my finger. "You've used the Gate-Ring to freeze time."

"Yes, but where are the others? And how are you...here with me, when everyone else is...?" I cast a gaze around me, then returned back to him.

His eyes saddened. "The survivors...we hid within a small alcove in the rear. I was chanting a shielding spell, until everything just...paused." He gestured toward me with his staff and I noted the azurite tip. "I'm here with you because of this. A relic of the gods, it offers protection to its wielder. Apparently, its power extends to the Ring's time manipulation when I'm close enough."

"Survivors?" I choked out, my voice raw with dread.

"They're in there." He waved a hand toward the back. "Just a handful of us. All frozen."

Despair threatened to drown me, a hopelessness I'd felt only one other time in my life. Five years ago after the massacre. "I've failed, Master Raman. I'm so sorry." My words sounded hollow, dead.

"Oh, Satya," he murmured, his eyes filled with sorrow. "We have all failed."

He placed a steadying hand on my arm as we skirted around the still devs, their mucus-yellow eyes staring vacantly, weapons frozen mid-strike. Stepping outside the healing quarters, the true scope of the devastation unfolded. My heart stalled.

The village, once bustling with life, was now a still tableau of horror.

Devs, trapped in various stages of violence, surrounded the crumpled forms of Azzi warriors. The air itself seemed to crackle with the weight of despair. A strangled sob escaped my throat.

Raman let out a choked gasp beside me. "Where are Rei, Mona…the others?"

Shame burned through me. "I…" I stammered, my voice barely above a whisper. "I hoped they were with you."

He shook his head, his face grim. "No, they never returned after you left for Dragon's Maw."

Oh, no.

"The Monster-King," I said, forcing the words out. "He met us at the entrance. Rei…he fought his brother, and then the King fell into the portal-cavern. I told the others to link, and they did. But the Ring…" A tremor ran through me as the realization dawned. "The Ring didn't allow them into Dragon's Maw."

Had I left them there unprotected? Had they been attacked, bitten, killed? I broke into a run, Raman struggling to keep pace with his staff tap-tapping against the ground. My knees ached, my legs spasmed. Gritting my teeth, I pushed down the path and past the frozen river, its crests as still as ice.

The clearing before the pulsating cavern came into view, eerily deserted. Only a handful of devs stood guard like grotesque statues.

A whimper escaped my lips as I turned to face Raman. "This is where I left them," I rasped as he approached.

Before he could respond, a high-pitched voice sounded across the ravine. "Satya Lumian, at last our paths meet."

A chill snaked up my spine. That voice—like icy wind carried through the darkest part of winter. Across the river, at the hill's crest framed by the brilliant blue sky, a tall figure stood amidst the trees. His head gleamed in the sunlight, a pale robe billowing around him.

The Enlightener.

He descended the narrow cliff path with measured steps, his eyes fixed on me. No demon-mouse graced his shoulder. Mona and I must have released it along with the others.

As he neared the water's edge, two objects glinted faintly in his outstretched hands. God-relics? Was that how he'd entered my own time-warp, while the rest of his army remained frozen?

"Light Weaver." His voice boomed, echoing eerily in the stillness. "You have one final chance to serve

Ahriman's will. Surrender your tools and join my cause, and I will return your companions."

I gritted my teeth. Mona, Rei, Tavid… *He's holding them hostage.*

Beside me, Raman tensed, gripping his staff with whitened knuckles.

"What have you done with them?" My jagged voice tore across the still water.

A chilling smile appeared on the Enlightener's gaunt features. "Come meet me and all shall be revealed."

"Where are they?" I demanded.

"That ring on your tiny finger, oh, sweet Light Weaver," the Enlightener said, chuckling, "is a time shield and quite a travel companion, as you've discovered. But did you know that using the Gate-Ring to enter or use a portal of the gods can only be done by *vessels* of the gods? You…" his smile widened. "…and me."

"You're Ahriman's vessel," I spat.

"Very good," he said, nodding with feigned approval. "And my keystone," he tapped his chest where a faint glow emanated, "allows me to manipulate relics, even at a distance."

Frustration, anger, and raw fear churned within me, a potent mix of desperation. That's when I noticed it. The massive tapestry. Its edges curled slightly, it leaned on the wet boulders beside the Enlightener, half rolled. Even from across the river, I could see that it was the same violent tapestry from the Golden King's quarters. Tendrils of smoke swirled around it. Not rising from it, but entering it.

A horrifying realization slammed into me. *He's buying time because…he's trapping spirits as we speak!*

Raman and I exchanged a horrified glance. He'd also noticed.

"Did you know," the Enlightener drawled, his voice laced with a sickening amusement, "that the energy of a single god-portal is enough to control an entire kingdom? Even from afar?"

My teeth ground together. "You're a monster."

He grinned. "Monster? No, Light Weaver. I am a man driven by a cause. Soon, I will rule the kingdoms, the world!"

The blood froze in my veins, leaving me cold and clammy. "What have you done to my friends?"

"I am merely offering them a lesson in history," he replied, a thin smile spreading across his features as he gestured toward the tapestry by his feet.

"You've trapped them."

A twisted satisfaction filled his gaze. "Little Light Weaver," he crooned in a sing-song voice that reminded me too much of the Monster-King. "You think you wield power? Do you have any concept of the raw godforce coursing through that portal-cavern? And all you managed was a time freeze? You're a child playing with artifacts far beyond your comprehension."

His words were a cruel echo of the doubts gnawing at me. I was a novice trying to use forces I barely understood. Shame burned my throat, but I forced it down. "Release them," I demanded.

He seemed to relish my distress, arching his nonexistent brows. "What lengths are you willing to go to save them?"

I loathed that question *so* much. Through gritted teeth, I said, "What do you want?"

He leaned forward, eyeing the writhing tapestry on

the ground beside him. His voice turned cold and calculating. "You. Your connection to the gods, to be precise. Surrender the relics and I will release your friends. Become my apprentice and I will teach you to become as powerful as I."

Raman had positioned himself beside me, his trembling grip on his staff betraying his fear. "Satya, don't," he muttered, sending me a warning look.

Not for a single second did I believe the Enlightener's empty promises. Even if I offered him the goddess herself, he would keep everyone hostage, a twisted leash to control me and my power for his own nefarious agenda.

Something the Enlightener had said earlier struck me as odd. He thought I'd used the portal-cavern to freeze time? Unless the Ring had warped my senses entirely, I'd released the spirits the Enlightener had trapped. But as I stood within the frozen village, with all the devs still in their monster-form, I knew it was a risk. I wouldn't know if I'd truly set the spirits free until I returned time to its normal flow. But if my plan hadn't worked, we'd be forced to face the devs…we wouldn't stand a chance.

"First release my friends," I said. "And then we'll discuss your…proposal."

The Enlightener's laughter ripped through the unnatural stillness like unexpected thunder. "That is not how it works, Light Weaver," he sneered. "The time for words is over."

His eyes glinted with cruel purpose as he raised one of the relics in his grasp. A ripple of dark energy spread across the water's surface. Then, defying the laws of nature, he stepped onto the still river. Beneath his feet, a thick sheen of obsidian materialized, solidifying into a shadow-bridge as he stalked toward us. Step by deliberate step, the bridge extended before him, a dark path defying the unnatural stillness of the water beneath. Shadowy ropes trailed behind, dragging the massive kork over the shadow-bridge in his wake.

"Master Raman," I whispered. "I'm about to do something reckless."

He shot me a sidelong glance. "Why am I not surprised?"

"I did something else in the portal-cavern," I said. "I think, I *hope*, I released the trapped spirits. But I won't know if it worked until I return time to its normal flow."

Raman's gaze flicked between me, the frozen devs, and the approaching Enlightener. The lines on his forehead deepened. He met my gaze, a silent agreement flashing between us. We were hopelessly outnumbered, trapped between a frozen army of the dead and a seemingly unstoppable sorcerer. With a resigned sigh, he whispered, "Do it."

I focused on the Ring's warmth against my finger. *Return time to its normal flow.*

The world lurched forward in a dizzying rush and erupted in sound. The air whooshed, rustling the leaves in a flurry of nervous whispers. The river gurgled, splashed, and rushed forward with a roar. From the bend in the river, shouts rose from the village center. A mixture of joy and confusion. The once-possessed Azzis stirred behind us, blinking and groaning as the world around them snapped back into focus. They scrambled to their feet, looking bewildered by their sudden release and the sight of the sorcerer seemingly floating over the turbulent water.

Raman's eyes snapped to mine, a shocked grin splitting his lips.

"Perhaps some encouragement is in order," the Enlightener boomed across the rushing river as he continued to stride forward. He was now halfway across the shadow-bridge.

Murmurs of an incantation left his lips. The dissonant spell rippled through the air. His stance, the tone of his voice, reminded me of how he'd called forth the darkness while I'd traveled the kork depicting the battle thirty years ago.

Raman gripped his staff like a spear, leveling it at the Enlightener. As he began his own chant, harmonic syllables resonated in the air, his voice ringing with power. A dome of white dust materialized around us, a protective shield against whatever magic the Enlightener brewed.

Fumbling in my belt pouch, I snatched the Spool. But what spell could I possibly cast against such power? My mind raced through the limited chants I'd recently learned, but each option seemed inadequate. I knew healing, not defense.

A raw energy extended from the Enlightener to Dragon's Maw. He was obviously using a god-relic with the portal-cavern to amplify his own magic.

An earsplitting roar exploded from the depths of the portal cavern, avalanching across the ravine. The ground trembled. My heart rammed against my ribs as if aiming for escape.

A creature materialized from the depths of Dragon's Maw. A colossal serpent-dragon with two—no, *three*—heads dwarfing even Vishap's, emerged with a primal roar that shook the mountain. Its serpentine body continued to unwind from the cavern entrance, silver scales glinting like blades. Its multiple heads spewed blood-red flames, scorching the surrounding rocks.

The massive creature's multiple yellow eyes glowed with a power both tangible and terrifying. As it fully extricated itself, its jagged tail trailing behind rose like a mountain range. Its colossal shadow cast a blanket of darkness across the ravine, and wherever its gaze fell, flames erupted in a horrifying dance of destruction. Bushes ignited, trees transformed into fiery pyres. The ground trembled under its earth-shattering strides; clouds of dirt spiraled in its wake.

Panicked screams shattered the air. Horror replaced my initial relief. The Azzis sprinted toward the village. I remained rooted at the river's edge beside Raman. Goddess, had I freed their spirits only to feed them to this herald of darkness?

"Muht-Vishap!" Raman gasped.

"The dark dragon?" I croaked.

Raman nodded, and continued to chant the shielding spell.

Unlike the legendary Vishap I'd encountered within Dragon's Maw, this colossal beast inspired primal dread, a nightmare of scales and flame. The only whisper of its existence was a solitary sentence in a dusty tome. A fleeting allusion to a foe that Vahagn, the Dragon Reaper, had never been able to vanquish.

Every able-bodied villager who could wield a weapon surged forward from the village center, aiming for the beast. Muht-Vishap's colossal tail lashed out with bone-jarring cracks. Its serrated edges, sharper than any blade, ripped through dozens of warriors in a single, devastating sweep. Screams rent the air, bodies flung in all directions. Some scrambled back in blind terror, while others lay broken and still. Azzis stood shoulder-to-shoulder behind us, faces etched with grim determination, spears leveled at the beast.

The colossal dragon's massive heads turned, yellow-mucus eyes scanning the ravine as if in search of something…or someone. Their search ended when six molten eyes locked on me.

My attention darted between the murmuring Enlightener who stood on his shadow-bridge at the river's center and the relentless creature behind us. My mind raced, desperately searching for a defense, *any* defense, against this unstoppable force.

My grip tightened on the Spool, ready to unleash one of the more powerful healing spells, when Raman lifted his staff. His incantation thickened a vortex of white mist that enshrouded us and spread over the village. But Muht-Vishap's resounding roar shattered the air, and a torrent of scalding spittle rained down upon the ravine. The protective mist sizzled and evaporated.

A chilling laugh erupted from the river's center. The Enlightener threw his head back, his voice dripping with cruel amusement. "You cannot defeat this creature of Ahriman, *Sacreds*."

"Your issue is with the Sacreds, not the villagers," I countered, my voice ringing out in defiance. "Withdraw your beast and we can settle this like rational *people*."

"Negotiations are over, little *Light Weaver*," the Enlightener sneered, his high-pitched voice stripped of all mirth. Raising his two relics, he launched into a cryptic chant. A thick, smoky luminescence erupted from the two objects, coalescing into a malevolent beam that surged across the shadow-bridge, sharpening to a point as it neared. Time seemed to slow.

The shadow-spear impaled Raman's chest.

A gasp escaped Raman's lips, his eyes widening in shock and disbelief.

"Master Raman!" I screamed.

Raman doubled over, a choked cry ripping through his throat. I lunged forward, arms outstretched to catch him. But the instant my fingers brushed his fragile shoulders, he dissolved into a swirling vortex of smoke.

Chapter 37

"Danger may lurk in the dark, but it also hides us."
~ Master Raman

My screams mingled with the Enlightener's grating laugh.

I stared at the ashen smudge on the ground where Raman had stood just moments earlier, and my heart splintered.

"Tell me, young *Light Weaver*," the Enlightener's voice dripped with menace. "Now that all your companions are unraveling their histories, nothing you do will match the power of a Dark Weaver. You have no other choice but to join us."

Weaver of Darkness. Vishap's words from the portal-cavern drifted into my thoughts.

Before me stood a figure no longer bound to humanity, a man mutated by Ahriman's essence. But if he had drunk from the Cup of Shadows, with Ahriman's godforce coursing through his veins, why did he need *me*? What could I possibly offer him in exchange for the freedom of those I cared for?

I recalled the thirty-year-old battle captured within my mother's carefully light-woven kork, where the Enlightener appeared unchanged. *Immortality.*

I sucked in a sharp breath. Maybe the Enlightener's time was running out. He could be desperate. Maybe he needed me, or more specifically, he needed my connection to the godforce to prolong his existence. Or maybe his aim was to gift Ayg's divine power to Ahriman, aiding the battle raging in the gods' realm.

"I will *never* join you." My words dripped with hatred, venom lacing each syllable.

Muht-Vishap towered over me, its three immense jaws curling in a snarl. *It's waiting to be commanded by the Enlightener.*

I stared into the Enlightener's mucus-yellow gaze across the surging water, beyond rage, beyond fear. This man had taken away everyone I cared about. How many spirits had the Enlightener ensnared within the tapestry that lay beside him? How many lives did he continue to trap using the portal-cavern's raw godforce?

"If you do not join me, then we are done here," the Enlightener growled.

Murky shadows rose from his body, circling him, then moving higher to enshroud the dark dragon. The noxious scent of his spell stung my nose. Muht-Vishap's three heads swiveled, and a silent message seemed to pass between creature and sorcerer. The beast parted three massive jaws, releasing a storm of darkness. An undulating mass of obsidian smoke spread and expanded outward, engulfing everything around me. It obscured the river, the mountain, the dwellings. The darkness continued to grow until it consumed the entire village in its inky embrace.

Visibility vanished. Screams erupted around me. Bodies hurtled through the fog as the beast ravaged one warrior after another.

Tightening my fingers around the Spool, I tapped into my connection to Ayg. At first, I sensed nothing but a void. Then, a faint glimmer, like the feeble flame of a candle. I seized onto it with all my focus. *Ayg, please help me!*

The Satya-dev within me stirred to life. It writhed, uncoiled, lashed out. Agony seared through my chest. I cried out.

The fog thickened into an oppressive shroud, muffling all sound beyond the tumultuous rush of air and the gushing river. I exhaled and the dense fog surged away from me and upward, morphing into dark clouds that veiled the sun. Sunrays glimmered, outlining the trees above.

"The fog, the mist, the shadows," I mumbled. There was something here I needed to understand, something I was missing.

My gaze shifted from the mist-wrapped surroundings to the play of light. The way the sun's rays contoured the fog's edges, creating a dance between radiance and obscurity. Just as the clouds concealed the sun, shadows eclipsed the light. The same way Eclipse obstructed the Luminous godforce.

Raman's recent teachings echoed in my mind. It was all about balancing the energies. But more than that. The immense primordial power thrumming in Dragon's Maw, the godforce in its purest form, now swirled around me, its touch like whisperweave. *This* was the elemental power that bridged and harmonized the Luminous and Eclipse energies. I could feel it weaving around me, flowing through me, merging with my essence.

The Enlightener craved dominance over the Eclipse godforce. All this time I thought I wielded Ayg's Luminous godforce, pure and potent. But that wasn't true. The Satya-dev was a part of me, so *it* wasn't just Eclipse. It was an amalgamation, a union of both light and shadow. A *balance*.

It had been right there all along, in the shielding spell Raman and Mona repeated while I used the Spool: *Luminous and Eclipse unite, in balance, harmonize the light.*

I finally understood what that meant.

As these revelations flitted through my mind, the dark fog stirred, converging into shapes. Figures materialized from within the misty walls. Shadow-devs.

They hissed and snarled, reaching with wispy claws. One struck out and scraped my arm, drawing blood. Another snagged at my cloak from behind.

Satya-dev snarled, her low growl escaping my own lips.

Clutching the Spool with trembling hands, I faced the shadow-figure standing before me. Its eyes, pools of darkness, bore into me, yet it seemed to hesitate, its assault held back by an invisible barrier. Was it the Spool protecting me? The Gate-Ring?

Satya-dev pushed at my chest, stretching my ribs. My eyes widened. It wasn't the relics. It was *her*, the one lingering inside, the one I'd been suppressing. Her energy seemed to resonate with theirs. An energy not of malice, but of shared existence. A strange kinship.

The shadow-devs continued to circle, punctuated by the Enlightener's dark spell, yet reluctant to strike a killing blow. The Enlightener's voice rose. Was that desperation in his tone?

I battled the urge to release my inner-dev, who prodded and pushed at the edges of my awareness. If I couldn't control her, I'd risk joining the shadow-devs instead of fighting them. The Enlightener's dissonant voice echoed through the fog. The shadow-devs continued to circle me, breaching in and out of the shadow-walls.

Spirits. My grip tightened on the Spool.

My father's voice echoed in my mind, grounding me, *"Be equipped..."*

Maybe my access to the godforce was blocked, but the Spool was a portal, wasn't it?

A spell. I needed one that was powerful enough. One that would not only divert the shadow-devs and the massive dragon but the Enlightener as well. Powerful enough to crumble this wall of thick fog.

"Be observant."

The roaring sounds from outside the shadow-walls was a grim reminder that Muht-Vishap continued to destroy the village, to kill.

My mother had given me a weapon during the battle in the kork. I'd already used it once to summon aid.

"Be quick."

I inhaled deeply and added a silent, *Be fearless*.

The spell poured from the center of my being, my chant resounding in harmony to my mother's tune that still resonated in my head: "Weavers of Light, empower this fight. The past and future must come together to end our plight."

Wrapped within the dense fog and surrounded by the shadow-devs that seemingly no longer posed a threat, my surroundings had grown as dark as night. From the walls of darkness, a form emerged. The Enlightener strode forth through the fog, his pale robe billowing as it brushed past the shadow-devs. Ten steps away. Seven.

I stumbled back, back, back.

The Enlightener's yellow eyes met mine and he grinned. "Are you prepared to succumb to the Archdemon of Despair and Chaos?"

The Spool clutched tight, I continued to sing the spell. The Enlightener's brow furrowed, his focus shifting to my moving lips. "What are you doing?"

Understanding flashed across his features, and he initiated his own incantation, an off-key, discordant chant.

Above the Enlightener, the massive heads of Muht-Vishap breached the shadowy barrier, its milky eyes pinned to me. Its tail swept straight through the encircling shadow-devs. Dark wisps seeped from the devs, momentarily dispersing before reforming into their former shapes. I jumped out of its way as a glinting scale missed me by a thread.

My heart rammed against my ribs in painful jabs. Unlike the shadow-devs, this creature had no reservations about harming me. The dark dragon opened its massive jaws and released a resounding roar. I lifted my voice and repeated the protection spell I'd heard Raman and Mona chant dozens of times.

"Conduit strong, take control. Power pure, shape and bind.

Bridge the realms and veil unwind.

Luminous and Eclipse unite, in balance, harmonize the light.

I call upon the forces deep, to shield the veil, the secrets keep."

But I skipped the last sentence, the one that would seal the doorway into the spirit realm. Instead, I opened it. And I repeated my mother's incantation inviting the spirits. "Weavers of Light, empower this fight. The past and future must come together to end our plight."

Wisps of light spiraled from the Spool.

The Enlightener's jarring incantation rose above mine.

The Spool's azure disks sprang to life with brilliant hues of reds, blues, greens and yellows, extending toward the shadow-devs around me, the Enlightener, even to Muht-Vishap.

The dark dragon froze mid-roar, its yellow-glazed eyes fixated on the relic.

Ribbons of rainbow-light surrounded me, forming into a multitude of shapes. Ethereal voices rang over the ravine—"Daughter of Light... Daughter of Light... Daughter of Light."

In a gust of forceful wind, the darkness receded, carrying away the shadow-devs. The air cleared. The scent of earth after rainfall wafted in the air. Brilliant halos emerged—the ethereal circle of Light Weavers from past and future. Hand in hand, their circle spread, expanding into a brilliant sphere that enshrouded the entire village, banishing the dense fog. They spanned the river's expanse, hovered by the cliffs, and behind the elms and weeping willows. Hundreds, perhaps thousands.

The Spool rose from my grasp, hovering and whirling in the air above my head like a spinning top. Its iridescent rays spread throughout the village.

Two hands found mine. The touch of the elderly woman and the child. I could feel their grips as solid as my own.

The Gate-Ring warmed my skin. The world around me warped.

I now stood at the heart of the village, the

Enlightener and Muht-Vishap frozen before me. The screams had ceased. The villagers became statues of suspended motion again. Even the air had stilled, not a leaf stirring.

Only the two ethereal beings beside me, and the encompassing spirits of Light Weavers, defied the frozen stillness. Maybe the Enlightener had attempted to block the Ring's space-warping powers, but he'd clearly not anticipated the relic's potential in this way. To be fair, neither had I.

Beside me, the spirits of the elderly woman and the child sent me identical encouraging smiles, their firm grips on my hands anchoring me. I glanced down at my own form, only to find that I was merely a wisp, a ghostly spirit made of shadows and light.

Satya-dev grew restless, writhing to be freed.

"Let her help you," the elderly Light Weaver's voice whispered in my mind.

I glanced at the Enlightener's still form before me, his frozen eyes. His fog-spell was broken. Finally, I could access the godforce freely.

I linked to Ayg. Golden energy immediately surrounded me, cocooning me like a safe haven in a storm. As if in this frozen realm of potentials, I was both the storm *and* the haven.

Ayg's voice echoed into my head. *"Brace yourself."*

Then it came. A cascade of energy crackled like lightning, as fragrant as my mother's patchouli oil, as sweet as nectar on my tongue. It poured over me, all-encompassing, filling me with pure bliss. This was more than Luminous or Eclipse, more than the primal energy of Dragon's Maw. This was Ayg's essence, the balanced power I'd been trying to create.

The harmonious energy poured through the Spool and into my heart. From the tempest emerged the Satya-Dev. My very own dev-worm. For a brief moment she stood before me, her golden-ringed gaze locking onto mine. Shadows exuded from her, a potent mix of darkness and light with coiling emotions. Rage, anger, fear.

"Release it," I urged, countering her bitterness with memories...

Of beauty. Of joy. Of love.

The darkness wavered. She raised a shadowy hand and brushed my cheek. Her powerful emotions sent a jolt through me. The Spool hummed, bathing her in radiant light.

I suddenly stood within the shadow-tunnel, but this time the Satya-dev hovered before me, and the Enlightener stood before the raging giant at the edge of the tunnel. I saw it then. The core of the magic at the sorcerer's center, a shadowy sphere with extended arms, threading him to Muht-Vishap who hovered above the tunnel's shadow-ceiling. And through the dark dragon, to a malevolent core I could not see, but *sensed.* An energy that pulsed like squirming, oily slugs. Ahriman.

A resounding chorus of voices rose around me. The spirits of past and future Light Weavers sang, their melody entwined with my mother's tune. Joined by the harmonious voices, my own voice surged forth.

Together, we chanted the spell, "Strands of light, threads of power, merge together in the final hour."

Strings of light coiled around me, swirling over my whispery arms, my body, transforming the dark tunnel into a channel of light.

The massive dark dragon's silhouette loomed above

me, frozen in time. Its form seemed insubstantial, as if woven from air, nightmares, and the essence of night itself. But within the shadowy outline, I could still see the glint of the Enlightener's mucus-yellow eyes at the shadow-tunnel's end.

As my mind raced, piecing together the puzzle Ayg's riddle had presented when we'd first met, a sudden clarity swept over me.

"Heed the night's truth to tell the story of dawn," I whispered.

The night's truth. The illumination of secrets concealed in darkness, even hidden in its name: *Muht Vishap.*

"Dark Dragon," I mumbled, the words carrying an air of revelation.

It was as if a veil lifted, revealing layers of meaning within Ayg's cryptic words. The Goddess of Dawn couldn't tell me what was clear to her, to all the deities. There must be some type of spell Ahriman had cast over them that prevented her from doing so. The night's truth was nothing more than a clever fabrication that Ahriman had orchestrated. A falsehood woven into our reality.

Ayg had said the realms of gods and mortals were intricately intertwined. The second part of the riddle crystalized. *Tell the story of dawn.* I saw it now, a beacon of understanding piercing through the darkness. To "tell the story of dawn" meant to shed light on the concealed truth in Ahriman's darkness.

These revelations flowed through me like a river over a precipice. I glanced up at the massive heads of Muht-Vishap. The truth lay within the dark dragon itself. The Enlightener was pouring his formidable powers into it. This was the heart of Ahriman's deceit, the hidden truth cloaked by lies.

Satya-dev stood before me like a guardian. She was *my* night's truth. The answer hid within her writhing shadows, a blend of darkness and light, now spinning and whirling as she drew the godforce from the Spool and Gate-Ring. A wild gush of energy coursed through the relics until the light tunnel expanded, encompassing the space around us.

The Enlightener's eyes snapped open. The Satya-dev burst toward him, weaving through him in a tangle of shadows and dagger-sharp spears of light. An inhuman screech tore from the Enlightener's throat. When Satya-dev emerged, she grasped a swirling, living shadow-sphere. The Enlightener's dead and blackened heart.

Embracing this newfound balance, I tapped into the Enlightener's volatile, raw Eclipse power. I blended it with the Luminous godforce pouring from the Spool. The two energies swirled, danced, weaved in a spiral around us. Satya-dev's gold-ringed eyes met mine. With a mischievous wink, she hurled the Enlightener's dead-heart skyward.

The swirling orb flew up, up, up…

And erupted into a cascade of sparkling stars, raining back to the earth in a shower of glittering dust. The Enlightener collapsed to his knees with a grunt.

Muht-Vishap reared up on its hind legs, its colossal form twisting and contorting as it unleashed an earth-shaking roar. The immense creature fragmented, shards of light beaming from its core. The massive beast splintered, shattered. Then it burst like the shadow-sphere, showering radiance over the sunlit village.

For a few heartbeats, it seemed as if the sun itself

had taken residence within the ravine, forcing me to shield my eyes against the explosion's overwhelming brilliance. When I blinked open my eyes again, the star-storm continued to swirl.

For a fleeting moment, Satya-dev stood before me, a flicker of challenge in her gold-ringed eyes. She angled her head, a silent question hanging in the air: *Are we still enemies, or have we transcended into mutual respect? Do you still hate me?*

This shadow-dev within me had always been there. She was my impulsiveness, my defenses, my *sarcasm*. She was also my caution, my distrust, my ambition and cynicism. Without her, I wouldn't be *me*. Ahriman had merely illuminated what had always existed within me. With a resigned sigh, I spread my arms in an embracing gesture, inviting her in.

With a playful grin, she moved closer, her shadowy form melding seamlessly into mine. Delicate particles of darkness danced across my skin as she settled. My body regained its solid, tangible form.

Whispers resonated throughout the frozen village as the circle of Light Weavers, spanning across time, also merged into the air, their gentle voices echoing before they faded... *Daughter of light...daughter of light...daughter of light.*

In the space occupied by the fearsome dark dragon now stood a towering warrior as tall as two men. Thick chains snaked around his massive form, binding his wrists and ankles.

With a ground-shaking movement, the giant warrior flung his head back and unleashed a primal roar. The chains responded with a sizzling whine, thick, acrid smoke billowing from them. With a final clang, the chains disintegrated.

The warrior stood tall, legs braced apart. His obsidian leather armor flowed from a mottled jacket to knee-high ebony boots. Waves of raven-black hair framed powerful shoulders, and a closely trimmed beard covered his strong jawline.

His eyes, a deep brown with golden-ringed orbs, locked onto mine.

Chapter 38

A towering mountain once asleep casts shadows tall and deep.

~ Ar-Haya Highlands Proverb

The giant towered over the Enlightener's frozen, hunched form.

"Light Weaver," the giant rumbled, his thunderous voice vibrating the ground beneath my feet, the very air around me. "You have my unending gratitude."

My knees weakened as I gaped at the deity before me. Ayg's ominous words from Dragon's Maw echoed in my mind. *"The gods are at war...our most powerful one is trapped...our worlds...linked intimately."*

I'd been wrong. It hadn't been Ahriman roaring at the end of the shadow-tunnel, trying to reach me. It had been a trapped god.

"Dragon Reaper," I said, sounding breathless.

Vahagn, the legendary Dragon Reaper, grinned. "You know your gods."

"Everyone knows of the mighty Vahagn, defender of realms, reaper of dragons," I said, my voice weak. "*You're* the one who was imprisoned by Ahriman?"

He grunted. "I'd prefer that detail not become common knowledge. I have a reputation to uphold." He drew his massive broadsword from the sheath at his side, the silver glinting in the sunrays. "First, I must ensure the cord is fully severed."

He raised his sword high, then brought it down in a mighty arc. As the blade met the Enlightener's stooped form, it shifted into vapor. Dark, smoky tendrils coalesced into the shape of a wide blade, slicing through the once-immortal priest—Ahri-Luys, the Enlightener—straight to his oily core, dissolving the final bonds that tied him to Ahriman.

Now stripped of immortality, the Enlightener crumpled to the ground. Vahagn straightened, the tip of his sword solidifying once more into gleaming silver, and leveled it at me.

I hunched trembling before him. My bones had grown brittle, my limbs weak. Knees buckling, I collapsed with a heavy thump. Gnarled hands rose to trace the deep creases and sagging skin of my face, my movement labored and stiff. *Are those my hands?* My hair, once a lush brown, had thinned to shocking silvery-white. *Sweet goddess, I'm ancient!*

Vahagn's eyes grew warm. "You are a beautiful soul, Light Weaver," he rumbled, his voice resounding across the silent ravine. He continued to speak into my head. *"Vessel of Ayg, I leave you with a gift."*

A thread of golden light extended from the sword's tip, weaving itself into my chest. I gasped at the impact, but felt no pain. The sensation of *karot*, a ripple of nostalgia and yearning filled my senses. It whispered of belonging, of *home's* warm embrace. For a fleeting moment, the scents of sun-warmed meadows, flower nectar and honeyed long-forgotten memories mingled with the breeze. My jaw quivered.

A surge of crackling energy spiked through me. Shadow-tendrils rose from the crescent moons on my wrist, delicately interweaving with the broadsword's golden light. I felt myself expand, stretch, as if my very bones were being remade anew. My hands flew to my face and I gasped. Smooth skin met my touch. A jolt of vitality coursed through me, banishing every lingering pain and stiffness. The world sharpened; colors became more vibrant. Tentatively testing my limbs, I rose to stand tall and straight.

The Dragon Reaper had reversed the Gate-Ring's curse and returned my body to its youth.

"Thank you," I whispered, my voice echoing into the still air.

"You are welcome, Daughter of Dawn," the deity said. "The gods are indebted to you." His eyes skimmed over the still-frozen village with deep understanding. "You have much work to do, Light Weaver."

My skin sizzled, crackled. Power fizzled over my hands, my arms. I nodded.

"The relic on your finger will not age you...for a day," he boomed. "Use my powers and your time...wisely."

I dropped to one knee, overwhelmed by the magnitude of his gift, and bowed to him in reverence. To be granted such a power, even briefly, humbled me beyond words.

With a fluid motion, he sheathed his massive sword. "And now, I have a long-awaited battle to wage against a certain archdemon."

With a brilliant, confident smile, Vahagn's colossal form dissolved into shimmering mist, rapidly dissipating into the breeze.

****

The world spun dizzily back into motion as time

resumed its regular rhythm. The villagers' frantic cries and shouts filled the air. Confusion and urgency swirled around me as people glanced about bewildered, searching for the formidable dark dragon that, from their perspective, had vanished in the blink of an eye.

My attention remained fixed on the motionless Enlightener. Was he truly dead? I cautiously approached him and nudged his shoulder with the tip of my boot.

He stirred with a faint groan. My jaw locked. Vahagn hadn't killed him, merely stripped him of his powers and his connection to the Archdemon of Despair and Chaos. Maybe, in a cruel twist, this now-mortal man's aspirations of immortality had led to a fate worse than death. A life devoid of his warped ambitions.

Beside the Enlightener's fallen form lay my dagger and a Weaver's Spool nearly identical to my own—the one he'd used to create and control the dev horde. My own Spool rested at my feet, looking like nothing more than an unimpressive clump of stone. I gathered up both Spools and my scarred knife, tucking them into my belt pouch alongside the folded tapestry of Vishap's prison and the other two daggers—Baba's, and the one Hampo had gifted me. The half-etched shield pressed against my back. My Light Weaving tools.

I finally understood what it meant to be a warrior-healer. We protected. We defended. We healed. And the Enlightener's tools? They belonged to the Sacreds now.

I kept my dagger in my grip and faced the Enlightener's stooped form. His eyes blinked open, fluttering as if waking from a horrible dream. He tried to move, but he appeared too weak and slumped back to the ground. "You will regret what you've done, Light Weaver," he rasped.

I took a step toward him, my hands shaking as my grip on the hilt of my dagger tightened. For a heartbeat, I considered plunging it deep into his empty chest cavity. But Vahagn, the great Dragon Reaper, could have taken his life and hadn't. I had to trust the deity's actions. There was only one place this man belonged, but I needed help to do it.

People cautiously emerged from their hiding places within dwellings, or rose unsteadily from where they'd fallen during the cataclysmic battle against Muht-Vishap. The aftermath was a tapestry of stark contrasts—the survivors, the slain, and those whose motionless bodies lay still on the ground, unclear whether they lived or perished. The once-devs lay in tattered clothes, their empty bodies healed and awaiting their trapped souls now that Ahriman's dark energy had abandoned them.

Through blurred vision, I scanned the faces of survivors, recognizing Pari and her parents, and many Azzi warriors. But not Rei or Mona. Not Raman. My heart squeezed, recalling how the Enlightener had sizzled my old schoolmaster into ashes.

Pari spotted me. On unsteady feet, she ran and engulfed me in a fierce embrace. "Satya, you're unharmed and…and young again!" She pulled back, eyes wide with disbelief. "And you're glowing."

If she only knew. She hadn't even seen the worst of my accelerated old age. I tried to smile, but my lips quivered. Pari's gaze found the Enlightener's depleted form at my feet and her expression hardened.

"You know where he belongs," I said.

Pari nodded, understanding filling her eyes. She gathered two Azzi warriors, and together, they hefted the Enlightener's frail body.

"You will regret this," the Enlightener said again in a hoarse whisper. "You will regret what you've done, Light Weaver."

This man had stolen so much from me and countless others. And now, this once-formidable agent of Ahriman had been reduced to such a pitiful state he could barely lift his head.

"You're a traitor, *royal priest*," I said, my voice rough with emotion. "What I'll regret is the countless innocent lives you've destroyed."

As soon as they hauled him toward Dragon's Maw, I sprinted toward the riverbank and the battle-kork that imprisoned the multitude of spirits the Enlightener had bound. Pari raced after me.

The massive light-woven tapestry lay across the wet pebbles, still tightly rolled. The Enlightener had carried it across the river with the intention of trapping more souls within it. As I drew closer, my heart jolted. A motionless figure lay crumpled beside it.

"Master Raman," I cried, hurrying toward him. Hope warred with dread in my heart at the possibility of finding my mentor, my friend—dead. Finally reaching him, I fell to my knees at Raman's side. His eyes were closed, face alarmingly pale. I placed two trembling fingers on the pulse at his neck and held my breath. Pari, who'd dropped to her knees beside me, watched me with a weary expression. There, faint but unmistakable. A heartbeat.

"He's alive!" I cried in relief.

Pari helped me lift him gently under his arms, and together we carried him to the healer's cavern. Yepo and Tereza, Pari's mother and grandmother, hovered over the motionless bodies of Rei, Mona, Hampo, Tavid, Souren, fervently chanting healing spells. Pari and I gently lay Raman beside them, my heart filling with dread. Had I hurt them, maybe killed them by trying to transport us all into the azurite cavern in Dragon's Maw?

"They find bodies everywhere," Tereza said to me. "Not awake."

I glanced back to the Enlightener's battle-kork abandoned haphazardly by the riverbank. My arms crackled with the temporary power the Dragon Reaper had bestowed upon me. I now understood why he'd done it as my gaze scanned the motionless bodies littering the village.

I said, "I know where they are."

Chapter 39

"Every journey is a different facet of the same truth."

~ *Ar-Haya Highlands Proverb*

Vahagn's energy sizzled over my arms, lending me strength. I dragged the battle-kork over pebbles and dirt onto the village center's dryer ground.

Unrolling the tapestry, I took in the horrific battle scene woven in vivid detail. Soldiers impaling innocents, taking slaves, their cruelty made eternal in every bloody thread. People began to slowly gather around me, their hushed tones a dull murmur in the background.

Pari pushed through the crowd and placed a hand on my shoulder. "What do you need me to do, Satya?"

What seemed like ages ago, the Enlightener's chilling words from the Golden King's quarters echoed hauntingly in my mind, *"Ahriman will be pleased with these countless Sophenian souls..."*

"Help me find them," I said, pointing at the kork.

I scanned the faces within the tapestry, some clearly part of the historic battle, others the recently bound spirits whose physical bodies remained lifeless in this village or back at the Enlightener's camp. Or goddess knew where else. How was I going to tell the difference?

Goddess, the sheer number of trapped souls!

My gaze roamed the kork, and slowly, face by face,

my memory began to stir as I recognized people from Sophene. Merchants we'd dealt with, neighbors we'd been friends with. People killed during the Mosatti massacre.

There—the elderly Murad who'd lived down the path.

And there—Anis, the baker's kind wife.

My heart ached as I spotted friends, loved ones, strangers. All ensnared within this cursed cloth. By now, dozens of people surrounded the tapestry, helping me search, including Yepo and Tereza. Some found captured loved ones, pointing them out to ensure I knew their location in the battle. One after another, I nodded, trying to recall every face, every placement.

How am I going to remember them all?

"There's Baba!" Pari cried, pointing at a dark-haired man clustered among a crowd at the chaotic battle scene's core.

And beside Tavid...

I gasped. "They're all together."

Within the cruel threads, Rei flanked Tavid, sword raised to fend off a soldier attacking them. The others surrounded them. Mona, Hampo, Souren...

Dread knotted my stomach. "Where's Raman?"

Yepo lowered herself to her knees beside me, her finger extending toward a sprawled figure with a long, silver beard, isolated from the rest. Raman. My heart quickened, throat tightening at Raman's prone form.

"Pari," I said, keeping my voice low. "Please make sure that I'm given space while my body 'sleeps' here."

"What do you mean?" she asked. Then her eyes widened in understanding. "You're going to go into this battle-kork."

I swallowed, nodding. "I need you to be my shield while my spirit travels this kork to free the captured souls."

Pari's jaw quivered, but she nodded. "I won't leave your side."

I envisioned Rei's handsome features, Mona's smiling eyes…and sang the incantation to enter the kork. "Woven light, strings of gold, grant me passage to times of old."

As I chanted the spell, iridescent threads of light danced and swayed above the tapestry in a vibrant display that drew the attention of everyone surrounding the kork. I tuned out their gasps and murmurs and allowed the spell to carry me forward.

The Gate-Ring pulsed warmly against my finger as my vision clouded. Reality warped. Brilliant threads of energy emerged, drawing me inward.

Light erupted from the azurite Ring, intertwining with the dancing threads hovering over the kork. The cacophony of distant battle cries echoed in my ears as the world spun dizzily.

A powerful brush of wind whipped against my face, my body, tossing me one way, then the other. The chaos of the battlefield materialized around me, a swirling tempest of clashing weapons, anguished cries, and the acrid scent of burnt wood, fear, and spilled blood. I scanned the frenzied turmoil, desperately seeking any sign of my imprisoned friends. I barely stepped aside in time to avoid a plunging dagger. Another mounted soldier rushed toward me, his sword raised high to strike. Although I knew the blade couldn't truly harm me, I recoiled by instinct and stumbled out of its path.

At this rate, I'd never locate them in this chaos. I

needed a better strategy. Once my friends were free, I still had so many others to rescue.

Then the solution struck me and I wanted to slap my palm against my forehead. The Gate-Ring had temporal powers over the stream of time. I could freeze the entire battlefield the way I'd done during my confrontation with the Enlightener.

"The relic on your finger will not age you...for a day," Vahagn had said. *"Use my powers and your time wisely."*

Raising my palm against my next attacker, I envisioned the scene around me as a still painting. My finger warmed. A concentrated surge of power poured forth from the Ring. Rapidly expanding in an outward sphere, it enveloped the entire battlefield within its grasp.

The clash of steel, the anguished cries, the chaos. It all froze into an eerie suspended dance. Soldiers caught mid-lunge hung motionless in the air, their expressions of rage or fear forever marking their faces. The swirling clouds of kicked-up dust hung frozen. Even the sharp, cloying scents of blood and seared metal seemed to crystallize in the air.

I moved cautiously through the uncanny stillness, maneuvering around the motionless figures of soldiers and victims. The sudden silence felt deafening, broken only by the whisper of rustling fabric as my ethereal form brushed past one frozen form after another. Each step sent distorting ripples through the time-shield, vibrating outward.

At last, I reached the cluster of frozen figures I'd focused on. There stood Rei, stance fierce, sword poised mid-arc as the pale sun glinted off his sweat-dappled brow. Beside him, Mona's face was frozen in a mask of furious determination, lips parted mid-shout, dagger gripped to strike. Tavid's fingers hovered just a handspan from wrestling a blade from an enemy's grasp, while Hampo had one hand raised as if to hold him back. Nearby, Souren and two other Azzi warriors had stilled in various poses of attack or defense.

I hadn't expected their forms to be so corporeal, so solid. The Enlightener's magic must have fused their spirits into the kork, forcefully making them join the fray.

I took Rei's free hand, surprised by the warmth of his skin against my spirit-touch. Placing it on Mona's shoulder, I guided Hampo's arm to brush Tavid's side, linking the others wherever contact could be made: shoulder, hand, arm, head, leg. Finally, I wrapped my fingers around Rei's wrist, focusing on the clearing before the Azzi healing quarters.

The frozen battlefield shimmered and warped as threads of light converged, cocooning us in pulsing energy.

One heartbeat…two…

The world shifted with a jarring rush of force. We stood in the Azzi ravine, air thick with damp earth and the battle's metallic aftermath. The river's soothing rush filled my ears as my senses adjusted to the abrupt transition.

I pushed off the mossy ground. Gasps echoed around us as Rei, Mona and the others scrambled to their feet before the healing cavern where their prone bodies had been.

"…and another thing, how dare you insult a Sacred, and…" Mona's voice rang out furiously, mid-tirade, before trailing off in confusion, finally registering our changed surroundings. "Oh, we're back." Her eyes widened with delight when she spotted me. "We're back!" Rushing forward, she pulled me into an unexpectedly solid hug.

Rei lowered his sword hand slowly, a flush coloring his cheeks. When our gazes met, his eyes brimmed with raw emotion. I offered a small smile, but joyous reunions would have to wait. Turning back toward the vile kork, I began the incantation anew, focusing my attention on Master Raman's crumpled form.

As the world warped, a reassuring hand settled on my shoulder. I turned to find Rei, eyes determined, as he gave me a quick, affirming nod. We entered the frozen battle again. The freeze-spell still held. As we reached Raman's fallen form, a distant figure in my periphery caught my eye. Broad shoulders, wide girth.

My heart stilled. Could it be him? But before I could search for my father, I needed to return Raman's spirit to his physical form before he withered away.

I placed a gentle hand on Raman's shoulder, and just as I focused on the Azzi village, Rei gasped, "Andreas!"

The Golden King stood a mere three steps away.

Emotions raged in Rei's eyes. Desperation, anger, love. For his brother.

A storm of indecision raged within me. The Golden King, the man who had cost me my family, needed retribution, not salvation. He deserved to forever roam this battlefield…

Yet he'd been corrupted by the Enlightener's darkness, and Ahriman's.

Beneath that tainted exterior beat the heart of Rei's brother, the Crowned Prince before his fall. I studied Rei's torn expression, a mix of emotions warring within me. Wouldn't I do anything to save my own family? Shouldn't Rei have the same choice?

I studied the King's confused ice-blue eyes, so much like Rei's, yet so different. Had he been on his way to seek Raman's aid? Maybe vanquishing the Enlightener had severed the dark tether that ensnared the King, as well.

Making a swift decision I prayed I wouldn't regret, I nodded to Rei. Relief flooded Rei's expression as he reached out to place one hand on his brother's still shoulder, and the other to my arm. The four of us whisked back to the physical realm, rematerializing before the Azzi healing quarters. A cry resonated from within the cavern. Unmistakably Raman's voice.

I scanned the area. No sign of the Golden King. Rei's brother was likely trapped in Dragon's Maw. Only the gods knew where his spirit went. But there was no time to search and wonder. Too many lives still depended on me. All around us, the bodies of devs lay still, like puppets without a master.

I forced myself to ignore Rei's devastated, frantic search for his brother. "I'm sorry," I whispered to him.

Without waiting for his response, I nodded to Pari, who sat beside the kork to watch over my physical form. Then I swerved back into the battle-kork's chaos, rematerializing amidst the furious battle that had begun to rage again. I froze the scene once more.

Where is he? He could be anywhere. If it was him at all...

I brushed past fallen soldiers and their victims. Some were woven depictions from the century-old battle, while others were trapped souls awaiting bodies in our world. Goddess, how was I going to tell the difference?

Above, the sky's vibrant hues seemed to be fading, the colors running together like wet dye on silk. Wisps of vapor trailed from the clouds. Spirits? The souls of the dead, no longer tethered to mortal bodies? I shuddered. Were Mama's and Caral's souls drifting among them?

At the horizon's edge, an inky blackness was spreading, devouring the frozen battle scene. The kork was unraveling without the Enlightener's power to sustain it. My heart raced. I had to work quickly before this realm disintegrated entirely.

I scanned the battlefield, now desperate to save anyone and everyone. There had to be a way to distinguish the trapped spirits from depictions. As the Gate-Ring's azure glow illuminated the threads around me, an idea struck. The Spool! It wasn't just a healing relic, but a portal-tool that channeled divine energy. Vahagn had gifted me with his power for a day. It *could* work.

The physical Spool rested in my pouch back in the Azzi village, yet its ghostly apparition hovered at my spectral belt in this kork-realm. I retrieved the relic's shimmering spirit-form, wrapping my ethereal hand around it.

Vahagn's loaned energy crackled across my ghostly skin as I whispered, "Show me the trapped souls."

Azure filaments lifted from the ancient relic and whipped outward into the frozen chaos of battle, weaving between the frozen figures. The traveling tendrils bypassed soulless forms, only marking those whose life-forces were severed and bound here, surrounding them in an azure halo.

I stared at the haunting field of flickering auras,

silently pleading for time. With a deep breath, I channeled every drop of Vahagn's power, urging the azure tendrils to reach the edges of the melee in time. I marked every ensnared essence, while keeping an eye on the kork's melting edges. The inky blight was devouring the tapestry at a terrifying pace. Figures began disintegrating into smoky threads at the melee's outer edges, their halos winking out one by one.

"No!" I cried, mouth dry with panic. Baba's spirit had to be here somewhere. I couldn't lose him again.

As a deafening unraveling sound like a roaring hearth bellowed through the air, I sucked in a deep breath. Gathering every last drop of divine power, I roared the words of the return spell with all my might…

…and willed every last essence back into the living world.

Chapter 40

Through wings unseen, the ballad tells,
Hidden within, a 'hreshtak' dwells.

~ Azzi folksong

The world reformed. My knees met the mossy earth with a muffled thud.

Confused shouts erupted. The scattered prone bodies who, moments ago had been lifeless and contorted, began to stir. They sat up, surveying their surroundings with bewilderment. Vahagn's power, channeled through me, had reversed every twisted dev back into their mortal selves, healing their bodies, restoring their souls.

As I stood, a wave of dizziness made me stumble.

Rei caught me with an arm around my waist. "I've got you," he murmured.

Leaning on Rei, I let my gaze roam the village. My heart swelled at the heartwarming reunions unfolding all around us. Friends, neighbors, strangers embraced with tears and laughter. My own eyes brimmed, silent tears streaming down my face. My friends were safe, the Enlightener defeated, and Muht-Vishap…a god I'd helped free. It was all too much. And not enough.

Rei's hold tightened as I wrapped my arms around his middle, pressing my tear-streaked face into his chest. I vaguely registered the rise and fall of his breath, the rapid beat of his heart.

My face warmed. *I'm hugging Rei. The exiled Aurean prince.*

But this was the boy who'd rescued me during the massacre. And now, the man who'd become more than a fleeting memory. Someone I trusted. Someone I was beginning to care for.

A hush descended over the ravine as all eyes turned skyward. There, amidst scattered clouds, floated the translucent form of a woman in a boat, cradling a golden plate. The Goddess of Dawn herself.

"Well done, my vessel," Ayg's melodious voice chimed across the village, drawing gasps from the awestruck crowd.

Angling the golden plate toward the kork, Ayg unleashed a beam of radiant light that pierced the tapestry, its energy rippling like sea waves over the fraying threads. Colorful wisps rose from the kork, swirling and coalescing into moving visions across the sky.

One after another, ephemeral scenes captured the soul of the Sophene Highlands, from the verdant valleys nestled between rolling hills, to the bustling towns alive with vibrant festivals. Tantalizing aromas of spices filled the air, mingling with the sweet notes of laughter, song, and the rich melodies of musicians. Families flung open their doors to neighbors and strangers alike, sharing abundant feasts bursting with the savory bounty of freshly harvested crops. Weavers and artisans crafted intricate rugs, tapestries, and tools, imbuing every detail with the essence of their skills and creative spirits.

These collective memories of the fallen rising from the kork painted a vivid canvas of Sophene's past, present and future. Despite our diverse walks of life, and hailing from distant corners of the Ar-Haya Highlands, we shared an unbreakable bond in heart, mind, and spirit. The ethereal tapestry swirled above us, brightening and expanding into a vast mural. Not a single eye remained dry.

I choked out a sob.

Wispy spirits rose from the illuminated kork. As the first few ghostly forms ascended, drawn toward the visions Ayg had painted in the sky, I understood. I hadn't freed all the ensnared souls. Only those whose physical forms still existed in the mortal world. Ayg was beckoning the trapped spirits of the dead with her evocative vignettes of memories to aid them on their final journey. Those without physical bodies to return to, those imprisoned for untold years, those whose mortal remains were lost—all rose, bathing the ravine, woods, and mountainside in a final illumination.

Eyes burning from exhaustion, lack of sleep, and grief, I disentangled myself from Rei, my eyes on the rising spirits, searching, hoping, waiting…

I'd nearly given up when two wispy forms materialized before me, hovering together with an overwhelming aura of love. A woman and a child.

"Mama, Caral," I whimpered brokenly before dissolving into racking sobs.

"Do not cry for the fallen," Ayg whispered into my mind. *"Their journey is not over. They merely move on to the next stage on their eternal path."*

I stared into the loving faces of my mother and brother. There was so much I wanted to say to them, so much I wanted to ask, but instead, the only words that tumbled from my lips were a plaintive, "I'm so sorry."

My mother's spirit smiled, radiating unconditional love. *"Be at peace, my sweet. I am always with you."*

Caral's face broke into a sunny smile that pierced my heart. *"Thank you, Satti, for being the very best of sisters."*

Satti. It's what he'd always called me. I tried to swallow, but a lump the size of an apricot blocked my throat. Caral placed a ghostly hand over my constricting heart. *"I am moving on to my next grand adventure."*

Blinking against the blur of tears, I whispered, "Goodbye."

With a gust of ethereal wind, hundreds of Ayg's flying steeds materialized in the sky. Their wings spanned the clouds as they descended toward the hovering spirits. Then each spirit took to the air astride their own flying steed.

I watched through blurred vision as first my brother, then my mother, rose on ethereal mounts. The sky opened like a window, revealing a dark, silent sea. Spirit after spirit vanished into the ether-waves beyond. I sucked in a breath. Ayg was showing me where the departed spirits dwelled, cradled within the submerged depths of the Night Sea alongside the sleeping sun—until it was their time to rise again.

But as my mother's mount reached the sky-window, Mama turned, met my gaze, and smiled.

For a fleeting moment, the circle of Light Weavers shimmered around her before she disappeared into their midst. The sky-window rippled and slurped closed.

The ravine grew hushed. People all around me craned their gazes skyward in stunned silence as the sky brightened again.

The world sharpened. Dappled sunlight pierced the

canopy on the ledges above. Rain had swollen the river, its current a frothing rush. The purged kork lay abandoned on the mossy ground. The once-vibrant images had faded into a carpet of charred gray, fraying threads.

I became aware of everyone's gaze turning to me. Rei's eyes roamed my face, his expression open, unguarded as if he only saw *me*.

"Child…" Raman's awed whisper carried across the hush. "You are a wonder."

Mona's smile trembled, her eyes glistening.

As if in a trance, I glanced down at myself. My mouth slackened. I was glowing. What I'd mistaken as the sun's radiance blanketing the village…was Vahagn's crackling power glowing within *me*.

Ayg's voice chimed in my head, *"The gods are indebted to you, Daughter of Dawn."*

From within the enraptured crowd, someone whispered, "Hreshtak…" *Angel.*

Then one by one, everyone around me bowed their heads, fist to chest.

Chapter 41

Though the night may linger, vast and cold,
Dawn's light will rise, a new story told.
~ *Azzi Proverb*

The divine glow faded from my body as Vahagn's power gradually waned, but a tumultuous tide of emotions continued churning within me. My heart felt so full that I couldn't speak for hours.

In the days that followed, I oscillated between grief and joy, contentment and heartache. I could still vividly see my mother's joyful expression as she joined the circle of Light Weavers, could still hear Caral's laughter as he submerged into the Night Sea. Could still feel the surging flow of emotion that had emanated from each ascending spirit.

The evacuated Azzis steadily returned home, hordes of formerly-trapped devs trailing in their wake. Kev dispatched scouts, Rei among them, to locate any others still roaming, lost. Despite the overcrowding, the Azzis generously offered shelter, food and provisions to the newcomers. Nets were cast into the lively river, yielding trout and carp aplenty. Goats were milked, fresh loaves of bread and sweet cakes baked, distributed freely. Blankets and garments were brought out and shared without reservation. Clusters of weary people settled throughout the ravine to rest, to sleep, to pray...or to simply *be*.

But as each day melted into night and stragglers continued trickling in, there was still no sign of Baba.

I threw myself into the healing rituals, my mind drifting back five years to the aftermath of the Mosatti massacre. Just like the Azzis, our town had rallied to support those who had suffered unimaginable loss. While Baba and I grappled with our own profound grief, our neighbors had brought us food and calming teas. Lana had spent her days and nights at our house for weeks, ensuring I ate, bathed, and eventually found reasons to smile again. It was a wonder how people bounced back, no matter what horrors they endured.

On the fifth dawn, as the sun's first rays bathed the ravine, the unmistakable cadence of many footsteps reverberated like rolling drums. People emerged from the forest shadows, weary and haunted, coalescing from the treeline under the scouts' guidance. My breath caught as a silhouette with massive girth limped among them.

Distinctive hunched gait. Broad shoulders.

I didn't realize I was running until the bridge's aged planks thundered under my boots, until clumps of loose pebbles rained down into the river below from the winding cliffside path. I didn't realize I was crying until my ragged sobs echoed over the ravine, until I crashed into Baba's trembling embrace.

Chapter 42

Through time's soft whispers, the tears will dry.
A once-broken spirit will learn to fly.
                                    ~ Ar-Haya Highlands Proverb

A somber silence hung over the Azzi village as it slowly stirred back to life. Many mourned those lost in the battle. I spent my days guiding the fallen spirits toward the ethereal plane as each pyre's melancholic farewell floated down the river's currents.

Baba surprised me with his near-perfect Azzian. He passed his hours swapping tales with Hampo about prized weaponry, ancient forging techniques, and invaluable tools. At every opportunity, Baba reached for my hand, draped an arm around my shoulders, planted a tender kiss on my cheek, or simply ran his fingers over my hair. His eyes shone with disbelief and relief, mirroring my own awe that we'd somehow survived.

Three evenings after Baba's arrival, Rei walked me back to Anahit's temple. We'd barely spoken since I freed him and the others from the battle-kork, both of us consumed with responsibilities.

"I never thanked you," he said, offering me a crooked smile.

I returned his smile. "You just did."

"What you did…" He shook his head, eyes growing distant with the memory. "It was incredible. I hope you know that, Satya." He stopped and faced me. "I wanted to…"

But then a faint, familiar bark reached my ears, that subtle hitch unmistakable. It sounded like…

I followed the sound, Rei trailing behind. "Satya, what is it?"

"I think…" My pace quickened, my heart raced. "Could it be…?"

Sprinting, I reached Dragon's Maw just as another joyful bark echoed from the pulsing cavern's entrance.

There he was. A small black dog with floppy ears and white paws, my beloved Vagrik. Kaleidoscopic spirit-wings fluttered on his back as he led a dazed procession of people from the cavern. Azzis and others from different villages, blinking against the light of the setting sun.

Vagrik dashed straight toward me, leaping into my arms as I crouched. I laughed, my first uninhibited laugh in far too long. Rei offered me a brilliant smile. Golden rings surrounded Vagrik's dark pupils, mirroring my own. Through his eyes, I glimpsed an ethereal realm of incomparable beauty. He whimpered and licked my face.

Ayg's whisper caressed my mind. *"He is your connection to the gods, just as Tatu is Mona's link to Anahit."*

I hugged Vagrik to my chest until he yelped in protest.

Amidst the crowd emerging from Dragon's Maw, a familiar tall figure stepped into a stream of sunlight. Matted yellow curls clung to his head, pale eyes squinting. The Golden King.

"Andreas," Rei gasped.

Rei strode forward with determined steps. The

brothers met halfway, embracing in a hearty thumping of backs as they clung tight.

Still clutching Vagrik, I watched their reunion, torn by a tumult of emotions. The Monster-King, corrupted by the Archdemon of Despair and Chaos, had caused so much profound loss and suffering. The scars would be etched into my soul for an eternity. Yet seeing the youthful King now, tears streaming as he hugged his brother, it was hard to reconcile him with the monster of only days ago.

In truth, I wasn't sure how I felt watching Rei, his face lit up for the first time since I'd known him with something akin to joy. The bonds of their brotherhood clearly ran deep, transcending the darkness that had consumed Andreas.

As the others who'd emerged from Dragon's Maw wandered in a daze toward the village center, guided by many Azzis, I returned to Anahit's temple, my fairy-pup in tow. Whatever Rei had been about to say before Vagrik's bark had interrupted him would have to wait.

My feelings for Rei remained a tangled knot I couldn't begin to unravel.

****

That evening, as we prepared to sleep, Mona and Raman cornered me by the round table beyond Anahit's temple.

Mona's gaze fell on my hair. "The blue-white strands become you."

I lifted a lock of my hair and squinted at it. A strip of white a fingertip thick, tinged with azurite-blue, had remained. "My battle scar."

Mona smirked. "So, what are your plans?"

"For my hair?" I teased.

"Your plans for your future," Mona said, her tone growing serious.

"I need to talk to Baba..." I glanced at my father, who sat on the cot at the other end of the small space.

"Satya," he said, "you are an adult. This was always your path, no matter how much your mother and I tried to protect you from it."

Baba still looked lost, beaten. But the determination in his gaze told me he had plans of his own. *Goddess, don't let it be another dangerous thieving mission.*

"What about the shop?" I asked.

"Let me worry about the shop."

"But..."

"We want you to stay," Raman said. Then clearing his throat, he added, "We would *like* you to stay."

"Stay?" I asked, surprised. My heart fluttered with newfound hope. I'd hoped to stay in the village for a while to help, but it seemed they were suggesting more.

A warm smile played beyond Raman's thick beard. "Yes, right here, at the heart of the Legion's new center."

Mona chimed in. "We want to rebuild, locate other Sacreds, and invite new initiates." She sent me a pointed glance.

My gaze drifted to my father, but he shook his head. "You don't need my permission, Satya. Do what feels right," he encouraged, thumping a fist to his chest.

My lips quivered. "I would be honored to become your first initiate."

"Our second," Mona said, clearing her throat.

"Oh, who's the other?"

"Me," Pari said from the doorway, a cast-iron pot in her arms and a grin playing on her lips. "My mother sent some warm mint tea for everyone."

I beamed at the young girl who had become a friend. The sudden warm feeling of belonging, of *karot*, washed over me.

"Once things are settled," Mona said, "we will initiate you both into the Legion, as Sacreds."

"But Satya," Raman interjected, "I need my student who is a sponge, not the impulsive one that pops up when I least expect it."

Baba grumbled something under his breath.

I sent him a glare, then turned back to Raman. "No promises."

Chapter 43

As dawn's light paints the eastern skies,
The Sacreds among us will rise.
~ The New Legion of Garni Motto

The next afternoon, I took the river path back to the temple after a morning of healings. Vagrik trotted beside me, his rainbow wings a wonder to everyone we passed. I spotted Rei sitting alone on a boulder at the river's edge.

My heart constricted. We'd never finished our talk, and there were things I wanted to ask him. As I approached, gravel crunched underfoot and Rei turned.

"Satya," he said, rising. "How do you feel?"

"I feel well. And you?"

"Fine."

I glanced away, then met his gaze again. "Why didn't you tell me that you were there…five years ago, during the Mosatti massacre?"

Shadows clouded his stormy eyes as he turned his gaze to the rushing waters. "I was on the run from my brother, from the Enlightener. I knew their plans were evil and I tried to stop them, but they tried to kill me. I disguised myself as a guard and followed them. I couldn't stop an entire army, but I did what I could…"

"You saved me," I said.

His eyes snapped to me.

"You saved me," I repeated. "My mother and brother had been killed, but you pulled me away. We were inside our shop…" I swallowed.

"I never forgot you," he said, his usually clipped voice cracking. "The way you stood up to the King's guards, the way you shielded your brother."

I searched for the anguish that always accompanied that memory, but I'd finally found peace when I guided Mama's and Caral's spirits onward.

"When I saw you again after all these years," Rei continued, "I recognized you immediately. You have a way about you that's hard to forget. I couldn't tell you who I was until…" He cleared his throat. "You hated me when you first arrived here."

"I didn't hate you," I said softly. "Not really. I only hated what you represented…what I *thought* you represented."

"Do you still…" He stepped closer. "Hate me?"

Hate? What I felt was the opposite of hate. *Complete* opposite of hate. But how could I feel this way for a man who should be my enemy?

I held his twilight gaze and whispered, "No."

He studied my face, sending a warmth radiating from my head all the way to the tips of my toes. I couldn't say who moved first, but suddenly we were locked in each other's embrace, our lips meeting with sighs. What began as a soft caress quickly deepened into a passionate dance of lips and tongues. Goddess, this kiss! I had never been kissed like this before. As if we were both pouring every unspoken word into this single connection. Our arms wound tighter, holding each other as if we had no intention of ever letting go.

When we finally parted, Rei kept me wrapped in his

embrace, our foreheads touching as our ragged breaths slowly steadied.

"I've wanted to do that ever since I first saw you," Rei confessed, his voice a gentle rumble resonating into my chest.

I raised a playful brow. "Five years ago?"

He chuckled, the sound a warm melody. "Weeks ago, when you arrived…and I recognized you."

"You knew who I was as soon as I arrived?"

Tracing his thumb over my cheek, he said simply, "You, Satya Lumian, are unforgettable."

His gaze spoke volumes, mirroring my own thoughts. "I never forgot you either. The boy who saved my life on that horrible day."

He swallowed hard, pressing me closer.

I lifted my palm to his face, cherishing his warmth. "What now?"

His eyes turned serious. "My brother needs my help."

I glanced over his shoulder, spotting the Golden King slumped on a boulder at the river's edge, head cradled in his hands. He looked so different now: young, defeated, a far cry from the terrifying monster who'd haunted my nightmares. I almost felt a twinge of sympathy for him. Almost.

"My brother may have returned," Rei said, "but he isn't truly back, not yet. There are changes that must be made if we're to steer the Aurean Kingdom in the right direction."

"Changes?"

His gaze briefly shifted to his brother and he lowered his voice. "Before the Enlightener corrupted the King, my father had planned to reform the kingdom. I want to help Andreas fulfill those original reforms. Andreas is talking about having been judged by some kind of creature in the portal-cavern, about being forced to delve deep into his life-choices and actions. He's talking about rectifying past wrongs…I want to leverage his newfound wisdom and empathy. To push for progressive laws that grant greater freedoms to all the kingdoms under Aurean rule…to keep the beautiful cultures alive…" The last he whispered, his gaze dropping to my lips.

My fingers clenched the fabric of Rei's shirt, the urge to draw him closer overwhelming me. I had so completely misjudged him when I'd first arrived. Despite his family history, and despite what his brother had become, Rei was intrinsically *good*. "Rei, that's admirable."

"Come with me."

For a heartbeat I almost said yes. Nearly let myself forget all the reasons why such a choice would contradict everything I believed in. All the responsibilities I still had. But the stark reality of my situation settled in the pit of my stomach like a mound of stones. I didn't belong in Rei's world. There was only one place where I felt truly whole, and it wasn't in the City of Vosk, nor was it in Mosatti. I dropped my hand from his chest. "I want to do that more than anything, Rei. But I can't."

His throat bobbed as he held my gaze, an unspoken depth giving weight to his next words. "Vosk and the entire Aurean Kingdom needs a Light Weaver to help shift perspectives on magic. The royals lack insight, they're clueless…" He swallowed. "*I* need you."

Oh Rei, if only we were different people from different worlds.

"There is still so much I must do," I said. "I want to help Raman and Mona reunite the Legion, aid my father in deciding our shop's future…" I swallowed, overwhelmed by all that lay ahead.

Rei's smile faded, a touch of sadness dimming his eyes. Goddess, I missed his smile.

He nodded, the silence stretching before he spoke again. "I've had years to think and plan. I never wanted my brother's throne, but if he hadn't survived…" He shook his head. "I've spoken to him about my role in the kingdom…and he agrees."

"Your role?"

"As the King's brother, I have options he never did. I could lead the royal guard, but I've seen enough battles to last me a lifetime. Or, I could serve as a diplomatic emissary for the Kingdom." A small smile played on his lips as he finished, his decision clear.

I thought about how effortlessly he'd assumed a leadership role among the Azzis, earning their respect. His thoughtful decisions, his integrity. The idea of him stepping into such a significant role sparked a seed of hope in my heart, hope for our kingdoms, hope for *us*.

I laced my fingers with his. "Does that mean…"

"Three months," he said, his smile returning. "Six at most. That's all the time I need in Vosk to establish a council to support Andreas. My role as emissary will take me to many places. I'd have to travel, regardless. I have wanted to escape this place since I first arrived, but now…"

He glanced around the ravine fondly. "It's grown on me…the place, the people. I could live anywhere. Here, Mosatti, it doesn't matter. I want to…" He stepped closer and released my hands to wrap his arms around me again. "I want to build something real with us. I want to make this work, whatever comes next. To give us a fighting chance."

My heart raced at his words, at their implications.

His brother devastated my family…Rei had nothing to do with it.

The massacre ruined us…Rei saved my life, saved many lives.

But he's an Aurean prince…it's all right to care for him.

I wrapped my arms around his neck and pressed my lips to his, pouring every unspoken word, every tangled emotion, into the kiss. He smelled of fresh earth after spring rains, of sunlit meadows.

When we finally parted, breathless, Rei cupped my face with his calloused palm. "Make your plans, Satya. Spread your beautiful light far and wide…and when you're ready, I'll be waiting. That's a promise."

Standing there, wrapped in Rei's embrace, I teetered between grief and joy. A euphonious sense of simply *being* enveloped me.

Six months. A mere fleeting dream in the sands of a lifetime.

The fortune teller's words drifted back, *"What you seek is seeking you. But what you seek now is not true."*

During my reckless race through Nurazard, I hadn't understood what I truly sought.

But now, with pristine clarity, I *knew*. I had been searching for *this*.

This profound sense of purpose and belonging.

Of becoming a beacon of hope for the conquered Sophenians and all peoples across the vast kingdoms.

This was my destiny, the gods' tapestry woven

before me, calling me forward.

I looked up into Rei's twilight eyes and whispered, "I will hold you to that."

A word about the author...

Lusine Torossian crafts young adult fantasy novels inspired by Armenian mythology. Drawing from her heritage, she weaves rich folklore into tales of adventure, magic, resilience, and hope. Her debut novel, *Light Weaver*, won the 2023 SCBWI-Florida Rising Kite Award for Young Adult Fiction.

When she's not creating magical worlds, Lusine finds herself contemplating the meaning of life by analyzing shapes in the clouds—often her story characters show up there. In her family, she's known for reading fortunes in Armenian coffee grounds, carrying on a generations-old tradition she's yet to master.

A New York City native, she now lives in sunny Florida with her husband, alongside her writing partner, a very brave Cavalier King Charles Spaniel named Finny.

Visit LusineTorossian.com for book news, events, and behind-the-scenes content. Connect with her on social media:

Instagram: @lusinetorossianauthor
Facebook: @authorlusinetorossian
Bluesky: @lusinetorossian.bsky.social